CHRONICLES OF

THE LONG WAR

THE BLACK GUARD
THE DARK BLOOD
THE RED PRINCE

THE
RED
PRINCE

A. J. Smith has been devising the worlds, histories
and characters of the Long War chronicles for
more than a decade. He was born in Birmingham
and works in secondary education.

THE
RED
PRINCE

A.J. SMITH

HEAD
of ZEUS

First published in the UK in 2015 by Head of Zeus Ltd

9 7 5 3 1 2 4 6 8

A CIP catalogue record for this book is available from the British Library.

ISBN (eBook) 9781784080853
ISBN (HB) 9781784080860
ISBN (XTPB) 9781784080877

Printed and bound in Germany by
GGP Media GmbH, Pössneck

Head of Zeus Ltd
Clerkenwell House
45–47 Clerkenwell Green
London EC1R 0HT

WWW.HEADOFZEUS.COM

For Simon

THIRD CHRONICLE
OF THE LONG WAR

MAPS
BOOK ONE:
THE RED PRINCE

THIRD CHRONICLE
OF THE LONG WAR

BOOK TWO:
THE GREY KNIGHT

THE LANDS OF
RANEN

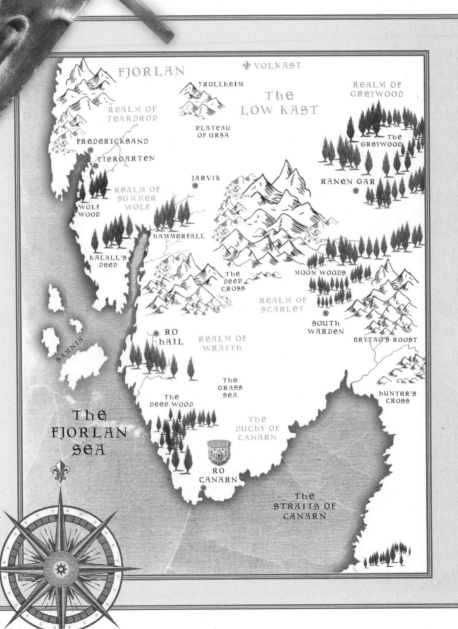

THE LANDS OF
RO

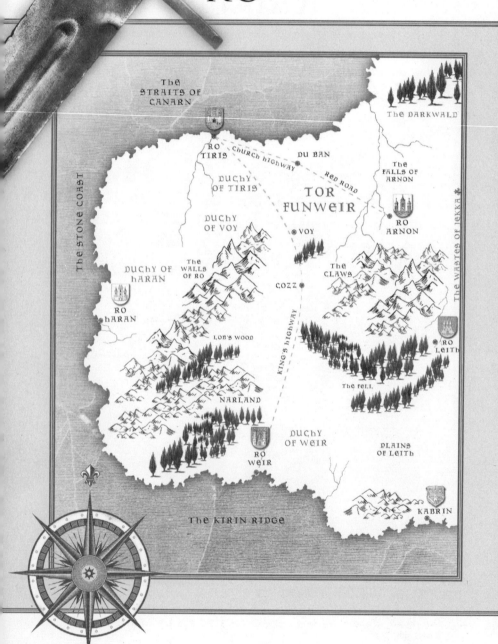

ARM OF THE RED

The
STRAITS OF
CANARN

The DARKWALD

RO
TIRIS   church highway   DU BAN

DUCHY
OF TIRIS

RED ROAD

The
FALLS OF
ARNON

TOR
FUNWEIR

RO
ARNON

DUCHY
OF VOY   VOY

The STONE COAST

The
WALLS
OF RO

DUCHY OF
HARAN

The
CLAWS

The WASTES OF JEKKA

COZZ

RO
HARAN

KING'S HIGHWAY

LOB'S WOOD

RO
LEITH

The FELL

NARLAND

DUCHY
OF WEIR

PLAINS
OF LEITH

RO
WEIR

KABRIN

The KIRIN RIDGE

THE LANDS OF
KARESIA

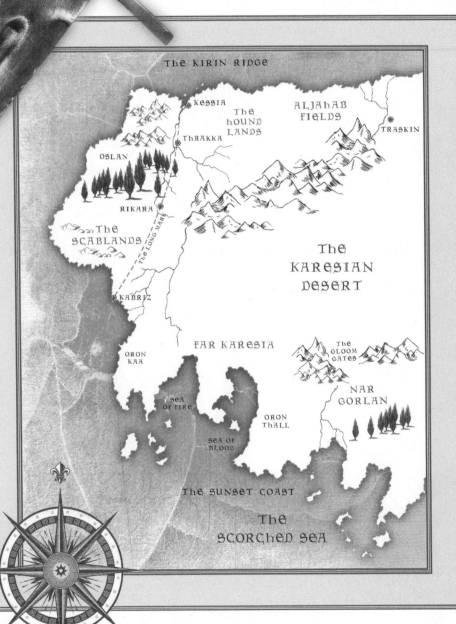

THE KIRIN RIDGE

KESSIA

The
HOUND
LANDS

ALJAHAB
FIELDS

THRAKKA

TRASKIN

OSLAN

RIKARA

The
SCABLANDS

THE LONG MARS

The
KARESIAN
DESERT

KABRIZ

FAR KARESIA

The
GLOOM
GATES

ORON
KAA

NAR
GORLAN

SEA
OF FIRE

ORON
THALL

SEA OF
BLOOD

THE SUNSET COAST

The
SCORCHED SEA

ARM OF THE RED

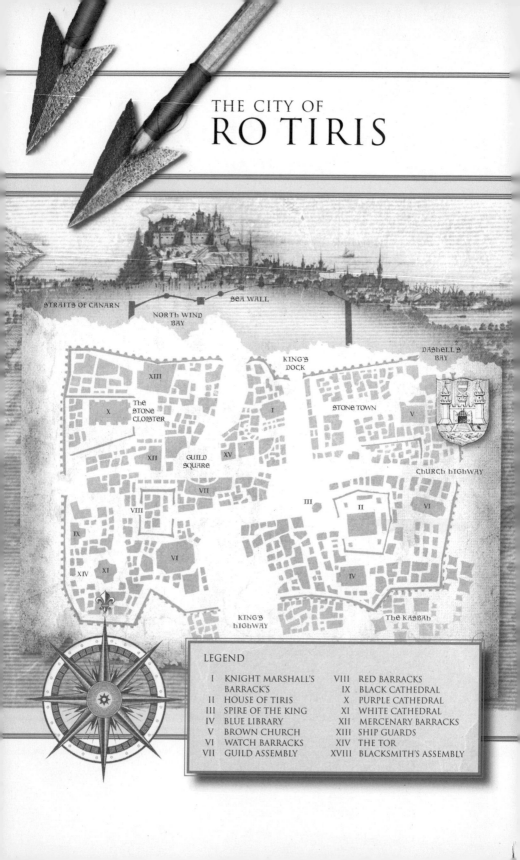

THE CITY OF
RO TIRIS

STRAITS OF CANARN

SEA WALL

NORTH WIND
BAY

KING'S
DOCK

DASHELL'S
BAY

XIII

The
STONE
CLOISTER

X

STONE TOWN

V

I

XII

GUILD
SQUARE

XV

CHURCH HIGHWAY

VII

VIII

III

II

VI

IX

XIV   XI

VI

IV

KING'S
HIGHWAY

The KASBAH

LEGEND

I	KNIGHT MARSHALL'S BARRACK'S	VIII	RED BARRACKS
II	HOUSE OF TIRIS	IX	BLACK CATHEDRAL
III	SPIRE OF THE KING	X	PURPLE CATHEDRAL
IV	BLUE LIBRARY	XI	WHITE CATHEDRAL
V	BROWN CHURCH	XII	MERCENARY BARRACKS
VI	WATCH BARRACKS	XIII	SHIP GUARDS
VII	GUILD ASSEMBLY	XIV	THE TOR
		XVIII	BLACKSMITH'S ASSEMBLY

THE CITY OF
RO WEIR

LEITH GATE

KING'S HIGHWAY

WARDER'S GATE

KING'S FOLLY

VII

III

VI

HAWKWOOD GATE

X

I

GRAND MARKET

OLD TOWN

II

PORT SIDE

VIII

IV

The DUKE'S HARBOUR

EASTERN HARBOUR

KIRIN TOR

IX

LEGEND

I   DUKE'S RESIDENCE
II KNIGHT MARSHALL'S OFFICE
III WATCH BARRACKS
IV PURPLE CHURCH
V   BLACK CHURCH
VI BROWN CHURCH
VII MERCENARY BARRACKS
VIII HARBOUR MASTER
IX RAINBOW POINT
X   MERCHANT'S GUILD

BOOK ONE

THE RED PRINCE

THE TALE OF THE OLD BLOODS

AS THE GIANTS became fewer and mortal creatures became more numerous, before ages had names and when time was still in its infancy, the blood was still strong.

The weak beings of this age took the blood gladly and mortal mated with Giant until mighty creatures rose to rule the rock, tree, earth and sea.

As the Giants disappeared, they left beings of strength and twisted form to rule their lands and fight their Long War. These old bloods were few and most bore a visage of madness which they used to cow the primitive men. Faces and bodies, half-twisted by the enormity of their blood, and minds with cunning intent.

As long ages passed, the old bloods waned until the blood was almost spent. They warred with the Great Race of Jekka and they warred with each other. Through the inexorable passage of time, mortals forgot about their masters.

The old bloods that remained bore children and the blood diluted until all that was left were abnormal remnants of Deep Time.

As the Jekkans left and men appeared, gaining their own power, naming their own lands, kingdoms and empires, the old bloods retreated to the darkness of the world. Some hid in forests, some in the deepest caves and some – those that could pass as men – walked paths of their own and kept alive the blood of Giants.

PROLOGUE

THE LADY OF Haran ducked behind a line of rocks and held her breath. The ground was hard and dotted with sharp stones. Beyond the rocks and across the northern plains of Haran rocky pinnacles rose, harsh and unyielding terrain where a thousand warriors could hide in a hundred places, anywhere from Ro Haran to the Walls of Ro.

'How many?' she whispered to Sergeant Ashwyn.

'Maybe a hundred, my lady. Another group of hunters trying to sniff us out.'

No more than forty paces away, the column of Hounds had not seen them and continued their march northwards, oblivious to the warriors of the fifth cohort.

'Not us, Ash . . . not us,' she replied. 'They don't know our names or who we are. They only know that Alexander Tiris, the Red Prince of Haran, is hiding up here somewhere.'

The Hounds clanked past, the noise of their marching masking any other sounds. She wondered about their training, or lack of it. To march into enemy territory in such a blatant fashion was ignorant, stupid, suicidal. The Seven Sisters didn't care about their troops – so long as they had more than everyone else. They're just a mob, she thought.

She peered carefully over the rocks to get a better look. Her long black hair, loosely tied in a topknot, brushed her neck as the wind picked up. It chilled her, finding the gaps in her leather armour and making her fingertips tingle. She wore no chain shirt or steel helmet, preferring to avoid blows rather than to bear them.

That set her apart from the prince's Hawks more surely than her gender or origin.

'Announce our presence, sergeant,' she said.

Ashwyn drew his short sword and signalled to the men. Two hundred, half the unit, poised to strike. The Hounds were now parallel to them, ambling northwards, a shining mass of black armour and scimitars.

The warriors of Haran moved as one as Ashwyn shouted, 'We are the Hawks of Ro, stand down or die.'

* * *

Although she had lived in the duchy of Haran for ten years, this campaign was her first prolonged stay away from the city of Ro Haran. It was a long way from Hunter's Cross, especially for a young woman untutored in the strict traditions of Tor Funweir, but then she'd never expected to be married to a duke of Ro.

Alexander Tiris had come to her land with an army of Red knights to purge a settlement of Dokkalfar. They met strong resistance from the warriors of the Cross. The knights floundered in the forests, but the fighting still lasted many months. The final battle against Xander's men left only two survivors. They huddled together in the deep woods, far from either camp and badly wounded.

He had told her he was a knight. He had told her he only followed orders. He was of the Red and did his duty for the One God. But his eyes were opened when the Dokkalfar found them.

He struggled at first, but his wounds were severe. He had no option but to accept their help. Over weeks and months they watched each other heal from the hidden branches of a Dokkalfar settlement. Each day she saw his glare softening, his conviction wavering. It wavered until he was no longer the same man. He stopped clutching his sword, stopped fussing over his armour, he even stopped calling them risen men.

At some point – she couldn't be sure when – they began to love each other. Endless days with each other for company meant they shared everything. War and death were a thousand leagues away, too distant to mean anything any more. So the king's brother and an unsuitable woman gave themselves to each other in the stillness of the forest. When they left, clutching hands, they were bound for life. He was handsome, tall and muscular, with strong hands and ardent brown eyes.

Alexander Tiris and Gwendolyn of Hunter's Cross married in a Darkwald village on their way back to civilization, with a vagabond Blue cleric to speak the words that united them.

Their first few months were difficult. Every knight of the Red has a story of a man he once knew who tried to leave. Without exception, those stories end in death: sometimes the noose, more often beheading. Xander was a Red knight who served no longer and neither of them wanted him to hang or lose his head. If he hadn't been of royal blood she might just have had enough time to watch him die in a military camp, north of the Falls of Arnon, before her own execution.

King Sebastian Tiris didn't even look at her as he made the proclamation. He wasn't a wicked man, just a pampered noble who couldn't conceive why his younger brother would wed a commoner in secret. Instead of death, he gave him a duchy, the most isolated in Tor Funweir, and dismissed them. The first and only man allowed to leave the knights of the Red, and his low-born wife, the Lady of Haran.

Ten years hence and time had only brought them closer. She had adapted to his world, knowing that he would never adapt to hers. He was tough on his men, but with her, in the quiet moments when the world went away, he was vulnerable and insecure, a man with great pain in his heart. He took on the role of general and duke, ruling fairly and beloved by the folk of Haran. A duke who had been a prince. A man who had cast away his god for the woman he loved. But he never forgot his family and he never forgot his name.

* * *

The Hounds startled, flailing scimitars and trying to move into a defensive formation. Gwen and Ashwyn led the Hawks in two waves, flanking the mass of black steel, and it was clear that the Karesians were outmatched. Their weapons were adequately forged but poorly wielded. Her first blow drove her Dokkalfar leaf-blade into a man's throat, sliding off his clumsy parry and deflecting the scimitar with little effort. The Hounds' plated black steel armour was not custom-fitted and gaps appeared as each man moved. At the underarm, the knee, the neck, a blade could be crippling or fatal, and the Hawks' short swords were designed to exploit such weaknesses.

Their bloody work was done quickly, with no survivors.

'That's the fourth patrol this week, my lady,' said Ash. 'Do you think they're getting bored of our city? Bored enough to come up here to die?'

'If the enchantress is foolish enough to stay in Haran and send all her Hounds to us . . . well, then we'll raise a glass to her stupidity. But we're not that lucky.'

'So if we can't go back to the city until she is gone,' asked the Hawk sergeant, 'when will that be?'

'Do you know a man who can kill them?' she countered. 'Xander won't return if there's any possibility he'll become thrall to Shilpa the Shadow of Lies . . . I'll kill him before I let that happen.'

'We've got five thousand Hawks of Ro, my lady, and every one of us would die rather than see the general a slave . . .'

'But . . .'

He smiled. 'But I'm sick of sleeping under canvas. It's been seven months.'

'Let's hope that assassin turns up soon, then,' she replied.

PART ONE

CHAPTER ONE

RANDALL OF DARKWALD IN THE TOWN OF KABRIN

THE HARBOUR WAS called the White Landing, though in the darkness it looked black. He'd never been this far south. It was hot, much hotter than he was used to. He wore a simple tunic, leaving his arms bare, and his belongings were stored in a heavy rucksack back at the inn. He was still sweating, even at night.

He had begun to trim his beard, and his master had remarked that the squire was turning into a strapping young man. Months of continual activity had turned him from wiry boy into well-muscled man of Ro. The sword at his side, the battered travelling boots, the visible scars – he felt older than his nineteen years. And it felt as if his conscience had added a year for each man he'd killed. It was a strange thing to admit. The bloodstains on his hands never seemed to disappear completely, nor did the nausea he felt whenever he pictured the men's faces.

A gust of warm air travelled across the black water and he closed his eyes, breathing in the refreshing wind. Somewhere across the Kirin Ridge was the city of Kessia. Beyond that, he didn't know. Their ship would be here soon and Randall was too impatient to join the others in sleep. He preferred to wait at the White Landing on the off-chance that the boat might arrive early. So far, it hadn't done.

He was also uncomfortable being around Ruth for any extended period of time. The Gorlan Mother had maintained her human form since they left the Fell, but he was sufficiently scared of spiders to struggle to alter his perception of the woman. She had slept when they'd slept, and eaten when they'd eaten, but Randall was certain that was merely a courtesy intended to make the two men feel more comfortable.

He had stopped trying to talk to Ruth and accepted that she simply didn't understand his desire for conversation. That was appropriate, because Randall understood nothing about her. She was an ancient spider and she was a woman. He shook his head and tried to accept that his life was likely to get stranger before it got any easier.

His mind was forced to stop wandering as a sail appeared out of the foggy sea. The ship was of Karesian design and emerged slowly, bobbing gently in the water and gliding towards the White Landing. The harbour was tiny compared to that of Ro Weir and catered mostly for private merchant ships and the occasional pleasure cruise. The king's harbour in Weir was flooded with Hounds, and so Utha had directed them to the small coastal town of Kabrin in order to take passage to Karesia.

Kabrin was one of the nicer places that Randall had visited since he had left the Darkwald, and they had found it easy to pass unobserved through the quiet town to a tavern overlooking the White Landing. If the captain of the ship proved trustworthy, they'd be in the city of Kessia in a week or so, and that thought terrified him. He knew that Utha had never been there and he doubted whether Ruth would have much local knowledge. None of them had a clue about Karesia or how to act around Karesians.

A bell was rung from the harbour to signal that the ship was approaching at the right angle. Men on board began to trim the sails and prepare to dock. Within a few minutes the ship had turned and the sailors were coiling ropes to throw across to men stationed on the landing.

Randall puffed out his cheeks and began to stroll down the wooden steps to the dock. He tried to adopt a tough demeanour for dealing with the ship's captain, imagining the man would react badly to a humble squire. They'd been told that the Karesian's name was Captain Makad and that he was amenable to chartering his boat to strangers. For a price. Randall had twenty gold crowns. Utha had told him to pay no more than fifteen for passage to Kessia.

The Karesian crew quickly roped the ship to the dock and rolled out a wide landing plank over which a dozen men quickly disembarked. They all had the rolling gait of men who had spent most of their lives at sea, and the hard faces of men who don't like other men. Randall thought briefly about going to wake Utha before he attempted to deal with the sailors, but decided at least to try and negotiate a favourable deal on his own. The worst they can do is kill me, he thought.

The sailors were joking and complaining among themselves as Randall approached. The main topic of conversation was the likelihood, or otherwise, of there being a brothel in Kabrin. Randall was fairly sure they'd be disappointed, but hopefully the preponderance of taverns would soften the blow during their time ashore.

'What do you want, boy?' asked a bearded sailor.

'Captain Makad,' replied Randall, keeping his voice even and unemotional. 'I have business for him.'

The dark-skinned Karesian sailor assessed the armed stranger in front of him before nodding in the direction of a man just coming ashore.

'There's your man,' he said, keeping his eyes fixed on the squire.

'Thank you.'

Randall thought that there was no reason to forget his manners, despite the impression he formed that Captain Makad and his crew were far from legitimate traders – something about their demeanour, the cutlasses in their belts, the glares they gave any man of Ro who came too close to their ship.

Randall smiled to himself as he realized how little he feared common criminals. The things he'd seen in the last few months had strengthened his confidence beyond the point where a few nasty glares could bother him. In fact, he found himself meeting them, and standing his ground before the sailors.

Captain Makad was a tall Karesian in late middle age. He was barrel-chested, with a smug look of self-satisfaction on his face. Wiping his mouth with a napkin, he looked as if he had just stopped eating. He was taking his first steps on the wooden dock as Randall approached.

'Captain Makad?' he asked, extending his hand.

The Karesian sailor looked down at the offered hand and then back up to meet his eyes.

'I don't shake hands with Ro.'

Randall snorted confidently, glad he found the insult amusing and not offensive.

'And I don't offer money to rude bastards that don't shake my hand,' he said with a smile. 'Shall we start again?' He extended his hand a second time. 'My name's Randall of Darkwald. Would you be Captain Makad?'

The Karesian sailor narrowed his eyes at the confidence on display and looked around to reassure himself that a dozen or so of his men were still present.

'I am,' he replied, no longer smiling. 'What do you want?'

Randall nodded down to his offered hand and broadened his smile, indicating that he wasn't going to respond until the niceties had been observed. Captain Makad considered his next move carefully and, after a moment, took Randall's hand and shook it half-heartedly.

'You see? We can always be polite,' said the squire, slightly surprised at his own confidence. 'Now, I understand that you are amenable to paying passengers.'

'I might be,' replied Makad. 'Who, and how many?'

'Two men and a woman . . . we're going to Kessia.' Randall wasn't turning away and he judged that his stare was making the barrel-chested captain a little unsure of himself.

'I could do that,' replied the Karesian, adopting a more business-like expression, 'for thirty gold crowns.'

'Ten,' countered Randall.

'Who do you speak for, boy? Who am I taking to Kessia?' Makad was obviously wary and, just as obviously, not a fool.

'Me and two friends of mine . . . twelve crowns,' replied Randall.

The Karesian looked around at his crew and nodded to the closest men. Four swarthy-looking sailors closed in round Randall and waited for their captain's order, nodding their heads suggestively.

Makad began to look even more smug. 'Give me a reason not to steal your shiny longsword and dump you in the harbour.'

Randall chuckled. 'I could give you a reason, a very good reason, or I could tear your head off and use it to kill your men . . . but then you wouldn't get twelve crowns for sailing to Kessia . . . which you're going to do anyway.'

It was a bold strategy, but the squire didn't back off a step, even when surrounded by men who would attack him in an instant if their captain ordered them to.

For a moment, Randall thought he'd pushed his confidence a little too far, until Captain Makad replied, 'Fifteen crowns . . . and I won't kill you.'

'Done,' he replied. 'When do you set sail?'

Makad looked back at his ship, then up into the dark night sky. 'With a good wind, we'll be out of here a few hours after dawn. I need to give my lads a chance to get drunk and fucked . . . assuming there are paid women in town.'

A few nods from his men indicated that they liked this plan.

'Whatever you want,' replied Randall, 'as long as they can sail when hung-over.'

A few of the sailors looked as if they were about to take offence, but Captain Makad shook his head.

'We'll be here two hours after dawn,' said Randall, beginning to turn and leave the dock. 'Oh, and just so we're clear, neither of my companions are as fluffy as me . . . so I advise you to take the money and not do anything foolish.'

He maintained his smile for a moment before striding through the Karesian sailors and back up the wooden steps of the White Landing. No one said anything as he left and he allowed himself a moment of self-satisfaction as he walked back to the tavern.

Randall didn't mind the uncertainty, he didn't mind the danger, and he didn't mind being the calm centre of his bizarre little world. He had accepted that his fate was bound to that of his master and where Utha the Ghost went, Randall would follow.

* * *

'Randall, I told you to wake me up when the ship arrived. I did not tell you to talk tough to a bunch of Karesian sailors.'

Utha was always grumpy in the morning and his squire no longer took it seriously.

'It was a sort of experiment,' replied Randall, opening the shutters to their room and letting the bright sunlight intrude.

'Are you trying to fucking blind me, boy,' grumbled the Black cleric, holding an arm up to his eyes and rolling over in bed. 'And what kind of experiment involves you picking a fight with a few dozen men?'

Randall shrugged. 'I thought that confidence was the important thing . . . the experiment proves I was right.'

Utha scratched at the huge scar running down his neck and sat up on the edge of his bed. He was grunting and rubbing his eyes, though looked otherwise fit and healthy. Randall was impressed at his master's constitution and confined himself to worrying mostly about his state of mind, leaving his physical well-being to take care of itself.

He had sensed a change in his master since they left the Fell. Utha now spoke of the halls beyond the world and, in his sleep, he murmured about a stairway, a labyrinth and a guardian. Randall didn't understand exactly where they were going or why they had to go there. He certainly didn't understand why it was necessary to take Ruth along with them.

The Gorlan mother, even in human form, was a constant worry in the back of his mind. As he looked at the dark-haired woman, just waking from sleep, he gritted his teeth and breathed deeply.

'You have done well, Randall,' said Ruth, sitting upright and seeming instantly awake. 'Your master does not appreciate you.'

'No, no he doesn't,' replied Randall.

'Gang up on me after I've had breakfast,' interjected Utha with a throaty growl.

Randall gestured to the tray of bread and fruit that had been placed on a small table by the door. It was far from a hearty breakfast, but was included in the price of the room and wouldn't dent their rather meagre travelling fund.

'What are we going to do for money in Karesia?' he asked. 'Do they use gold crowns?'

Utha began to munch on a fist-sized apple and considered the question. 'I'm actually not sure.'

Randall didn't like this answer. 'So I'm in charge of such things?'

'You're my squire, boy. It's your job to look after me,' he said, between mouthfuls of apple.

'I don't know how much bed and board costs in Kessia, but we're not exactly rich.'

Randall opened his small coin pouch and counted the gold crowns within. He counted to ten and estimated that, were they in Tor Funweir, they'd be able to pay their way for a few more days. He hoped that things were cheaper in the capital of Karesia.

'I don't like Karesian food,' said Utha. 'Lots of spicy meat, makes my stomach churn.'

'We won't be able to afford lots,' replied Randall. 'Maybe a small amount of spicy meat.'

Utha glared at his squire but said nothing. Randall hoped the occasional bit of teasing would help lighten his master's bad mood. If the joking helped, he'd take it on board as another of his duties.

'What was the captain like?' asked Utha.

'Fat. Suspicious.'

'In your professional opinion, young Randall, is he likely to kill us and dump us off the coast?' asked the cynical albino.

He shook his head. 'Doubt it, he seemed like a coward. I don't think he's too bright. He has a crew of nasty-looking sailors, though. I'd say they don't always ply an honest trade.'

'Very few Karesian sailors are entirely honest, my dear boy. Smuggling is far too easy to do and far too difficult to stop.'

'And we don't sail too well . . . as a race, I mean.' Randall had heard a hundred jokes about the notoriously poor maritime skills of the Ro.

'Armoured men on armoured horses are not best suited for sea combat. You can't lead a heavy charge across the deck of a ship.'

'The captain didn't seem too concerned that we were Ro. Maybe he's not expecting an armoured cavalry charge.'

Randall had begun to gather up their belongings while Utha was eating. Ruth had remained seated on the edge of her bed, looking impassively at the two men.

'So, where to after Kessia?' asked the squire.

Unexpectedly, it was Ruth who answered. 'The Hound lands lie to the south of the capital city – also called the Spider's Web, incidentally – then the city of Thrakka. An interesting place of spires and viziers.'

'Viziers?' questioned Randall, who had heard the term but did not know what it meant.

'They're diplomats, I think,' answered Utha. 'The noble classes of Jaa. They make sure the merchant princes and mobsters stay polite . . . well, polite-ish.'

'It's a little more complicated than that,' said Ruth. 'The viziers are not to be trifled with, even by the mighty Utha the Ghost.'

'Who says I want to trifle with anyone?' replied the albino, glaring at Ruth.

'It seems to be in your nature.'

Randall chuckled involuntarily, causing Utha's glare to turn towards him.

'What?' said the squire. 'It's a fair point, master.'

'I haven't finished eating yet. You're not allowed to gang up on me.' To emphasize the point, he took another large bite of apple.

* * *

They said nothing more while Randall packed, Utha ate, and Ruth looked on without blinking. Within twenty minutes they had paid their bill at the inn and were walking through the warm morning air of Kabrin. They shared the streets with few other people, though an occasional commoner did spare an extended glance for Utha. True to form, the cleric paid them no attention.

As they neared the dock, a thin, well-dressed man of Ro, carrying a longsword, appeared suddenly out of a side street. His eyes were red and his skin pasty, though a black mark on his cheek seemed to be obscuring a tattoo. He stumbled into Randall, losing his footing on the cobbled road, and fell over.

'Easy, friend,' said the squire gently. He offered a hand to help him to his feet.

'Get away from me,' sneered the man, slapping away Randall's hand and pulling himself up. His movements were sluggish and uncoordinated, suggesting he was hung-over, or maybe still drunk.

Randall backed away and Utha grabbed the collar of the man's cloak, roughly pulling him into a standing position. He wore well-tailored clothes which, though dirty and creased, marked him as a nobleman of some kind. The longsword at his hip was not a decorative weapon and he had scarred hands.

'Better get home,' said Utha, straightening the man's cloak.

For a second they locked eyes. The man showed a flicker of recognition as he looked at the albino. Utha didn't react with more than a raised eyebrow and in a moment the man had left, weaving a chaotic path along the dawn-lit streets.

'You should keep your head covered,' said Randall, wishing his master was more aware of his distinctive appearance.

'You should keep your mouth shut,' replied Utha.

Randall decided to stay quiet while the three of them completed their short journey to the harbour. Captain Makad's ship was the tallest at anchor and bobbed gently in the morning wind. The sea was calm and the Kirin Ridge stretched over the horizon, and Randall felt strangely tired as he searched for Karesia in the distance. All he could see was a rippling line of blue at the limit of his field of vision.

'I get seasick,' muttered Utha, as the smell of salt water hit them.

Randall looked at him, trying to stifle a laugh. 'Okay, that is . . . not at all funny.'

The squire ducked under an attempted back-hand from his master and quickly chuckled his way down the street.

'Come here, you cheeky fucker,' barked Utha, running after him.

The chase ended with the squire, desperately trying not to laugh, cowering against the steps leading to Makad's ship.

'Okay, I'm sorry, master,' he said, biting his lip.

Utha stood over him and narrowed his eyes. 'You only call me master when you've done something wrong or are trying to be funny.'

Randall let out a laugh, unable to help himself. 'Yes, master.'

'Right, you little bastard.' Utha grabbed his squire by the back of the neck and hefted him upwards. He raised his hand as if to strike, but the anger quickly disappeared from his face and was replaced with a reluctant smile.

Randall turned to look down the steps and saw a dozen Karesian sailors looking at them.

'Er, this might damage my tough reputation,' he said, nodding towards Makad's men.

'What the fuck are you looking at?' Utha snapped at the Karesians.

'They're looking at our passengers.'

The words came from Captain Makad, who was once again wiping food from his mouth. The barrel-chested Karesian had a half-eaten chicken leg in his fist. 'When you're done beating the boy, the tide is waiting.' He turned back to his men. 'Stop gawking and get to work, you worthless cunts.'

Utha released Randall and stepped back from the steps. 'Fifteen gold crowns, huh? Well done, my dear boy.'

'It wasn't actually that difficult. I just acted a bit like you,' replied the squire.

With pride rather than anger, Utha motioned down the steps. 'After you, sir.'

'Thank you, master.' He received a light cuff to the back of the head as he walked towards the tall ship and Captain Makad.

Ruth, who sauntered slowly behind them, was given special attention by the Karesians, who leered at her. She didn't react, but kept her eyes forward, gliding along the wooden dock and weaving between the gruff sailors.

'She with you?' asked Makad as Randall reached the gangplank. He nodded. 'I told you, three of us. Me, him . . . and her.'

Utha smiled up at the captain and pushed back his hood to reveal his bone-white hair, pale skin and pink eyes. 'A fair wind for the Kessian dock, captain?'

Makad was startled at the intimidating man before him, but showed no sign of recognition. As Randall had hoped, Utha's celebrity had not spread to Karesia.

'Three days,' replied the captain. 'The winds are pretty constant along the Ridge.'

'And make sure our friend isn't bothered by your men,' said Randall, glancing at Ruth.

'They'll behave.' Makad was suspicious, but the gold was a good enough reason to keep his word for now. 'Come aboard. The three of you will be sharing a cabin.'

Utha boarded first, leaving Randall to wait for Ruth, who was taking her time walking along the dock.

'I've never been to sea,' she said calmly.

'Something we have in common,' replied Randall, realizing that he didn't know whether or not he got seasick.

It took a few minutes for the crew to cast off and ready the ship to make way. Randall and his companions were left on deck to stand by the railings while Makad shouted at his men. Utha said nothing and his thoughtful gaze was directed across the Kirin Ridge to the shimmering southern horizon. Somewhere there was a strange new country. Jaa's land. Karesia.

The three of them stood in a silent line, looking out to sea, as the ship – the name of which Randall had not noticed – began to lurch out of the small harbour. Kabrin was a modest place, remarkable primarily for its dock, and he hoped that anyone searching for Utha would not think to look here. A quick glance at his master made it clear that the squire was alone in his worry. Utha was as oblivious, as always, lost in his complicated thoughts.

The Karesian sailors moved with a certain professionalism and the ship began to bob smoothly over the calm sea. Randall knew nothing about sailing but he was impressed with the spectacle of sails unfurled, ropes uncoiled, orders shouted. Within minutes they'd caught the wind and the three passengers looked up to see the billowing white sails tense and pull the ship out to sea with a sudden lurch of speed.

'This is how it starts,' muttered Utha, holding his stomach and puffing out his cheeks. 'Soon there will be headaches and vomit.'

'So, if Captain Makad is less than honest, I'll have to fight his crew on my own?' joked Randall.

'Get her to help.' Utha waved at Ruth, who was ignoring the two men and gazing up at the wind-filled sails.

As the ship moved swiftly away from Kabrin, the sailors slowed down. The back-breaking part of sailing seemed to lie in the bits that involved the harbour, and now that the ropes were tied and the sails in place the Karesians visibly relaxed. A few of those Randall had encountered earlier displayed hostile looks and muttered comments, as if they were more confident at sea, but they still had work to do and Makad kept them too busy to cause problems.

'Out the way, boy,' snapped a gruff sailor, reaching for a coil of rope next to Randall's feet.

The squire moved along the rail and nearly fell as the roll of the ship caught him by surprise.

'If we're both sick, my dear boy, Ruth will have to defend us on her own,' said Utha, smiling at his squire.

They were eventually led below and shown to their cabin. Randall slowly began to get the hang of walking on the ship and was glad that he didn't suffer from seasickness. Unfortunately, Utha was not so lucky and his pale skin was turning green by the time he lay down in his hammock.

The wooden frame of the ship was solid and well cared for, and Randall found its construction interesting. From the wide crew quarters through which they had to walk, and the stairs that interlocked between decks, the ship felt like a creaking mansion, with large empty spaces and cosy compartments. It was strangely empty, with only provisions taking up any space and no obvious cargo. If these men were smugglers, they had already deposited their goods.

'I'm going to be face-down on this hammock until we reach Kessia,' slurred Utha.

'How long will that take?' asked Randall, glancing round at their new living quarters. There were four hammocks and a low table, with everything closely packed and no open floor space.

'Couple of days,' he replied.

'Should be enjoyable,' said Ruth.

'Not for me.' Utha was looking very unwell. Even for an albino who normally looked strange, his appearance was a mess.

'We've only been at sea fifteen minutes,' said Randall.

'Don't pity me, I'll die quietly,' Utha replied, burying his face in the hammock and clasping his hands behind his head.

'The mighty Utha the Ghost,' said Randall, with an ironic smile. 'If your enemies could see you now.'

'I'm going to break your fucking nose when we're on dry land.' It was said so feebly that all Randall could do was laugh.

* * *

Being at sea was a calming experience for Randall. He had nothing to do and nowhere to go. Captain Makad was true to his word and kept his men polite, though the underlying current of aggression remained.

The first night was peaceful, with Utha's moaning the only sound, and Randall slept better than he had in months. The hammock was more comfortable than it looked and the air was fresh and clean. By the time he awoke, to the gentle ripple of waves and the calling of sea birds, the young squire was surprisingly well rested.

One of Makad's men, one of the few who actually spoke to the young man, had told him that they would reach the main shipping lane within a day and then turn south towards Kessia, passing the broken ridge of jagged islands that gave the sea its name. Hoping to be on hand when they sighted another ship, Randall was spending his time on deck, enjoying the sea air and watching the Karesians go about their work.

'You worry a great deal,' said Ruth suddenly. 'Things happen in their own time and in ways we can only accept and rarely predict.'

Randall snorted with little elegance, showing his scorn for the words. 'That's one of those annoying things that sounds profound, but is basically rubbish.'

'You are cynical beyond your years,' replied the Gorlan mother.

He laughed, more genuinely this time. 'That is a commonly held opinion.'

The ship was alone, bobbing gently southwards on an empty blanket of blue. Randall and Ruth stood alone against the railings of the forecastle, far from the sailors, who went apathetically about strange tasks that Randall didn't understand.

'We should mate,' she said, as if she'd been thinking about it for a while.

The squire raised an eyebrow at her.

'You'll forgive me if I don't agree,' he replied. 'And the suggestion is a little . . . er, disconcerting.' He looked at her. 'You're a spider.'

Her thin lips curled into the merest hint of a smile. 'Actually, I'm a Gorlan, not a spider.'

A shiver travelled up his spine as he remembered their first meeting. She was, as far as Randall could tell, a huge, talking spider. He'd never liked spiders, even the small ones that killed chickens throughout the Darkwald, and Ruth was a terrifying specimen.

'Have you known women?' she asked.

Randall's life had moved quickly over the past year and he had been forced to miss out on the usual stages of a young man's experience. 'It's strange to think that I haven't . . . and that it doesn't bother me.'

'I haven't known another's flesh for time beyond your understanding,' said Ruth.

Another shiver of nerves, tinged a little with revulsion. 'Don't you . . . mate with other spiders . . . er, Gorlan?'

'Only when the need to procreate is paramount. We eat our males after mating.'

He took a step away from her and his eyes widened.

'Do not worry, Randall of Darkwald,' said Ruth. 'We mate in other forms purely for pleasure. The instinct to consume applies only to male Gorlan. That is why there are no remaining Gorlan fathers.'

'You are seriously scaring me,' muttered the young man. 'I'm no expert on seduction, but I think you're going about it the wrong way.'

'I understand that humans often use alcohol to aid seduction. Perhaps we should try that.' She wasn't joking and Randall wasn't laughing.

'Can't we just forget about it?' he asked.

She attempted a smile. It didn't quite work and her narrow face looked harsh and angular. 'No, I don't think so. Maybe I'll try another method of seduction. What do you think would work?'

Randall suddenly found the situation funny. He snorted with amusement, his face cracking into a broad smile. Ruth was slim and would be attractive to a man who had not seen her true form. As he looked at her, his smile became softer and he leant forward over the railing.

'I don't think any attempt at seduction would work. I'd be nervous having sex anyway, and adding the Gorlan element to the equation would probably make me catatonic.'

'I could relax you,' replied Ruth.

'It would probably take a lot of booze.' Randall instantly realized that this comment would offend a normal woman. He found it reassuring that Ruth was immune to petty annoyance.

'I'm sure the captain has plenty of wine.'

'Wait,' Randall said, shaking his head. 'Are we seriously considering this?'

She gazed out to sea. 'We have little else to do. The ship can sail without us.'

They locked eyes. The young squire was taller than the Gorlan and his shoulders, broad and muscled from months of activity, made Ruth appear rather petite. She had a vulnerability in her eyes that disconcerted him, a low gaze from green pupils and dark irises.

'We would enjoy each other,' purred Ruth, causing him to shiver with involuntary arousal.

'Stop it,' he said.

'No.' She stepped closer to him until they were virtually touching.

'Please,' he murmured with little confidence.

Ruth lowered her head and looked Randall up and down. Her eyes moved slowly, making him even more uncomfortable. She paused for a second, looking at his chest, before returning her gaze to his eyes. It was a deeply sensual look, loaded with hidden meanings. Randall understood his rapid breathing, his sudden arousal and his nervousness, but he didn't understand seduction.

She gently ran her fingertips along his forearm and lightly cradled his hand. 'Do you still want me to stop?' she asked, a gust of wind catching her hair.

'I . . . I don't know,' he stuttered in reply.

* * *

It was a strange hour, spent largely naked and filled with constant apologizing from the virginal squire. Sex seemed to be a matter of not trapping your hair, skin, legs, hands and private parts in a manner that caused pain. When this was accomplished, the melding of flesh was a deeper and more fulfilling experience than Randall would have thought possible. He fell in love a little as Ruth, straddling him, rose in apparent ecstasy and caused her new lover to become utterly lost in sensation. He couldn't see beyond her skin, the smooth and dusky flesh that swayed on top of him. He didn't think about her true nature; it was further away than the gentle rippling of the water or the surge of the sails.

The sex ended quickly, but the naked sprawling on the floor of the small cabin lasted nearly an hour. Ruth had pulled down two unused hammocks to act as a blanket and they had been quiet enough not to disturb the sailors. Utha, still seasick in the next cabin, had been silent, probably asleep, and the two naked, sweaty bodies that adorned the wooden floor were undisturbed.

'You have much to give a lover, Randall of Darkwald,' purred Ruth. Her dark hair was wild and wavy, spread across her naked back. Their bodies glistened.

'Do you mean other than you?' he replied, still breathing heavily.

She leant on her hand and ran a finger down his chest. 'It would seem selfish to keep your talents to myself.'

She kissed him and Randall lost himself again. He felt naive, young, stupid and, for the first time in weeks, out of his depth. He had found it easier to deal with swords, blood and death than with a woman and sex. Even in the warm afterglow he was wide-eyed and light-headed, not fully trusting himself to speak without sounding like an idiot.

Ruth craned herself over him, looking down into his eyes as he lay on the white linen hammock. 'Even now you can't relax,' she said plainly.

'Especially now,' he replied.

'We have nothing to do at this moment, no commitments or responsibilities. The Ghost is occupied, the sailors are sailing. We are alone.'

She kissed him again. This time it lingered. Her lips parted gently and he closed his eyes, letting the sensation ripple through his body. They remained there for what seemed like days.

* * *

Utha the Ghost dreamt. When he wasn't awake and vomiting, murmuring quiet insults to the waves, he was lost in his own mind. When Ruth had touched his mind in the Fell, she had awoken something within him. Now, his sleeping hours were filled with visions and dreams of obscure places and bizarre beings for which he didn't have names. Creatures lived and died in worlds of imagination and realms of fantasy.

He believed that he saw the halls beyond the world, but he couldn't understand what he saw. His eyes were not equipped to translate the vistas of castles, mountains, halls and caverns that his dreams showed him. He saw ethereal roads, arcing through the eldritch sky. He saw patterns and silhouettes colliding together.

The upper and lower void, the faded pathways, the fragment of R'lyeh, the flesh halls, the dreamlands, the plateaus of Leng, the sea of urges. None of it made sense, but he could see it and it did not drive him mad. He was unique among men. He could perceive beyond the world and keep his mind intact.

The only thing that made sense was the pull southwards, the desire to find the staircase, the labyrinth and the guardian. Utha believed that he could reach beyond the world – that he was the last being who could do so. He wasn't given to selflessness, or to follow vague intuitions and dreams, but someone – or something – was summoning him.

He'd always been an outsider, since before he joined the church, since before he cared about his pale skin and pink eyes. He didn't belong and he'd always assumed that was his calling from the One God, a part of being infused with death.

But what his dreams told him was that he didn't belong because he was not entirely human. If for no other reason than to discover who he was, Utha the Ghost, last old-blood of the Shadow Giants, would walk up the stairs, traverse the labyrinth and defeat the guardian.

CHAPTER TWO

KALE GLENWOOD IN THE DUCHY OF HARAN

T
HE WALLS OF RO were an impressive sight to a man who had never been to the western lands of Tor Funweir. The path through the mountains had been easy. It would have been dangerous, but Rham Jas had effortlessly seen off three bandit attacks. Glenwood had given the third group a chance to run, but they'd stubbornly refused to believe that the diminutive Kirin was dangerous.

The assassin had chosen to ride in the lead for the last few days and had actually stooped to talk to his companion. It seemed that Rham Jas Rami, arguably the most infuriating man he had ever met, was actually looking forward to their arrival in Ro Haran. He'd even spoken at length about his intention to get blisteringly drunk once he'd killed Shilpa the Shadow of Lies. After the events of the last few months Glenwood thought they both deserved it . . . assuming that for once they weren't running away from their enemies.

As they followed the trail down through the mountains, the river lands of Haran came into view. In the valley were clusters of wooden villages where fishermen lived peaceful lives, isolated from the rest of Tor Funweir by the mountain range known as the Walls of Ro.

They were not yet within sight of the city, but it was no more than a day's ride away. He had never seen the high banners of Haran, but the heraldry of the red hawk was well known, as were the city garrison, the Hawks.

'Do you think the fishermen will have anything to drink?' he asked, as the path dropped below the reach of the biting wind that lashed the higher altitudes.

Rham Jas turned in his saddle with a dubious grin. 'Goat's milk, maybe home-brew . . . nothing worth paying for.'

'Anything worth stealing?' countered Glenwood.

'There might be some buxom young farmers' daughters down there,' said Rham Jas with a chuckle.

'You're not that charming, Rham Jas.'

They both laughed at that.

'Where do we go from here?' asked Glenwood, as the trail grew steeper. 'From Haran, I mean. Assuming you kill Shilpa with your customary style and grace.'

'Well, we'll need to tell the duke that his city's free . . . assuming he doesn't kill us on sight . . . and then it's off to Ro Weir.' The Kirin was grinning broadly as he spoke.

'And that Saara woman, yes?'

'That's the idea,' replied the assassin. 'If all goes well, you should be back in Ro Tiris and plying your nefarious trade within a couple of months.' He patted his companion on the back in comradely fashion. 'It's okay, Kale, no need to thank me.'

'Fuck you, Rham Jas,' responded Glenwood, with an ironic smile.

'Aren't you sweet?'

They rode for a while until the ground levelled out and the wind dropped away completely. Some way to the north, across the rugged plains, Glenwood could see riders heading away from them at a trot. Otherwise the two men were alone in the duchy of Haran.

'See those riders?' asked Rham Jas, pointing. 'We've been spotted.'

'Who are they? Friend or foe?'

'They look like Hawks to me.'

The assassin raised his head as if he'd caught a scent on the wind. 'I think we'll know in a minute.' He gestured to the south.

Glenwood turned, just as six more riders emerged from a rocky outcropping.

As the riders approached, Glenwood was relieved to see their weapons were sheathed, though all were dressed in full battle armour. Rham Jas pulled back on his reins and wheeled his horse to a halt on the gravel path. Glenwood followed suit and the two men waited for the news or, more likely, confrontation the riders would bring.

All six wore the heraldry of Duke Alexander, a tabard bearing a red hawk volant, and well-maintained chain mail underneath. They wore short swords and rectangular shields, and the hard expressions of professional soldiers. Their faces suggested they had seen neither a bath nor a bed in some time.

'The road is closed, friend,' announced the lead rider.

Nudging his horse forward, Rham Jas held his empty hands wide. Glenwood followed. Their leader was a man of Haran of middle age and the chevrons on his shoulder suggested an officer's rank.

'We have business in Ro Haran, captain,' said Rham Jas, showing more knowledge of the Ro military than his companion would have credited.

'Not today you don't, Kirin . . . any business you have can wait until the city is open to travellers. No exceptions,' replied the soldier.

The assassin nodded and glanced to where the other riders had disappeared northwards. 'You are the duke's men?'

A chuckle erupted from some of the Hawks, though the captain looked unimpressed. 'We are Hawks of Ro, Kirin,' he replied scornfully.

'I know that,' said Rham Jas. 'What I mean to ask is, are you still the duke's men or do you follow . . . a new mistress?'

Worryingly, Glenwood noticed the Kirin's hand rest casually on the hilt of his katana. Well, if Rham Jas intended to fight half a dozen men of Haran, he was welcome to do so . . . without Glenwood's aid.

'We follow General Alexander Tiris,' replied the captain. 'The Karesian witch holds no sway over us.'

At the mention of the enchantress, the faces of the Hawks became ominous.

'That's good, then,' said Rham Jas, with a disconcertingly friendly grin. 'Would it be possible for us to have a little chat with your general?'

The captain frowned. 'Why?' he asked.

'I'm here to kill your witch,' replied the assassin cheerfully. 'It's only polite to let the duke know that he'll soon be able to return to his city.'

The Hawks were silent. The captain nudged his horse forward until he was as close to Rham Jas as their horses would allow. Glenwood felt the Hawk assessing the Kirin, taking particular note of his katana.

'I'm Captain Brenan of the Walls,' he said. 'What is your name, Kirin?'

'I'm Rham Jas Rami, friend to Lord Bromvy of Canarn and enemy to the Seven Sisters.' He wasn't grinning now and Glenwood caught a rare note of seriousness in his voice.

Brenan nodded slowly. 'Bromvy's a Black Guard and you're wanted by the Crown,' said the captain. 'They say you killed an enchantress in Tiris in front of a hundred armed men.'

Glenwood coughed. 'Probably a few more than that, but most of them weren't armed.'

'And who are you?' asked Brenan, turning to face him.

'Me? No one really, just a loyal companion . . . well, a companion. My name is Glenwood. I'm mostly just here for the scenery.'

A few of the Hawks chuckled, but the captain shook his head and returned his attention to the assassin.

'Well, maybe you and your pet here,' he gestured at Glenwood, 'should come and meet the general.'

The Kirin's grin returned. 'Excellent. Just one thing, though, what do we call him?' He pouted and there was a note of cheek in his voice. 'You Ro are obsessed with titles and your general seems to have more than most people. What is he, duke, prince, general, what?'

Captain Brenan smiled wryly. He seemed not overly impressed with Rham Jas. Glenwood thought his men looked even less impressed by the slight against their general.

'You can call him whatever you like, but he'll likely kill you if you piss him off,' replied the captain. 'So be on your best behaviour.'

Rham Jas smirked as though he were about to say something caustic. Thankfully, after a moment's thought, he merely nodded.

Brenan motioned them to follow, wheeling his horse off the path and towards the north. The others paused until Glenwood and Rham Jas had nudged their mounts after the captain, and then closed in formation behind. They broke into a gentle trot, travelling smoothly on to the lowlands of Haran.

'No matter what soldier-boy says, I'm not your fucking pet, okay?' whispered Glenwood.

'I actually liked the sound of loyal companion,' replied Rham Jas, with a smug grin. Glenwood felt like punching him.

* * *

It was several hours before they saw signs of life, albeit just abandoned fishing huts on the banks of the Red River. Captain Brenan said something about it being too cold for the trout this far inland. It was odd that a captain would trouble himself with such a mundane fact. The other Hawks, once they had become accustomed to their new travelling companions, filled the journey with equally trivial matters of weather, hunting and the seasons. By the time they reached a wooden watchtower that marked the edge of the duke's lands, Glenwood knew more than he wanted to about the winter migration of the local cattle and the hardy men who herded them.

For a man who had spent little time outside the city, he felt he was becoming strangely accustomed to this rough life. Since he and Rham Jas had left Ro Tiris, what seemed like a hundred years ago, he had not slept in a bed for more than a night at a time. As they had traversed the wilds of Tor Funweir he'd even learned how to light a campfire and to skin a rabbit. He still left the business of catching and preparing Gorlan to his less squeamish companion, but he shared all the other duties.

He hoped they wouldn't be required to spend a night in the company of Captain Brenan and his soldiers. But Rham Jas believed they'd sight the general's camp well before nightfall.

'What are you going to say to the duke?' asked Glenwood, as they rode through a wooded gully. 'He's a Tiris, they're not known for being nice to Kirin . . . or any common folk.'

'Just tell him you're a noble from Leith. I'm sure he'll be impressed,' replied Rham Jas with a smirk.

'I'm serious, you contrary bastard. He's a duke, or a general or whatever . . . and you're a Kirin scumbag. You don't have much in common.'

'I can kill the Karesian bitch. He'll be interested in that before he thinks to question my birth,' replied the assassin. 'Well, I might need to drop Brom's name a few times.'

Glenwood didn't really understand the Kirin's association with the lord of Canarn. 'Isn't he a traitor to the Crown?'

'A quality that may well be appreciated by the Red Prince,' said Rham Jas, with a reassuring grin. It was one of his rarer grins, and Glenwood wasn't entirely sure he trusted it.

'I'll let you do the talking.'

He wanted a bed, a drink and a warm woman. What he didn't want were any more complications in his life.

'Well, you'd better keep your mouth shut, then, because I think we're here,' said the assassin, pointing over the plain.

Just coming into view on the horizon, casting shadows as dusk descended on the duchy of Haran, was a large military encampment. Set back, next to a line of low caves and flanked by several newly built watchtowers, was the pennant of Lord Alexander Tiris. The Hawks of Ro had set the rest of their tents and fortifications in organized lines.

'There's a shit-load of them. What if they just arrest us and we end up in the stocks?' Glenwood asked, instinctively nervous around so many soldiers.

'They'll never take us alive,' replied Rham Jas with a mocking sneer. 'Just relax, we'll be fine.'

The forger was not reassured. 'Relax, the man says.' His words were directed skywards, to whichever god was listening.

Captain Brenan led them towards the centre of the camp. As they passed the first watchtower, a small town of tents spread out in front of them and a hundred grim faces turned to observe the two outsiders. These were not clerics or watchmen, but professional soldiers, loyal to Haran and their general. The Hawks of Ro were spoken of with the same respect as the knights of the Red. Indeed, their prowess was said to match the warriors of the One.

'They look pretty tough,' he whispered.

'In the long run, that's probably a good thing,' replied Rham Jas, grinning confidently at any Hawk who met his stare.

A bell rang insistently as the small group rode through the camp. Glenwood nervously watched dozens of soldiers emerge from their tents and come to attention as they passed. At the edge of the camp, nestled against the sheer cliff face, was a small hexagonal command pavilion flanked by the hawk banners of Haran.

'Watch your manners, Kirin,' said Captain Brenan as three figures emerged.

No ceremony or guardsmen accompanied Alexander Tiris. Of his two companions, one was a woman and the other a corpulent older man wearing the robes of the Blue church. Glenwood's first impression of the general was of his shaved head, focused dark eyes and simple steel armour with numerous minor alterations and repairs – chosen for efficiency rather than style. He was tall and cut an impressive figure, though his manner was relaxed. Glenwood had never seen the king but had been told that he bore some resemblance to a sweaty goat. If this were true, the Red Prince of Haran did not look like his brother.

'That's a big sword,' Rham Jas whispered, pointing out the oversized blade at the general's side. 'Man must have strong wrists.'

'General!' the captain saluted, striking his breastplate. 'A man with an interesting tale wishes to speak to you.'

The general looked past his captain at Rham Jas and Glenwood. He took in their faces, clothing and weaponry with no sign that he was concerned by their presence. The woman at his side regarded the mounted strangers more suspiciously. She was black-haired and attractive, but her movements were too cautious and her eyes too mistrustful to be beautiful. Glenwood noticed she was wearing leather armour and carried two leaf-blades of Dokkalfar design.

'Who are you, Kirin?' asked the general, looking up at Rham Jas.

'Shall I dismount so we can talk more comfortably . . . my lord?' asked Rham Jas.

'You can dismount once I've decided whether or not you're staying.' He turned to Glenwood. 'Do you carry that sword for show or does it mean something?'

'A bit of both, my lord,' replied the forger. 'But he's the one you want to talk to.' He gestured towards Rham Jas, smiling weakly.

'Is he now?' said Xander. 'Speak your name, Kirin.'

'I'm Rham Jas Rami,' responded the assassin nonchalantly.

'You are reckless, Rham Jas Rami,' said the general, almost indifferently.

The Kirin considered this. 'I suppose I am a little, yes.'

The fat Blue cleric approached Tiris and whispered something in his ear. Exactly what he said wasn't clear, but the churchman looked at the Kirin as he spoke.

'Ah, I see,' said the general. He smiled thinly. 'I hear my cousin Archibald has put a bounty on your head large enough to fill Oswald's Bank.'

Rham Jas shrugged. 'I try not to listen to what others say about me,' he replied with a grin. 'Archibald Tiris is a fucking idiot.'

A curl of amusement showed upon the general's stoic features. It was clear that Xander was not overly fond of his cousin.

The cleric whispered something else in his ear.

'And you know young Bromvy?' he asked.

'I do. He's one of my oldest and truest friends,' replied Rham Jas.

'Well, then,' said Xander, 'you'd better dismount and come and have a drink.'

He didn't move away from Rham Jas. In a display of courtesy that took Glenwood by surprise, the general extended his hand and offered to help the Kirin down from his horse.

The assassin paused, wrong-footed, but then he grasped the general's hand and allowed himself to be assisted.

'Welcome to Haran, Rham Jas Rami,' said Xander, thumping the Kirin around the shoulders. He frowned. 'You need to repair that armour, it's split.'

The assassin lowered his eyes mischievously. 'I prefer not to get hit at all.'

The Blue cleric roared with boisterous laughter. 'A man after my own heart,' he said, slapping Xander on the back.

'This is Brother Daganay, my confessor,' said the general. 'And this beautiful creature,' he gestured to the woman, who still watched them with wary eyes, 'is my dutiful wife, Gwendolyn.'

She frowned, then smiled, blew a kiss to her husband and turned back to the pavilion.

'Well, she's sometimes dutiful,' said Daganay. 'The rest of the time she's a hard-nosed bitch.'

Xander chuckled and the Blue cleric walked after Gwendolyn.

'Thank you, Captain Brenan,' said the general suddenly. 'Why don't you go and get some breakfast? Report back here in an hour.'

'Aye, my lord.'

The captain led his unit away as Glenwood dismounted with a hand from the general. With no ceremony he led the way into the large tent.

'This guy's like no Tiris I've ever heard of,' whispered the forger as they followed him into the pavilion.

'Brom always liked him,' replied Rham Jas.

Once inside, Xander seated himself in a large, comfortable-looking canvas chair. Daganay and Gwendolyn remained standing. In the centre of the tent were the remnants of a simple meal on a long wooden table. The rest of the pavilion was homely, with few of the customary noble trappings. It had a lived-in quality which spoke volumes about the time these people had been away from their city.

'Drink?' asked the general once Rham Jas and Glenwood had taken seats on the opposite side of the table.

'That would be pleasant,' replied the assassin. 'Darkwald red by any chance?'

Xander smiled. 'Afraid not, we're simply soldiers.' He reached for a bottle of dark liquid on the table and pulled out the cork with his teeth. 'The grapes on the southern slopes of the Walls make a tangy but not unpleasant vintage.'

He moved two brass goblets in front of the newcomers and poured each a generous measure.

'So, Rham Jas Rami,' said the general, 'what brings you to my squalid piece of Tor Funweir . . . just passing through?'

The assassin gulped back his wine and wiped his mouth on his cloak. 'It's a flying visit. Arrive, kill someone, fuck off. At least, that's the plan,' replied Rham Jas.

'And the target?' asked Xander.

'Her name's Shilpa. I understand she's an enchantress of sorts,' he replied smugly.

Xander snorted with amusement.

Daganay spoke before the general, leaning over the table and meeting Rham Jas's eyes. 'I'd advise you this is not the time for games, Kirin,' said the cleric quickly.

'And I'd advise you to take a step back, cleric,' replied the assassin mildly.

The general laughed, but there was steel in his laughter. Glenwood shivered.

'Watch your mouth,' said the general. 'We can have this conversation with or without my hand round your throat.' He kept his voice even. 'Daganay's comment was a fair one.'

Rham Jas turned back to the general, nodding slowly. 'Okay, I suppose it was. I'll try to . . . soften my tone. Okay?'

'I'd appreciate that,' replied Xander. 'Now, you claim the power to kill the witch. The report from Tiris supports your claim and I clearly have need of someone with your . . . abilities.' He leant back in his chair and glanced across at Gwendolyn and Daganay. 'I suppose I didn't actually believe that you did what they said, killing Katja in front of half a hundred lords and clerics.'

Glenwood cleared his throat and nervously raised his hand. 'It was probably a couple of hundred people, but most of them weren't armed. But I saw him kill her. He stuck a goblet into her skull while your cousin watched.'

Xander turned back to a grinning Rham Jas. The assassin's arrogant attitude had frequently made Glenwood want to punch him. However, in this case, it did seem to be justified. Whatever else this strange assassin may be, however annoying he may get, he does have an uncanny ability to kill people otherwise considered unkillable.

'How?' asked Xander. 'Why can you kill them?'

Rham Jas puffed out his cheeks. 'That, my Lord Tiris, is a very interesting question.'

'So answer it,' said Daganay.

'You'll excuse my confessor,' interjected Xander. 'He can't stand not knowing something.'

'If it's worth knowing,' answered the cleric.

'Oh, this is definitely worth knowing,' said Rham Jas, 'but I'm not going to tell you.'

Xander laughed again, more genuinely this time. 'I respect that . . . though it'll torture Dag here.'

'What's wrong with wanting to know?' asked Daganay indignantly.

'Enough,' barked Gwendolyn. 'You can argue later. If it's all the same to you, I'd like to return to our home. If this man can help, we listen to him.'

The general and the cleric looked as abashed as scolded children. Glenwood glanced at Rham Jas, both of them enjoying the situation. Alexander Tiris was clearly used to treating both his confessor and his wife as equals. There was none of the casual arrogance or misogyny that Glenwood would have expected from a duke of Tor Funweir and a member of the family of Tiris.

'Gwen's right,' said Xander. 'You may be just what we need, Rham Jas.' He paused. 'If we can trust you.'

'Well, I wouldn't leave me alone with your daughter,' replied the assassin with a lazy smile, 'but you can trust me to kill Shilpa the Shadow of Lies.' He took a gulp of wine and shifted position in his chair, moving his Dokkalfar war-bow from behind him and leaning it against the table. 'I understand that you and your good lady have spent time among the forest-dwellers.'

They both nodded. 'Gwen more than me,' replied the general. 'That's one of the reasons I have a Blue cleric with me . . . they do not preach about the Dokkalfar.'

Daganay spread his arms wide. 'I've read a lot about the risen and nothing has convinced me there is any credible evidence that they are undead monsters.'

Rham Jas frowned. 'I've never met a cleric of knowledge before,' he said curiously.

'It's simply a question of evidence and logic,' said Daganay. 'We do not trust things just because a cardinal decrees it. We study and learn to understand the world better.'

Gwendolyn snorted in amusement. 'Those of the Blue do not care about conquest or privilege, they care only for knowledge.'

'That's not strictly true,' said Daganay. 'I also care about Tor Funweir . . . and ale.'

'I think she means that you're less annoying than the Purple,' translated Xander, giving his confessor a playful punch on the shoulder.

'Well, the evidence would suggest that is undoubtedly true,' replied Daganay.

Glenwood didn't know how to react to the Blue cleric. Like his Kirin companion, he'd never met one before and had thought they were confined to dusty old libraries.

Xander turned back to the two outsiders. 'How long will it take you to kill the enchantress?'

Rham Jas was clearly gratified that the topic of conversation had returned to assassination. 'If you tell me where she is and what guard she has . . .'

The general nodded. 'And how are Brom's sea legs?' he asked mischievously.

The Kirin frowned. 'No idea, but he's never been much of a sailor. Will he be taking a voyage soon?'

'Of course,' replied Xander. 'Once I can return to my city I'll be loading as many men as I can spare on to ships and sailing to Tiris . . . via Canarn to pick up young Bromvy.'

Daganay raised a hand as Rham Jas opened his mouth to reply. 'Two nobles of Tor Funweir make a much better statement than one, wouldn't you agree? Especially when the nobles are planning to sail into the king's harbour with an army.'

Glenwood and Rham Jas looked at each other. By reputation, Alexander Tiris was single-minded and tough. However, to hear so bluntly that he intended to sail his army into Ro Tiris was startling.

'I'd imagine that Lord Archibald may be a little . . . unhappy about that,' said Glenwood, wincing at the understatement.

'Our sailing into his harbour should be the least of his worries. He should concern himself with what I'm going to do when I'm face to face with him,' said the Red Prince, his lip twitching.

'Well,' said Rham Jas, 'your family issues are no concern of ours . . . and I'm sure Brom would be delighted to accompany you.' The assassin paused, realizing that everyone present was looking at him. 'If you just tell me where Shilpa is hiding, we can be on our way.'

The general leant forward and locked eyes with Rham Jas. It was strange to meet a man who was not the slightest bit afraid of the Kirin assassin. It was stranger still when Rham Jas looked away from Xander's gaze.

'Don't worry, Rham Jas,' said the Red Prince, 'you'll be on your way soon. Dag, tell him what he needs to know.'

Xander rocked back in his chair and motioned for the Blue cleric to speak.

'Well, the logical place for her to be using as her headquarters would be Ranolph's Hold, the old knight marshal's office. With us gone, Marshall Trego is in charge, so she'll need to keep him close. It's also in the centre of town and next to the watch barracks. You should probably enter via the wood gate, they won't have guards on it. Head for the high towers.'

Daganay spoke as if what he was saying should have been obvious to anyone with a brain. His manner was of a man who had to concentrate to control the immense amount of knowledge he possessed.

'Just be sure to swing back this way and tell me when you're done,' said Xander.

* * *

Ro Haran was on the coast, but quite far back from the harbour and perched high on sheer cliffs above the rough seas. Its thick walls and high battlements could be easily defended by a handful of good soldiers – even a lowly forger like Glenwood could appreciate its design.

'Now that's what I think of when I imagine a city of Ro,' joked Rham Jas, as they approached the wooded gate. 'Why is it here, though? Who's going to invade this place?' He looked around at the rugged coastline and mist-shrouded plains. 'There's not much here.'

'It's an old, old city,' replied Glenwood. 'Back when Weir was far too dangerous to attack, the Hounds used to unload thousands of soldiers along this coast. The dukes of Haran have always been . . . the guardians of Tor Funweir.'

Rham Jas smirked. 'A scholar of Ro history now, are we?'

'Fuck you.' It was said without aggression. 'Stories from when I was a kid, I suppose. When my dad wasn't drunk he liked telling me about history . . . don't get me wrong, I'm no expert.'

'You had a father?' teased the Kirin.

'Not much of a father.'

Rham Jas stopped at the wood gate. It was heavily overgrown with brambles and all but invisible except for an arched doorway. It lay in a small depression next to the northern wall, leading to an equally overgrown tunnel of moss-covered brickwork.

'In we go,' said Rham Jas, pushing his reluctant horse through the tall brambles and into the dark tunnel.

'Oh dear,' replied Glenwood, 'another stealthy incursion into another hostile city.'

They passed through and dismounted, edging forwards beneath the thick walls of Ro Haran, until they emerged in a dusty back alley, stinking of rotten food and sewage.

There was a handful of guards on the main gate, but no crossbow-men patrolled the battlements and the two companions were barely noticed as they skulked from the alley on to a narrow, paved road. If Shilpa was worried about the Kirin paying her a visit, she wasn't showing it.

The paved road opened out into a huge courtyard, framed by a high inner wall. Beyond, the tall spires of the city perched on a hill.

Glenwood turned up his nose at the smell of rotting vegetation. He glanced around at overflowing sewage trenches and food left out to spoil. The common folk of the city – those who had not already fled – scratched around in the filth, piling it away from their homes in an attempt to stop the spread of disease.

Rham Jas covered his nose and mouth, coughing into his hand. 'Well, this is a bit fucked up,' he murmured.

'That's one way of putting it. The Seven Sisters aren't famed for their administrative skills, it would seem.'

'I think this particular sister is a bit of a bitch.' Rham Jas screwed up his face and waved away the noxious smell.

'These people are going to start dying,' said Glenwood.

He had seen pestilence before, when he was a child in Ro Leith, and the streets before him had the same whiff of lingering death.

'Do you think the general knows what she's doing to his city?'

Rham Jas led the horse away from the central courtyard, waving the forger after him. 'Xander struck me as the kind of man who cares about his people. He'd have told us. And I don't think he'll be pleased when he gets back.'

'Shall we kill the enchantress and cheer him up?' joked Glenwood.

'We? Are you an assassin all of a sudden?' replied the Kirin with a friendly grin.

'Fuck you, Rham Jas.'

Ranolph's Hold was well away from the wood gate, in an area of the city that was clean and well patrolled. It was positioned as a vantage point over the harbour and incorporated a colossal lighthouse as well as the town's main barracks, a building now empty of Hawks. The remaining guards went about their work with the apathy and casual violence of men who cared little for their duties. The common folk, stricken by hunger and disease, were dealt with harshly by the watchmen, but most were wise enough to stay away from the high towers of Ro Haran.

'Want me to do the talking?' he asked the Kirin.

'If you would be so kind,' replied Rham Jas, without looking up.

'I'll try the bold approach.'

'Just get us in, Kale.' This close to Shilpa, Rham Jas was acting with cold efficiency.

Glenwood rode straight for the line of carts acting as a barricade between the slums and the high towers. There were half a dozen men standing guard, each casually holding a crossbow. Shilpa and the remaining officials of Ro Haran had a simple approach to administration. Keep the commoners out. This, it seemed, was the way the Seven Sisters kept order. It was efficient, but cruel.

'Are we saving these people?' he asked Rham Jas, instantly realizing how stupid it sounded. 'Are we on the right side here? Because, if we are, it feels novel. Good.'

'I might be doing the right thing,' replied the assassin, 'but I'm not the good guy. Neither are you.'

'Still . . . it's nice to make a difference.' Glenwood showed his companion a broad smile. The Kirin chuckled in spite of himself.

'Okay, we're big fucking heroes,' joked Rham Jas.

'Hush now, time to spin some horseshit.'

Holding the reins indifferently with one hand and setting an imperious look on his face, Glenwood approached the watchmen. He'd seen plenty of officials in his time, but these were a little on the pathetic side. Most of them were unshaven and a few had the drooping red eyes of men the worse for drink.

'Ho there,' called Glenwood authoritatively. 'Clear this cart out of the road. I'm not going to clamber round it in order to get home.'

The watchmen roused slowly, directing confused expressions towards the man of Leith. His feigned confidence stymied refusal, but still they were suspicious of the rough-looking nobleman before them.

'Don't know your face, sir,' muttered a watchman.

'I don't know yours,' barked Glenwood, 'but I'm not lazing around impeding your journey home.'

Rham Jas coughed politely. 'Master, shall we report these men for impudence?' He spoke just loudly enough to be heard by the watchmen.

'Let's not be hasty, now.' Glenwood puffed out his chest. 'You have one chance to get out of my way before things get unpleasant.'

They were just cowardly, or apathetic, enough for the threat of trouble to do the trick. They hadn't seen the Kirin's face, and they wheezed and grumbled but removed the cart from the road.

'On you go,' puffed the watchman, barely mustering the effort to speak.

'Why, thank you, you're very courteous,' replied Glenwood, affecting his best expression of vacuous snobbery.

As they rode past the barricade the city changed radically. The noble mansions of Ro Haran that flanked the high towers were all spotlessly clean, and watchmen patrolled the streets between opulent residences. The rich citizens were still rich. A gift from Shilpa, perhaps.

With the Kirin's face still obscured, they made their way towards the Hold. Glenwood's clothing was poor and travel-worn, but his longsword averted any curiosity.

'What's going on over there?' Rham Jas was pointing towards the base of Ranolph's Hold where robed figures were advancing in single file towards the inner keep.

'Don't know,' replied Glenwood. 'Peculiar.'

The line moved slowly and disappeared behind the high, castellated walls into the bottom level of the Hold. Above them the building rose sharply, from the wide lower levels to the narrow watchtower, a fortified stone block overlooking the coast.

'Are you finding that grim procession as sinister as I am?' he asked.

Rham Jas was peering at the figures, his lips pursed in concentration. 'They're nobles,' he muttered. 'Expensive shoes.'

Glenwood took note of the array of leather boots and heeled shoes peeking out from under the anonymous robes. These were no commoners, and the watchmen of Haran were avoiding the area completely. A few armoured Hounds patrolled the battlements above, but, save for the silent line of figures, an eerie emptiness pervaded the central square.

Rham Jas was assessing the wide side streets, craning to see where the procession began. 'Some of them are coming from houses over there.' He smiled suddenly. 'This way, quick.'

He nudged his horse out of the road and dismounted. Glenwood followed. Rham Jas tied his horse to a wall bracket and darted into an alley, staying close to the wall, while Glenwood remained with their mounts, trying to appear casual. He heard two muffled grunts. A moment later, Rham Jas climbed back with two sets of black robes and a smug look on his face.

'Slick,' said Glenwood, looking along the street to make sure they'd remained undiscovered.

'I thought so,' agreed the assassin. 'Put it on and try to look sinister.'

'And then what? Have you got any idea what the place is like on the inside?'

Rham Jas shook his head. 'No clue. Let's wing it, shall we?' The accompanying grin was one of his worst.

Once adorned in billowing black robes, the two men walked to the end of the wide boulevard and joined the procession. The nobles moved at a shuffle, making it easy to infiltrate their ranks.

Glenwood kept his head down and focused on the figure in front of him. No one spoke. Soon they were approaching the wide gate that led into Ranolph's Hold. The gate was open, revealing a line of guards on either side of the courtyard. They were guiding the nobles of Ro Haran into a stone passageway leading downwards. The two interlopers moved silently forward with the slow column.

If they were going to be exposed, it would happen now. But it didn't. It had all occurred too quickly for Glenwood to be afraid. He was nervous, but not afraid.

Walking through the doorway, they entered a cold, high-ceilinged stone cloister. Thinly spaced torches illuminated a red-carpeted corridor along which the line of figures walked. Karesian women were positioned between pillars on either side. Each wore an elaborate, blood-red robe displaying twisted, sinuous symbols. When the women began to laugh the sound was shrill, but the nobles did not react.

'Step to your left,' whispered Rham Jas sharply, placing a hand on Glenwood's shoulder and pulling him out of the line.

The man of Leith was not quick enough to react to the assassin's instruction, but the Kirin pulled both of them behind a pillar in a single movement, attracting no attention from the walking nobles or the laughing women. The former were hooded and looking at their feet, and the latter seemed manic and unfocused.

Rham Jas shoved Glenwood into the shadow against a stone pillar, while he scanned the cavernous space. He crouched down and his eyes flickered rapidly, focusing in the darkness. Only the central carpeted walkway was lit; beyond the pillars the stone chamber melted into shadows.

The procession of Ro nobility kept moving and the Karesian women continued laughing. Glenwood tried to slow his breathing and stay as quiet as possible. Rham Jas pulled him backwards and they were enveloped in darkness. Groping around with his hands, Glenwood found the far wall and slid down it to sit on the cold stone floor.

'Now we wait,' said the assassin.

'Why couldn't I wait outside?' muttered the forger.

The laughter suddenly abated and the robed women began a bizarre undulating dance. Their robes were slashed at the arms and legs, and dark skin was exposed with every sensual movement. More torches were lit along the walkway and a raised platform came into view in the flickering red light. The cloaked nobles stopped before the platform. More appeared and the line grew into a column, four deep. The darkness obscured some of them, but a hasty count revealed at least fifty.

Glenwood jumped as the doors to the catacombs slammed shut. In the darkness beyond the platform a woman's voice could be heard. 'Friends, old and new, you are welcome.'

'There she is,' whispered Rham Jas. His focused gaze brought to mind a cat watching its prey.

The hoods were thrown back. Each face showed its own variation of wide-eyed euphoria. Men and women of Ro intoxicated by . . . something . . . maybe a drug, maybe devotion, certainly enchantment. They dropped to their knees and prostrated themselves before the enchantress. The dance continued, increasing in speed and intensity as each worshipper reached out towards their leader. Shilpa closed her eyes and moved along the line, letting her fingertips caress each outstretched hand. They flailed and cried, coming together as a mob, fighting for pride of place and a touch from the enchantress.

How quickly the weak-willed are swayed, thought Rham Jas. A few months before these people had been loyal to the One God.

Now, with a new, decadent religion to explore and a new mistress to follow, they had betrayed the god of their land and the ruler of their city. What had she promised them? Money? Influence? Maybe nothing. Maybe just a glance from this woman was enough to buy their allegiance.

'We come together in pleasure and blood,' she intoned breathily.

The Karesian women flung off their robes and the dance became frenzied and overtly sexual. Legs parted and flesh twisted into a mockery of sensuality – vicious, hateful, uncontrollable rapture.

'Give yourself to me . . . and to the Forest Giant of pleasure and blood.'

Pleasure and blood, pleasure and blood, cried the kneeling congregation as they removed their robes and clothing. Even Shilpa removed her dress and joined in the dance, in isolation on her raised platform.

'Stay here,' whispered Rham Jas.' And remember . . . don't look at her for too long.'

The assassin edged along the wall until he was past the platform and hard to see. Glenwood was alone with nothing but the rapidly escalating orgy for entertainment. It was a curiously unenjoyable sight. Something about the violence of the encounter – perhaps the way the acolytes surrendered to their primal impulses, biting, scratching and shrieking, like wild animals. There was no affection or intimacy, just deranged devotion to a god that demanded wanton excess.

Pleasure and blood, pleasure and blood. The ritual was equal parts both.

As the minutes stretched, he ceased watching. The worshippers were now violating one another in ways he was sure weren't legal in civilized lands. Why didn't the bloody assassin just stick his blade between her perfectly formed breasts? She was cavorting in a nimbus of light – Glenwood thought even he could have got close enough to her. The darkness beyond her appeared distorted, as if a tree were swaying in the wind – a trick of the minimal firelight.

Then she stopped writhing on the platform. Shilpa turned towards him. As if she had divined his thought, her eyes narrowed. Across layers of darkness, through legs, arms and bodies twisting in perverse rapture, he met her gaze. She saw him. Just for a moment, but it was enough.

Her silvery laugh made him smile, despite his fear. She sat up and her eyes were predatory. To look at her was both calming and arousing. She was naked, she was beautiful, and she was in his mind.

'I am called Shilpa the Shadow of Lies and you are most welcome here,' she whispered in his thoughts.

His head suddenly felt heavy. He rose and stepped towards her, vulnerable and naked under her attention, utterly absorbed by the desire to please her, barely registering the dark, grinning face that had appeared behind the enchantress.

'I don't enjoy doing this . . .' said Rham Jas.

The woman gasped and looked down at the katana blade protruding from her chest.

'. . . but you bitches killed my son and took my daughter.'

Shilpa's eyes widened. As she tried to draw breath, the Kirin assassin wrapped an arm round her neck and twisted the blade. Glenwood saw the life disappear from her face.

The bloodied, breathless worshippers stared in shock at the twitching body of the enchantress.

'Kale, your sword might be useful,' snapped the Kirin, kicking the dead woman away from him and scowling at the acolytes.

Glenwood's thoughts were confused. He drew his longsword, compelled by an urge to attack Rham Jas, and approached slowly from behind the crowd.

'Don't waste your lives,' growled Rham Jas, stepping over Shilpa's body and pointing his sword towards the assembled devotees. 'Go worship the One God or some other fascist idiot. The Dead God has no use for you any more.'

Glenwood was enraged. It was only the extreme fatigue clouding his mind that prevented him from attacking Rham Jas.

Instead, the defenceless acolytes of Shilpa the Shadow of Lies fell upon him. They screeched, sobbed, tore at the air, but each one died swiftly at the edge of his katana.

Those who turned towards Glenwood were frenzied and had no sympathy for the pain he felt at Shilpa's death, nor his hatred for the assassin who had killed her. He lashed out, killing a man with bite marks on his chest. His thoughts focused on reaching the Kirin and ending his life in vengeance.

'We're leaving, Kale,' shouted Rham Jas, darting off the platform.

A Karesian woman drenched with sweat stepped in front of him, swinging an iron torch-holder. She struck Glenwood on the side of head and his vision went dark. He lost consciousness as a biting pain enveloped him.

Calm, sweet Kale, let your mind be calm . . . our time will come. The beautiful voice echoed through his mind.

CHAPTER THREE

TYR NANON IN THE FELL

L ONG AGO HE had lived in the Drow Deeps. Far to the south
and the east, beyond the lands of silence. It was peaceful
and timeless, an early life spent in play and mischief. Nanon
couldn't remember exactly how old he was, but he had pieced
together twelve centuries of memory. The first two were in the
Drow Deeps, among his own kind. The next five in the Heart,
learning his craft. He was a Tyr, a warrior, and a Shape Taker.
He had mated, sired children, fought in wars, battles and duels.
He had learned to be cautious and considered. He had survived.
Nanon was older than any other Dokkalfar he had met and he
saw the world as a river of endless conflict. It was the Long War
and he was its soldier.

His last few centuries had been spent among men, walking
the paths they considered important and learning their ways. He
liked them and their short-lived, obsession-filled lifestyles. They
were foolish, passionate, capable of tremendous honour and rather
amusing. They had taught him humour, a concept rare among
the Dokkalfar.

He smiled and returned to the present. They had been fighting
for a week. Nanon had lost count of the days he had gone without
rest and the friends he had seen die. His ally, Tyr Dyus the Daylight
Sky, had made sure that the Dokkalfar of the Fell Walk had come
to their aid, and Nanon's host had stayed at around fifty warriors
despite the losses.

It was early morning and the Hounds of Karesia had not
attacked for several hours. The old Tyr had not taken any rest,

preferring to allow his fellows to meditate while he stayed on guard in the branches of a tall tree.

Their advantage was twofold. First, as long as they stayed in the Fell, the Hounds couldn't use their full force. Second, the humans needed sleep and the forest-dwellers didn't. A few hours' quiet meditation every few days was enough for the Dokkalfar, and this advantage made their defence of their forests more stubborn and effective than their numbers would suggest.

Fresh arrows and black wart were delivered each day, and the humans had not crossed the line set by Nanon. The first Dark Young they had killed still stood, in the form of a withered tree, a short way from where he sat. Beyond it, a few hundred dead Hounds lay in the smouldering ash of the Fell, and many more had been retrieved or burned by the Karesian army. The fires had stopped and it appeared that even the whip-masters of the Hounds wouldn't bombard their own troops with flaming boulders. Nanon mourned the loss of so many ancient trees from the Karesians' initial bombardment, but he was stubbornly refusing to let any more burn.

'Shape Taker!' The voice came from a Tyr skulking in the darkness below.

'I'm busy.'

'Vithar Loth asks for your presence in the Fell Walk,' said the voice.

Nanon frowned and turned from the tree line, directing his dark eyes towards the younger forest-dweller.

'As a Kirin friend of mine once said, you fucking what?' demanded the old Tyr, evoking Rham Jas.

The Dokkalfar was confused by the cursing, but grasped the tone.

'He was very insistent that you return to take counsel from the Vithar.'

Nanon considered swearing again, but decided not to shoot the messenger and merely waved him away.

A few trees to his right, Tyr Dyus sat, strumming calmly on the string of his war-bow.

'My friend, I am required to leave,' Nanon said to his ally. 'Loth wants to flex his muscles at me again.'

Dyus didn't turn from the tree line. 'We are Tyr, we fight. They are Vithar, they talk.'

'We have an hour or two before they attack again,' replied Nanon. 'I can get to the Fell Walk and back.'

'I will lead in your absence,' said Dyus. 'No human will pass your line.'

Nanon jumped down from the tree, leaving his short bow on a high branch but keeping his Ro longsword in its scabbard.

'Maybe I can bring a few hundred warriors back with me . . . and keep my line where it is.'

He backed away from the tree line and darted into the deep shadows, keeping low to the ground. Within minutes he was hopping over fallen logs and making his way swiftly through the dense forest. It was nice to be in the woods again after his time in Ro Canarn and he chuckled to himself, enjoying the excitement of his current battle in the Long War. The last time he'd been needed was four hundred years before, and that conflict had been rather tedious, involving a lot of sitting around and talking to unpleasant things. Whatever the downside of Shub-Nillurath's attempt to reassert his power, at least the old Tyr wasn't bored.

It was a brisk jog back to the Dokkalfar settlement and the Fell Walk was buzzing with activity when he arrived.

As with all forest-dweller havens, it was built below a constructed forest floor, using the roots of huge trees as pillars between which to construct buildings. Nanon considered the Heart, far to the north in the Deep Woods of Canarn, to be his home. It was a much smaller settlement, with a few hundred Dokkalfar rather than a few thousand, and he disliked the densely populated southern haven.

After so many years spent among men, Nanon quickly became frustrated with the slow and steady ways of his people, which were annoyingly prevalent in the Fell Walk. The pace of life was the hardest thing to adapt to. His short time in Canarn had included much activity, a daily dance of nice conversations and broad smiles. Nanon had thoroughly enjoyed his time with Brom and the other men of Ro and he had to acknowledge that he preferred their company to that of his own people. Even the Dokkalfar of the north, who had come to live in Ro Canarn, were better company than the Fell Walkers.

'Tyr Nanon, you have been summoned.' The voice was female and harsh.

Turning round, he looked up into the eyes of a Vithar. She was armed – unusual for a shaman – and wore a brown robe, covering her from head to toe.

'Hello,' replied Nanon with a smile. 'Who are you?'

The Vithar didn't react and her face showed no emotion.

'Please excuse my manners.' He bowed his head respectfully. 'Just escort me to the auditorium . . . I assume that's your job.'

She stepped past him and extended her arm to show him the way, evidently intending to follow close behind.

'I love a good chat,' said Nanon drily, as he walked in the direction indicated. 'Again, excuse my manners.'

Closer to the centre of the Fell Walk, Nanon saw multiple Dokkalfar wearing armour and packing their personal belongings into woven satchels. The activity was strange. They were preparing for something, and he doubted it was a stint on the front line against the Hounds. Whatever Vithar Loth had planned, it would likely annoy Nanon. He prepared himself to bite his tongue rather than shout and swear. He needed to remember who he was . . . what he was. Now was not the time for the bluster of men.

With the Vithar still behind him, Nanon stepped on to a long and winding platform leading to the auditorium. It wove upwards, providing a clear view down into the settlement and confirming that a thousand Dokkalfar were packing their belongings. A hundred buildings of wood and earth at a dozen levels encircled the largest tree trunks, each one now empty of its inhabitants.

Nanon slowed and ran his hand along the twisted wood that formed a railing. Every few inches a leaf sprouted from it.

Some had grown into small shrubs or produced flowers, and they would continue to grow, a symbiosis between nature and forest-dweller.

'Keep walking,' said the Vithar.

'I didn't stop.'

'You slowed down. Please hurry up.'

The Vithar stepped close to Nanon and glared down at him. She was several inches taller than him.

'I don't like you, Shape Taker, so hurry up and I won't need to force you.'

He smiled and walked slightly faster, not caring to argue with the Vithar. It was odd behaviour for a shaman and Nanon wondered if she was actually prepared to use force. He decided that he didn't want a fight and that it was easier to just do as she said. Vithar Loth would cause more than enough irritation. Remember not to swear. Remember not to swear, he repeated in his mind.

At the end of the walkway a circular balcony hung over the settlement and housed the auditorium. The last time Nanon had been there he'd defied Loth and rallied allies against the Hounds. It was also the last time he had seen Rham Jas Rami and Utha the Shadow. The space was now mostly empty, with no Tyr guarding the perimeter and only four Vithar seated at the far end.

'Tyr Nanon, you will approach,' said Loth.

'I approach in friendship,' he replied, strolling casually into the circular auditorium. 'You have more supplies for me? Maybe a hundred more warriors?'

A moment of silence. 'We have not,' replied Loth.

'A shame, we are hard pressed.'

Nanon reached the raised seats at the far end and came to a stop in front of the seated Vithar. Next to Loth was a senior Tyr named Hythel who had refused to accompany Nanon to the line. On the old shaman's other side were two more Vithar, both of whom were expressionless.

'I can't be away for long, my attention is needed on the line,' said Nanon, keeping his tone even.

'Tyr Dyus can kill in your absence,' replied Loth. 'You are required here.'

'If I am required to talk . . . you can do that without me.'

'Insolence,' sneered Tyr Hythel. 'You are not a Fell Walker and you have spent too much time among men. The cycles turn and, despite your age, you see nothing.'

Nanon refused to laugh. He wanted to, but it would have been lost on the forest-dwellers before him and would have showed more disrespect than he felt. He tried to think at their pace, slowing things down to a crawl in his mind.

'Why is your settlement enveloped in such activity? And why do I now need escorting?'

Hythel tilted his head. 'You see? He is arrogant and thinks only of his own now. The forever of your people is at stake, Shape Taker.'

Vithar Loth raised his hand and silenced Hythel. The old shaman turned his eyes to Nanon and attempted to communicate with him silently. Nanon refused to open his mind, not wanting to give the wily old forest-dweller access to his thoughts. After a moment, Loth tilted his head as well.

'The ages of this land turn. We have seen this before and wish to wait out this battle of the Long War.'

'That will not stop the lands from turning,' replied Nanon, 'or the Long War from raging.'

'You misunderstand.' Loth was impassive and difficult to read. Nanon was used to being able to sense motivation among his people, but those of advanced age were strong of mind.

'You were escorted because we no longer trust you,' said Hythel. 'You misunderstand because you are ignorant. You kill because the stench of man has infected you.'

He shook his head, fighting bad habits. The Tyr before him was powerful but he was beginning to irritate him. 'Please tell me plainly, what do you want?'

Hythel stood up and displayed his full height. He stood much taller than Nanon, flexing his shoulders and clenching his fists.

'Plainly? What is this, impatience? We have meditated on a problem and wish you to join our meditation.'

'Sit in silence with us and remember who you are,' said Loth.

Nanon closed his eyes. He wanted to do as they asked and be a Dokkalfar again. He was angry with himself for his impatience, but he knew that sitting in silence for three days was a luxury he couldn't afford.

'I can't. I am needed,' he murmured.

'If you will not sit as a Dokkalfar, we will at least speak to you as a Tyr,' said Loth.

'I am still Dokkalfar,' he snapped.

Instantly, he knew he'd confirmed their suspicions. He'd become angry and let impatience govern his actions.

The Tree Father stood and softened his hard gaze with a minuscule smile. He was too controlled to appear smug, but now he felt superior and Nanon could sense it.

'This land has changed and we have stayed the same. We have no hall to which we can flee, our ashes will not travel beyond the world, they will return to the earth we could not save.' Loth was quoting from *The Edda*, an ancient tome written by the Sky Riders of the Drow Deeps. It was a somewhat ponderous treatise on the history and self-sacrifice of the Dokkalfar. Nanon had read it many times, especially the sections dealing with the Long War, but the majority of the book was a meditation on the inevitable destruction of the forest-dwellers.

'I can quote from *The Edda* as well,' he replied. 'It also says that the trees of the Fell were planted by Giants, but we don't let that inform our thinking.'

Loth stood before Nanon, his dark green robe catching in the soft breeze.

'We will never be at peace. This battle of the Long War will turn into another and another and another, until the Giants have left nothing but a smouldering wreck for us to inhabit. Our trees will burn, our people will flee or be turned into Dark Young. It is the slow pain and it is painful indeed.'

59

'The loss of hope can be a dangerous disease,' replied Nanon.

'We are not talking about hope, Shape Taker. This is about the legacy of our people.'

The wind picked up, catching their clothing and adding a low whistling accompaniment to the Vithar's words.

'But you don't speak for our people,' challenged Nanon. 'Not all of them.'

'I speak for the Fell Walkers,' replied Loth, with deep sincerity.

Tyr Hythel interjected. 'We are with the Tree Father. His word is our word.'

Nanon let his annoyance take over. 'Tell me what you intend to do. Don't quote from old books or hide behind rhetoric, just tell me . . . please. If you must treat me as an outsider, at least respect me as a soldier of the Long War.'

Loth closed his eyes and spread his arms wide, slowly turning his face upwards. 'We will burn. Our ashes will return to the world we could not save. Every Dokkalfar of the Fell, every one will stand in the divine flame of the Shadow Giants.'

Silence. Nanon had no words to call upon. He stood there, looking at the old Vithar, trying to find something to say in response. Loth planned to light the Shadow Flame and lead his people to their deaths. It was the ultimate act of martyrdom, but one that Nanon thought was apocalyptically foolish. *The Edda* spoke of a time when the world no longer had room for a godless race of forest-dwellers, but it never specified the time and was read by most as a parable. Certainly not as a call to mass suicide.

'Have you contacted the Heart about this?'

'We have not.' Loth's reply was maddeningly simple.

'Maybe you should. Vithar Joror will meditate with you.'

'His woods are not under siege,' stated the Tree Father. 'It is not his decision to make. Joror will slowly realize that the Shadow Flame is the only path for our people. I expect him to follow us into the dust of the world.'

Tyr Hythel, who had resumed his seat, clenched his fists and craned his neck forward with an expression of anger. 'It will be our final victory against the Dead God. We will deny him his Young. You should join us, Shape Taker.'

Nanon tilted his head. 'I don't think so.'

'Tyr Dyus and your forces at the line will be called back to the Fell Walk,' said Loth, also resuming his seat.

'To die?' asked Nanon with incredulity. 'That's not a message I'll deliver.'

'Our intentions will reach their minds anyway, you know this. Whether your human sensibilities allow it or not, the Shadow Flame will be lit.'

The collective memory and consciousness of the Dokkalfar would gradually inform all the Fell Walkers that their elders planned to die. Nanon could do little to stop the thoughts from influencing them.

'It has not even occurred to you that we can win, has it?' he asked.

'Who are we fighting? What can we win?' Hythel asked.

'Well, I thought we were fighting for the survival of our people, and the survival of the gods of men. Was that ever in your mind?'

'We are old, our time to die should be a time of our choosing. Our people deserve more grace than to be turned into monsters. The wars of men will bring ruin to us.'

Nanon took a step back and bowed his head, thinking quickly. He was not foolish and he doubted rational argument would be of much use with the stubborn forest-dwellers before him. But he could not concede.

'It will take time to light the Shadow Flame, it has been cold for centuries.'

'I have a dozen Vithar working on the fires, coaxing them to life with their blood,' said Loth.

'So I ask for time.' Nanon let his human smile appear. 'The Dark Blood still lives, the Red Prince enters the war, the gods of men have allies, we should be among them. '

Loth leant back and his eyes darted from side to side as if his thoughts were troubled. Once again he tried to enter Nanon's mind and once again the Shape Taker refused to let him in. The Tree Father had never lit the Shadow Flame and had probably only ever glimpsed the Twilight Grove from afar. He was uncertain how long it would take to light the fires. As he looked at the smiling Tyr before him, Loth had to concede that Nanon knew more than he did.

'The last time the Flame was lit,' began the Shape Taker, 'was six hundred years ago. Vithar Duil and ten of his shamans walked into the fires after they lost a settlement in Narland. They killed themselves in shame. That's illustrious company to join.'

'You mock us,' stated Hythel.

'It seemed the appropriate response to your idiocy,' Nanon snapped. 'But I'm serious about the time it'll take. If you have any strength left, you'll wait until I return. If the enchantress falls, then your suicide is unnecessary.'

The wind picked up again, a steady breeze swirling across the empty space. The auditorium felt hollow and cavernous. Loth was in command of everything in the Fell, he ruled in a way unknown to many other Dokkalfar settlements, but he was unsure when challenged by an older forest-dweller. In the Heart, the Vithar were advisers, wise and respected, but they made no claim to leadership. Nanon preferred it that way. The Fell Walkers, however, looked to their Vithar for more than just counsel. The Tree Father was the eldest and he held authority over the settlement in consequence.

'Talk to Joror, kill the human woman, it makes no difference. When the Shadow Flame is lit, we will enter the void,' the Tree Father pronounced stubbornly.

'We are agreed,' Nanon replied, knowing that the fires would take much longer to light than Loth realized.

* * *

Nanon took his time walking back to the line. The Vithar had escorted him to the edge of the Fell Walk and remained morose the entire way, though, on this occasion, the Shape Taker was deep in his own thoughts and less talkative.

He'd begun to project his words to the north and was slowly contacting Vithar Joror in the Heart. The transfer took time and was only possible because Nanon and Joror had known each other for many centuries. Both were old enough to have forgotten their earliest days of life.

'How long will the Shadow Flame take to light?' he asked into the air, hoping that Joror would hear.

Now he was alone, walking across the dense undergrowth towards the line. He could hear no sounds of combat and hoped that the Karesian Hounds had not attacked in the time he'd been away.

'Is that how humans say hello?' came a soft reply.

'Sorry. Time is short, my friend,' said Nanon. 'Loth seems to be taking *The Edda* literally.'

Silence. He could sense deep thought from his friend.

'Is the Fell lost?' asked the Vithar.

'No, we are holding them. The Daylight Sky stands with me.'

'Then why the Shadow Flame?'

It was a hard question to answer. Nanon wanted to say that Loth was a fool, but thought better of it. 'Apparently the Fell Walkers think that our end is inevitable. Worse, in fact, they think we'll all be turned into Dark Young.'

'Loth is a fool,' said Joror, making the Shape Taker feel better for a moment. 'Has he begun lighting the fires?'

'He said so, yes,' replied the old Tyr.

'Then you have thirty days. The Shadow Flame does not spring into life with a simple touch of fire. It takes blood and exertion to bring it back.' He paused. 'Do you know what it is, Nanon?'

'Not really . . . but neither does the Tree Father. He's more interested in his suicide.'

As their connection strengthened, Nanon felt himself in two worlds. He was standing, alone and still, in the forests of the Fell, and he was sitting in the auditorium of the Heart, next to Vithar Joror.

'What is it?' he asked.

The Vithar tilted his head in greeting.

'The Shadow Flame is a doorway of sorts, to a hall beyond the world. It is a shadow and an echo of the ones we loved. To light it, a Dokkalfar must give enough of himself to reach beyond, to rekindle the last ember of memory that yet remains of the Shadow Giants.'

Nanon took in the air as he listened, unsurprised by what he heard. 'The memory is not strong, though, and it fades.' He looked down at leaves and grass. 'Maybe there's a tiny piece of me that agrees with Loth.'

'When the Shadow Flame can no longer be coaxed to life, our race will truly be godless,' said Joror, sensing the melancholy that had enveloped his friend. 'But we still live. We have lived without a god for millennia. You would be the first to tell me this, Nanon.'

'And I'd be right, but it's still a depressing idea,' replied the Tyr.

'Depression is a human trait, one of many you are exhibiting these days. Is that a longsword I see at your side?'

'I prefer the weight,' he replied. 'So, thirty days, yes?'

'Indeed. I assume you have a counter-strategy,' prompted Joror.

'I do. I'm going to help the Dark Blood kill the enchantress . . . then see what the Ro can do about a host of Karesian Hounds.'

'I'd say good luck, but it would be rather human to do so,' said the Vithar, showing more humour that most Dokkalfar were capable of.

'We'll talk soon.'

Nanon closed his eyes and felt grass beneath his feet. When he opened them, he was alone in the Fell with only a slight smell of jasmine to remind him of where he had been. Any sense of relaxation or calm that he may have felt was gone now. In the near distance he could hear troubling noises: the sound of bowstrings and metal armour. The Hounds were once again pushing the line. He broke into a run and within a few minutes he could see the dead Dark Young marking the boundary.

A cacophony of grunts and moans arose from the massed ranks of Hounds as arrow after arrow smashed into the Karesian column.

They had been advancing for a few minutes. The Dokkalfar war-bows had, once again, stopped them cold.

Above him was Tyr Dyus the Daylight Sky, his hands blurring with motion, firing arrows into the enemy. Either side, forest-dwellers sat in the branches of trees or behind dense brush, hurling leaf-blades with deadly accuracy. Each Tyr was the worth of a dozen Hounds. At least, that was the case so long as they remained in the Fell.

'Tyr Nanon,' greeted Dyus, 'Your bow is most welcome.'

The Shape Taker smiled up at his friend and drew his bow. With a few long strides he bounded over fallen logs and stood, bathed in lancing shards of sunlight, in full view of the Hounds. There were more than before, as if the Karesians were making an effort to overwhelm the defenders, but their dead were quickly mounting up from the relentless barrage of arrows and blades. Commands were being shouted and the whip-masters were trying to stop their troops from breaking. Nanon suspected that retreating from the Fell would mean execution and he felt slightly sorry for them. The feeling lasted barely an instant as the Hounds formed up for a concentrated assault.

'Here they come. The faceless masses know not when they are beaten,' announced Dyus.

'Prepare for the melee,' added Nanon, expecting that a few Hounds would get past the sheet of arrows.

Over a hundred Karesians plunged through the trees, pushed forward by callous commanders all too willing to throw away troops in order to secure the line. Nanon set an arrow to his bowstring and loosed it in one motion, hitting a charging man in the forehead. Another fell, then another, then more as the Dokkalfar rose from their places of concealment and blunted the Karesian advance.

The whip-masters funnelled them into a narrow column. A few dozen would make it to the defensive line.

'Blades!' shouted Nanon, dropping his bow and drawing his Ro longsword.

Dyus kept firing, as did a handful of defenders, while the majority drew leaf-blades and moved to flank the Shape Taker. All that remained between the armies now was the dead tree, standing in a bizarre contortion amidst dead Hounds and broken arrows.

'Let none pass the line,' said Nanon, crouching to meet the attackers.

The Hounds that reached them were sweating and terrified, their scimitars held in shaking hands and their advance more of a chaotic rabble than a charge.

'Strike,' commanded Nanon, causing the Dokkalfar to whirl into motion and cut at the Karesians. With a line of graceful movement, two dozen Hounds were maimed or decapitated.

Beyond them, a small force was holding its position past the line. Nanon suspected that they were a group of better-trained warriors, perhaps waiting for the expendable front rank to fall. A moment later, as the forest-dwellers pulled back behind the old Tyr, a cry sounded from above.

'Dark Young,' roared Dyus. 'Two of them.'

Nanon puffed out his cheeks and glanced either side of him. 'If I hear one of you so much as mutter the priest and the altar, I'll kill you myself.'

'We are not afraid.' The words came from Dyus and were spoken in a rumble of conviction.

'Black wart,' commanded Nanon, as two undulating shapes appeared between distant tree trunks.

The Dokkalfar steeled themselves and retreated to their cover, crouching behind fallen logs and drawing black wart arrows from hidden caches. A few were quivering, their eyes fixed in fear. Nanon could not hear any muttering and hoped his strength would transfer to them.

Without moving from his position on a tree trunk, in plain view of the enemy, Nanon slowly sheathed his longsword and picked up his short bow. He peered into the darkness and identified the two creatures advancing towards them. The Hounds had moved out of the way and were every bit as disquieted by the Young as the forest-dwellers. There was now a mound of dead Karesians forming a clearing, and the surviving men were flanking the open ground, giving the beasts space to advance. Their bodies rippled forward, tentacles grasping at trees and earth as they pulled their blackened shapes towards the line. Two maws, each wide and pulsating with sickly venom and bile, reached forward and emitted shrill, repeating cries.

Nanon didn't move, though several of his force tilted their heads at him, indicating he should take cover. He remained still and allowed the other Tyr to see him, standing unafraid in front of the Dark Young. His confidence began to flow into them. Even as grotesque sounds echoed around the forests, the assembled warriors were not afraid.

He placed a black wart arrow to his bowstring and smiled at the other defenders of the Fell.

'We kill them. They send more and we kill them, too. We kill every beast they send against us. We are Tyr and we will fight.'

The words travelled in a low echo through the trees. Each Tyr rose, abandoning cover and forming a line of archers, each with a flaming black wart arrow nocked and ready. Faces of anger and courage appeared either side of the Shape Taker. For perhaps the first time, there was no fear,. He knew it wouldn't last, but for now his strength was enough.

The two Dark Young moved over the dead Karesians and towards the line. The torpid remnants of their fellow blocked the way, but they twisted and contorted their bodies past the obstacle, reaching towards the forest-dwellers.

'Bring them down!' Nanon shouted.

A synchronized sound of bowstrings flexing drowned out the beasts' guttural cries, before fire engulfed the Dark Young. Each arrow struck and exploded, causing globes of sudden flame to ignite and pulsate against the writhing black creatures. Both rose to their full height, their maddening cries flowing into shrill howls of pain.

'Again,' shouted Dyus, already nocking another black wart arrow.

The second barrage dropped the huge beasts to the ground as fire quickly spread across their cracked flesh. They kept moving, but slowly became little more than smouldering, blackened parts, twitching on the grass. He wouldn't call it a vulnerability, but Jaa had made sure that fire was more dangerous to the Dark Young than any blade.

'Let your mistress send more,' muttered Nanon. 'She won't be breathing much longer.'

He gritted his teeth and began to calm his mind. Explaining to Dyus that he'd have to leave would be difficult, but meeting Dalian and Rham Jas in Ro Weir and killing the enchantress was as important as defending the Fell, though he feared that his strength would be missed on the line.

* * *

Saara the Mistress of Pain was tired. She had not slept properly in a month, since Lillian had died in Ro Arnon. She might have recovered, but then Shilpa had died in Ro Haran and sleep left her entirely. Her head was a whirlwind of names and faces, many she didn't recognize. Her phantom thralls, as she'd begun to see them, occupied most of her attention. Four of her sisters were dead and those they had enchanted were now a constant burden to her.

She knew Rham Jas Rami was in Haran, but was powerless to act against him. She believed everything that she could do to protect herself was being done, but still she was on edge. Elihas of Du Ban was acting as her personal bodyguard, her flock grew stronger each day, her Hounds were everywhere, and her sister, Sasha the Illusionist, had managed to buy the Kirin's daughter. Was it enough? Had she thought of every eventuality? Saara hated the fact that she couldn't be sure.

She was sitting in Duke Lyam's office, attempting to distract herself from her phantom thralls. She'd seen an endless line of wind claws and Ro officials, testing her patience by asking petty questions about the security of Weir and delivering reports from other cities. Elihas had dealt with the men of Ro, but the Karesians didn't respond well to the Black cleric and required Saara's attention.

Her next appointment was with Sir Hallam Pevain. The mercenary knight had recently risen from his sickbed after having had his throat opened by Utha the Ghost. By all accounts, the wound had soured his disposition even more, making a vile man even viler. He remained rather useful, however.

The door opened and three men entered. The wind claws flanking the door recognized Pevain and allowed them entrance. One of the others was Parag, an unpleasant mercenary and Pevain's second. Saara did not know the third. He was a thin man of Ro in tarnished steel armour and with an ugly red brand on his cheek. Elihas of Du Ban, who stood over Saara's shoulder, was impassively scanning the newcomer but remained still.

'My lady,' said Pevain, the smooth scar across his neck making him rasp as he spoke. 'This is Yacob Black Guard of Weir.'

The thin man nodded with only the barest hint of deference.

Saara moved round the table and smiled at Yacob. She was wearing a white dress, less revealing than those she customarily wore, but more appropriate for Tor Funweir and the stiff-necked Ro. She lowered her eyes and seductively touched the man's chest.

'Good day,' purred Saara. 'I apologize, but I need to speak to Sir Pevain alone.' She smiled girlishly. 'And if you enter my chamber unannounced again, I will have you skinned and salted.'

Yacob blinked several times and turned to Pevain. 'I . . . was told that you'd welcome my assistance.'

'He does not make my decisions,' replied Saara.

Pevain laughed, his face splitting into a grotesque mask. 'He has some knowledge you might find useful, and a few skills, too. Maybe talk to him before you skin him.'

She backed away demurely and perched on the edge of the table. She thought the Black Guard had probably been scared sufficiently by her initial threat and could be allowed to stay.

She gave him an open smile of apology. 'What knowledge do you possess?' she asked gently.

Yacob was hesitant now, but the smiling mercenary beside him nodded and showed little fear of the enchantress. Parag directed his slack-jawed gaze at Saara's breasts. She inferred he was not overly encumbered with brains.

'I think we should discuss payment first.' The Black Guard did not speak with any confidence.

Elihas walked round the table. With a dutiful look at Saara, he punched Yacob squarely on the nose. The blow was delivered with minimal strength but had the desired result, mangling the man's nose and dropping him to the floor.

'I warned you,' joked Pevain.

'Keep your mouth shut.' Elihas turned to the mercenary knight. 'When I hit you, it's with a blade, not a fist.'

'So draw your steel,' challenged Pevain, looking down at the broad-shouldered Black cleric.

Saara clapped her hands excitedly. 'As intoxicating as this display of aggression is, I have little time and I need both of you.'

She allowed Pevain to relax, but made no effort to sway the cleric, knowing that he would follow her commands without argument.

'And as for you, my dear Black Guard.'

She placed a finger under Yacob's chin and raised his bloodied face. He had a hand clamped to his nose and blood was seeping out from between his fingers.

'I will not pay you, but I will give you a great gift.'

She looked deep into his eyes and penetrated his mind. Yacob's eyes widened, his hand falling from his broken nose to hang limply at his side. His body shook as extreme pain flooded his senses, but he was helpless to react or speak. Saara began to feel intoxicating pleasure as his pain flowed into her. His mind became malleable and open. His thoughts and memories were hers to enjoy.

She saw his upbringing in the city of Ro Weir. He was the son of the previous duke, an infamous nobleman called Rafe.

Yacob had been an arrogant child. A bully and a sadist, he had followed in Rafe's footsteps, taught by an abusive father to view the peasants as if they were insignificant cattle. By the time Yacob was eighteen he was his father's finest assassin and would kill on command. Noblemen, businessmen and clerics, all died at his hand. Saara felt his lack of empathy and his need to prove that his own life had worth by taking the lives of others. When Rafe was executed for his numerous crimes, the boy had been spared and branded as a Black Guard. Duke Lyam had wanted him killed, but the Purple clerics insisted that his father was to blame and had merely exiled Yacob.

'You have suffered much, sweet Yacob,' said Saara, feeling the man's depthless self-loathing and anger. 'But I can help.'

She softened her grip on his mind and allowed him to sense euphoria. After a moment, his eyes rolled back in his head and his mouth contorted into a vacant smile.

Pressing into his memory, Saara identified the knowledge he wished to share. Somewhere to the east, in the town of Kabrin, Yacob had seen an albino man of Ro boarding a Karesian ship. The captain was a smuggler called Makad and he was bound for Kessia.

Saara gasped with pleasure and saw the pale face of Utha the Ghost. He was accompanied by his squire and a dark woman who was not as she appeared. Yacob had recognized him, and the last old-blood was certainly heading towards the capital city of Karesia.

Saara released his mind and fell back against the table. Neither Elihas nor Pevain moved to help her and the Mistress of Pain breathed heavily with a contented smile on her face.

'Thank you, Yacob,' she said between panted breaths.

The Black Guard was unconscious now, slumped in a heap on the floor, but completely under the sway of the enchantress. He was a skilled assassin and could prove useful beyond the information he had just supplied.

'Is he dead?' asked Pevain.

She laughed. 'He will recover, my dear Hallam.' She pointed to one of her guards. 'You, take him to a bedchamber.'

The wind claw opened the wooden door and dragged out the torpid Black Guard. It was not unusual for men to be carried out of her office – though, for a change, the man was still alive.

'He has interesting news,' said Saara, licking her lips.

'He told me,' replied Pevain.

The mercenary growled. Utha had evaded him before and this would wrangle badly. Pevain saw himself as an unbeatable fighter who had been defeated and left for dead by the albino. He would relish the opportunity to resume his pursuit. Parag nodded excitedly and emitted a throaty chuckle. Neither of them cared about Yacob, and Saara figured they'd already been paid for introducing him to her.

'My sister will meet you in Kessia,' she said. 'Sasha will make sure you do not fail again.' Her smile was disarming enough for Pevain not to recognize straightaway the threat implicit in her words.

'I'll find him,' snarled the mercenary, rubbing his scar. 'And I don't need your sister looking over my shoulder.'

'I don't need you to find him. Sasha can find him. I need you to kill him. Kill him, kill his squire, cut out his eyes, cut off his cock . . . just kill him! Do you understand?' The venom flooded out in her words, and immediately she pulled herself back.

Pevain scowled, fighting his involuntary fear. 'I understand.'

Elihas stepped in front of the knight. 'Shall I remove something from him to ensure loyalty? Perhaps a hand?'

Pevain was scared enough of Saara not to react to the cleric's threat, though his eyes narrowed. For an instant, she saw a man who regretted his life. He had served her for money, power and influence, but occasionally he saw the dark heart behind her honeyed words. He would always fear her.

'I don't think so,' whispered Saara, licking her lips at Pevain.

The two men were now nose to nose.

'Do as you're told. And have the sense to know how small you are,' growled Elihas, making Saara's chest heave with desire. The man of Ro was not attractive but his stern manner and upright posture made him desirable in that moment.

Pevain did not turn back to meet the cleric's gaze. He patted Parag on the shoulder and pointed to the door. 'Let's go, there's a ghost that needs killing.'

As the mercenaries left, Saara panted and bit her lower lip, looking hungrily at Elihas. For a moment she considered grabbing the cleric and making him satisfy her, but she didn't want to hurt him. The last few men she'd taken to bed had died in extreme pain. She needed to consume the energy of others in order to maintain control over her phantom thralls, but Elihas was too valuable to waste in such a way.

'It's a pity you're not a man.' She was breathing heavily.

He looked impassively at her. 'You could not possibly begin to understand what I am,' he replied. 'But what I am not is interested in your cunt.'

Saara threw her head back and laughed. It was blunt, but coarse humour did amuse the enchantress and few people would have dared say such a thing to her.

'You're very droll, my dear Elihas.'

'I wasn't trying to be.' The cleric walked round the table to stand by the window, looking out over the harbour of Ro Weir.

'Can we use the Black Guard?' asked Saara, musing.

'Were you asking me or talking to yourself?' Elihas did not turn to her and again showed that his compliance was not devotion.

'Maybe you need to relax, my sweet.'

Now the cleric looked at her. His eyes were dark and expressionless. 'I am sufficiently relaxed.'

Saara felt her headache return. 'I need to go to worship. There are many who require their high priestess.'

Many Karesians had arrived in Weir and an elite group of the richest merchant princes and mobsters had been turned to worship of the Dead God. Even a few Ro noblemen had seen the benefits of following Saara. Her flock was growing each day. Her gospel of deviance and power was seductive to the weak-willed elite.

'Maybe you should accompany me. The One can do without you for a few hours of ecstatic agony.'

'I do not need your god,' he replied.

'You might enjoy him.' She licked her lips and gently projected images of exquisite pleasure and pain. Elihas baulked ever so slightly and his mind hardened. Saara had never tried to enchant him and she knew he was too strong to influence casually.

'Go and fuck your flock,' he said with a sneer, 'but leave me out of it.'

She giggled and rubbed her hands together sensually. 'I have some Ro followers now and our numbers swell, even in other cities. But I will not rush you, mighty cleric.'

With a twirl of her skirt, Saara the Mistress of Pain left the office and began to prepare for her sermon. More than usual she needed a release and looked forward to an hour or two of beautiful deviance.

CHAPTER FOUR

FALLON OF LEITH IN THE CITY OF SOUTH WARDEN

HE FIRE HAD burned down to embers and the simple wooden house was growing colder. The residence had been stripped of homely comforts and was being used as a prison by the occupying knights of the Red. The five thousand knights and clerics had quickly subdued the city and made themselves at home in acquired houses and stolen buildings, while the populace were kept under close guard in the ruined chapel of Rowanoco. Maybe five hundred Ranen were still alive. The able-bodied had been divested of their weaponry and put to work.

Fallon knew the strategies employed by the knights back to front, and the occupation was proceeding to schedule. First, they'd suppress any resistance, being deliberately brutal to discourage disobedience, then they'd establish their defences and, once the city was utterly broken, they'd execute their prisoners and move on.

Aside from the two bound men standing guard outside the door, Fallon's only company for a week had been an alcoholic nobleman and a timid cleric of the Brown.

Vladimir Corkoson, the Lord of Mud and commander of the Darkwald yeomanry, was good company when he was awake and not slurring his words, but the cleric, Brother Lanry, was a little too pious and naive to be a good conversationalist. The cleric had at least attempted to console his two companions regarding their forthcoming execution for betraying the Crown, but his counsel had mostly involved talk of the One.

Corkoson's crime had been to try and stop the slaughter of his men as Cardinal Mobius and King Sebastian repeatedly ordered them to assault the city. The Lord of Mud was a good man who cared about his people. Unfortunately, such emotions had no place here and Vladimir had been beaten and chained up for his interference.

Fallon's crime had been simpler. He'd merely disagreed with a Purple cleric and stopped a friend from dying. Their crimes were different, but their punishment would be the same – to be hanged from the gates of South Warden in front of the army. Lanry was too insignificant to kill and even Cardinal Mobius was not arrogant enough to execute a humble Brown cleric.

Fallon had much to ponder, but he was calm and was thinking more clearly than ever. He had maintained his honour when to do so had endangered his life and the One had rewarded him for it. The shade of Brother Torian of Arnon had been a shadowy companion since Fallon had been imprisoned, and the apparition lent him resolve enough to be sure that he wasn't destined to die at the end of a rope. He was the exemplar of the One and he had faith that his sword would soon be returned to him.

'How long do we have . . . roughly?' asked Vladimir, who was no longer asleep.

It was the dead of night and Fallon stood gazing through narrow slots in the shuttered window.

'How's your head?' replied Fallon, thinking that two bottles of strong Ranen mead would have been enough to induce a serious hangover.

'Don't know yet. The trick is to stay horizontal after waking up. It fools the brain into thinking it's okay.'

The Lord of Mud did not look well. His eyes were narrow and the remaining light from the fire was too much for him. 'Answer the question, old boy,' he prompted.

'It's been a week since they cleared the last resistance.' Fallon tried to focus through the narrow slots and into the darkness of South Warden. 'I'd say that sunrise this morning is a likely candidate for our execution.'

'Marvellous,' replied Vladimir. 'I'm sick of waiting around.'

The two of them had been exchanging gallows humour for a week now and Fallon had found himself becoming fond of the lesser noble. He was a shrewd man, not given to hysteria, and had slowly begun to accept his fate.

'I don't suppose you have a genius escape plan?' asked Vladimir, rubbing his eyes.

Fallon smiled thinly, nodding towards the sleeping form of Brother Lanry. 'Change clothes with him and hope they don't notice that you've put on weight and lost a few inches in height.'

Vladimir chuckled, wincing in pain as the laughter caused his head to throb. 'Don't make me laugh, it acts against my cunning method of avoiding a hangover.'

'Your own fault, you idiot,' Fallon responded with a broad smile.

At least he'd found his sense of humour again. Fallon was beginning to see the inherent comedy in the invasion of the Freelands, the occupation of Ro Hail and South Warden – even the king's increasing madness.

'Will we be strung up next to each other?' asked the Lord of Mud, turning over on his bedroll to stare at the wooden ceiling.

'Unlikely,' replied the former knight. 'I'm a vow-breaker, you're just a traitor.' He smiled again. 'They'll stretch you first and then probably make a big deal out of stretching me. There are a lot of men out there who know who I am. They'll milk it for all they can.'

'Shame,' muttered Vladimir. 'It would have been nice to have a friendly face up there next to me.'

Fallon turned away from the window and perched on the edge of an armchair he'd been using as a bed. 'Have you ever seen a man hang, my lord?'

'Nope, luckily I have not. I saw a man have his hands cut off once. He'd stolen from a Purple chapel in Du Ban . . . or something like that. Actually, he might have just been drunk and relieved himself on the steps, I can't quite remember.' Vladimir rubbed his eyes again and turned over awkwardly, trying to get comfortable. 'How long till sunrise?' he asked.

'An hour or two at the most.'

'So . . . should I expect to be dead in three or four hours?'

The Lord of Mud had closed his eyes and screwed up his face. He was rubbing his temples and fidgeting, and occasionally moaning.

'Unless something strange happens before that,' was Fallon's cryptic response.

Vladimir snorted in amusement but said nothing further. The lord of Darkwald was puffing out his cheeks and feeling the full effects of his hangover. He began to turn a funny colour.

Fallon returned to the window. Bound men were beginning to stir, going about their morning duties. The sun appeared later each day and was a constant reminder that the men of Ro were no longer in Tor Funweir.

'Be ready, exemplar,' said Torian's shade.

Fallon blinked at the sudden pain in his head. 'Can't you give me some fucking warning before you appear? Your words still hurt.'

Vladimir snorted and told his companion to be quiet. Fallon figured the lord's state had progressed far enough for him to be not really listening.

'Are you well rested?' asked the shade.

'No, not especially, I've had too much to think about,' Fallon whispered.

'You will need your wits about you.' The shade's voice was as hollow and monotonous as ever.

Fallon did not have a clue what he was talking about. 'I always have my wits about me, but if you're suggesting I run . . . I think you underestimate the number of people I'd have to kill in order to escape.'

Individually, he could best any knight, but to hack his way through several dozen was beyond even a swordsman of his skill. And he didn't have a sword.

'Look out of the window,' said the shade.

The knight peered through the slotted shutters. A dusty alleyway ran alongside the house, with a sewer trench parallel to it. The wooden fences that separated the houses in South Warden were solidly constructed and no obvious avenue of escape was in evidence.

'What exactly am I looking for?'

A moment later a hand appeared from the sewer trench. Fallon had paid little attention to the sunken trough, which would likely be full of blood, dead bodies and effluent. Lime was generally thrown into such places to stop the contents from festering.

The hand was shivering as it groped tentatively in the darkness for something to hold on to. After a moment, another hand appeared.

'Vladimir,' said Fallon sharply. 'Get your arse up and come over here.'

'I can't, I'm dying,' murmured the Lord of Mud, filtering his response through a layer of bile.

'Pull yourself together. That genius plan is taking shape.'

Fallon narrowed his eyes, trying to focus on the dark figure slowly emerging from the sewer trough.

The two guards at the front of the house had their backs to it. Whoever it was, he was moving with impressive stealth and had not been seen by the bound men.

Vladimir Corkoson rolled on to his front. With considerable exertion, he pulled himself to a sitting position.

'I think I may rob the hangman of his prize,' he muttered. 'The mead seems to be doing his work for him.'

Fallon put a finger to his lips and motioned for the nobleman to join him at the window. He crawled the first few feet, wincing in pain as he did so, before hauling himself uncomfortably to his feet and staggering forward.

'What?' he asked in a feeble whisper.

Fallon pointed to the figure crouched next to the deep sewer trench. The man was dripping wet and favouring his right arm, as if his left had recently been wounded. He was staying in shadows, close to the ground, but Fallon could make out distinctly Karesian features.

'I know that man,' he whispered to Vladimir. 'His name's Al-Hasim.'

The Lord of Mud shook his head wearily. 'Friend or foe?'

'He was captured in Ro Canarn and we took him north after Lady Bronwyn. I assumed he'd died at Ro Hail with Wraith Company.' Fallon paused for a moment and turned to look at the snoring form of Brother Lanry. 'He may not be a friend to us, but he's certainly a friend to him.'

The Karesian was obviously wounded, but just as obviously the wounds weren't life-threatening. He had a vertical cut down the side of his neck, wrapped in a makeshift bandage, and some heavy strapping around the left side of his chest. As he inched closer to the window, his face came out of the shadows.

'He's coming this way,' said Vladimir.

'Get back,' replied Fallon. 'Tell me if the guards see anything.'

The Karesian knew what he was doing. He silently crossed the ground and stood next to the window with his back to the wall. Removing the locking bolt from the window was accomplished quickly. He pulled one of the shutters outwards, as wide as he dared, and nimbly squeezed through the gap, turning to sit on the window sill.

'Close the window and stay quiet,' said Fallon. 'There are two guards outside.'

'Sir Fallon of Leith, I do believe,' murmured the Karesian. 'A prisoner . . . now there's an unexpected surprise.'

'Al-Hasim, Prince of the Wastes . . . still alive,' he replied.

'I'm not burdened with the Ranen need to fight until death,' replied the wounded man, taking a seat on the floor with his back to the window. 'I came here for Lanry, didn't expect to see you.'

The old Brown cleric was still asleep, oblivious to their situation. Vladimir was fighting back a need to vomit and staring at the Karesian in confusion.

'Sorry, where are my manners?' said the nobleman. 'Lord Vladimir Corkoson at your service.'

He attempted a bow, but pulled up halfway down and clamped a hand to his mouth. He had turned an unpleasant green colour.

'I've seen more noble-looking nobles,' said the Karesian.

Vladimir flapped his hands, asking for a moment to compose himself, before sitting down on the floor. 'Just carry on without me,' he burped out. 'Oh, and just so we're clear . . . if you're escaping, I'm going with you.' The Lord of Mud then clutched his knees and huddled up, closing his eyes and moaning quietly.

Fallon raised his eyebrows before turning back to the wounded Karesian. 'How did you survive?' he asked. 'Judging by that sword wound on your neck and the one in your chest . . . what is that, a crossbow bolt? I'd say that you were fighting with Scarlet Company.'

'I was,' replied Hasim. 'We lost.' The man's face was more serious now, as if he cared more for these men of Ranen than many would guess. 'A lot of people I liked are dead because of your Red friends.'

Fallon sympathized. 'If it helps you see me in a better light, I was locked up for oath-breaking weeks before the first trebuchet was fired.'

'As I remember,' said Al-Hasim, 'you and Verellian saved my life in Ro Canarn. That means you get the benefit of the doubt.'

Fallon nodded. 'You've been out there . . . in the city?' he asked.

'For a week or so now,' replied Hasim. 'Your knights are nothing if not predictable. They have a habit of ignoring things like sewer trenches.'

'Where are my men?' interjected Vladimir, leaning back and trying to control himself.

'After the king moved into Long Shadow's hall, your Cardinal Mobius ordered the yeomanry to picket themselves outside the walls. Only the knights and clerics are in South Warden . . . and a lot of angry Ranen prisoners.' Hasim shifted uncomfortably and rubbed his wounded neck.

'You need to get that seen to, it'll fester,' said Fallon.

'If it was going to fester and kill me, it would have done so by now. Remember, I've been crawling around in shit and piss for days,' the Karesian replied.

Fallon turned back to the unlocked window to give himself a chance to think. With knowledge of the troop placements between their makeshift prison and the outer walls, it would be possible to sneak out, although they had no weapons except Al-Hasim's light scimitar.

'How many of the yeomanry are left?' asked the Lord of Mud in a quivering voice.

'Not sure. They were wasted pretty badly at the breach.'

'Give me a rough estimate?' pressed Vladimir.

Hasim considered it. 'Maybe six thousand . . . once the wounded get better or die.'

Vladimir bit his lip and huddled up again. He had marched north with ten thousand men. To hear that four thousand had died in the breach at South Warden was almost more than he could bear. He sobbed, holding his sweaty hands to his face. The king had thrown away his men, using their bodies to break the lines of South Warden.

'Vladimir,' said Fallon, 'cry later. Your men are picketed outside the walls. That means we can get to them without the clerics interfering. Assuming we can get out of the city.'

'We can,' said Hasim. 'As long as you don't mind getting dirty.'

'Wake up the cleric.' Fallon pointed at Lanry. 'And at some stage I'll need a sword.'

Hasim glanced at the main doorway, beyond which the two bound men had their backs to the closed door. 'Perhaps you should wake up the cleric and I'll keep skulking over here.'

Fallon lightly shook Brother Lanry's shoulder. The old cleric shuffled uncomfortably and batted away Fallon's hand. Another shake of his shoulder and the churchman rolled over and opened his eyes.

'What . . . ?' he mumbled incoherently.

'We're leaving,' stated the tall swordsman. 'Get up if you want to come with us.' He turned back to Hasim. 'Where are Mobius and the king?'

'The senior knights and clerics got very drunk in Long Shadow's hall last night. They'll be rather ill right about now.'

'And Tristram?' continued Fallon.

'He wasn't with the others . . . maybe he respects his vows.' Al-Hasim was clearly knowledgeable about the lax attitude many knights took towards alcohol.

'Good for him,' said Vladimir, attempting to drag himself to his feet. 'I wish I had vows to follow.'

Fallon went back to the window and waited for Brother Lanry to rouse himself. They still had an hour or so until sunrise. Plenty of time to leave South Warden, provided they weren't interrupted by too many bound men who needed killing.

'Hasim,' said Lanry with a weak smile, 'you're alive . . . The One be praised.'

'Let's praise him later,' replied the Karesian. 'For now, we need to leave. They're going to kill you in the morning.'

'Me?' asked the Brown cleric incredulously.

Hasim nodded.

'What are you thinking, sir knight? Is it doable?' he asked Fallon.

'Maybe. But don't call me that. My name's Fallon.'

He peeked through an open sliver in the shutters and could see a clear path to the sewer trench. It ran under wooden walls and houses to the outer palisade. There would be guards stationed by the outer walls, but Fallon thought the escape route a good one, provided Al-Hasim was right and the knights were mostly in the central ground of South Warden.

'Any of the Ranen captains still alive?' asked Fallon.

'Horrock got his stomach opened by a Purple bastard, but he's still alive. I didn't see what happened to his axe-master, Flame Tooth. Everyone else is locked up or being put to work.'

'My Lord Corkoson,' Fallon said to the Lord of Mud, 'can I trust you to look after Brother Lanry?'

'Only if he looks after me in return,' he replied, without humour.

'I can look after myself,' mumbled the Brown cleric, rubbing sleep from his eyes and blinking rapidly to try and wake up. 'Just point me in the direction of safety and I'll follow you youngsters and be as quiet as a mouse.'

'Let's move then, shall we?' said Fallon, beginning to climb out of the waist-high window.

His boots made little sound as he landed on the muddy ground outside. Hasim followed and the two men hugged the wooden wall, helping their less mobile companions to clamber out of the building. Both Lanry and Vladimir needed help. The Brown cleric in particular had to be told to be quiet several times before he made it into the alleyway.

'Extricating myself from imprisonment via a window is not a part of my usual clerical duties,' said Lanry as Hasim helped him to stand upright next to the outer wall.

'Just stay behind Vladimir,' replied Fallon in a dismissive whisper.

Al-Hasim tiptoed across to the sewer trench, keeping his eyes on the front of the house. As long as they were quiet, the two bound men on guard would have little reason to investigate, and Lanry's lack of stealth told Fallon that the guards were not the most observant of men.

Hasim waved Fallon across. With light footsteps, the exemplar of the One approached his escape route.

Hasim pointed down to a ledge that ran along the side of the trench. 'That'll keep your feet out of the shit at the bottom . . . just don't fall off the ledge.'

The ledge was narrow but far enough underground for Fallon to remain unobserved. He doubted how quickly they'd be able to move with Lanry in tow, but it was a clear route to the western stockade of South Warden.

They climbed down slowly, helping Lanry and Vladimir to get a good footing on the stone ledge. They were no more than three feet from the sewage that ran along the bottom of the trench and the

Lord of Mud began to retch again as he took in the rancid smell.

'I'm hung-over and expected to escape through a river of shit . . . lovely.'

'It's probably Ro shit,' joked Al-Hasim, 'if that makes you feel any better.'

'Strangely, it doesn't.' The Lord of Mud had a hand across his mouth and had now turned a pasty-white colour.

'I must say,' said Lanry, 'the smell is not making it easy to balance.'

Hasim had extended an arm across Lanry's chest to keep him braced against the stone wall of the trench and the Brown cleric looked to be in no immediate danger of falling in.

Within ten minutes, they'd passed underneath two walls and several buildings. The sewage trenches of South Warden were well designed and of more solid construction than many of the buildings. Also, something in the nature of the Red knights meant that they were not inclined to check such places, as if it would be beneath them. It was an ideal, if disgusting, escape route.

The sun was not yet visible when Fallon first heard the sound of talking from above. 'Men up ahead,' he whispered behind him. 'Probably guarding the outside wall.'

'Point me towards danger, sir knight,' panted the Brown cleric. 'I'll assist in any way I can.'

'Just stay quiet,' responded Fallon. 'Hasim, give me your blade.'

The Karesian didn't hesitate. He swiftly removed his scimitar and offered the handle. It was lighter than Fallon was used to and the blade was top-heavy, but it would be enough to defeat bound men.

Chancing a look above the lip of the trench, Fallon saw four men standing round a small cook fire. Just beyond them was a hole in the outer stockade, probably caused by the initial bombardment. No other men were nearby and the four guards were well away from the centre of town. They were chatting boisterously about wine and women, with little care for the campaign of which they were a part.

'Four men,' he whispered to Al-Hasim.

'Can you handle them?' asked the Karesian.

The exemplar narrowed his eyes. 'Another four guards might make it a fair fight,' he said, barely thinking how arrogant it sounded.

He vaulted out of the sewer trench and landed in a crouch on the gravelly surface above.

The men made no movement and were too engrossed in their banter to notice the armed man who had appeared no more than a few feet from them. Each wore a red tabard over chain mail and carried a longsword.

He kept low to the ground, holding the Karesian blade in front of his chest as he stepped towards the fire. He whistled sharply to alert the guards and then thrust forward into the nearest man's ribs.

'Who the fuck . . .?' spluttered a bound man, fumbling to release his sword.

Fallon stood upright and looked down at three terrified faces. He kicked the dead man off his scimitar and stepped forward, answering a clumsy thrust with a fluid parry, running the man through.

Two of the guards were dead and the other two barely had a chance to stand before they were expertly killed, too. One had his chest opened as he tried to lunge, the other was kicked in the groin and decapitated before he could utter a word of alarm.

Fallon paused and surveyed the dead bodies. There was no sound or movement and all four had died cleanly.

'Smooth,' said Al-Hasim, poking his head up.

'Get them out of the trench,' he said, kneeling down and picking up a fallen longsword.

The Karesian smirked and disappeared below. There was grumbling from Lanry and moaning from Vladimir. It took a few minutes and by the time they were all standing by the stockade the horizon had a slight blue tinge to it. Fallon wanted to be out of the city and with the Darkwald yeomanry before the day watch began.

'Who's in command out there?' he asked Vladimir, as the four of them skulked by the stockade of South Warden.

'Dimitri, I'd imagine,' replied the Lord of Mud. 'He didn't want to come here in the first place. Good man, though . . . loyal, honest.'

'What is he, a wine-maker?' asked Al-Hasim with a smile.

Vladimir made a show of mock offence. 'Not just any wine-maker. I'll have you know that Major Dimitri Savostin makes a sparkling white that would have you weeping, my good fellow.'

'Major? In charge of six thousand men? Don't you have a general?' asked Fallon.

'My father established the chain of command. I think he may have been drunk.' He frowned. 'Thank the One I never touch the stuff, hey?'

'Yeah, you're a model of purity, my friend,' replied Fallon. 'Shall we move?'

Al-Hasim poked his head out of the breach in the outer wall and looked upwards. 'Will they have sentries up there?' he asked.

'Possibly, but they'll be looking down into the town and not out on to the plains,' responded Fallon. 'And it's still dark. Even if they do see us, they'll likely assume we're yeomen who sneaked out of camp for the night.'

He sheathed his new longsword and took the lead, crouching down to squeeze through a low gap in the stockade. Al-Hasim was a step behind, holding his scimitar low to the ground as if expecting trouble. Vladimir was next, hating every moment of his escape, and bringing up the rear was Brother Lanry of Canarn.

The ground beyond the wall was muddy and Fallon's boots made an unpleasant squelching sound as he crept away from the wall. The others followed and within a few minutes they were trotting across open ground and into the darkness. In the distance, a good way from the city and lit up by a hundred fires, was the encampment currently occupied by the Darkwald yeomanry. Formerly, it had been the king's camp, until the clerics and knights moved into the Ranen settlement, with Fallon as their prisoner.

They heard no words of alarm from behind them and the small group remained invisible in the dark morning that enveloped the Plains of Scarlet.

Fallon began to smile as the camp fires ahead of them grew closer. Then he stopped suddenly. The others did the same and they stood wordlessly looking at two dozen large wooden stakes standing in an orderly line in front of them. The stakes had been obscured by the darkness and the group had virtually run into them.

The wooden pillars were dug well into the ground and each stake had a bloodied figure tied to it. There were a few signs of movement and Fallon narrowed his eyes to bring them into focus. They were knights.

'Hasim,' he whispered, 'what do you know about these men?'

The Karesian stepped next to Fallon and squinted. 'I think they were strung up when one of them challenged a Purple cleric to a duel.' He glanced at Vladimir. 'It was the man commanding the yeomanry . . . the Purple fucker that opened up Horrock's belly. Didn't seem like he wanted to fight, so Mobius declared them traitors and . . . there you go.' He gestured at the twenty or so figures staked out in front of them.

'Brother Jakan,' said Fallon. 'That Purple fucker is called Brother Jakan.'

He was silent for a moment as the faces in front of him grew clearer. Tied to a stake several feet off the muddy ground and wearing the barest of bloody rags was Sir Theron of Haran, Fallon's former adjutant. He turned sharply, and Al-Hasim saw his alarm as the other figures revealed themselves to be the rest of Fallon's unit.

'He strung them up for supporting me and showing . . . honour.' Fallon whispered, and turned to see Vladimir looking up at the bloodied figures.

'I say, isn't that Lieutenant Theron?' spluttered the Lord of Mud.

He ignored him. 'Lanry, what is their condition?'

The Brown cleric was hesitant, but after a little encouragement he stood next to Fallon and studied Theron's injuries. The knight lieutenant was shivering and his face and chest bore deep whip marks, but he was alive. Lanry turned to the other men and made a swift but practised assessment of their condition.

'Well, I'd estimate that a few won't survive . . . a few are dead already. Sorry, Sir Fallon.' He pointed at Theron. 'This one is still breathing.'

'We have to cut them down,' stated Fallon.

'Um, I grant you I'm not a military man,' replied Lanry, 'but is that wise . . . given the daylight?'

'Just cut them down,' repeated the exemplar. 'Hasim, Vladimir, cut their bonds.'

Neither man argued and both swiftly went about the unpleasant business of releasing the battered knights. They had been displayed like common criminals, but Fallon tried not to let his anger show. Lanry merely looked at him with pursed lips. The old cleric probably understood as well as Fallon that the justice of the Purple could be brutal.

'They were your men?' asked the cleric.

'Indeed.'

'Perhaps we should hasten to the camp over yonder and get some assistance. They will need to be treated properly or we may make their wounds worse.' Whatever else he might be, Lanry was a skilled healer and Fallon was thankful for his counsel.

'Very well,' replied the exemplar.

His blood boiled, his mind raced, but he stayed outwardly calm.

Within a few minutes Al-Hasim had cut down most of the men. Vladimir was slower and had obeyed Fallon out of politeness more than actual desire to help. After a token effort, the Lord of Mud had returned and sat down on the grass.

From a little way to the west, the yeomanry had noticed activity on the plain and a detachment of soldiers was moving towards their position.

'Vladimir, you might want to make yourself known,' Fallon said, gesturing to the approaching yeomanry. 'Ask them to assist with these men.'

He had almost called them *my men*, and he felt a heavy sense of responsibility for what had been done to Theron and the others.

The soldiers approached tentatively, with their weapons drawn. There were five of them, with crossbows. Fallon raised his arms to show that he wasn't hostile and motioned for Vladimir, who was still slouching on the grass, to rise and address his men.

'Yes, yes,' grumbled the Lord of Mud. 'I may get some rest at some stage . . . just not yet.' He hauled himself to his feet and stepped past Fallon to greet the approaching men.

'Easy, lads,' said Vladimir, with a note of relief in his voice, 'don't you recognize your commander?'

The soldiers paused ten feet from the wooden stakes.

'Identify yourself.'

Dawn was breaking but it was still too gloomy for faces to be easily made out. Hasim skulked back to stand next to Fallon, wearily holding the hilt of his scimitar.

'You know, it's possible that these men will have a cleric or two in their camp,' whispered the Karesian. 'We should be cautious.'

'Nonsense,' stated Vladimir. His voice rose in volume and was directed towards the soldiers. 'I am Lord Vladimir Corkoson, commander of the Darkwald yeomanry . . . and in desperate need of a drink.'

* * *

Luckily, Al-Hasim's suspicions proved baseless. Within half an hour they were sitting in Vladimir's pavilion in the middle of the camp. Fallon's order that his men be cut down and cared for had been obeyed quickly. He formed the impression that fear of Brother Jakan had been the only thing stopping the Darkwald folk from doing so already.

At the pavilion entrance were clustered a dozen of Vladimir's senior staff. Behind them, the majority of the six thousand-strong army were awake, having heard the news that their commander had escaped. Exactly what this meant for the Darkwald yeomanry was the main topic of conversation and only the steady hand of

Major Dimitri had stopped the men from rushing the pavilion to give thanks.

Theron, Ohms and the survivors from Fallon's former unit were being cared for in a nearby tent, Brother Lanry using his healing arts to pull them back from the brink of death. Al-Hasim, Fallon and Vladimir were taking a hard-earned rest in the Lord of Mud's pavilion. With the sun now casting a dull glow over the misty Plains of Scarlet it would be only a matter of time before their escape was noticed and Fallon needed to come up with further strategy for staying alive. Strategy. He hated it.

'My lord,' began Major Dimitri, a man in late middle age with dusty blond hair to his shoulders and an ill-fitting chain shirt, 'I am thankful to the One that you are alive and unhurt, but we need to come up with a plan. The Purple cleric will return this morning and want answers.'

The Lord of Mud glanced at Fallon. 'Strategy is not my forte, major. Perhaps we should ask our resident knight of the Red.' He gestured to the seated exemplar.

Fallon coughed politely and leant forward. He was perched on the edge of a comfortable couch which had clearly been used as someone's bed in the recent past. To his left was the Karesian scoundrel, Al-Hasim, taking the whole situation in his stride and taking the opportunity to fill his belly with a hastily prepared breakfast of hard bread and even harder cheese.

'I am not a knight,' said Fallon. 'Neither are the dozen men we pulled down from those stakes.'

'You're Sir Fallon of Leith,' stated Dimitri, with a hint of reverence. 'You are famous, even in the Darkwald. I assume you have a plan?'

Al-Hasim grinned, spilling crumbs of bread from his mouth. 'Er, major, I think the plan was to escape South Warden . . . I don't think Fallon had a plan beyond that.'

Dimitri frowned, unsure why a Karesian was present. It also occurred to Fallon that Al-Hasim had been fighting in the breach at South Warden and would have killed men of the yeomanry.

'When does Jakan arrive?' asked Fallon.

Dimitri puffed out his cheeks and looked at the lightening sky through the tent flaps. 'A few hours after dawn usually. He brings a guard of other clerics with him. They have a strange obsession with inspecting the men. They're the same today as they were yesterday, but still we must line up and be inspected.'

'We need to be gone before they arrive, surely?' asked Vladimir, drinking deeply from a brass goblet.

Fallon considered. The yeomanry were not a match for the knights, no matter how loyal they were to Vladimir. But he did not feel like running. His honour was now all he had, and the One had more in store for him than a pointless death on the fields of Scarlet.

'We stay,' he said.

Vladimir frowned, Al-Hasim laughed and Major Dimitri looked confused.

'I think I'll get drunk again,' said the Lord of Mud, with a laboured sigh.

'I might join you,' agreed Hasim.

Dimitri glanced at both men, clearing his throat. 'I have nothing but respect for you, Sir Fallon, but do you think your strategy a wise one?'

'Don't worry, major, that is not the limit of my strategy,' replied Fallon, thinking quickly as he spoke. 'Tristram would not risk a battle against the yeomanry. His knights will rant and roar, cursing your names and your home, but they won't force a confrontation.'

'Er, they'd likely win, though,' interrupted Hasim.

Dimitri looked offended at this, but confined himself to a frown.

'That's not the point,' said Fallon. 'Win or lose, they'll end up a long way from home with a small army. With no yeomanry to rely on, they're vulnerable against the northern Ranen. Tristram knows that, even if the king and Mobius don't.'

Vladimir cleared his throat and placed his goblet on a table. 'Fallon, my men are common folk. Maybe a few are true fighting men, but you can't lead them against the knights.'

'I don't plan to,' Fallon replied, locking eyes with the Lord of Mud. 'You need to trust me, Vladimir.'

Dimitri coughed hesitantly. 'The knight general has been summoned from Ro Arnon. He'll be here soon. I don't know how many men Sir Malaki Frith commands, but I doubt the king will need the yeomanry.'

'How far is Ranen Gar?' asked Fallon.

Hasim considered. 'Three weeks travel, maybe. There are a lot of Ranen between here and there. Moon clans, Free Companies . . .'

'And that's where Lady Bronwyn is bound?' Fallon was beginning to form a plan.

Hasim nodded. 'Long Shadow wanted the help of the Moon clans, and Dominic Black Claw commands three or four companies at Ranen Gar. He'll fight if given the chance.'

Fallon had heard of the Black Claw family. They were the protectors of the Freelands and, by all accounts, deranged followers of the Ice Giant. They had no legitimate claim to nobility but were known in Tor Funweir nonetheless. They were no allies of the Ro.

'And me?' asked Fallon. 'How will the captain of Greywood Company look upon me?'

'Don't know, never met the man,' replied Hasim. 'But he won't like the knights being in South Warden.'

'I think you should go and ask him, my friend,' said Fallon.

'Me? I'm no diplomat.'

'You don't need to be, you just need not to be a Ro. Catch up with Bronwyn and carry my greetings to Black Claw and any other Ranen you meet. Tell them I wish to get the Red knights out of Ranen . . . just as much as they do. It's the same deal, they're just making it with me rather than Long Shadow.'

'Well, there are a lot of Moon clans between here and Ranen Gar,' replied Hasim.

'If they're close enough, we'll need them soon. If Malaki Frith wants to pick a fight.'

They were all looking at him. He really hoped that he knew what he was doing, but he didn't let any doubt show in his face.

Time slowed and Torian's shade appeared to Fallon. The Purple cleric was armed and armoured, though still indistinct.

'You have made a strong decision, exemplar.'

Fallon didn't respond aloud, letting the words form in his mind. 'People are going to die here, this is not a time for half-measures or weak words. This is a time for conviction, and for honour.'

Torian thrust out his chest and held his head high. 'You are no longer a knight of the Red.'

'No, I am not,' he replied. 'I don't know what I am.'

The shade drew his incorporeal sword and placed it on Fallon's shoulder. 'You are a knight of the Grey, you follow the aspect of honour. Know that you and you alone speak for the One . . . not the king, not Mobius.'

Thus knighted, Fallon the Grey stood and saw the world through different eyes. The others looked at him, as if some tangible difference had become evident in his demeanour.

'Vladimir, muster your men – fully armed and armoured – and have them stand to at the eastern edge of camp. You and Major Dimitri will accompany me to speak to Brother Jakan.' He spoke with a note of command, powerful and in control. 'Hasim, you get going before the Purple fucker arrives.'

The three of them paused, looking at each other, until Hasim smiled and gave a mock salute. 'Major, could I trouble you for a horse?'

* * *

The light barely penetrated the black clouds as Fallon made his way to the front of the column. The Darkwald yeomanry fanned out behind him in organized ranks, crossbows to the fore, standing above two thousand crouching pikemen. Cavalry guarded the flanks and columns of swordsmen stretched across the Plains of Scarlet.

Vladimir's men numbered six thousand. Tristram and the king commanded five thousand, though they were far better trained. It was a gamble, but not a bluff. The yeomanry had trebuchets and could, if Vladimir ordered it, bloody the king's nose – but any confrontation, however stubbornly they fought, would inevitably end with the knights victorious.

'My head doesn't hurt any more,' muttered Vladimir, coming to join Fallon.

'Stress has that effect, my lord.'

'Also makes me want a drink. It's sort of a cycle. A never-ending cycle,' replied the Lord of Mud. He glanced around, seeming to realize for the first time that he was standing at the very front of his army. 'Shouldn't we have horses? Might make us look more serious.'

Fallon smiled at him. 'Do I not look serious to you?'

Vladimir patted the swordsman on the shoulder in a comradely manner. 'You look fucking terrifying. I, on the other hand, look like a puddle of sweat.'

As if answering his query, Major Dimitri rode into view. He led two horses and was accompanied by Sir Theron. Fallon's former adjutant was battered and bloodied, but had a look of hard determination in his eyes.

'Much better,' joked Vladimir, pulling himself awkwardly into a saddle.

'Captain,' said Theron, throwing Fallon a second set of reins.

'No longer. It's just Fallon now,' he replied. 'How's your faith?' It was a complicated question, but being tortured and tied to a stake was one of the very few things that could make a Red knight begin to question his place in the One's design.

'I have decided that, as I am still alive, I should do what I know to be right,' replied Theron. 'The One and I will need to have a long and difficult communion should I ever leave the Freelands.'

Fallon mounted the horse and adjusted his newly acquired leather armour. 'I'm not pious, my friend, but we are doing the right thing. Stand by me and let's tell Jakan what we think of him.'

This made Theron smile. He wheeled his horse next to Fallon's, resting his hand on the longsword at his belt.

'I don't suppose you know who has my sword?' asked the exemplar.

'Commander Tristram took it,' he replied. 'I think he wanted to keep it from Jakan, my lord.'

Fallon laughed at the title. 'It's going to take some practice to use my name, isn't it . . . Theron?'

A bugle sounded from the gates of South Warden and they all looked towards the city. Dimitri and Vladimir sat astride their horses just behind Fallon and Theron. Fallon waved his hand, bringing the nervous noblemen into a more equal position.

'Okay, but you're doing the talking,' grumbled the Lord of Mud, shifting uncomfortably in his armour.

Horses emerged from the repaired wooden gates and a guard of several dozen men rode quickly away from the city. Two flags were carried – the clenched fist of the Red and the sceptre of the Purple. The sound of their armour and their horses' hooves carried across the Plains of Scarlet. Fallon did not need to look behind him to know that the Darkwald yeomanry would be nervous as Brother Jakan approached.

'He's got more company than usual, sir,' announced Major Dimitri.

'So have you,' replied Fallon. 'They're not idiots, they've been watching your men assemble for an hour.'

'Are you going to kill Jakan?' asked Theron.

He didn't answer. Breathing deeply, he focused on the approaching riders. As the point of mutual recognition approached, he smiled.

Jakan had seen him. The cleric was fully armoured and a look of sudden panic came across his face. Word spread quickly among the approaching riders and each man moved a hand to his sword hilt in readiness.

'Fallon of Leith!' roared Jakan, bringing his panic under control. 'Throw down your sword and submit to arrest.'

'No!' he shouted in reply.

'Very witty,' whispered Vladimir. 'Just try not to start a massive fight.'

Jakan and the knights fanned out and came to a stop ten feet in front of them. The cleric registered surprise at Theron and Vladimir, but anger at being face to face with Fallon kept his face harsh.

'Brother Jakan, what can we do for you?' asked Fallon casually.

'You are a vow-breaker,' announced the cleric, wheeling his horse theatrically. 'Lord Corkoson, you are a traitor.' He drew his sword with a flourish. 'Major Dimitri, arrest these men.'

The minor nobleman held himself upright. His eyes flickered at Vladimir and Fallon, making him look unsure in spite of his best efforts.

'I defer to Sir Fallon,' replied Dimitri, holding his breath with nervous tension.

'You will pay with blood for your treachery,' snapped Jakan. 'We will eradicate your feeble army. You, Lord Corkoson, have doomed your people to death under the boot of Tor Funweir.'

'Enough!' roared Fallon, silencing the cleric. 'This is the situation – we will fortify this camp and stand ready. If I see any attempt to muster the knights, we will bombard you until you weep. You have no artillery, and don't pretend Tristram would launch a frontal assault. He, unlike you, cares for the troops under his command.'

A grunt of angry agreement came from Vladimir, as he recalled the manner in which Jakan had wasted so many men in the breach at South Warden.

'You can't win, vow-breaker,' snarled the cleric. 'We will kill any man who stands against us.' He addressed the last words to the front ranks of yeomanry, trying to scare them into submission.

Fallon nudged his horse forward until he was close to Jakan. Theron followed, and the exemplar was glad to have the man of Haran at his side.

'I'm not trying to win, you fucking idiot, I'm trying to stop men from dying. Ranen and Ro, enough have died for no purpose. If the king wants to follow the whim of an enchantress, he'll have to do it without the Darkwald yeomanry . . . and he'll have to do it without me.'

Jakan still held his sword and glared at Fallon, a look of arrogant entitlement in his narrow eyes.

'You can't stay here forever,' he muttered. 'Cardinal Mobius and the king will stamp out your little rebellion.'

'Rebellion?' shouted Fallon, cowing the cleric with his sudden ferocity. 'I do not recognize your authority. I do not recognize the authority of the king.' His voice rose in volume and carried across the Plains of Scarlet. 'You do not speak for the One!' He lowered his voice, breathing heavily. 'As for what I'm waiting for . . . when General Malaki Frith gets here, I'll speak to him about our collective forces leaving the Freelands and you answering for the people you have slaughtered. If he is an honourable man, he'll listen. If not, more men will die.' With a confident smile, he addressed Jakan directly. 'I still plan to kill you, cleric. Don't give me a reason to do it today. I trust you will deliver my terms to Tristram and Mobius. I don't give a shit whether you tell the king, his mind is not his own.'

'Heresy!' barked Jakan.

In a move that surprised even Fallon, the cleric was knocked from his horse by a lightning-fast punch from Theron. The former knight was twitching with rage.

'YOU DO NOT SPEAK FOR THE ONE,' he bellowed.

'You!' Fallon pointed to the second Purple cleric, a man of the sword called Rathbone of Chase. 'Take him back to South Warden and ensure he delivers my terms.'

Chase hesitated and Jakan looked up from the grass blearily. His eyes were unfocused and his jaw was beginning to swell and turn red. Slowly, Chase dismounted and helped his brother cleric back into the saddle. The Red knights that followed them were all staring at Fallon in awe, but none of them acted.

'Brothers,' said Fallon, talking to the knights. 'Please realize that you have been led astray by a mad king under the sway of a witch.'

He knew his words would fall on deaf ears, but he had enough residual respect for the knights of the Red that he felt he had to try – much as William of Verellian had done with him.

'That is all I have to say. We will parlay when the knight general arrives.'

He wheeled his horse round. With Theron of Haran close behind, he returned to the forces of Darkwald.

CHAPTER FIVE

BRONWYN OF CANARN
IN THE MOON WOODS

THE SNOWY TREE tops thrust up from the rugged landscape, pushing their way out of the canopy as sharp pinnacles of white. South Warden was a week to the south and they were deep within the Moon Woods. The terrain rose and fell like a choppy sea. The going was tough.

Bronwyn had taken to wearing two cloaks once they left the city of Scarlet Company. She had worn the same clothes, day and night, for the last five days. She was further from home than she had ever been and she had not seen her brother for months. She knew the city was secure and that Brom was safe, but she longed once again to be the lady of Canarn.

She had always thought of her home as a bitterly cold place, constantly lashed with freezing winds from the sea. However, the cold she felt now was a world away and ten times worse than anything Ro Canarn could offer. She hadn't known it was possible to be this cold.

Her travelling companions, two men of Ranen, were more accustomed to the weather and teased her whenever she shivered or complained. Micah Stone Dog, the young warrior of Wraith Company, was a dry-humoured, sarcastic man who had come with her on the orders of his captain, Horrock Green Blade. The implication had been that she, as a noble of Ro, would probably get herself killed without an axe-man to rely on.

Dragneel Dark Crest, a priest of Brytag the World Raven, was an infuriating man to travel with. He had only one leg but was inhumanly dextrous with his crutches. Even when the terrain became rocky and unyielding, he was faster than Bronwyn and Micah. Annoyingly, he was vocal about her need to keep up with him and frequently chuckled when she stumbled or needed a break.

'Don't worry about him,' said Micah, as they neared the end of a day's travelling. 'He's better than some of the bird men I've met.'

The sun had disappeared behind the trees and they were at the end of a wooded valley, sheltered a little from the wind.

'I grew up with the greatest respect for Brytag, but his priest is an idiot.' She was feeling petulant. She was sick of eating boiled roots and dried meat, and she hadn't taken off her boots for a week.

Stone Dog nodded. 'Without doubt.' He stopped walking by a rocky outcropping with a slight overhang. 'Time for food,' he said, removing his large rucksack.

Dragneel had already stopped and was perched on the top of the rocks, scanning the forest on either side of the valley. The priest had estimated that they'd run into the men of the Crescent in a day or two and he was eager that they shouldn't be seen as enemies. The Moon clans were dangerous and unpredictable, men who worshipped Rowanoco as the Earth Shaker. To them, he was a spirit of nature rather than an Ice Giant.

'Does he know where he's going?' asked Bronwyn, settling down on the cold, snowy ground and helping to build a fire.

Micah didn't answer straightaway. He was laconic, but pleasant company. 'Northwards . . . I suppose.'

She glared at him. 'Yes, very clever. I mean does he know anyone in the Moon Woods or are we just hoping to run into someone?'

'I met a man of the Crescent once,' replied Micah. 'He came to Ro Hail. Strange man, lots of tattoos.'

'That's not an answer.' She piled wooden shards together while Stone Dog gathered some dry wood.

'Wasn't supposed to be,' he said unhelpfully.

Bronwyn stopped building the fire and shook her head at him, pursing her lips in anger.

'Okay, I'm sorry,' said Micah, slouching down in the snow. 'We're going to Ranen Gar, that's all I know. If that mad bastard knows a few men of the Crescent who can help South Warden, all the better.'

She was tired and had no further appetite to be annoyed. They were on their way to the realm of Greywood with the vague hope that help could be found for South Warden. How exactly a noble of Tor Funweir had ended up on a diplomatic mission for the Free Companies was somewhat of a mystery to Bronwyn, but she was too proud to admit that she was still out of her depth. She had been so ever since she had fled her home so many months ago, and she doubted she'd feel any different for many more months to come.

Dragneel threw his rucksack down to land next to the small fire. 'Food!' he demanded, pointing to his bag.

Micah directed his eyes up at the priest. 'Make it yourself, bird man.'

'I need to stay on watch, wraith man. I've got better eyesight than you,' replied Dragneel. 'I don't want anyone to sneak up on us.'

'And who will be sneaking up on us, Master Dragneel?' asked Bronwyn.

'Hopefully, someone friendly,' was the unhelpful response.

With no further words, the priest disappeared beyond the overhang, his crutches making little sound on the snowy ground.

Bronwyn and Micah huddled under the rocks, leaning forward to warm themselves by the small fire. A few embers flickered into low flames and within minutes a satisfying crackle could be heard. Micah opened Dragneel's bag and produced some dried goat's meat and hard bread. It was filling, salty and lacking in flavour, but she had long since stopped complaining about their diet. Weeks of harsh living had taught her that flavour was a luxury and of secondary importance. It was not that the Ranen didn't know how to make nice food – their hearty mutton stews, usually served with dumplings, were particularly pleasant – but when travelling they thought of food as a necessity rather than a luxury.

As they ate, she was glad that Micah was not a particularly talkative travelling companion. Bronwyn liked the young warrior of Wraith but was happier sitting in silence, contemplating her situation. She knew little of the Moon clans and was apprehensive at the prospect of meeting them. Luckily, she was becoming hardened to new experiences and was no longer surprised at strange Ranen behaviour. She chuckled to herself at the thought, thinking it a little snobbish.

'What's funny?' asked Stone Dog.

She smirked at him. 'I just realized how little I knew about your people. Since I rode into Ro Hail, I've seen things I didn't know existed. Even in Ro Canarn we had a slight arrogance about the Ranen, as if they were . . . I don't know, lesser men or something.'

Micah didn't show any sign of offence at the comment. 'You must have known we had towns and people. You're a Ro, not an idiot.'

'I just didn't realize how big it was,' replied Bronwyn, remembering the huge distances she'd travelled since leaving her home. 'And I've only seen a tiny bit of it.'

'You don't want to go to Fjorlan,' muttered Stone Dog, 'it's fucking cold there.'

'It's cold here,' responded Bronwyn, shivering under her cloak as the cold night took hold of her limbs. She gestured to the overhang. 'Is he going to come back, do you think?'

'Don't care,' was Micah's simple response. 'Hopefully, something big and scary will eat him during the night.'

She smiled and her lips cracked in the cold. During the day the glare from the snow was difficult to bear, but at night the darkness was almost comforting. Bronwyn was glad that the gloom didn't reach much beyond twilight and never became total, though the temperature dropped even further when the blue skies disappeared. Her limbs shivered, her fingers ached and her face stung, but she still smiled.

'Sleep, I think,' yawned Stone Dog, exposing his hands in front of the fire and clenching each fist.

'Indeed.' Bronwyn puffed out her cheeks and huddled up next to the fire.

* * *

She dreamt. Somewhere in the shadowy corners of her mind a raven called to her, its voice sharp and insistent. She often dreamt of Brytag, but never did the World Raven call to her in such a way. It now seemed as if time was short and events were colliding faster and faster. She didn't know why he was calling to her. She was a scared Ro noblewoman, far from home and ill suited to interpret the will of a god, be it a bird or a Giant.

'What do you want?' she asked.

The raven cawed louder.

'I don't understand.'

Silence for a moment. Then the raven flapped its wings extravagantly and let out a series of short, sharp sounds, snapping its beak and hopping up and down. The World Raven became fully visible in her mind, perched on thin air and flexing its vicious talons. Behind it was a vague impression of riders in dark blue.

It stopped cawing, but its deep black eyes regarded her. Whatever she was seeing and whatever the raven wanted, Bronwyn felt small and confused. She wondered how much was a dream and how much was real. Or maybe none of it was real and she was simply the scared Ro noblewoman she was trying not to be. The raven wanted her to know something, but its call was incomprehensible and came from far away beyond the world. The riders in blue were fanned out and plunging across snowy ground.

Then another sound began to drown out the cawing. It came from closer and Bronwyn thought it was the growling of a dog.

* * *

She awoke sharply and with a gasp. Across the low embers of the flickering fire, Bronwyn saw two green dots, flecked with red. The eyes were widely spaced and, although the beast remained in darkness, she could tell it was a large creature. Next to her Micah

Stone Dog was still asleep, curled up under his cloak. She didn't dare to look up to see if Dragneel was there.

A louder growl and Micah spluttered awake. The young man of Wraith rubbed his eyes and sat up quickly.

'What's that?' he asked in a whisper, directing wide eyes across the fire.

The creature shuffled slowly round the fire, its head emerging into the small globe of light. It was a huge, broad-shouldered dog with a squat muzzle and massively muscled forelegs and shoulders. Its eyes were striking and the flecks of red appeared to pulsate as the dog snarled at them.

'It's a Volk war-hound,' said a voice from above. Dragneel had reappeared and there was a catch of fear in his voice. 'Don't piss it off.'

'It looks pissed off already,' replied Micah. 'And it's got a lot of teeth.'

A sudden movement caught Bronwyn's eyes and dark figures emerged on the opposite bank. A moment later, before she could alert her companions, an arrow thudded into the ground next to their fire. Micah sprang backwards and Dragneel rolled out of view as more arrows narrowly missed them.

The war-hound leapt at her. The beast was huge and heavy enough to pin her to the snowy ground without apparent effort. Bronwyn had the wind knocked out of her and was utterly helpless as the dog growled over her exposed neck. But it didn't kill her. It merely kept its hypnotic eyes on her face.

She held her breath and saw Micah draw his locaber axe and dart forward. An arrow in his thigh slowed the axe-man, but he reached the other bank and swung up at the legs of one of their attackers. The shapes had been silent, but now a sound of pained anger erupted from them. She saw a dozen or more jump down from the bank. They were all bare-chested, with blue tattoos covering their bodies. Each man wielded a short bow and a curved sword.

'I don't die easy,' barked Micah, parrying an attack and opening a man's chest.

Dragneel appeared again, waving his arms in the air. 'Friends, we're friends.'

His words were cut off by an arrow striking him solidly in the stomach. The priest dropped his crutches and fell from the overhang. He landed next to where the war-hound had pinned down Bronwyn. Another arrow hit Micah in the side and he fell to one knee. Then the dog howled. It was a deep-throated rumble of a sound that cut through the melee.

The tattooed men backed away from Stone Dog and held their bows ready. The axe-man was breathing heavily and grasping the arrowhead in his side, but he did not appear badly hurt. Dragneel's wound was worse and he was barely moving.

The hound growled at the tattooed figures and clamped its teeth around the neck of Bronwyn's cloak. With great strength, the dog dragged her away from the overhang and into the middle of the gully. She wailed as snow-covered rocks assaulted her back and she rolled into an undignified seated position before the war-hound.

One of their attackers stepped to the front and began to stroke the huge hound. Bronwyn was surprised to see a woman looking down at her, wearing tight-fitting leather.

'Who are you?' asked the woman in a gravelly voice. 'Why are you here, under the Moon?'

Bronwyn looked over at Stone Dog. He still held his axe in one hand and was surrounded by armed men. A steady trickle of blood came from the arrow in his thigh and the wound in his side had made him double over in the snow.

'We're not your enemies, you stupid bastards,' spat Micah.

The woman looked at the two men killed by Stone Dog. 'You look like enemies.'

The hound growled again, craning its neck towards the woman. The red flecks formed a pupil, showing a worrying intelligence in the dog's eyes.

'Okay, okay,' said the woman. 'I'll try politeness.'

She moved closer to Bronwyn and sheathed her sword. The weapon was simple and appeared to be made of lacquered wood rather than steel. She had black hair, in a tight knot, and dark blue warpaint covered her face.

'I am Dawn, called Sun Runner. What is your name, woman?'

Bronwyn shook. Her back was torn up from the rocks and her teeth were chattering. 'My friends are wounded.' The words were hesitant.

'Two of mine are dead,' replied the woman of the Crescent.

Stone Dog laughed. 'Shooting arrows at people in the dark is not the way to make friends.'

'I asked you for your name, woman . . . I'll kill you before I ask for it again.'

The tattooed men numbered almost two dozen and most of them held arrows notched to their short bows.

'Bronwyn,' she said quietly, 'of Ro Canarn.'

'And your companions?' asked the woman.

'Micah Stone Dog of Wraith and Dragneel Dark Crest of Brytag's Roost.' She blurted out the names, stumbling over each syllable. 'We hoped for a more friendly introduction.'

The Volk war-hound backed away and sat on its haunches, looking at Bronwyn. The dog was no longer growling and the flecks in its eyes were dancing from side to side. Most of the men of the Crescent were focused on the dog, as if waiting for something.

Dawn Sun Runner nodded. She was absently stroking a hand along the hound's back, ruffling his ears playfully.

'Okay, I think we can lower the bows. You!' she pointed to a man behind her. 'Fetch Barron, he can help the young axe-man.' The tattooed warrior disappeared quickly into the dark Moon Wood.

Bronwyn turned to look at Dragneel. The priest was shuffling in pain and his fists were grasping at the snowy ground.

'And him?' she asked.

Dawn looked over at the one-legged man lying on his back with an arrow protruding upward from his stomach. 'I don't think ointments and bandages will help him,' she replied impassively.

'You shot an unarmed priest in the dark,' barked Micah. 'He's an annoying bastard, but still a priest.'

The men of the Crescent didn't react to this news. They all displayed a similar impassiveness to that of Dawn. Bronwyn and Micah looked at each other, finding their behaviour strange.

'What's the matter with you?' asked Micah. 'He needs help.'

The man who had been sent into the trees poked his head back round a tree. 'Barron says that the wounded need to come to him.'

The men quickly moved to pick up Dragneel and Micah, while Dawn offered her hand to Bronwyn. She allowed herself to be helped to her feet and winced as the wounds on her back flexed and split. The war-hound pawed at her cloak, shaking off the snow and straightening her clothing. It looked at her and panted happily, a nonetheless intimidating gesture, given its size.

Micah shoved away the help and stood defiantly on his own. Dragneel was barely conscious and had to be lifted from the ground. Stone Dog limped over towards Bronwyn, holding his axe and resisting any attempt to take it from him. The young man of Wraith was very attached to his hook-pointed locaber axe and scowled at the men of the Crescent who circled him.

'Dragneel's in trouble,' said Stone Dog. 'They'd better have a priest, or he's done for.'

'They're Moon clan?' asked Bronwyn, whispering the words.

'Hope so.'

'You okay?' She frowned in sympathy, looking at the two arrows sticking out of the young axe-man.

'Well . . . I'm leaking blood all over the place, but I'll live.' His eyes were darting from side to side, keeping track of the movements of the warriors around him. 'I could do with some help, but don't worry about me. These bastards still follow Rowanoco.'

'Mouths shut,' demanded Dawn.

Bronwyn and Micah moved slowly away from the gully, flanked by tattooed warriors and leaning on each other to make walking easier. They were led into the trees, away from the glow of their fire and into the glow of another. Their attackers were camped close by, obscured by the ridge and with their fire placed out of sight.

Several more men of the Crescent stood flexing their bowstrings round the fire. An older man, not displaying any tattoos, was reclining against a tree.

Dragneel was placed on the snowy ground, while Micah and Bronwyn were shoved, under guard, into a wooden corral where the men of the Crescent had several packhorses tied up.

'These two are Ranen,' said the man sitting by the fire. His tone was disapproving. 'You said they were Ro.'

'We saw the woman, she was Ro . . . we assumed . . .' replied Dawn.

'Not exactly an invading army of Red knights, though.' The older man stood and flexed his back, muttering under his breath about sleeping rough.

'They're spies . . . or scouts.' Dawn showed no emotion in her voice and spoke in a matter-of-fact manner.

'We're not,' barked Stone Dog from the corral. 'We come from South Warden seeking aid.'

'Silence,' snapped Dawn. 'You do not speak here.'

'I clearly do, you fucking idiot,' replied the young man of Wraith. A nearby man of the Crescent slapped the arrow in Micah's side, making him recoil in pain.

'Stop it,' shouted Bronwyn. 'We're not your enemies. You people have plenty to contend with without inventing more.'

'If she speaks again, kill her,' ordered Dawn, and several men aimed arrows at the noblewoman.

Bronwyn began to sweat and her hands shook. She knew nothing of the Moon clans and didn't know whether or not they were likely summarily to execute her.

The older man sauntered casually over to the corral and stood before the two prisoners. Like Sun Runner, he'd largely ignored the body of Dragneel. Bronwyn could no longer see any movement from the priest of Brytag.

'Who are you, woman of the stone?' asked the man.

He had long, straight brown hair, flecked with white, and his beard was surprisingly well groomed. His clothing was made of leather and furs and was more suited to the cold weather than that of his companions.

'Bronwyn of Canarn . . . we are not people you should be fighting.'

'Dawn thinks you are,' he replied. 'But Warm Heart isn't sure.' At the sound of its name, the huge war-hound loped into the glow of the fire and growled playfully at the man.

'I'm Barron, called Crow Friend. I decide whether or not we kill you.'

She looked nervously at Micah, who had kept quiet since the wound in his side had been aggravated. He was pale and obviously in pain.

'We were sent by Johan Long Shadow to seek aid for Scarlet Company. If you kill us, you kill people trying to help the Freelands,' said Stone Dog.

Another growl from Warm Heart and the men of the Crescent lowered their bows.

'Okay,' conceded Barron. 'Perhaps I am not the ultimate arbiter of your fate.'

'My friends need help,' spluttered Bronwyn. 'He's going to die.' She pointed a shaking hand at Dragneel.

Barron puffed out his cheeks and shook his head. Slowly, he turned from the corral and approached the unconscious priest. Kneeling down, he inspected the arrow protruding from his stomach and gently pushed at the bloodied flesh. A lank mop of hair obscured Dragneel's face and his arms were splayed across the ground.

'Hmm, he's in trouble,' said Barron.

Absently, he swept the hair out of the priest's face and looked at his features for the first time. His expression changed completely and he craned forward to get a better look at Dragneel's face.

'I know this man.' He quickly turned the priest on to his side and took note of the man's missing leg. 'Dark Crest, you silly bastard.'

'He's a priest, I told you,' said Micah weakly.

'He's not just a priest,' countered Barron. 'He's a man of the World Raven.'

Even Dawn narrowed her eyes and showed concern at this news. It was the most animated she had appeared since they had fired their first arrow.

'Pick him up, gently,' said Barron. 'Dawn, bring the other two, and try not to kill anyone. Warm Heart.' The Volk hound's ears flickered and he looked eagerly at Barron, panting and wagging his short tail. 'Go and tell Federick that we have guests.'

Quite how the huge dog would convey this news was unclear, but Bronwyn saw him bound off into the dark woods.

* * *

Bronwyn did not know the organization of the Moon clans. She didn't know how many clans there were, or whether they followed a single chieftain or a group of lesser captains. What was clear, as they were led through the snowy gullies of the Moon Wood, was that they talked little and moved in eerie silence. Their tattoos were patterned by some kind of blue ink and she saw Dawn reapply her designs as she walked.

'Some kind of mushroom,' muttered Stone Dog, limping along next to her.

'What is?'

'The blue stuff. Freya used to say that the Moon Wood was filled with hallucinogenic mushrooms which make them a bit . . . unpredictable. I think these ones are called night-raiders.'

'So they're drugged up?' asked Bronwyn.

'Think so, they dry it . . . rub it on their skin, smoke it in pipes.'

Micah had removed the arrow from his thigh, but a wooden shaft still jutted from his side and made walking awkward. He was tough and she knew he wouldn't complain, but Bronwyn could see droplets of sweat on his face.

They were now deep within the woods and far from the central trail they'd been following. She had no skill at tracking, but even a young Ro noblewoman could tell that they were now entering the outskirts of a rude settlement. In the high branches of trees were disguised platforms, with archers hidden under grassy nets and other kinds of camouflage. The ground was dotted with pit traps and tripwires, though most of them were not primed.

'Stay in the middle of the path,' ordered Barron Crow Friend from the front. 'If you break the tree line, they'll shoot you.'

More faces appeared at ground level. Many carried wooden swords, curved and covered in some kind of hard lacquer that gave them a serrated edge. They were mostly bare-chested and untroubled by the cold. Those that were wrapped up warm were also bereft of blue tattoos, and Bronwyn wondered whether the mushrooms protected them against the weather.

Ahead of them, Warm Heart appeared from between the thinly spaced trees and panted happily at Barron. The war-hound confused Bronwyn, who was unsure how intelligent it was, though she was pleased that it seemed to like her. He led the way through forested clearings, now wide and open, protected by a high canopy and dense undergrowth on either side. It was wilder here than in the southern woods and the terrain was more up and down, with craggy rocks providing the men of the Crescent with ample cover in which to build their primitive settlements. They built almost exclusively out of wood, which the Moon clans had shaped and twisted into homes, staircases and walkways that snaked between the trees. Their craft was strange and Bronwyn could see no nails or joints, so that the structures had an organic appearance as if they had been shaped out of single pieces of treated wood.

'Wooden swords,' muttered Stone Dog. 'I was captured by people with wooden swords. How embarrassing.'

'I promise I won't tell Horrock,' said Bronwyn. She took in her surroundings, seeing numerous eyes looking her up and down. 'Don't the Free Companies have any contact with these people?'

'Not that I know of. The Moon clans were originally escaped servants from the Ro work gangs. When the Free Companies rose up, those under the Moon stayed in their woods.'

'Do they care about the Freelands?' she asked.

'You'll have to ask them.'

'That's not helpful.'

Barron and Dawn led them into a shallow depression in the ground. The snow was sparse here and various wooden platforms served as a piecemeal roof across the edges of the large space. Warm Heart scampered forward and ran down the incline to the large fire that sat in the open space. Around the sides of the depression, under the wooden roof, sat various men and women, lying back on comfortable-looking cushions and talking boisterously. For the first time since she had entered the Moon Wood, Bronwyn saw people at rest, maybe even enjoying themselves. These Ranen were not tattooed and all wore thick furs, though a few were barefoot and warming their feet by the fire.

'I see a Ro,' grumbled a man.

'A Ro with a nice arse,' joked another, receiving a playful slap from a nearby woman.

'And a beautiful young boy,' sneered a third, licking his lips at Micah.

The men of the Crescent who had escorted them stopped at the edge of the incline, with only Barron Crow Friend moving into the depression. Bronwyn and Stone Dog stood in the light, in plain view of those seated below. Micah was glaring at the man who'd spoken, a man with a piggish face and an unpleasant sneer on his fat cheeks.

'Stop looking at me, pretty boy,' said the man. 'You've already got an arrow in you, you don't want my cock as well.'

Micah, more confident than Bronwyn, slumped down the incline, favouring his right side, and stood in front of the man. 'Talk to me again, you fat fuck, and I'll stick my foot down your fucking throat.'

A few people of the Crescent laughed, but most looked angry. Barron turned to look at Stone Dog with raised eyebrows, but didn't intercede. The fat man spat out a lump of hard bread and pulled himself forward into a seated position.

'You aren't scary, pretty boy,' he said, with a vile leer on his face.

With surprising speed, given his injury, Micah kicked the man in the face and leapt on to him, smashing his fists into the piggish man's jaw.

'Am I scary now, you troll cunt?' he roared, taking out his frustration on the unlucky man. Blood was seeping from the wound in Micah's side, but anger was overriding the pain.

Others moved out of the way, surprised at the man of Wraith's ferocity, but Barron and several others darted forward and grabbed him by the shoulders. He ignored them and didn't stop punching the fat man until he was pulled out of range. By the time he was upright, the man on the floor was a bloody mess.

'That was a mistake, boy,' shouted Barron, as Micah, still swearing, was thrown to the floor.

Warm Heart, who had watched the fight with interest, let out a low growl and pointed his head towards Dragneel's unconscious body. Bronwyn was again surprised at the way the Ranen responded to the hound, as all those present grew silent at his growl.

'Barron, are you upsetting my friend again?' said a voice from the far side of the depression. The speaker was obscured by the fire, but spoke with an impossibly deep voice and made Barron look nervous.

Warm Heart rose from his haunches and loped over to Stone Dog. The huge hound nudged him upright and lapped gently at the arrow protruding from his side.

Barron helped him stand. 'Sorry, I didn't even ask your name, lad.'

Micah, still seething with rage, was desperately trying to ignore the wound in his side and appear strong, but his legs gave way and Barron had to catch him. Weakly, through gritted teeth, he said, 'I'm Stone Dog,' before passing out from loss of blood.

Suddenly everyone was looking at Bronwyn. The war-hound was nudging his muzzle against Micah's chest, but he was unresponsive. The nervous Ro noblewoman realized that she would have to do the talking now.

'Don't worry, my dear,' said the deep voice. 'We won't hurt you.'

Barron left Stone Dog and offered his hand to help Bronwyn down the incline. His eyes kept darting across to Dragneel and she was glad that he was showing concern for the priest's survival. Around the edges of the depression, standing above the others and armed with their bows, were Dawn Sun Runner and the other tattooed raiders. In total, Bronwyn could see several dozen men and women of the Crescent looking at her.

'Come round the fire, love,' said the deep voice. 'Sit by me.'

She walked with Barron past many faces. Most were curious or friendly, though some muttered insults at her. Bronwyn had never been more aware that she was a Ro.

'Lady Bronwyn, may I introduce you to Federick Two Hearts,' announced Barron, coming to a stop in front of several cushions.

The far side of the depression was covered with wooden planks and the deep-voiced man was reclining on his back, smoking a pipe. Four women, all armed with multiple small knives, joined him on the cushions. They looked similar enough for Bronwyn to suppose they were his daughters.

Federick Two Hearts, Ranen chieftain of the Moon Wood, was a grey-haired and muscular man. His height was difficult to gauge, but she thought he was tall and his arms, exposed across his chest, were bulky and scarred.

'You are . . . the leader here?' asked Bronwyn hesitantly.

'Chieftain,' replied Two Hearts, his voice even deeper at close range. 'Call me Federick.'

'Very well.' She looked again at Micah and Dragneel, neither of whom was moving. 'I don't wish to be rude, but my friends need help.'

'One-leg is familiar to me,' said Barron. 'He's a man of the World Raven.'

This made Federick sit up and give his pipe to one of his daughters. 'He's a priest? And you shot him . . . why?'

'Dawn was being impetuous,' replied Barron, dropping his head and focusing on the floor.

Federick glanced round, looking at the eldest woman sitting next to him. 'Aesyr, go and fetch some rowan oak sap and help Barron save the priest's life.'

The woman nodded and sprang to her feet, directing a challenging glare at Bronwyn as she did so. 'Yes, Father,' she said respectfully.

Barron followed after Aesyr to help Dragneel.

'You can stay here, my love,' said Federick, retrieving his pipe and patting the cushion next to him.

'What about Stone Dog?' she asked.

'Why should I help him?' It was said casually and the deep rumble conveyed scorn. 'He attacked one of mine.'

She was uncertain how to respond. Her confidence, fragile for months now, was beginning to crack. Suddenly she felt like crying.

'Just help him,' she cried, her voice rising.

Two Hearts' mouth slipped into a smile. His face wrinkled up and he moved into the firelight. The chieftain was around fifty years of age and had a wild glint in his eyes.

'We're not a Free Company, love. I do what I want, not what I'm told.'

'You're still Ranen,' pleaded Bronwyn.

'And you're Ro. You're lucky I don't skin you, given what the bastards did to South Warden.'

She paused, the tears disappearing. 'You have word from South Warden?' They'd left weeks ago and had no idea what had transpired on the Plains of Scarlet.

'Birds and beasts speak to Warm Heart,' was the cryptic response from Federick. 'We know what happens around our woods.'

The hound appeared at her side. It had been silent and made her jump as it began to lick her hand.

'He likes you,' said Federick. 'He can smell Brytag on you.'

She nodded, finding the presence of the hound strangely calming. 'Brytag likes twins.'

'I see.' There was no reason Two Hearts would know anything of Tor Funweir, but he was clearly interested in her connection to the World Raven, though it was a connection she didn't fully understand herself.

'Tell me of South Warden,' asked Bronwyn, not sure whether to talk to the chieftain or the Volk war-hound.

'They sacked it,' replied Federick plainly. 'Killed everyone and moved in.'

She was stunned. Her legs felt weak.

She thought of Wraith Company, of Horrock and Haffen. She thought of Scarlet Company, of Johan Long Shadow and his warriors. And, with tears returning to her eyes, she thought of Al-Hasim and Brother Lanry.

'I don't know how many survived, maybe a few hundred. Most of Long Shadow's men were massacred. Last we heard, the knights were still there, thousands of them.' Two Hearts did not appear callous, but the tone of his deep voice was unemotional. 'There is no Scarlet Company, not any more.'

Bronwyn had no words. She was alone in a strange land and her reason for being there was gone. The people she'd got to know over the last few months, people she'd grown to respect and even love, were most likely all dead. The king's invasion was doing its work well. First Canarn, then Ro Hail and now South Warden. Ro Canarn had recovered, but it had not been the goal. She wondered how long it would take the Freelands of Ranen to recover – if they ever did.

'You're in danger,' she said, through quivering lips. 'They won't stop. I don't know what they want, but they won't stop.'

Two Hearts again patted the cushion next to him. 'I'll have the young lad cared for if you come and sit by me, love.'

She shook her head, maddened by the man's casual attitude. 'Do you not care what's happening to Ranen?'

He shrugged and his remaining three daughters started to giggle. 'She needs to relax, Father,' said the youngest, a girl of perhaps eighteen.

'She does,' agreed Federick. 'Have a smoke, Bronwyn.' He offered her his pipe.

'I'd rather not,' she said pointedly.

Two Hearts chuckled, more of a rumble than a laugh. 'Okay. Ossa, go and help the young axe-man.'

Another of his daughters stood up and crossed the depression. Bronwyn watched her move towards Stone Dog and was glad that he looked to be slowly regaining consciousness. She also noticed that the people of the Crescent were no longer looking at her and had returned to their boisterous drinking and smoking.

With a deep breath, and beginning to feel light-headed, Bronwyn sat down on a plump green cushion. Her head began to throb with pain as the hours of intense and painful activity caught up with her.

Two Hearts put a casual arm round her shoulder and she was too tired to object. 'The world moves without you worrying about it, love. The worry doesn't change anything.'

She looked up at the muscular chieftain and was greeted with a twitchy grin. Whatever he was smoking was having an effect and she, too, wished for the oblivion such things provided. She had never been exposed to drugs, her upbringing in Canarn had been rather sheltered, but she thought that if she were to develop a drug habit it might be a rational response to her situation.

'Maybe I should just stop trying to be a good person,' she muttered, causing a ripple of drugged laughter from Federick's remaining daughters.

'Well, you'll have some time to reflect on it, my sweet. You'll be with us for a while,' announced the chieftain, removing his arm from Bronwyn's shoulders and touching a flame to his pipe. 'A noblewoman of Ro doesn't just go for a walk under the Moon. What are you doing here?' He exhaled. 'And if you lie to me, I'll cut something off you and ask again.'

She looked at him. For a moment Bronwyn was angry. She knew she should be anxious, or even scared, but after so long away from home she was too tired to be intimidated.

'I'm going to Ranen Gar to ask Dominic Black Claw for . . . something. Help, I suppose.' The words felt hollow.

Two Hearts smiled and coughed. The sound was a gravelly snarl and produced phlegm that flew into the fire.

Bronwyn breathed in deeply. 'The king has invaded. He's taken Ro Hail and South Warden. He'll march north next.'

'And why would he do that?' he asked, wiping his mouth.

'How should I know? Why would he invade in the first place? But do you think he'll stop?'

'I think he'd be a mad man to march into the Moon Wood,' stated Federick.

'He's got an army. You, as far as I can tell, have trees,' she replied, not caring if he took offence.

'Cheeky bitch,' he replied, showing her a wild smile.

'You're not used to talking to nobility, are you?'

Federick's voice contorted into an intermittent growl. It was perhaps a laugh, but sounded like an animal's snarl.

'What makes you noble, young lady?' he asked.

Sudden anger. 'My father, my brother, my family. The weight of responsibility I feel for my people.'

Two Hearts looked at her and stopped laughing. 'You're sincere, my love, so I won't mock you, but your lands, your family and whatever else you care to mention mean nothing here.'

'I'm not the one who's ignoring an army of Red knights. If either of us is delusional, it's you.' She paused. 'And stop calling me love.'

'I call everyone love, don't take it personally.'

'Well, call me Bronwyn, if you would be so kind.' Her words came with a curtness that made the Ranen smile again.

'When and if the Red men enter the Moon Woods, we'll know. And when and if they do, we'll kill them. Do you think this happy gathering is the only camp we have?'

She felt like swearing at him, but remembered her manners. 'It would seem prudent to at least call the other Moon clans.'

'Would it now? Prudent?' asked Two Hearts, trying not to laugh.

'Oh, just . . . be quiet,' she snapped.

The chieftain leant forward and looked at her. 'Worry doesn't change anything,' he repeated. 'I'm not going to kill you . . . if that helps.'

'It doesn't,' she replied. 'Not at all.'

She tried to tune out the chattering voices and retreat into the peace of her mind. Warm Heart loped away and disappeared into the southern trees. Federick Two Hearts carried on smoking and making vulgar conversation. Micah and Dragneel were taken away and transferred to high tree houses.

Hours may have passed as she sat in the Ranen settlement, but she was too tired to notice and too alert to sleep.

* * *

Al-Hasim was sick of running. He'd lost his horse to a few well-aimed crossbow bolts several hours ago. Since then, he'd been running through the Moon Woods. Somewhere ahead of him, hopefully not too far away, was Bronwyn, and he was determined to find her before the knights found him.

Fallon's genius plan – to send him ahead as a makeshift diplomat – had hit an early snag when a large patrol from South Warden had spotted him and given chase. Their armour had slowed them down, but Al-Hasim was now on foot and was not able to gain any distance on the Red knights.

All he could see was trees and snow. The trees were tall and looming, and the snow was deep and freezing cold. He had been further north, having spent much time in Fjorlan, but he'd only ever visited Fredericksand and rarely strayed far from the fire-pits. Trudging through a snowy forest in the middle of nowhere was arguably the most unpleasant thing he'd ever done.

'Karesian, halt!' The horseman had appeared from behind a tree. He was an armed knight of the Red, wrapped in a thick cloak and holding a longsword across his chest.

'Er . . . no,' replied Hasim, darting to the left and raising his knees high to gain purchase in the deep snow.

'Halt!' the knight repeated, wheeling his horse and trying to manoeuvre after the fleeing man.

Hasim drew his scimitar and kept a wide tree trunk between him and the knight. He couldn't see or hear any others in pursuit and he hoped the man was an advance scout of some kind. The Red knight was a skilled rider and kept his horse under control, cutting off Hasim's escape and driving him towards a dense bramble thicket.

Hasim swore under his breath as the snow hampered his escape. He couldn't run quickly and any movement required considerable exertion.

'Right, come on then!' he snapped, when all avenues of escape had been explored and discarded.

The knight pulled back on his reins and the large warhorse reared, kicking out at Hasim. He rolled out of the way, narrowly missing a downward sword stroke. The knight wheeled round, keeping Hasim trapped.

'Just forget you found me,' he said, doing an ungainly forward roll into the snow.

'Submit to justice,' replied the knight, pressing his advantage.

Through a combination of agility and blind luck Hasim managed to avoid being trampled by the horse. He got to his feet, his back to a tree, and stood ready.

The knight turned his horse sharply, knocking Hasim back and spilling the air from his lungs. Face down in the snow, he rolled sideways, pulling himself under a dense mass of brambles.

'Just fuck off!'

The horse trampled forward, crushing the brambles and driving Hasim back into the open.

Then a dog barked. Or maybe it was a dozen dogs barking. Either way, it was loud and alarmingly close, cutting through the sound of armour and horse.

Hasim rolled out of the brambles and lay face to face with a huge, snarling dog. It had massively muscled shoulders and a squat muzzle, but he didn't register much past the slobbering mouth and abundance of teeth.

'Good dog,' he stuttered, forgetting about the horse and backing away.

'Back, beast,' shouted the knight, pointing his sword at the dog.

The warhorse stamped at the ground in alarm and shook its head violently. More barking and the horse stuttered backward, nearly throwing its rider. Hasim crawled through the snow, his face and hands cut by brambles, trying to get clear of the dog and the knight. Luckily, they seemed more concerned with one another than with the cowering Karesian.

The dog pounced. Its back legs braced for a moment, displacing the snow, then it leapt at the knight. As big as it was, it couldn't reach the knight's body, so settled for a mouthful of leg. The chain skirts that protected his legs proved no impediment to the beast's powerful jaws. A scream, a spray of blood, and the knight was yanked from his saddle. He flailed at the snow, trying to force open the dog's mouth as it shook him violently, biting deep into his thigh. The knight was tiny compared with the dog and his strength waned quickly. His laboured screams became gargles as the dog flung him around, mauling the fallen man.

'Well, you two seem to be getting on well. Don't let me get in the way,' muttered Al-Hasim, crawling slowly away from the spectacle.

The gargling ended and the knight stopped moving. Hopefully, he tasted good and the dog would not feel the need to turn round and add Karesian to his diet.

'Stay on your belly, man of the sun,' said a voice.

Hasim rolled over swiftly, bringing his scimitar to bear. In front of him, half hidden in the snowy brush, were a dozen people. They were bare-chested and marked with the blue designs of Crescent night-raiders. He had heard of them, and he hoped they were friendly.

He didn't stand. 'There's a fucking big dog over there.'

One of the Ranen whistled and the huge dog bounded away from the dead knight. It was the biggest dog he'd ever seen. Bigger than the wolfhounds common to Fjorlan and much larger than the hunting dogs used in Tor Funweir. It nuzzled up to one of the men and received a playful scratch behind the ears.

'Is that a Volk war-hound?' he asked.

A few of the night-raiders looked at one another impassively, in muted acknowledgement that Hasim did know something.

'Er, shall I introduce myself?' he asked, when none of them answered him.

More silence.

'I'm Al-Hasim. I come from South Warden seeking allies against the knights of the Red. And looking for an attractive young lady.' He smiled cheekily, hoping they would have a sense of humour. 'She's called Bronwyn. I think she came by these parts.'

PART TWO

CHAPTER SIX

HALLA SUMMER WOLF
IN THE CITY OF JARVIK

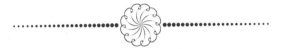

THE MOOD OF Jarvik matched the rugged terrain in which the city nestled. The City of the Green-Eyed Lords was at the highest point of the plateau of Ursa and dominated the barren, rocky terrain. It was far from the coast and relied on snow melt and underground rivers for its fresh water, while its livestock was kept in heated buildings on the northern edge of town. The predominant colour was grey and it lent the city a harsh and humourless edge. Living so long under the house of Ursa might also have contributed to the people's sour disposition.

The gullies that stretched from Hammerfall, through the Bear's Mouth, and ultimately to the Low Kast, were at their narrowest in Jarvik and looked like nothing so much as jagged fissures in the icy ground, through which fresh water bubbled up from vast underground lakes. The city was encircled by a seemingly bottomless gully which acted as Jarvik's natural defence, though much of it had now been built over or covered in, leaving just a few sheer drops into blackness. Although the outer walls were built of stone and dug into the natural rock, most of the inner buildings were constructed of wood and thatch, with the more important structures built half underground in order to protect them against the cold winds that lashed the city.

Jarvik wasn't as large as Fredericksand, or as impressive and ancient as Tiergarten. It was a lump of a city, which gave the impression of having simply been dumped in the most hospitable area of an inhospitable plateau.

'It's time,' said Wulfrick from the window.

They'd been in the city of Ursa for almost two weeks, slowly moving their five hundred-strong company through the gullies and quietly into Jarvik. The majority of the city's battle-brothers were either with their thain in Fredericksand or at the Bear's Mouth with Grammah Black Eyes, the bastard currently razing Hammerfall. Halla and her captains had met no resistance and the remaining chain-masters evidently didn't consider a stealthy incursion to be a threat. There were no gate guards and many of the streets were devoid of life, making it easy for Halla's company to put things in place.

Rexel Falling Cloud had taken men to secure the city's ballistae. Oleff Hard Head had quietly moved men into position round the chapel of Rowanoco. Heinrich Blood and Anya Lullaby had met with disgruntled citizens all too willing to throw in their lot with Halla, and the axe-maiden herself had remained close to the Ranen assembly while the large spider bite in her chest healed.

Wulfrick, the huge axe-master of Fredericksand, had remained with her and ensured that their men were spread throughout the city, waiting quietly until Halla judged it was time to reveal themselves.

The non-combatants among her company had been the last to enter Jarvik. They had picked up women and children from burning villages in Hammerfall and placed them safely in the farming and livestock areas away from the assembly. Halla expected them to remain in the city when she left with her battle-brothers. She silently thanked Rowanoco that she would no longer be responsible for those too weak, too old or too young to fight.

'Is everything in place?' she asked Wulfrick, rising from her chair and retrieving her walking stick.

The Gorlan venom had been a persistent foe, not easily defeated. Even now, her muscles ached and her mood was dark.

'Everything was in place a week ago,' he replied. 'We've been waiting for our leader to be able to walk by herself. I didn't want to have to carry you when we reveal ourselves . . . it sends the wrong message.'

They were in a small stone house next to the assembly. They'd found the building deserted and had moved in, using the house as a central point from which to coordinate their incursion into the hostile city. Halla, Wulfrick and twenty of her toughest axemen had watched the comings and goings of the city's populace closely, identifying those that would need killing and those that could be potential allies. The senior loyalist left in Jarvik was the chain-master David Emerald Eyes. He was one of the few men left over from before the family of Ursa took the city. By all accounts, the old warrior was no friend to Rulag Ursa or his loathsome son.

'Give Rexel the nod,' she said, testing her aching limbs, 'and tell Oleff to enter the chapel.'

'Aye, my lady,' responded the axe-master with a shallow nod.

Wulfrick turned from Halla to the waiting men, standing eagerly by the door to their acquired headquarters.

'You heard her, lads . . . it's time. Get to it,' he said with quiet authority. 'Quick and quiet, by the time they know what we're doing it'll already be done.'

They all saluted and split up, Rudolph Ten Bears taking men northwards to the chapel of Rowanoco, and Lars Bull taking others westwards to the outer wall. Five stayed with Halla and Wulfrick and waited for the next order.

Halla felt stronger than she had since leaving the spider caverns, but she was not yet fully mobile. The ice spiders had potent venom which had only been counteracted by the combined craft of the wise woman Anya and the novice of the Order of the Hammer, Heinrich. She could walk unaided now but still preferred to use a walking stick to keep herself upright. It was more dignified than leaning on Wulfrick's huge shoulders.

'Shall we go?' asked the axe-master, picking up his two-handed axe from the floor.

It was early morning and their plan was to march up to the Ranen assembly and announce their presence to the few remaining lords of Jarvik. Most of those who remained were old men. She hoped that a few well-placed threats would make their coup a bloodless one.

They stepped out of the building and on to the hard stone streets of Jarvik. The morning was freezing cold, with a crisp wind. The cold made the wound in her chest throb and she grumbled quietly, realizing that if there were a fight she would be unable to take part. She still carried her axe, insisting that it remained at her hip, but she was too weak to heft it with any force.

'Who do we have to worry about?' she asked.

The small group made their way across a wide avenue towards the stepped building that lay at the centre of the city. There were no guards, but the lords would be in attendance. Rowanoco's Stone had to be occupied during the hours of daylight, and deliberations took place from dawn till dusk.

'The Blood Fists are still here,' replied Wulfrick. 'I don't know which one is in charge, but he'll be in there and likely be an arrogant bastard.'

'Thran,' said another of her men. 'His name is Thran Blood Fist. He's a pig.'

'Well, let us hope he behaves himself,' responded Wulfrick, with a violent grin.

Halla limped up the steps and approached the heavy wooden doors. Wulfrick and the others were polite enough to stand behind and let her lead. The axe-master had his great axe slung casually over his shoulder and the other men were similarly armed. She held her walking stick tightly and used her other hand to push the doors inwards. A grunt of exertion showed the others that her strength was insufficient to move the heavy oak and Wulfrick moved to assist her.

'The hinges get stuck in the cold,' he said, showing a rare tact. 'Let me.'

He put a huge hand against the door and flexed his shoulder, causing a sudden creak as the door inched open. The others approached and within moments both doors were flung open.

'What is the meaning of this intrusion?' shouted a voice from within.

Halla stood in the doorway, flanked by warriors and the axe-master of Fredericksand. She had to squint to see through the dark entrance to focus on those seated within and was gratified when she saw barely twenty men in the stone auditorium.

Moving slowly forward, her walking stick announcing her presence with a rhythmic thump, Halla kept her single eye on those within. They were mostly old men, white-bearded and barely awake, but a number of them stood and glared down at the intruders.

'I am Halla Summer Wolf, lady of Tiergarten. I claim this assembly and these lands in the name of Teardrop and Summer Wolf.'

A moment of silence. Wulfrick stepped forward and the assembled lords of Jarvik exchanged looks.

A green-eyed man, seated in the centre of the stepped auditorium, had not stood up but seemed more alert than most of the lords. He was of advancing years and bore an old red tattoo over his left eye. He glanced either side of him, frowning at the man who had spoken first, and then nodded politely at Halla. 'I am David, called Emerald Eyes, and I will speak for Jarvik,' he said in a deep voice.

'Silence, chain-master,' roared the other man, who held two throwing-axes in indication that he was in charge of the assembly in the absence of a thain.

'I am Thran Blood Fist,' he shouted, 'and I will speak for Jarvik. By what right do you step on Rowanoco's Stone?' He stood defiantly upright and hefted both his axes. 'Speak!'

Wulfrick smiled at Halla. 'My lady, would you like me to teach this man some manners?'

She returned the smile but waved away the offer.

'Lord Blood Fist, you are an axe-master of Jarvik and I don't wish to shut you up, but I'm not asking for an election. I'm taking your city. It belongs to the house of Ursa no longer.'

Blood Fist held his axes across his chest, but his eyes betrayed conflict. He was considering casting an axe, but was not sure this was worth dying for. He looked at Emerald Eyes, confirming that he would have little support, and then laid both his axes on the marble stone in front of him. 'I will not shed blood on Rowanoco's Stone, but I do not recognize your claim to the realm of Ursa. The battle-brothers of Jarvik will not stand for this treachery.'

Wulfrick snorted with derision. 'You're short on battle-brothers. We have more. It's simple.'

'Don't be a fool, Thran,' insisted David Emerald Eyes. 'This was inevitable.'

'I remain loyal to Ursa, even if you do not.'

Blood Fist stepped down from his raised seat and spread his arms wide to signal his submission. He stood face to face with Halla, sizing her up, though he kept glancing at the huge figure of Wulfrick.

'I knew your father, girl. He'd be proud of what you've become. A traitor and a rebel.'

Halla's men tightened their fists around their axes and Wulfrick growled. Just as she was about to retort to the insult, five men entered the assembly from behind the raised seating. They wore the red bear claw of Ursa and hefted glaives. From their chain-mail armour, Halla guessed they were the guards of Rowanoco's Stone, though they appeared to hesitate at the sight of Halla's men.

David Emerald Eyes stood and held up his hand . 'Stand down, there is no fight here.'

Thran did not smile, but his eyes betrayed a new confidence.

'Wulfrick,' said Halla quietly, conveying meaning with a serious look.

'Aye, my lady.' He moved to stand before the five men of Ursa and held his great axe at the ready. 'Do you know who I am?' he asked.

They exchanged glances, but all shook their heads.

'I am Wulfrick, axe-master of Fredericksand and servant of Teardrop. I have killed men and beast by the thousand and I stand here ready to kill you.' He paused. 'Do not give me a reason.'

The show of strength startled the battle-brothers, doubly so as no more of Halla's men had advanced. The huge axe-master was confident he was more than a match for the five guards. Thran, who had heard of Algenon's axe-master, now backed away from Halla and approached the raised seats.

'For the sake of our men, our families and our city, I surrender to you, Lady Summer Wolf.' He bowed his head in shame.

The man was not a fool and Halla breathed a sigh of relief.

'You are wise, Lord Blood Fist,' she said, with a respectful nod.

A whistling sound reached her ears as a signal arrow was fired from Falling Cloud's position.

'We have the ballistae and the walls, my lady,' said one of her men.

'Let's hope young Rexel was met by equally wise men.' Halla directed her words at Thran. 'Your walls are ours.' Another signal arrow from the centre of the town. 'As is your chapel.'

'I bet Oleff found a way to get his axe wet,' joked Wulfrick. He held his great axe in one hand and pointed it at the armed battle-brothers of Ursa. 'Drop. Your. Weapons.'

A word from behind told her that Heinrich, Lullaby and two dozen of her company were approaching the assembly as arranged. The reinforcements were not needed but she was glad of the extra support.

'Do as they say,' commanded Thran. 'We will not throw our lives away.'

David Emerald Eyes allowed himself a thin smile, reflecting his allegiance to the city rather than to its Ursa rulers. He stepped down from the seating and bowed his head to Halla.

'And now I will speak for Jarvik,' he said, as battle-brothers flooded into the assembly and a tingle of pride travelled up Halla's spine.

* * *

Halla was tired. She had risen early and her chest ached. The strength in her arms, tested by permanently leaning on her walking stick, was beginning to wane and as she walked along the southern battlements of Jarvik she desperately needed to sleep.

Wulfrick, Rexel Falling Cloud and David Emerald Eyes accompanied her. Her men had met little resistance. Aside from a small fight at the chapel of Rowanoco, the city was now theirs. Thran Blood Fist and a handful of others were being guarded in the assembly and those who wished to join Halla's company were being organized by Oleff Hard Head. Several hundred men and women had greeted them with enthusiasm, shaking their hands and thanking them for deposing Rulag Ursa. This in itself assured Halla that she had done the right thing.

'It's a shame you can't stay,' said David, stopping at a ballistae turret. 'This city needs some leadership.'

'Jarvik was never our destination . . . just a necessary stop,' replied Halla, struggling to keep her mind alert.

Falling Cloud pointed to a broken limb on the huge ballistae. 'They fouled the artillery for some reason.'

'Maybe they thought we were an invading army,' quipped Wulfrick. 'Halla, how long do we remain here? The Bear's Mouth beckons.'

Emerald Eyes shook his head and frowned. 'More death, my lady? You don't need to leave. Keep Jarvik strong and fight Rulag here.'

'And abandon Hammerfall?' replied Halla, glancing at Falling Cloud. 'We saw first-hand what Grammah Black Eyes was doing to the cloud-men.'

'A lot of your people agree,' said Wulfrick. 'Our company gets larger and I have not had a proper battle since my thain was killed.'

Halla rubbed her eye to relieve her tiredness and tried to smile at David. 'I'm sorry, but Fjorlan needs us to fight, not to wait. We take loyal men from Jarvik, we kill Grammah Black Eyes, we take loyal men from Hammerfall . . . and we fight Rulag at Tiergarten.'

Wulfrick smiled. 'Where sits Alahan Teardrop.'

'He lives?' asked Emerald Eyes with incredulity.

'He killed Kalag Ursa,' replied the axe-master with pride. 'Make no mistake, David, we are not beaten.'

Falling Cloud, who had the most invested in seeing Hammerfall freed, stood next to Halla and nodded. 'If we can muster the cloud-men, we have an army. If we can get to Tiergarten, we have a thain.'

'I understand,' said David. 'But I'm an old man and I want some peace.'

Halla laughed at this, causing the men to look at her in confusion. 'Peace is hard won, it seems. You will have little, I'm afraid, if you are to be Jarvik's lord.'

'I'm a chain-master, not a thain.'

'Would you prefer I invest Thran with the lordship of your city?' Halla knew there were many logistical problems in leaving Jarvik, but she had no doubt that David was the right man to lead the city. 'You don't need to pledge your allegiance, just rule fairly.'

'If you lose, my lady, Rulag will kill anyone here who didn't fight you.'

David was a wise man and he made a good point. All she could think of to say was, 'We won't lose.'

He let a pained laugh escape his lips. 'Confidence is admirable, but I have already done enough to be killed . . . should you lose.'

Wulfrick and Falling Cloud looked at him. 'We won't lose,' they repeated.

Emerald Eyes shook his head and puffed out his cheeks, the expression of a tired old man who knows he can't win. 'Very well. I will trust in blind optimism.'

'Trust in Rowanoco,' replied Wulfrick. 'The Ice Giant doesn't want a troll cunt like Ursa ruling Fjorlan.'

'Unfortunately, the Earth Shaker won't be joining your army, master Wulfrick, so I fail to see how he can help. You have no priests.'

He was right. Halla's company contained only an novice of the Order of the Hammer. To go into battle without a priest was considered not just a bad omen but presumptuous. Without the Order it was impossible to know whether Rowanoco approved their actions.

'Old Father Brindon Crowe,' said Halla after a second. 'He sits in Tiergarten with the high thain. We will talk to him before we leave your city.'

David narrowed his eyes. 'Our cloud-stone went missing some weeks ago.'

'That's because I stole it,' replied Falling Cloud, with a mischievous smirk.

'I hate to say it, David,' began Wulfrick, 'but the cloud-stone was the reason we came here. It was a bonus to snatch Jarvik from under Rulag's nose.'

The chain-master shook his head again, this time slowly and with evident frustration. 'So, we're just a by-product? Has the crest of Jarvik fallen so far?'

Halla rubbed her eye and prevented Falling Cloud's response. 'David, this is not the time. Fjorlan is what matters, not Tiergarten, Fredericksand or Jarvik.'

The sound of running feet and Oleff Hard Head bounded up the nearby steps to join them on the battlements. He was out of breath and his axe was held firmly in his fist.

'Easy, man,' said Wulfrick. 'You're too old to be running around.'

Oleff panted and leant on his knees. 'We have a problem, Halla.'

'Another one?' she replied.

'Afraid so,' he said between laboured breaths. 'To the north, an enclave of Low Kasters who don't like being told what to do.'

'Ah, yes,' said David. 'I expected trouble from them.'

Halla and Wulfrick both glared at him, the axe-maiden wearily and the axe-master with frustration.

'Why are men of the Low Kast in Jarvik?' she asked.

David smiled thinly, perhaps realizing that he should have warned them. 'Rulag used to say that they're the best hunters and trackers in all of Ranen. And they have a way with trolls. He conspired to use them as his ranger corps. During the winters it's rather hard to keep larders stocked and the trolls at bay. They have a knack for finding food and grain in any weather.'

'How did he persuade them?' asked Wulfrick. 'The berserkers of Varorg are not easy to sway. As Oleff said, they don't like being told what to do.'

'He killed their chieftain and all of his family.' It was said plainly. 'The way I understand it, if a clan has no hereditary leadership, they pledge themselves to someone of strength.'

'Rulag? He was the best they could find?' queried Falling Cloud.

David shrugged. 'They had just seen him massacre their leader and his entire family. That certainly says strength to me.'

'Will this be a problem?' asked Halla, barely mustering the energy to listen to the response.

'I should expect so, yes,' replied David. 'They're not loyal as such, but they respect strength. I suppose you need to show equal or greater strength . . . prove you're more worthy than Rulag Ursa.'

'How many of them?' asked Wulfrick.

Emerald Eyes considered the question. 'Hard to tell, they come and go as they please. I'd say that thirty or so actually make their homes in Jarvik. They bed down in an old cattle shed against the northern wall. The place stinks of troll piss, but it keeps them away from the rest of our people and stops them randomly butchering the populace.'

Halla knew little about the berserker clans of the Low Kast. They came from the wildest area of Fjorlan, a place not easily travelled. Despite this, the men of that land had a terrifying reputation and a highly honoured place among the faithful of Rowanoco. They called the Ice Giant by the name of Varorg, for reasons she was unclear about, and her father had told her a hundred stories about grotesquely deformed men frothing at the mouth and revelling in bloody combat.

'We could just kill them,' muttered Falling Cloud. 'If they don't behave, I mean.'

'Sounds reasonable, if a bit aggressive,' said Wulfrick. He turned to Oleff. 'Did you speak to them?'

'No, but they beat up a couple of our men who tried. They've barricaded themselves into the cattle shed.' The chain-master panted a few times and caught his breath. 'Some fellow called Rorg said he'll only speak to our leader.'

Halla and Wulfrick looked at David.

'Rorg?' she asked.

'I know the man,' he replied. 'He's called the Defiler. You probably don't want to know why.'

Halla leant heavily on her walking stick. Her chest hurt, her leg ached and her body felt as if it needed a few days' sleep.

Breathing heavily, she heard Wulfrick and David arguing about the berserkers. Their raised voices were distant and the words flowed into a muddle of sounds. The axe-maiden would never admit that she needed rest – the previous few weeks while she was fighting off the Gorlan venom had been enough – but Halla, strong as she was, needed to sleep.

'Will they wait until morning?' she asked.

'I don't think they're going to burst forth in a rampage,' said Oleff. 'They're happy in their shed for now.'

'So, keep an eye on them. Take a few dozen men and stay at a safe distance. I'll speak to them when the sun rises.'

None of the men argued and Wulfrick went so far as to assist Halla in walking down the stone steps.

The axe-master turned back to David and the others.

'Get some rest,' he said, 'and, Falling Cloud, stop looking for a fight. You'll get one soon enough.'

* * *

Sleep helped, but only a little. Halla was thinking more slowly and her decisions had become sharp and decisive over the last few months. No one questioned her authority and her captains reinforced every word she spoke, but the lady of Tiergarten was a woman conflicted. She had pledged herself to Fjorlan and to keep her company alive, but she still doubted whether she was up to the task.

What if a decision got men killed? What if she was wrong and they couldn't beat Grammah Black Eyes at the Bear's Mouth? She'd taken Jarvik in a bloodless coup and had increased their number considerably, but what if these men were just more bodies to pile up when they lost?

These thoughts disturbed her, but they also kept her sharp. It was a long trek to Tiergarten and she would need every ounce of wit and intelligence.

A bang on the door roused her. Anya Coldbane, still called Lullaby by most of her company, strode into her chamber without waiting to be invited. The old wise woman walked straight up to the shuttered windows and flung them outwards, letting freezing air and bright light stream into Halla's chamber. She baulked and tried to burrow further into her straw-filled mattress.

'Anya, this is not the most pleasant way of being woken.'

'You should have been up hours ago, young lady. Light means action. It's been light for hours, so we need action.'

The crotchety woman of Hammerfall was oblivious to the comfort of others, but her healing abilities and her piety had proven useful since they had first encountered her.

'I have met with men of Varorg before,' said Anya. 'Perhaps I should accompany you. To stop you saying anything stupid.'

'Such as?' asked Halla, pulling herself upright.

'Trying to appease them. It's a sign of weakness.'

'Anything else?' she prompted, rubbing under her eyepatch and padding her feet on the cold stone floor. 'Perhaps my sex will be an issue.' She delivered the comment with sarcasm, not caring what the men of the Low Kast thought.

'Women are not treated well in their culture,' replied Lullaby. 'Except wise women, obviously.'

Halla smiled. 'I'm likely to kill any man who doesn't treat me well. I've trudged through too much blood to be put off by a berserker.'

'And his thirty friends,' offered Anya. 'Don't be silly, my dear. These men could be good allies.'

'Thirty warriors I can do without,' she replied.

Anya made a throaty grunt.

'What?' demanded the axe-maiden, standing up from her bed and retrieving her walking stick.

'They have craft unknown in the rest of Fjorlan. They can tame the beasts of the ice, communicate over long distances without cloud-stones, and fight harder than any man you know.' She paused, squinting at Halla. 'I think I will come with you.'

'Suit yourself.'

Halla dressed quickly, pulling on her leather armour over sore limbs. Within a few minutes she was feeling much more alert than she had the previous day. A cursory smell of her underarms caused her to take a sharp breath of fresh air from the window. Perhaps a bath later in the day, she thought.

She could hear Wulfrick and Oleff in the next room and both men were in good humour. The taking of Jarvik had gone well and she hoped that morale would be high among her men. She had heard cheering and drunken revelry as she had drifted off to sleep, which made her smile. They only got drunk when they felt safe.

With Anya following her, she exited the chamber and greeted her battle-brothers. Along with Wulfrick and Oleff were six other warriors, each man armed as if expecting trouble. They knew that the men of the Low Kast were violent and unpredictable. She had ordered Falling Cloud to gather a hundred men to encircle the cattle shed at a distance, in case their negotiations did not go smoothly, but otherwise she planned to approach them openly and with as few men as possible.

* * *

Wulfrick had assembled a large breakfast and made sure that they waited for Halla to wake before eating. Once the hearty mix of porridge and honey, bread and fruit, and rich beef sausage had been consumed, they set out into the chill morning air of

140

Jarvik. Lullaby came with them, sheltered behind Wulfrick's huge shoulders.

The cattle shed was against the northern wall of the city and was much larger than she had expected. The underground springs kept the area warm and the houses free of snow, though the area was still grim and lifeless, with the continual grunting of cattle. Oleff directed them to the most remote area, down a steep road and against the lowest part of the outer wall.

'They live here?' asked Wulfrick, turning up his nose at the smell.

'Apparently,' replied Oleff. 'They have tunnels that lead into the underground caverns.'

'What, they don't like using the gates?' asked Halla.

'I think it's the other people that don't like them using the gates.' Oleff pointed to a barricaded opening that led into the low-ceilinged shed.

'Do we knock?' asked Wulfrick, slowly unsheathing his great axe.

A gruff voice came from within. 'We can hear you. Don't need to knock.'

Halla raised her eyebrows and came to a stop directly in front of the barricaded doorway.

'Who am I talking to?' she asked.

There was silence for a moment. Wulfrick and Oleff moved to flank Halla, and Lullaby poked her head round the axe-maiden's shoulder.

'You are a woman,' said the voice.

She snorted with amusement. 'I am. Are you a man?'

An angry growl sounded from within. 'I don't talk to the weak,' said the Low Kaster.

'Watch your manners,' barked Wulfrick. 'We both have axes, so let's both be polite.'

'You are a man, we will talk to you,' said the voice.

Wulfrick turned to Halla. She paused, allowing her anger to rise and her mouth to curl into a sneer.

'You will talk to me!' she shouted. 'I am Halla Summer Wolf and I command Jarvik. If you are truly a man, you will open this door and face me.'

Her men grunted in agreement and hefted their axes behind her. She could hear movement within. After a silent minute which seemed to stretch, the barricade was opened and several men were suddenly visible.

Each man had a malformed head, bulbous and red, with split veins barely contained behind tight leather strapping. They wore mismatched and poorly maintained leather and fur clothing, with heavy woollen cloaks. Their appearance was both strange and startling, causing Halla to pause in surprise before she could speak. The berserker men of Varorg lived up to their reputation, in appearance at least. Their axes were oversized and several were made of deep ice rather than steel.

Halla and her men moved into the cattle shed and found themselves standing under low, wooden beams. The shed went back a fair distance into the caverns below Jarvik and nothing but darkness lay beyond the berserkers standing before her. She could count twenty-five men of the Low Kast in the cattle shed.

'You are the Daughter of the Wolf?' asked the lead man.

He was tall and his huge arms were mostly bare, covered only at the elbows and wrists with more leather strapping. His eyes were red and Halla thought he was twitching.

'I expected a mightier being. You are a small girl.'

She was confused and irritated by the man's words. He knew who she was, but still insulted her.

Wulfrick, angered at the insult, stepped up next to Halla and glared down at the berserker. 'I told you once to watch your manners. If I have to say it again, I say it with my axe.'

The reaction was almost instant. Each one of the men of Varorg began to laugh. The sound was hearty and good-humoured, though their malformed skulls made the spectacle somewhat grotesque.

'You think I'm fucking joking?' shouted Wulfrick.

The lead berserker stopped laughing and met Wulfrick's eyes. 'I am Rorg, called the Defiler. We laugh because you don't understand our ways. If we were in the Low Kast I would kill you.'

Wulfrick frowned, unused to people standing up to him. He paused, allowing Halla to take over.

'You know who I am. Now I know who you are. Don't push me and we can stay civil. If you have a desire to die in a no doubt glorious but nonetheless futile battle, please attack us.' Halla wished she didn't have to use the walking stick and could truly stand up to the man.

Rorg snarled and his twitching increased. He hefted his ice-axe and lunged forward. The move was sluggish but powerful and Wulfrick had to drop his shoulder to intercept the attack. The two men clashed violently and Rorg's strength gave way as Wulfrick grunted with exertion. Both men had huge shoulders and Halla had to sidestep to avoid the berserker as he fell to the dusty floor. His eyes were black and he vibrated with anger.

'Come on!' challenged Wulfrick, waving for the man to rise.

An inhuman growl sounded from the darkness of the cattle shed. It was a bestial sound that cut through the air and caused Halla's men to take an involuntary step backwards.

In the darkness a shape rose from a gap in the floor behind Rorg. The flagstones were broken at regular intervals, giving access to the icy depths of Jarvik. The sound rumbled upwards as the figure pulled itself to a crouched position, hunched under the roof of the cattle shed. It was undoubtedly a troll, but smaller than those Halla had seen and it did not look poised to attack.

'No!' shouted Rorg, holding his hand up to Wulfrick and Halla. 'Do not attack, he is a friend.'

Halla's men gathered themselves and held their weapons ready. They were shaking at the sight of the huge, hairy beast, but they were men of conviction and would not back down.

'That's a fucking troll,' said Oleff, staring wide-eyed at the creature, as his eyes took in the huge tusks and the foot-long claws. 'It's in a city . . . trolls don't come to cities.'

The Ice- Man of Rowanoco bellowed again and craned its head into the light. It had dense brown and black fur covering every inch of its huge body and sparkling green opals for eyes. It was hard to determine its height, but Halla guessed at around ten foot tall.

Rorg stood up quickly and his rage dissipated. He waved his arms at the troll, drawing its eyes away from Halla and her men. 'Down!' he said in a commanding voice, causing the beast to grunt and plonk itself into a seated position.

Halla was stunned. The Ice Men were chaotic eating machines, rampaging through anything in their way. To see one essentially tamed was bewildering.

'How the fuck did you do that?' asked Wulfrick.

'He is an awakened troll,' replied Rorg, as if that explained everything.

'Hmm, interesting,' offered Lullaby in a raspy whisper. 'It seems that the Ice Father has given us a gift.'

The troll grunted again, this time at Lullaby, and banged its huge fist on the shed floor at the mention of Rowanoco. Dust rose, indicating the beast's enormous strength, and Halla panted nervously.

'His name is Unrahgahr,' said Rorg. 'The Ice Father has decreed that his family should no longer eat men.'

'A name!' said Halla. 'He has a name?'

Lullaby shuffled past them and stood a few inches from the troll. Wulfrick moved to stop her, but the wise old woman waved away the intrusion. She reached out a hand to Unrahgahr, appearing tiny next to the bulky troll.

'They all have names,' she said. 'Though they only have so many sounds, so their names are all similar, made up of the same few grunts. Body language is important.'

'Un rah gahr,' grunted the troll. 'Yal ul rah.'

Lullaby chuckled to herself as the beast nuzzled her hand, as a dog would allow a man to pet it.

'Yal ak gahr,' she replied, letting the sounds come from her throat and be coughed out rather than spoken.

'They have language?' queried Wulfrick. 'I thought they barely had minds.'

Rorg the Defiler, amused at their reaction, sheathed his ice-axe and approached them, leaving Lullaby to pet the huge troll behind him.

'Their language is minimal,' he said. 'They speak in three sounds at a time. They only have twenty sounds, but they understand body language.'

'This is not unusual for you?' Halla asked him.

'For ages beyond counting, we have welcomed the Ice Men to our fires,' he replied. 'They are attracted by the troll crystals we snort before battle. Sometimes an Ice Man will remain with a clan for months, believing he has found a new family of trolls.'

'And this one?' she asked, hesitating to point at Unrahgahr.

'This is new,' he replied. 'But welcome.'

'I don't feel like fighting any more,' said Wulfrick as Lullaby scratched Unrahgahr behind his oversized, shaggy ears.

'We will fight again,' stated Rorg. 'I must kill you to maintain honour. But your bone reader has bought you some time.' He pointed at Anya.

Wulfrick, too distracted to register the threat, merely nodded.

'You know what is happening to Rowanoco's land,' said Halla. 'You have a tame troll and Anya says you are faithful to the Ice Giant. Perhaps we are allies.'

Rorg grunted, still dismissive of the axe-maiden before him. 'I knew your father, girl. One of my people pledged their fate to him. Your name is strong.' He looked her up and down. 'But your body is not.'

Again, Halla wished she didn't have the walking stick. 'My father travelled to the Low Kast many times. I am not him, though I am a Summer Wolf.'

'She is our captain,' offered Wulfrick. 'Each of us would die for her. We would kill for her.'

'Aye!' agreed Oleff. 'Halla is a better leader than any I have known beyond Algenon Teardrop himself.'

She tried not to blush with pride. She kept her head upright and her eyes hard. 'Ally with us and fight back against the betrayer . . . or we fight and you die.'

Rorg motioned his men to stand, though Unrahgahr kept out of the way, lulled into contented growling by Anya's petting. The men of the Low Kast assembled behind their chieftain with axes held in grimy hands.

'We will travel with you, Daughter of the Wolf, and give you a chance to earn our fate, as your father did.'

'And the troll?' she asked.

'He and his family go where we go. They are a gift from Varorg, a means to defend the land of the Ice Father.'

'His family?' queried Oleff. 'Mums and kids and stuff?'

Rorg nodded. 'Ten of them, though Unrahgahr is the patriarch.'

'Halla,' asked Wulfrick, 'are we seriously considering adding ten trolls to our company?'

'They do not eat men,' offered Rorg. 'They are as much children of Varorg as you or I.'

Halla considered. She had a significant force now, hardened battle-brothers ready to die for Fjorlan, but there was still doubt in her mind. The Bear's Mouth would be a hard fight and thirty berserkers and a family of trolls could only assist their efforts.

'Okay, you come,' she said. 'We are fighting for Fjorlan. As long as you remember that, we'll get on fine.'

'Agreed,' replied Rorg. 'I will give you notice when I intend to kill the axe-master.' He thrust his chin forward at Wulfrick.

Halla laughed. 'Very well, but I don't think he'll die easily.'

Wulfrick frowned. 'Why do you want to fight me? Basically, I just pushed you over.'

'You don't understand,' Rorg said. 'We will fight, face to face and honourably, and I will kill you . . . but not today.'

Oleff chuckled and Halla raised her eyebrow. Wulfrick said nothing.

'We are leaving Jarvik within the week,' said Halla, trying to prevent Wulfrick reacting. 'Grammah Black Eyes holds the

Bear's Mouth and we need to punch through it before we can enter the Wolf Wood.'

Rorg thrust his chin forward. 'We will contact more men and beasts and they will meet us in the realm of Summer Wolf.'

'Contact them how?' she asked. 'You have cloud-stones?'

'No. The Ice Men have means of talking to each other. We call it the keening chain. The words pass from one troll to the next until the message has reached its destination.'

'Interesting,' was all Halla could think to say.

CHAPTER SEVEN

GWENDOLYN OF HUNTER'S CROSS IN THE DUCHY OF HARAN

THE KISS WAS hard, deep and passionate. She closed her eyes and melted into Xander's embrace. She didn't understand love, but knew that she felt it. From her head to her toes, her body rippled, trying to get as close as possible to the warm flesh that pressed against her. She ached for him – his mind, his warmth, his being. Whatever he would give, she would take and lose herself in ecstasy as she took it.

He paused and their eyes met for a second.

'I need you,' he murmured. 'I've never needed anything. But I need you.'

She tenderly touched his face and gasped as he thrust forward. Grabbing the back of his neck, she smiled. 'Talk is for daylight, my love.'

Clamping her teeth to his chest, Gwen wrapped her legs around his waist and growled in longing. Xander responded and the only sounds to come out of his mouth were primal sounds of passion.

* * *

Gwen never woke gently when she slept under canvas. The command pavilion she shared with her husband was cold and kept out no wind or nightly noise. No matter how much she tried to shut out the sound of soldiers at their rest, the five thousand Hawks were loud throughout the night.

She always rose before her husband, enjoying the morning air and solitude that an early start provided. For company during these quiet hours she had the camp servants who built fires and prepared food for the officers. Most of the Hawks looked after themselves, but some traditions – such as the reluctance of the nobility to erect their own tents – made servants a requirement.

Her own body servant, a naive young girl called Lennifer, was constantly following her around and asking strange questions about her hair and clothing. Lennifer had not yet grasped that Gwen was not particularly interested in clothes and preferred to be clad in simple leather. On the rare occasions when she had to make an effort, she wore her long black hair down and a simple blue dress.

When at Xander's court in Ro Haran, Lennifer was a constant and reassuring presence. She gave Gwen good advice regarding the nuances of noble life for which her upbringing in Hunter's Cross had not prepared her. However, the young girl had not adapted well during their extended absence from the city.

'My lady.' Lennifer was smiling the vacuous smile of a girl unsure of her place in the military camp. 'A pleasant morning.'

'You don't need to get up at the same time as me. I'm aware I rise earlier than most,' said Gwen, placing a hand gently on the girl's shoulder.

Lennifer wore a brown smock – not quite a dress – and woollen trousers, gathered at the waist with a silvery brocade. She'd abandoned any attempt at formal or feminine dress within a few days of leaving Haran, primarily on the advice of her lady. The last thing soldiers need around them is a young, unobtainable woman.

'It is a pleasure to serve, my lady,' replied the girl.

'Indeed.'

Gwen continued her wandering, content that Lennifer would follow her whether she requested it or not.

Looking southwards from the camp, past a hundred tents, dozens of carts and numerous small smithies and cooking fires,

Gwen could see the slight shimmer that marked the location of Ro Haran. The river men, who normally made the flat lands a vibrant and friendly place, had retreated back to their isolated farmsteads and left the duchy to the wind and the beasts.

It was a strange and lonely sight, a natural vista of green, grey and brown, from the Walls of Ro to the Stone Coast. Gwen loved this land. She had been here for ten years and felt a bond with the simple folk of Haran beyond anything she had experienced elsewhere in Tor Funweir. She disliked Tiris and found Arnon too reserved, whereas the westernmost duchy of the Ro was isolated and less arrogant.

'There is a rumour, my lady,' muttered Lennifer under her breath.

Gwen smiled. 'Soldiers gossip as much as courtiers, it would seem.'

'They say . . .' The young girl was nervous about repeating the rumour and leant forward as if she were being naughty. 'They say that we'll be returning to the city soon. Is it true?'

'It depends how much you trust the skill of a Kirin assassin,' replied Gwen.

'One of the cooks says that he's killed two already.' Lennifer was more in tune with the gossip of the Hawks than her mistress.

'He claimed three, but he may not be trustworthy. That is also the answer to whether or not we're going home – he says so, but he may not be trustworthy.'

'And then?' asked Lennifer. 'When we get home. What happens then?'

Gwen smiled warmly. They both knew that Tor Funweir was slowly imploding, annexed by the Karesian Hounds and swayed to a dark new religion by the enchantresses. The answer to these myriad problems was more complex than Xander believed and Gwen could not bring herself to trust in strength of arms, whether or not Rham Jas could do as he claimed.

'I think a war is brewing. I think it may have started already. We've just yet to take the field,' she replied. 'Our lord will act with equal parts passion and conviction. Hopefully, we'll find victory between the two.'

The serving girl frowned, not fully understanding what Gwen said. 'I've never been to war.' Her words were spoken through a sheen of barely disguised fear.

'I wish I could say that I hadn't, but Hunter's Cross spent years fighting Red knights and yeomen. War is loud and bloody. It gets under your skin and stays there.' She softened her eyes and looked at the young girl. 'Don't worry, I won't need you to dress me on the battlefield.'

'It's my duty to accompany you, my lady.'

'It's not your duty to die, Lennifer. I'll have a tent. You can stay in it while I kill Hounds.'

Gwen was not eager to fight anyone, but she took her vows seriously. She had made vows to Xander and to the people of the duchy. Those obligations weighed heavily on her shoulders, and the lady of Haran knew that the Hounds were a threat to them both. They would hunt and kill their people and turn Xander into a slave. She would not allow either while she had strength.

Lennifer giggled, her cheeks turning red in embarrassment.

'What's funny?' asked Gwen.

'Sorry, my lady. It's hearing you talk of fighting. My father was old-fashioned, he didn't allow me to wear trousers, let alone a blade.'

The men of Ro were a notoriously misogynistic bunch, believing in the One God's principle that women were to be the gentle counterpoint to the warrior men of Tor Funweir. That ignorant horse shit had never fully penetrated the northern lands of Hunter's Cross, the Darkwald or Canarn. Gwen had been raised as the equal of any man she knew. Her Dokkalfar leaf-blades were always at her side and she knew how to kill with them. It was a simple matter to cut flesh and an easy lesson to learn where would cause the most damage. She was skilled at opening a man's neck, slicing his tendons, rupturing his groin. It was Dokkalfar fencing, a style designed to kill, and it had served her well.

She continued her wandering, past tents and cook fires, gazing across the plains. Lennifer followed, but said nothing more, leaving her mistress to her silent contemplation. To the south, far across the duchy, lay Ro Haran, her home for ten years. If the Kirin assassin could truly do what he claimed, they'd be able to return home soon. The small comfort this provided was eclipsed by the sure knowledge that they would not be staying long in the city. Xander intended to muster his army and sail to Canarn. After that, Gwen could only guess at their ultimate destination.

The Hawks of Ro would go to war. They would liberate Ro Tiris, and then what? She hated the idea of a long campaign but she could not see any alternative for Tor Funweir. Her husband was stubborn and he had made up his mind. She'd always known that his name was a heavy burden, but it was a burden he'd so far been able to ignore. As the king's younger brother and a man not gifted with the skills of courtly intrigue, Xander had never been destined to rule. Being duke of Haran was difficult enough for him and he chose to style himself a general rather than a noble. But things were different now. His brother had been led astray and the Ro needed a Tiris to follow.

The sound of approaching horses dragged her back to her surroundings as a small patrol returned to camp. She had wandered as far as the southern stockade. A deep bugle sounded a muted note from a watchtower and Gwendolyn strode out to meet the Hawks. A few guards approached and, with Lennifer running along behind, they escorted the lady of Haran to greet the patrol.

'My lady,' greeted Captain Brennan, striking his breastplate. 'We have news.'

'From the city?' she asked, trying to contain her eagerness to return home.

He shook his head and began to dismount. The other four Hawks did the same and started to lead their tired horses back to camp.

'Best we speak to the general, my lady,' said Brennan, shaking the dust from his cloak. 'The Kirin's on his way back.'

Her eyes widened. As the group hastened back to camp she began to feel a touch of optimism. If Rham Jas was alive, he had either run away or succeeded.

'He fired a signal arrow an hour ago. Should be here soon.' Brennan gave his reins to a nearby guard and left his patrol to rest and eat while he accompanied Gwen to the command pavilion.

The bugle had alerted some of the Hawks and word was spreading through the army. Men emerged from their tents and started to whisper about returning to the city. Brennan waved away their queries and ordered them to go about their duties. He was the general's senior scout, commanding a unit of rangers and he was harsh towards the common soldiers. He was also rather miserable and consumed with duty, making him poor company but an excellent soldier.

'I don't suppose the signal arrow indicated success . . . in any fashion?' asked Gwen.

Brennan looked at her. 'No, my lady. It was just an arrow.'

She smiled politely as they approached the pavilion. The guards on duty saluted and banged their fists in unison on their red breastplates. She swept aside the tent flap and strode inside, with Captain Brennan a step behind.

The pavilion was split into a number of chambers and they had emerged into the main tent, adjoining the bedchamber that the duke shared with his wife. Xander was slouched inside, his right hand clasped round a mug of steaming fruit tea and his feet up on a stool. It was still early morning and he had only recently woken.

'General!' said Brennan with a salute.

'Morning, captain. Can I interest you in a mug?'

'Thank you, no.'

'I'll have one,' interjected Gwendolyn.

Xander chuckled. 'You can get it yourself,' he said with a flirtatious smile. Turning back to the Hawk, he stood and straightened. 'Report, captain.'

'Signal arrow sighted, sir. The Kirin returns.'

Xander nodded and his eyes betrayed the same hope that Gwen was feeling. He thought for a moment, deciding how to react to news of Rham Jas's return.

She poured herself a mug of sweet-smelling tea and glanced behind to see whether Lennifer had followed her. The serving-girl had gone straight to the bedchamber and was busy arranging Gwen's leather armour.

Xander rose from his seat. 'Assemble a guard of men, captain. Let's go and meet Rham Jas Rami.'

'Aye, general,' replied Brennan, striding from the tent and leaving Gwen alone with her husband.

'What do you think?' she asked, warming herself with the mug in her hands.

'I think he's still alive,' replied Xander. 'That's a good start.'

'But does it mean we can go home?'

He crossed the tent and lunged in for a kiss, his face split into a tender smile. 'I have no idea.'

'He's killed her,' she responded. 'How else would he have left the city alive?'

'He could have run away.' Xander was not given to needless optimism.

'Did he strike you as the kind of man who would run away?' she countered.

'No, but I'd still rather wait until we know either way.'

She chuckled, stroking his face playfully. 'Get your armour on.'

He kissed her again, slower this time. 'Yes, my lady.'

* * *

Captain Brennan had assembled fifty Hawks to accompany them and, mounted on armoured horses, they rode slowly southwards. Daganay, the Blue cleric, had risen only reluctantly but insisted on accompanying them to meet Rham Jas Rami. The rest of the army were striking their tents and preparing to march.

Brennan had sent five men on ahead to check that no surprises awaited them and the patrol was now returning.

'What have we here?' mused Daganay, peering at the hastily approaching Hawks.

Xander held up his hand and the men accompanying them slowed their pace, forming up behind the general. They were an hour or so from the city and their camp was no longer visible behind them.

'General!' shouted one of the returning patrol. 'The Kirin is being pursued by Karesians.'

The company of Hawks drew their short swords in unison and retrieved their shields from their saddles. Xander rose in his stirrups to look further south. After a moment of searching across the plains, he smiled thinly and drew Peacekeeper from its scabbard. The bastard sword made a metallic sound as it was drawn and he held it effortlessly in one hand.

Daganay let loose a throaty chuckle. 'Are we killing Karesians, my lord?' he asked, drumming his fingers on the hilt of his mace.

'Unless they surrender,' he replied.

Brennan motioned for the returning patrol to rein in their horses. 'How many warriors pursue the Kirin?'

'Around twenty riders.' The soldier was out of breath.

Xander nudged his horse and advanced. Gwen followed, drawing one of her heavy leaf-blades, and the fifty Hawks fanned out behind them. Daganay stayed next to the general, wearing only his thick blue robe. He was skilled with his mace, but rarely wore armour.

Gwen caught her husband's eye and nodded, blowing a subtle kiss. It was a ritual they had been through many times – on every occasion they'd been in battle together. They had agreed that he would never hold her back or tell her what to do, and the trust between them meant she had saved his life as often as he had saved hers. Gwen knew he worried about her and would have asked her to stay behind if he could.

The sound of hooves silenced him but Xander mouthed the words, 'Stay alive,' with an intense smile.

They rode quickly now, covering ground at speed, until a single horse appeared before them. The rider was kicking the flanks of his mount vigorously and had a motionless body slung across his saddle. The Kirin held his bloodied katana in one hand and the reins in the other. His Ro companion was unconscious.

'I could do with some help,' he wailed as they appeared over an incline.

Behind him, riding in a disorganized mass, were several wind claws and a significant force of Hounds. They numbered two dozen and were accompanied by several riderless horses, indicating that Rham Jas was a dangerous man to follow. They wielded scimitars and kukris, though the wind claws had large, wavy knives and black armour.

Xander motioned to Brennan. 'Ask them to surrender, captain.'

He raised his chin. 'We are the Hawks of Ro, stand down or die!' he bellowed.

The Karesians were outnumbered, but the fanatical glare in their eyes made it doubtful that they would surrender. They shifted their focus from the fleeing Kirin to the mounted Hawks and the wind claws barked orders.

'Now we're killing Karesians,' shouted Xander, when it became clear that they were not going to stand down.

Rham Jas grinned broadly and pulled back on his reins. Kale Glenwood, the man of Leith, was hanging limply over the forward pommel of the Kirin's horse and the extra weight was hampering their escape. The assassin rode straight past the Hawks, without turning to help.

Gwen held her weapon with the blade pointing downwards and clamped her thighs to her horse, maintaining balance as they plunged forward. The ground was covered quickly as the two groups neared each other. She hunkered down on her saddle, lining up the nearest Hound. Xander was in front and standing tall in his stirrups, holding Peacekeeper steady.

The first blow was struck slowly. A wind claw, his reins held in his teeth and wielding two long knives, met the Red Prince of Haran. Xander drove his bastard sword through the man's chest with precision and strength, sending the spluttering and bloodied Karesian to the grass.

Then the forces clashed. Gwen ducked under a scimitar and cut at the man's neck, taking a chunk of flesh as he rode past her.

Horses in distress and metal striking metal made the melee a confusing one. Xander removed a man's head. Daganay and Brennan flanked the general and killed two more with effortless skill. The Hounds were outmatched and most of them died as the line of Hawks rode them down. Heads were severed and horses maimed, many of the beasts bolting across the plain. Bodies were flung to the ground and blood covered the grass, staining the green with vibrant red. A few Karesians survived the initial clash and were now duelling with Hawks. Two men of Ro had fallen already, but no more of them met their deaths as their heavy short swords ran skilfully through the remaining Hounds.

'Yeah!' offered Rham Jas, mockingly raising his arms in celebration.

'Keep your mouth shut, Kirin,' grunted Daganay, finishing off a Karesian with a solid strike of his mace.

'Get this finished,' ordered Brennan, dismounting and putting a bloodied wind claw out of his misery.

The wailing of men in pain was quickly silenced as the wounded Karesians were swiftly despatched. Apart from a few cuts and bruises among the Hawks, and two men who had been run through, the encounter had ended swiftly and decisively.

'You!' Xander pointed Peacekeeper at the Kirin. 'Report?'

Rham Jas looked confused for a second. 'I'm not a soldier, you can talk to me properly.'

This comment caused several of the Hawks to glare at him, but the general merely laughed. 'Did you kill her?' he pressed, silencing a rebuke from Brennan with a wave of his hand.

The assassin nudged his horse round and, with a vacant grin, approached the company of Hawks.

'Yup,' he replied casually. 'Dead as a dog with no head.'

A ripple of smiles passed over the faces of the men of Ro, and Gwen found herself eager to hear how Rham Jas had accomplished such a thing. The Kirin dismounted and carefully removed his torpid companion, laying him on the grass. His head was bloodied, with a torn length of cloth round his forehead.

'What happened to the forger?' she asked, sheathing her leaf-blade.

'Too much sea air, I think,' he replied. 'And he got hit on the head by a metal torch-holder. He'll live.'

'Tell us of the witch?' demanded Daganay, accompanying Xander and Gwen to meet the Kirin.

'She was in some catacombs under Ranolph's Hold – chanting and shit with a load of followers. I shoved my sword through her chest. She's dead.'

'Followers?' queried Gwen. 'Who?'

He shrugged. 'Some Karesian women and a whole lot of Ro nobles.'

Gwen and Xander locked eyes. This was troubling news. They had known that the Seven Sisters could sway people's actions, but not that they could convert so many in so little time.

'She's built herself a cult,' guffawed Daganay, emphasizing his disgust with a chesty laugh.

'This is serious, Dag,' snapped Xander. 'I don't want to have to kill the nobles of my duchy.'

'You won't need to,' interjected the Kirin. 'I don't know how the enchanting works exactly, but the ones I didn't kill looked scared and ill after a few seconds of frenzied violence.'

The Red Prince glared at him, and the assassin turned away. Xander nudged his horse close to the Kirin. 'You killed nobles of Haran? I assume you had no choice?'

'Well, I gave them a choice. A few took it and a few just curled up on the floor. Don't worry, your dukeness, you still have plenty of up-their-own-arse nobles to suck your royal cock.'

Daganay put his hand to his mace and looked ready to strike the Kirin, but Xander raised his hand again. 'I owe you thanks,' he said through a pained smile. 'And I will remember that. Though I ask you to show more respect. This may just be another kill for you, but for us it's our home and our people.'

The assassin's face contorted into the caricature of a guilty child and he averted his eyes. 'Sorry,' he mumbled, clearly not meaning it. 'Have I been bad?'

'Look at me, Rham Jas Rami,' said Xander.

The Kirin raised his head. His skin was swarthy and his hair lank, making him appear grubby and low-born. The katana at his side and the Dokkalfar war-bow across his back were both of fine materials and of considerably more value than his clothing.

When Xander regained eye contact with the Kirin, he sheathed Peacekeeper. 'I hope you are telling me the truth. If not, I won't forgive the insult, or the lies.'

'She's definitely dead,' he replied. 'Whether either of us like it, we're on the same side. You, me, her, him, them . . . Brom, who's my friend, remember?'

The general narrowed his eyes and a slight smile appeared on his lips. Gwen could read her husband well and she knew he believed the assassin's words.

'Very well,' he replied. 'But excuse me if I don't let you leave just yet.'

'I have an important appointment in Ro Weir,' said Rham Jas, with a mischievous smile, showing no fear of Xander. 'If my appointment goes well, things in your country should improve rapidly.'

'Do you want a fucking knighthood?' spat Daganay. 'You're going to our camp until we have the city back.'

'Easy, Dag,' interrupted Xander.

'I don't trust him. The witch is probably still alive,' offered the Blue cleric.

Rham Jas's grin grew even more mischievous as he looked through his dirty hair at Daganay. 'I go where I like, fat man. She's dead . . . go minister to her body.'

An eruption of expletives came from Daganay's mouth. He hefted his mace and Xander wheeled his horse sharply to cut off the cleric's attack.

'Enough!' ordered the general. 'Rham Jas, do as we ask . . . if you're a truthful man, you'll be on your way tomorrow. Brennan, back to camp and rouse the men. March them here. Dag, you too. Move!'

'Yes, my lord,' he said solemnly, grasping the reins of his horse.

'Seriously? I have to go with this idiot?' asked the Kirin, blowing a kiss at Daganay.

'He's my friend. Be nice,' said Gwen.

'Can I bring my friend?' asked Rham Jas, pointing to Glenwood. 'He'll only grumble if I leave him here.'

Brennan and Dag pointed their horses northwards and waited for the Kirin to heft his companion back into the saddle. Rham Jas was reluctant, but Gwen suspected that his insufferable cockiness masked a keen mind.

'They were in the catacombs,' said the Kirin, more serious now. 'If you want to see if any of your nobles are alive, they'll be there.' He paused, looking at the grass. 'Something else, maybe. I heard a weird sound and . . .' He trailed off.

'Make sense, man,' prompted Xander.

'Do you know what a Dark Young is?' asked the assassin.

* * *

Five thousand men rode across the plains of Haran. With Alexander Tiris in the lead and Gwen riding next to him, they plunged south towards the city. Dozens of supply wagons and smithing equipment followed, guarded by their auxiliaries, and the Hawks of Ro moved with a rare purpose. Ro Haran was now visible and she felt a warmth enter her body at the thought of a hot bath and cosy bed.

The city looked small, with only the High Towers standing out against the grey sky and blue ocean. Steam and smoke rose from the dark stone and the castellated lump looked ominously quiet. No guards were visible and, though a few carts could be seen around the main gate, the city had no life.

'What's she done to it?' mused Xander as the army approached. 'No banners, no guards. They should have seen us coming and sounded a horn by now.'

'There'll still be Hounds there, my lord,' said Daganay.

The general nodded in agreement. 'Set cover round the main gate,' he ordered.

'Dag, Gwen, come with me. Brennan, let's go and see how welcome we are.'

Gwendolyn joined the detachment that broke off and two hundred Hawks rode slowly towards the main gate. The rest of the army crawled into line across the eastern plains, taking up position in organized ranks facing Ro Haran. The camp servants and supply carts moved behind the lines.

Xander kicked the flanks of his horse and reached the road, hooves clattering on stone. Looking up at the guard towers, Gwen could not see men on duty or any indication that the city was defended.

'Careful,' she muttered to her husband.

Xander scanned the walls, but didn't slow down as he rode straight for the main gate. 'Brennan, announce our return.'

A loud bugle was blown by one of the accompanying Hawks and Captain Brennan roared, 'General Alexander Tiris returns.'

'Onwards,' grunted Xander.

Their pace slowed as they formed into a column narrow enough to pass through the gates. Once inside, Gwen gasped and held a hand to her mouth and nostrils.

'Plague,' growled Daganay. 'What has the witch done?'

All around them lay festering people. Many were dead; others groaned in pain, with sores covering their skin and flies massing around their bodies. Rotting meat and vegetables were piled up in the street and the sewer trenches were stagnant and overflowing. A few commoners tried to stand, but most just looked at the returning army through dying eyes, filled with despair.

The Seven Sisters had much to answer for. Shilpa the Shadow of Lies had all but destroyed the common folk of Ro Haran. As they rode slowly through the fetid streets, no one spoke. Xander practically vibrated with anger, Gwen felt a tear of anguish fall from her eyes and Daganay wept openly.

'Too many to heal,' the cleric said through his tears. 'We need a White cleric.'

'We don't have one,' replied Xander.

Dag spluttered and wiped his eyes. 'Then many will die, my lord.'

They continued their grim ride through the streets and towards the High Towers of Haran. Buildings were in bad repair, streets hadn't been cleaned and no watchmen patrolled the city. Within sight of Ranolph's Hold was a barricade, solidly constructed from upturned carts and barrels.

Xander ordered a halt. 'Brennan, get word outside and tell them to minister to the sick and start clearing the streets.'

The captain hesitated, his eyes wide, seemingly overwhelmed at what had happened to his home. 'Aye, general. At once.' He wheeled his horse round and hastened back to the main gate.

Xander addressed the rest of his men in a voice full of conviction. 'Strength, brothers. We must continue on. Get this barricade out of the way.'

A handful of soldiers rode past their general, dismounting as they reached the upturned carts.

'You okay?' Gwen asked, moving close to her husband.

He smiled, though his eyes were red with emotion. 'No,' he replied. 'But I need to be.'

'General!' shouted a voice from behind.

They turned to see Sergeant Ashwyn, the blacksmith, riding fast towards them.

'Report,' replied Xander.

'Looks like some of the Karesians have fled, my lord. Three ships are hugging the coast, heading south. They're moving slowly, trying to stay hidden.'

The Red Prince turned back to the barricade. 'Get this shit out of the road, there'll be men left in the city . . . they need to die.'

He kicked his horse and rode forward at speed. Gwen and the others followed and those on the ground hastily tipped over two of the carts to create an opening.

'Ash, take men and secure the harbour. The rest of you, with me.'

The sergeant broke off with twenty men, while the remainder rode for Ranolph's Hold.

The streets here were cleaner, with no pestilence or bodies. It seemed that Shilpa was kinder to men and women of station, perhaps because she needed them to join her growing flock.

Gwen rode close to Daganay. 'Keep an eye on him, he's getting very, very angry.'

'Good,' replied the tearful Blue cleric.

'When he's angry, he tends to be stupid,' she countered. 'Just keep an eye on him.'

'Always, my lady,' he conceded, trying his best to smile. 'I just hope someone keeps an eye on me . . . to stop me being stupid.'

'That's my job, Dag,' she replied, returning his smile.

The company rode in tight formation behind the general, clattering along the cobbles towards Ranolph's Hold, the highest tower of Haran. A few nervous faces regarded them from windows, peering from behind floral curtains and over steel fences and well-tended lawns. These were the noble folk of Ro Haran, the courtiers and landowners who constantly sought Gwen's favour and her husband's notice. She had little time for them but after several years she had realized that they were an important element in the duchy. Now they all looked afraid, as their duke, his face a mask of rage, rode through the streets of his city. At least they weren't all dead. Some had been sensible enough not to join the new order.

They took a sharp right turn and entered the lower courtyard of Ranolph's Hold. The area, formerly a marketplace, was now empty, and the wide doors of the catacombs were flung open. If the Kirin could be believed, the grain silo beneath the Hold was where they'd find the dead enchantress . . . and a creature of some kind, perhaps related to the darkwood trees that the Dokkalfar feared. Gwen could see lights coming from within.

'Dismount!' ordered Xander, jumping to his feet and drawing Peacekeeper. 'You!' He pointed to a nearby unit. 'To the left, check the building.'

He directed two more units to other areas of the Hold and then gestured for the rest to follow him into the catacombs. 'Eyes open, lads. The Kirin was afraid of something down there.'

Gwen drew both her leaf-blades and ran to join her husband. Daganay, his face still wet with tears, also joined the general and twenty men strode into the torch-lit grain silo while the rest of the Hawks secured Ro Haran.

'If there is anyone in here,' bellowed Xander, 'show yourselves now!'

They walked over a central carpet, between thick pillars and torch placements. After a moment the daylight glow from the entrance was behind them and they walked in an ominous glow. On either side Gwen could see women, mostly Karesians, naked, with ugly scratch marks on their bodies. Some had killed themselves within the last few hours, though several were lying on the carpet and had died from katana wounds.

Before them the torches stopped and the last globe of light illuminated a chaotic pile of naked, twisted bodies. Their death blows had been swift, but each body was cut and marked with fresh bites and scratches. Gwen recognized most of them as noble folk of Haran, mangled together in an orgy of flesh and blood.

'So this is a chapel,' grunted Daganay. 'What kind of god demands this?'

'A dead god,' replied Xander. 'Keep moving.'

An attractive Karesian woman came into view. She lay face down, with her eyes staring off a raised platform. She had a tattoo of a flowering rose on her cheek. This was evidently the enchantress, and Gwen allowed herself a smile because the Kirin had not been making an idle boast.

A cracking noise sounded from before them and Xander ordered them to halt. In the shadows, away from the main carpet, she could see a large shape, slowly swaying in the darkness.

'What the fuck is that?' whispered Daganay, raising his mace.

'A Dark Young,' replied Gwen, a catch of fear in her voice. 'A darkwood tree.'

Xander turned to her. They had listened to the Kirin and believed that he feared the thing of which he spoke. But it was impossible to imagine that such a thing actually existed. The priest and the altar, Rham Jas had said, a beast, terrifying to look upon. The Dokkalfar had said less. Our doom was all that they would mutter.

Several men retrieved torches from sconces and stepped forward, carrying globes of light into the darkness. The others followed. A moment later, illuminated before them was a grotesque mockery of a tree, a huge, black maw surrounded with greenish needles and propelled forward on thick tentacles.

Howls of alarm came from the twenty Hawks, and even Xander took an involuntary step back. Gwen held her breath, frozen immobile by fear of the thing, and Daganay prayed loudly.

The tree darted forward, its tentacles reaching a man of Ro and stuffing him into its waiting maw. The Hawk appeared to dissolve and disappear into the noxious mouth, leaving nothing but a short sword that clattered to the stone floor.

Men fled, howling as they ran. Several more fell to the floor, dropping their blades and staring at the tree. Gwen was in the latter group and was rooted to the floor in the path of the beast. She hadn't dropped her leaf-blades, but she was helpless to strike or to flee as the maw reached for her.

A hand grabbed her shoulder and pulled her firmly out of the way behind a pillar. Xander held her tightly with one hand, keeping Peacekeeper at the ready with the other.

The beast consumed another man. It slobbered over its meal, dropping bile on to the floor and making a shrill, repetitive noise.

Its tentacles writhed in the air, striking men and wrapping around pillars.

'Cover!' roared the general, a crack of fear in his deep voice.

Daganay, still praying, was not frozen, but he could do nothing but shove men out of the way and try not to look at the thing. He held his mace ready but he was not about to attack. The remaining men followed Xander's orders and, assisted by the Blue cleric, they dragged themselves out of the way and behind pillars. One man was swept up by a tentacle and torn in half.

Seven warriors remained, all taking cover out of reach of the beast's tentacles. Xander had pulled Gwen to the floor and they crouched behind a stone pillar, clutching their blades tightly. They locked eyes and the general nodded to the right, indicating they should move round the pillar as the tree advanced, staying out of its field of view. She couldn't respond with anything more than a feeble nod, but moved with him when two huge tentacles reached round their pillar.

Xander stood up and grabbed a flaming torch. 'Stay here,' he grunted to Gwen.

With willpower showing on his face, the Red Prince of Haran attacked the beast from behind. He swung the torch first, wedging it between the bark-like plates on the creature's trunk and eliciting a deafening cry of anguish from the tree. Then he swung Peacekeeper. Roaring with exertion, Xander hacked at a tentacle and cut a chunk of blackened flesh from the thing. It couldn't turn round quickly and it seemed less frightening when its maw could not be seen.

'To arms!' ordered Xander. 'Torches, blades . . . burn it, cut it, bring it down.'

Daganay responded with a desperate battle cry and circled round the beast, swinging his mace in controlled circles. Others grabbed torches and flung them at the thing, causing it to howl in pain as the fire caught on its back.

Gwen's knuckles had turned white as she gripped her leaf-blades, but she held her breath and forced her legs to move, emerging next to her husband and between the undulating tentacles.

Joined by Daganay, the three of them struck repeatedly at the creature's rear, severing tentacles and causing the thing to lose its power of locomotion. It wailed, pulsated and reached into the air, but the fire had spread quickly and with missing limbs it had no chance of escape.

'Back . . . stand clear,' shouted Xander, as the tree turned into a massive ball of fire.

Gwen stumbled back on to the carpet and stood with the others as the fire rose high, engulfing the thing and causing them to back further off. Everyone who remained was wild-eyed and panting, but they looked more clear-headed now as they watched the beast burn to death.

'I think I'll trust Rham Jas in future,' muttered Xander to his wife.

'I didn't know,' she replied. 'The Dokkalfar fear them . . . but they never said exactly why.'

Daganay stepped forward and forced himself to look at the tree as it burned lower and lower, turning to ash and sickly green slime. 'If this is part of the Sisters' new religion, Tor Funweir is truly in danger,' said the cleric, his face a mask of fear.

'Let's leave,' said Gwen. 'I feel the need of daylight.'

'Agreed,' offered Xander.

* * *

They didn't talk about the darkwood tree. Two hours later, Gwen and Xander were standing on a balcony halfway up Ranolph's Hold, looking out over the city. The surviving Hawks from the catacombs had been released to get some rest, though each of them, Gwen included, would feel darker and more solemn after their encounter with the thing in the chapel. Daganay had returned to his church, muttering something about the need to pray, and Xander had busied himself ordering men around and assisting the pestilence-stricken population of his city.

No Karesians remained and the escaping ships were too far south to be caught. The razing of Ro Haran had been a vile, slow and clinical operation. Thousands would be dead by the time the toll was truly known. Gwen had no words to describe how she felt.

'I love you,' said Xander suddenly.

She frowned. 'Good . . . but why tell me now?'

'Because I don't know anything else at this moment . . . and knowing that I love you makes me feel better.'

She held his hand and rested her head on his armoured shoulder. They could see into the city, both the noble quarter and the old town where Hawks were clearing the streets and assisting the plague-ridden to the Blue church. Dag would be able to help some of them, but many would die before the week ended.

'Tell me what to do, Gwen . . . I don't know,' he said, with a tear rolling down his cheek.

'Look at me,' she snapped, causing him to turn and face her. 'You are duke of Haran, general of the Hawks . . . and my husband.' She touched his cheek tenderly. 'We sail to Canarn to get allies. We take back Ro Tiris, and then we take back Tor Funweir.'

CHAPTER EIGHT

RANDALL OF DARKWALD
IN THE CITY OF KESSIA

EVEN WHILE HE was still at sea Randall had decided that
Karesia was the hottest place in the world. He was also
reconciled to the fact that he was travelling south and it
would only get hotter. The wind was abrasive and the rain, when
it came, was sudden and like lancing shards of water. Combined
with the dust that constantly hugged the surface of the sea, the
last few days had been decidedly unpleasant.

They had joined a queue of slow-moving ships travelling from
Tor Funweir to Karesia and had been crawling along under the
boiling sun for days. Utha had remained below deck for the
majority of the journey. Other than occasionally shouting about
his imminent death from seasickness, he had been largely silent.
This had left Randall, who was ignored by the sailors, with ample
time to smile awkwardly at Ruth.

The Gorlan mother came to him at least once a day and
conveyed her need for physical contact through a complicated
array of smiles and glances. Randall had slowly become
more comfortable with sex and even engaged in post-coital
conversation without feeling the need to say thank you. Their
daily trysts had simply become another, more pleasant, part of his
routine.

'Young man,' bellowed Captain Makad from the hatch that
led below.

'It's Randall . . . as I've told you a few dozen times,' he replied, sauntering across the slowly rocking deck towards the Karesian sailor. 'Is he awake yet?'

'He's awake, but still not forming complete words. I thought that clerics were supposed to be tough.'

Makad had been trying to talk to Utha about their destination for several days now. Unfortunately, he'd refused to rise from his hammock to do anything other than visit the piss-pot or vomit.

'Okay, talk to me instead, captain,' Randall reluctantly conceded. 'What do I need to know about Kessia?'

'Come and have a drink, young man,' said Makad, disappearing through the hatch.

'It's Randall . . . not difficult to remember.'

He walked down the wooden stairs and under narrow beams towards the captain's cabin at the rear of the ship. Sailors lounged around, sipping strong Karesian liquor and munching on hard bread. They didn't glare at him any more. The squire's reluctance to back down in the face of intimidation seemed to have impressed them. More than once, he'd stared down a Karesian who had sought to bully him.

'Come in, boy,' said Makad, taking a seat behind his cluttered table and reaching for a bottle of dark liquid.

The squire rolled a little as he walked, though the movements of the ship were easier to negotiate than when he had first boarded. He sat opposite the captain.

'My name is Randall. Yours is Makad.'

'I know,' he replied with a toothy smile. 'I like teasing you, boy.'

A snort of amusement. 'What is this?' he asked, pointing to the glass of liquor Makad had placed before him.

'Skaven brandy. It keeps longer than wine.'

He sniffed the thick liquid and winced. 'Smells like Utha's breath.'

The Karesian pursed his lips and rubbed his ample belly. 'I still haven't figured you out,' he said, gulping back a generous measure of brandy. 'On one hand, you're barely twenty years old and nothing but a squire. On the other, you hang around with a cleric of death and don't put up with shit.'

'Comes from experience, captain.'

'Oh, really?' he replied, unimpressed. 'Well, that confidence may be tested when we reach Kessia tomorrow.'

'What do I need to know?'

Makad relaxed back into his chair and poured himself a second drink. Randall tried a small sip of his own and instantly coughed, feeling the liquid burn his throat.

'You get used to it,' joked the Karesian. 'You won't find any Darkwald red in Kessia.'

'Okay, so what will I find?'

'Most Ro who find their way across the Kirin Ridge end up as slaves. Karesians don't see you as equals.' Makad sneered. 'Pretty lad like you will have plenty of interest. Your master will likely just get himself killed.'

'How do we go about not being taken as slaves?' asked Randall, attempting to hide his concern.

Makad chewed on a fingernail and peered across the table. 'Tricky,' he replied unhelpfully. 'Most merchants who make the journey are careful not to leave the docks. You three intend to go on a little trip south . . . that is not safe. Ro don't travel the Long Mark.'

'That's a road?' pressed Randall.

'The only road.'

He narrowed his eyes. 'Why are we having this conversation?'

'Well, my boss could help you . . . I suppose I wanted to talk to the cleric to find out whether or not it was worth my while.'

Randall could not match his master when it came to threats or intimidation, but he believed that he had the edge on brains. 'What do you want in exchange for help?'

Makad grinned. 'The woman.'

If Randall had been drinking he would have spat out the liquid. As it was, he merely burst out laughing. 'You'd be better off asking for the albino. Ruth is . . . powerful,' he replied.

'She'd fetch a lot of money on the slave docks. I know a merchant prince who likes just her type.' He was confused by Randall's sudden outburst of laughter.

Randall nodded, suppressing his mirth. 'Trust me, no amount of money is worth the aggravation it would cause should you try to do her harm.'

There came a knock at the door – a single thump, accompanied by muffled Karesian voices.

'Come in!' bellowed the captain.

The door swung inwards and Ruth glided into the cabin, ignoring the comments the Karesians directed at her. She closed the door and glared at Makad. How could she have known what was being said? The Gorlan mother was largely a mystery to the young squire, but she had vaguely hinted that she knew things no one else could know.

'Captain Makad,' she said by way of a greeting. 'I wondered if I might join your discussion.' It was a demand rather than a question.

The Karesian spluttered in the manner of a man who has been caught red-handed.

'Of course,' he said hesitantly.

'This is how we will proceed,' began Ruth. 'You will introduce us to the mobster you work for. He will provide us with a writ of passage for the Long Mark and we will part as friends.' Her eyes conveyed a threat and she walked round the table to Makad as she spoke. 'Do you understand?'

He frowned, looking from Ruth to Randall and then back to Ruth. A young man and a slim woman would not normally be very frightening, but the Karesian was not a fool and he realized all was not as it seemed. However, he was not going to give up a lucrative business deal easily.

'What makes you think I give a shit what you want, sweetheart?'

'I'd be polite if I were you, captain,' said Randall. 'We had a deal. Probably best that you stick to it.'

'What is your mobster's name?' asked Ruth, perching on the edge of the table.

'Claryon Soong. Not someone you want to cross,' he replied, staring at Ruth. 'But he'd like you. If your friends want to go south, all you need to do is let him . . . buy you.'

She darted forward, flickering from her seat. No exaggerated movement or overt skill was in evidence as the Gorlan mother grabbed Makad's throat and held him in the air with one hand. His eyes bulged at her unnatural strength and he grabbed feebly at her arm, unable to catch his breath.

'Told you to be polite,' said Randall.

Ruth looked angry. It was not an emotion she often displayed, but the prospect of slavery has a strange effect on people – and Gorlan, it would seem.

Her hand was tightening round the man's throat and Randall could see dense black hairs sprouting on the back of her neck. She swayed, a throaty gurgle coming from her mouth, more like a spider's hiss than a woman's cry. He gasped and stopped smiling as he stood up and put his arm round her shoulder.

'Easy,' he said. 'There's no need for that.'

Despite their relationship, he was still terrified of the prospect of her changing back to her natural form.

She looked at her lover, the anger slowly dissipating. 'He would sell me as property,' she muttered, as if that explained everything.

'I know, and he's a scumbag as a result, but we need him for now,' offered the squire, pulling her towards him, oblivious of the fact that she still held Makad in mid-air.

Slowly, making sure the Karesian was in no doubt as to who was in charge, she lowered him to the ground. The sailor coughed and grabbed at his throat as she released him, rushing round the table to the opposite side of the cabin.

'Are you an enchantress?' he spluttered, his voice cracking with fear.

'Of a kind,' replied Ruth, stepping closer to Randall. 'All you need concern yourself with is introducing my two friends and me to Claryon Soong.'

Randall smiled. 'Assuming Utha doesn't die of seasickness.'

* * *

The Kessian dock was a huge, sprawling mass of floating platforms and sails. Hundreds of troop transports lay at the jetties and more were already sailing north. The Karesian army of Hounds was on its way to Ro Weir, and Randall felt sadness at the war that was going to engulf Tor Funweir. The young squire had never been particularly patriotic – growing up in the Darkwald, well away from Tiris – but he didn't like what the Seven Sisters were doing.

He hoped that Tyr Nanon, Dalian Thief Taker and the Kirin bastard who had killed Torian would have a plan, but he also feared that his own path would take him far from his home just as it was engaged in the struggle with the Hounds. Not that he would have been a good soldier – but, try as he might, Randall couldn't shake off the feeling that he was travelling in the wrong direction.

They had been in dock for an hour while Makad dealt with paperwork and Utha wandered around, showing how much he liked being on dry land. Ruth sat nearby, looking across the hazy vista of buildings and smoke that was the capital of Karesia. The three of them were all looking southwards and, Randall thought, probably seeing three different things. Utha was probably thinking about the halls beyond the world and his duty as the last old-blood. Randall was thinking about how to keep themselves alive and fed as they travelled through unfamiliar territory. He had no idea what occupied Ruth's mind, but he doubted it would be any of the usual things that concerned travellers on the road.

'Randall, get down here,' said Utha from the wooden dock.

The squire slung his travelling bag over his shoulder and left the ship, resting his hand on the sword of Great Claw.

He wandered over to Utha. 'Feeling better?'

'Don't be cheeky, lad,' replied the former cleric.

He was wearing a simple brown shirt and had his weapons – a longsword and a mace – strapped across his back. For a change, realizing that they were in a land where the Seven Sisters held sway, his distinctive pale face was covered by a hood.

'So, we're being introduced to a mobster?'

Randall nodded. 'Apparently it's the only way to avoid becoming slaves. We need to travel along something called the Long Mark. I think it's a road.'

'Slaves, huh?' said Utha, raising his eyebrows. 'That would be an interesting encounter. I don't think I'd be a very good slave.'

'Which is why we need to speak to the mobster. Makad works for him, so I'd guess he's a smuggler.'

Utha smiled at his squire. 'Becoming something of an expert, are we?'

Randall blushed a little. 'Just observant. You were dying in your cabin . . . I had to deal with the travel arrangements.'

Utha looked at the young man to ascertain whether or not he was being cheeky.

'Okay,' he said. 'Let's see what happens. From what Dalian Thief Taker said, most of the Seven Sisters are in Tor Funweir, not skulking around Karesia.' He gestured towards Ruth, sitting cross-legged on the dock. 'Did the sailors behave themselves around her?'

Randall blushed again, this time his cheeks turned a bright red and he spluttered, not actually using words.

'Okay, different question,' began Utha, a thin smile on his face. 'Did you behave yourself around her?'

The young squire considered his answer, not wanting either to be crude or to give his master any further reason to tease him. In the end, he simply said, 'I may have misbehaved.'

Utha erupted into laughter, causing several nearby sailors to look at him in confusion. He didn't stop laughing and had to wipe his eyes after a few moments of raucous amusement.

'Shut up!' said Randall, in the manner of small child.

'First time?' asked Utha, trying to control his laughter.

'None of your business,' muttered the squire.

The muscular albino put an arm round his squire's shoulders

and showed him an affectionate smile. 'And now you are a man, Randall of Darkwald.'

'And you're a . . . bastard,' barked the young man petulantly.

'That I am, my dear boy,' he replied. 'But, right at this moment, I feel a certain fatherly affection for you.'

Randall sneered at him. 'You'd be a terrible father.' He shoved his master's arm away. 'Get off me, we need to go and meet a criminal of some kind.'

'Mobster,' corrected Utha. 'They don't see themselves as criminals.'

Randall ignored him and walked quickly away from the ship to meet Captain Makad as the Karesian sailor returned along the wooden dock. He had several others with him, mostly grey-robed men with curved scimitars and raised hoods. The captain looked nervous and the men with him had stern expressions on their dark faces.

'Randall, I'm coming with you,' said Utha, no longer laughing. The old-blood had seen the approaching men and his mood changed quickly. Ruth also stood and glided over to join her two companions.

They walked in silence along the sturdy wooden planks and towards the distant stone walls of Kessia. Makad and his companions were coming from the other direction and the two groups met between slowly rolling ships at dock.

'Captain,' said Utha, coming to a stop in front of the ten armed men.

'You are well, my friend?' asked Makad.

'I'm glad everyone's concerned for my well-being,' he replied, showing no fear of the grey-robed Karesian men. 'Shall we get on with this?'

One of the men threw back his hood and shoved Makad out of the way. He smiled – a forced grimace with no humour or warmth to it – and stood facing Utha.

'My name is Walan, I am servant to my master, Claryon Soong.' His eyes moved to Ruth and a sneer appeared. 'Your woman will be ample price for a writ of passage.' His voice was deep and his hands, rubbing together in front of his chest, had tattooed fingers and brown nails.

Ruth didn't react, perhaps knowing that Utha would never accept such a thing. She did, however, step behind Randall's shoulder, which made him feel protective.

Strangely, it was Captain Makad who spoke in defence of the Gorlan mother. 'Don't be hasty.' His hands were raised in a placating gesture. 'The woman is . . . not to be trifled with.'

Walan wasn't concerned by this and continued to sneer. 'I know my master's tastes and the woman would do nicely, my lord Ro. If you turn us down, we will give you to the worst kind of Kirin slaver.'

Utha chuckled. 'We aren't asking, we are demanding. Take us to Claryon Soong or I will turn you inside out.'

Randall rolled his eyes.

'That won't be necessary,' spoke another Karesian voice from behind Captain Makad.

'This man does not deserve your intervention,' snapped Walan, turning his head to glance at the unseen speaker. 'They are of no worth to Claryon.'

Utha chuckled and stepped forward. 'And you're of no worth to me. I'm sure someone else can take us to your mobster.'

Walan flushed with anger and moved to draw his scimitar. The former cleric didn't hesitate and punched the Karesian in the throat, making the man cough violently and grab at his neck, before stumbling backwards on to the dock.

'Anyone else?' snarled Utha, kicking Walan in the side and making him curl into a foetal position.

With Walan still coughing and the other warriors drawing weapons, a single figure emerged from behind them. He was dressed like the others, but had no sword at his side. Instead, slung across his back was a long spear, tipped with a serrated edge.

'There are ten armed men before you,' said the stranger, keeping his face hidden under his hood. 'This does not concern you?' He raised a hand that stopped the others from attacking.

'Men with swords don't scare me,' replied Utha, not even deigning to draw his own weapons.

Walan grunted, wheezing loudly and rubbing his throat. 'You will regret your arrogance, my pale friend.' His voice was gravelly.

'Enough, Walan,' said the spearman. 'This man of Ro is expected.' He raised his head, showing the face of a weathered Karesian in his mid-fifties. He wore a black tattoo of a scimitar across his neck and his smile appeared genuine.

'And you are?' asked Utha.

'I will take you to Claryon Soong,' he replied, ignoring the question.

* * *

Whatever authority the spearman had, it was sufficient to prevent Walan and his men from attacking them.

As they left the dock and made their way through one of several narrow gates and into Kessia, Randall was taken aback to find the people of Karesia overt in their dislike of foreigners, though that did not seem to apply to the huge population of Kirin that he could see. He had never seen so many and he felt exposed and vulnerable under the numerous hostile pairs of eyes.

'We may be the only Ro in Kessia, my dear boy,' said Utha, with a reassuring smile. 'Doesn't that make you feel special?'

'Special? No,' replied Randall. 'The Seven Sisters are in charge here, master.'

Once inside the city, they were treated to an impressive vista of stone buildings and high minarets. Kessia was huge and stretched away from them in clearly marked circles, displaying the status of those who lived there, from low-rent wooden signs to opulent marble storefronts. The city was dirty and crowded, but had a bustle that Randall had never seen before, a colourful vibrancy that made the young man think legality must be a rather fluid concept in Karesia.

'They call it the greatest city of men,' said the spearman, gesturing across the endless horizon of stone.

'They say the same thing about Ro Tiris,' countered Utha.

'And I'm sure the Ranen say the same about their own cities,' he replied. 'But Kessia is certainly the biggest. Though it has experienced something of a religious conversion of late.'

The spearman led them past the outer circle and beyond the worst of the filth into a cleaner street connecting directly to the docks. The street had numerous small warehouses and servants were unloading crates from newly arrived ships. Randall was startled to see the slaves who formed a large part of the workforce. Men and women in chains, wearing tatty rags and with dirty faces, were going about their monotonous work with passive compliance.

'Slaves,' said Utha, with a disapproving scowl.

'A way of life, I am afraid,' offered Ruth. 'The Karesians have different values from the Ro.'

'An ex-cleric I may be, but I still hate slavery.' He had spent his life following the One God, a master who detested the Karesian practice of human bondage.

The spearman stopped in front of a busy warehouse where men and slaves hauled heavy crates. Several armed warriors stood nearby and Randall casually rested his hand on his own sword, feeling better at the feel of the wooden grip. As they were led inside, he was surprised to see that no one questioned the spearman, as if he held some important office that he had not yet revealed.

Walan exchanged whispered words with several guards, but didn't question the man who led them. Within moments they were walking up a wide staircase towards pillared corridors and ornately decorated doors. The facade of the warehouse gave way to white marble and there were no slaves on the upper level, but scantily clad young men and women instead.

'Avert your eyes, my dear boy,' joked Utha as they were led into a sweet-smelling bath-chamber.

Randall was used to the rough stone of Ro bathhouses and found the polished floor and crystal-clear water strange. Several older men lounged around naked on smooth benches while slaves poured water and scrubbed their skin with bricks of yellow soap.

The spearman dismissed Walan with a shake of his head, motioning for the other warriors to leave, too. Walan glared at Utha and bit his fist in a threatening display before he marched off. The spearman then drew his long spear and struck the marble floor of the bath-chamber, causing a dull thud to echo away from them.

'We may enter,' he said to Utha, gesturing forwards.

'Are we about to see a naked mobster?' asked the old-blood.

'Only if he likes you,' replied the spearman.

They stepped on to the damp floor and the three of them were led past rich-looking and gaudily dressed men and women, some naked and being cleaned, others talking rapidly about business matters or their status in Kessian society. Most spared a glance at the three strangers, but none was concerned enough to stand up or remark on the Ro visitors. Utha had his face hidden, Randall was a young man and Ruth was a woman – hopefully they would not be remembered.

In an adjoining room, larger and filled with steam, was a bulky Karesian man. He was seated, but clearly tall, and his naked shoulders and chest were heavily tattooed with dark green designs. There were no guards in the room and the man sat alone, with his head bowed and a black towel wrapped round his waist. The steam was coming from a small stone slate in the corner upon which he poured scented water. Randall felt light-headed as the odour entered his nostrils.

The spearman struck the floor again. 'Claryon, a guest,' he said, showing his familiarity with the mobster.

'I count three,' replied Claryon Soong, looking up at them. His face was also tattooed and his neck was thick and muscular. Randall felt intimidated by the man.

'We need a writ of passage for the Long Mark,' said Utha, showing no fear of the man.

'Ro don't travel the Long Mark,' replied Claryon.

'That's why we need a writ of passage.'

He chuckled, his tattooed face wrinkling up. 'You're the Ghost. Heard of you . . . been offered money to kill you.'

'By whom?' asked Utha casually, displaying a confidence his squire did not share.

'Wind claws,' he replied. 'The new god of the Seven Sisters wants your head.' He leant back, showing a huge chest tattooed with faded green spires. 'But they're all in your lands currently, so I think I'll remain faithful to Jaa for the time being.'

'Good to hear. Now, that writ of passage?' asked the old-blood.

The spearman stepped past them and took a glass of red wine from a low table.

'He's insistent, isn't he?' Claryon asked the unnamed warrior.

'I think eager is the word,' replied the spearman. 'I suppose you don't stay alive in his situation without being a bit of a hard case.'

Something else was afoot here. These men knew who Utha was. Although he doubted they meant the old-blood any harm, Randall wasn't sure of their motives.

'Well, if the enchantresses don't know you're in Karesia, I'd say you're fairly well hidden,' said Claryon. 'Only a fool would come here.'

'Which one of you is going to speak plainly?' asked the former cleric coolly. 'I can make a lot of mess in here before your guards arrive.' The threat was delivered casually, with a menacing smile.

The spearman glared and the mobster stood up. Randall was more intimidated by Claryon Soong now that he was standing. The man was close to seven foot tall and hugely built, with tattoos over most of his visible flesh.

'You wish me to speak plainly, Utha of Arnon, last old-blood of the Giants?' asked the spearman. 'I have a simple one for you.'

Utha's face turned to a mask of irritation at the Karesian's manner. 'Speak!'

'I am Voon of Rikara, high vizier of Karesia and exemplar of Jaa,' said the spearman. 'And I need your help as much as you need ours.'

Out of the three of them only Ruth reacted to this news. The Gorlan mother knew what an exemplar was, even if Randall and his master did not. Her face showed surprise and confusion as Voon revealed his identity.

* * *

An hour later and they were in less obscure surroundings, seated round a small fountain with drinks being poured by slaves and Claryon Soong fully dressed. The fountain sat in the middle of a wide courtyard at the base of the mobster's domicile and Voon had successfully conveyed to them that no harm was intended to any of them.

'Are tattoos a big thing for your people?' asked Randall, unable to take his eyes from the huge mobster's green-inked neck.

'Don't be rude, my boy,' said Utha, sipping from a goblet of red wine.

'It's fine,' replied Claryon. 'I don't mind indulging youth. My marks are from my time among the Hounds. With no identifying marks on our armour, those of us who served long terms chose to cut our bodies instead. Each tattoo signifies a battle or a mission.'

'I didn't know anyone left the Hounds,' said Utha, more relaxed now he had alcohol in his stomach.

'It's rare.' Claryon grinned, as if there was a story behind his survival among the imprisoned army of Karesia. 'My life sentence was . . . shortened.'

Voon was not seated. He stood next to the mobster, throwing small stones into the fountain. He had not removed his spear and was not drinking the wine on offer. 'Claryon is a faithful servant of Jaa,' he said. 'Such men are needed at this moment.'

'I heard that the Dead God was undergoing something of a renaissance in these parts,' offered Utha.

'The Fire Giant is still master of Karesia,' snapped Voon, displaying annoyance for the first time. 'The Seven Sisters' treachery will not go unpunished. They have torn down the cloisters of Jaa, made his worship illegal, turned the wind claws into their servants and planted the dark altars of a tentacled god in the fire lands.' He bowed his head and took a deep breath. 'Apologies, but I have not been able to hear the voice of my god for almost a year – since the Sisters killed the last Fire Giant old-blood.'

'The last . . .' Utha began.

'You are now the last. There was one in Ranen, recently slain, and another lost in the Wastes of Jekka.' Voon was speaking of strange things which made Randall's head hurt, though both Ruth and Utha were listening intently. 'You are the last. The only method by which I can talk to Jaa.'

'And how am I supposed to do that?' asked Utha. 'I'm bound for the south. There's a staircase, a labyrinth and a guardian. That is all I know and it's a mystery how I know that.'

'Then I will accompany you,' said Voon, 'and assist you if I can. We want the same things, brother Utha.'

The former cleric and last old-blood stood up from his chair. He breathed in deeply several times and took a large gulp of wine. Thus calmed, he spoke. 'What do I want?' mused Utha. 'I want . . . to live. I want to know who I am. I want Tor Funweir to remain. I understand what I am, but I fear that I need guidance.' He looked at Ruth, sharing a thin smile with the Gorlan mother. 'But I have never spoken to a god other than my own.'

'That was before you knew what you are,' said Voon. 'I am the Fire Giant's general in the Long War and I ask for an alliance.'

'And I'll give you a writ of passage,' interjected Claryon, with a smirk, taking a deep swig of wine. 'Sorry, just trying to keep the conversation light.'

'You sound like my squire,' said Utha, trying not to smile at the interruption. 'He often says stupid and unnecessary things, too.'

Randall frowned with indignation. 'I'm the rational one,' he said to the two Karesians. 'That often gets confused with stupid and unnecessary.'

'Interruptions aside,' began Voon, 'we have a long way to travel and many enemies who will seek to impede us.'

'Other than the Seven Sisters?' asked Utha.

'Their allies control Karesia. The wind claws and the viziers are slowly being turned to the worship of the Dead God,' offered

Voon. 'The faithful of Jaa are becoming fewer by the day.'

'Voon is hidden, but I am watched,' said Claryon. 'Paranoia is a way of life in Kessia and my faith is not going to stay hidden for long.'

'We should listen to the exemplar,' said Ruth, nodding with respect towards Voon.

'Hmm,' interjected Randall, raising his hand. 'I don't really know what an exemplar is.' They all looked at him. 'Might be important . . . at some point.'

'I am the Fire Giant's general in the Long War,' replied Voon. 'Each Giant has one. Though we are ineffective without your kind, Utha the Ghost.'

The old-blood snorted with amusement, gulping down his wine and pouring some more. 'I really wish I could, but I have no idea how I can help you. If it's a power, a spell or a trick, it's not one that I've learned.'

Voon was expressionless. 'Then I will teach you. You are a channel to the halls beyond . . . my last opportunity to talk to Jaa.'

The sound of running feet intruded and Randall looked across the fountain, over flagstones, towards the entrance. The inner courtyard where they sat was at the back of Claryon's warehouse, obscured by interior walls and separate from the main building. He could see a slave, easily identified by his simple white loincloth and neck shackle, running into the courtyard from one of several arched doorways. The man was agitated and heading straight for the mobster.

'Master Soong,' he said, bowing his head and spreading his arms wide. 'There are men in the warehouse.'

'What men?' asked Claryon coolly.

'I believe they are wind claws, master. They wish an audience.'

Voon shared a look with the mobster. Both men were now concerned and Randall saw Claryon tense up slightly and crack his tattooed neck.

'How many?' he muttered.

'Walan says five, master. With guardsmen, maybe fifteen in all.'

'I assume there is a back way to this place?' asked Utha.

More noise, this time raised angry voices. Claryon, standing up from his seat, glared at the entrance.

'There is,' he replied. 'Perhaps you should use it. Voon, show them the way.'

A gurgle of pain sounded from another archway and a figure was thrown into the courtyard. A bloodied body, his throat cut, slid across the flagstones. They all stood up and Randall reached for his sword. Sounds were now coming from all around and he guessed that there were more men than simply a few in the warehouse.

'Does that make us surrounded?' asked Utha, lowering his eyes at the twitching corpse.

Claryon strode round the fountain and retrieved a two-handed scimitar from the wall. Voon unslung his long spear and the two Karesians exchanged another look. It seemed to Randall that they had a certain rapport and could convey significant meanings with simple looks and gestures. On this occasion, he saw them frown at each other and glance with concern at Utha.

'Yes, I think we are surrounded,' replied Claryon. 'They must have been closer than I thought.'

'Is there a fight here or should we run?' asked the albino.

'You should stay back,' offered Ruth. 'You are too valuable to die in a petty fight in Kessia.'

'I concur,' agreed Voon.

Utha chuckled. 'I get the impression you'll need my help.'

As if in answer to his query, men began to appear at all four of the archways leading into the courtyard. Several of them wielded wavy-bladed knives, reminiscent of the weapons Dalian Thief Taker carried, and Randall knew they must be wind claws. Most were simple Karesian guardsmen, however – but simple or not, there were twenty or so of them.

Claryon's slaves scattered, leaving their master and the others to come together in a defensive circle next to the fountain. Ruth was not armed, but the others held their weapons low and ready.

'Too late to run?' asked Utha, with a smile.

Voon looked unimpressed at his attempt at humour, but Claryon laughed, swinging his broad-bladed scimitar from side to side. The mobster was a huge man and showed no sign of fear.

'You will all come with us,' announced a wind claw. 'We will kill any that resist.'

'Wrong man to threaten,' boomed Claryon, advancing towards one of the doorways and the five men who had entered through it.

When it became clear that none of them was going to surrender, the guardsmen attacked. Randall was startled at how quickly things escalated and he found himself involuntarily on the back foot while Utha, quicker to react, rushed past him.

He paused as Voon, Claryon and Utha attacked the intruders with ferocity. The mobster drew first blood, slicing a man across the chest with a mighty swing of his sword and throwing the body backwards. Voon was more guarded and whirled his spear with great speed and skill, darting from side to side with nimble steps.

Utha, true to form, seemed to come alive now that he had an enemy to fight, and Randall's master had run a man through and kicked another in the groin before the squire had even thought about moving.

Ruth simply stood and watched Utha attacking five men. The Gorlan mother showed an interest in the albino's manner, pouting as he roared insults and laughed. Then she glanced at Randall, standing next to her, sword in hand. 'I think you should help him,' she said calmly.

The young squire nodded and took a deep breath before joining his master in combat. The wind claws were the more dangerous opponents and, once several of the guardsmen had been slain, the kris-wielding Karesians became more defensive. Randall advanced on one of them, meeting an incoming thrust with his sword and stepping back to parry the off-hand strike. To his left, Utha fought two guardsmen, keeping them at bay with kicks and punches while his longsword parried their scimitars.

The wind claw was faster than Randall and he wasn't used to fighting a man with two long knives. He tried to keep his forward momentum, but the Karesian was quicker than him and a backhand attack caught the squire's neck, opening up a glancing wound and causing him to retreat several steps.

He saw a headless body fly into the fountain behind him as Claryon chopped his way through the guardsmen, and to his right Voon had skewered a man through the mouth. The young man grabbed at his neck and felt blood seep over his hand, though the wound was not deep. He held his blade up as the wind claw nimbly covered the ground between them, crouching down and lunging at Randall's chest. He couldn't bring the sword of Great Claw down quickly enough to parry and the attack would have killed him had Ruth not intervened. She reached out and grabbed the man's wrist. With effortless strength she pulled him away from the squire and flung him across the courtyard.

'Thanks,' he said breathlessly.

'Welcome,' she replied, returning her gaze to Utha as if nothing had happened.

Randall glanced behind him and saw Claryon duelling a wind claw. The mobster was driving him back as he negotiated the small pile of bodies spread across the flagstones. Voon was less violent, but no less impressive, as he somersaulted across the fountain and barrelled into two of the remaining guardsmen. The exemplar of Jaa was too quick to be pinned down and Randall thought none of the three warriors really needed his help. With a slight sigh, he grabbed a goblet of wine from the table behind him and took a large gulp.

'Very impressive,' remarked Ruth. 'Utha the Shadow is strong.'

The young man took another gulp and nodded, watching his master decapitate a man and throw another head first into the wall, before turning round for someone else to fight. Randall looked round and saw Claryon kill the last of the men in front of him. Voon was catching his breath off to one side and finishing off some wounded men with swift downward strikes of his spear.

Within a few minutes all the intruders had been killed and Randall stared wide-eyed in astonishment at the spectacle he'd witnessed.

The three warriors eventually realized there was no one left to fight and strolled back to the central fountain. All were out of breath, though Claryon and Utha both seemed revitalized by the encounter.

'I don't like being threatened,' grunted Claryon.

'Evidently,' replied Utha, wiping his sword with the cloak of a wind claw. He looked at his squire, noting the shallow wound in his neck. 'You're still over-extending your sword arm, my dear boy.'

'One still lives,' said Ruth, pointing to a motionless wind claw.

Claryon placed his scimitar on the table and hefted the unconscious man back to the middle of the courtyard. The wind claw was bleeding from a head wound and his leg was deeply cut, but he was still alive.

'We don't have long,' said Voon. 'More will be here. We need to leave the city.'

'After I talk to the traitor here,' replied Claryon, dumping the man head first into the fountain. 'Right, boy, wake the fuck up.' He grabbed him roughly around the neck and held his head under the bubbling water. After a moment the wind claw began to flap his arms, grabbing at the mobster's hand and trying to free himself. Claryon pulled him up and shook him. 'Good morning,' he said.

The man was pale and his eyes bloodshot, but he focused on the huge man holding him. 'The Sisters will eat your heart.'

'They're all in Tor Funweir. All you've got are swords and we've got them as well,' replied Claryon. 'Tell me how many are watching and you won't have to taste your own eyeballs.'

Randall baulked at the comment. 'A little unnecessary,' he blurted out, and everyone except Ruth looked at him. 'I'm sure hitting him or something would have the same effect.'

Without taking his eyes from Randall, the mobster punched his captive in the side, making him breathe in sharply and struggle even more. Claryon then held his head back under the water.

'Any experience with torture?' he asked the squire.

'Er, nope. This would be the first time.'

'Keep your mouth shut, then,' said Claryon.

'Watch it, mobster,' interjected Utha. 'That's my squire you're talking to.' He pointed to the wind claw. 'And that man is about to drown.'

The mobster allowed his victim to breathe, but he continued to glare at the two men of Ro. Randall didn't consider himself particularly squeamish, but the thought of Claryon making the man eat his own eyes was too much for the young squire to bear and he felt slightly nauseous. He found it strange that the sight of blood and mangled bodies didn't bother him any more, and yet the prospect of torture was abhorrent.

'Who's watching?' repeated the mobster.

The wind claw smiled, spitting out bloody water on to the flagstones. 'Sasha the Illusionist watches. She will find the Ro scum.' He spat again, this time in the direction of Utha.

Voon reacted quickly to the news that one of the Seven Sisters was returning, swearing under his breath and looking at the various exits from the room. 'We should leave. Now! We need to get some distance on the enchantress.'

'Thrakka?' asked Claryon.

Voon nodded. 'Shadaran Bakara owes me a favour.'

'Is that another mobster?' said Utha.

'No, he's a lesser vizier. The old fool is too stupid to do what he's told by the wind claws. If anyone is still a follower of Jaa, it's him.' He darted forward, drawing his spear and thrusting its point through the soaking wind claw's neck, killing him instantly. 'I believe I said we leave now!'

* * *

Claryon Soong was a stubborn man. Years as a Hound had given him a violent resolve, a dark determination never again to be beholden to another man. He had risen through the webs and deceits of Kessia, killing men by the hundreds, as he cemented his place as one who would never kneel, never beg, never have a master.

He looked up from the table against which he was restrained. 'I can survive torture,' he snarled, spitting blood at the black-armoured man of Ro who stood over him.

'I don't care,' replied the knight. 'I like seeing powerful men all bloodied and broken.'

A light and airy chuckle filled the room as Sasha the Illusionist returned. She had left Claryon in the company of Sir Pevain while she arranged to travel south. The enchantress was more determined to find Utha the Ghost than Claryon had realized. The mobster had thought he'd have at least a day to resolve his affairs before they caught him. As it turned out, he'd had barely six hours.

'My sweet, Master Soong,' said the enchantress. 'We have severed your head from your body. You are already dead and I know everything I need to know. The torture is over, you have no cause to resist further.'

Claryon looked around him and remembered. First they'd cut off his hands, throwing them into a wooden basket. Then his arms, feet and legs. His mind had been lulled into a blissful euphoria by Sasha's enchantment. Even when Pevain sawed through his neck with a serrated blade, he'd barely woken. But neither had he died.

'I hope you understand,' said the enchantress. 'Claryon Soong is a mighty name. You are an ideal example for the other mobsters not yet . . . compliant.'

Pevain scratched his straggly beard and slapped Claryon's face. 'You listening, boy? We're gonna display your meat around Kessia as a warning.'

'Except for your head,' offered Sasha. 'That will stay in the Well of Spells. In time, your madness may yield great wisdom. Until then, your screams will be as music to us.'

Claryon laughed. It was his only remaining weapon.

CHAPTER NINE

DALIAN THIEF TAKER IN THE CITY OF RO WEIR

THE MAN WAS tough. Dalian realized he'd underestimated his opponent. Saara the Mistress of Pain had sent out dozens of wind claws and Ro servants to find Dalian, ever since he had carelessly let his face be seen outside the duke's residence. The man who faced him was standing over two dead guardsmen who had foolishly attacked the Thief Taker, but the survivor was a skilled swordsman and Dalian needed to concentrate.

'I'll be well paid for your head, old man,' grunted the man of Ro as he circled the old Karesian.

They were in an alley, several streets from the northern gate, a place where Dalian had been staying while he waited for the Kirin assassin to arrive. He'd spent the last week scouting out the situation in Ro Weir, a situation that was growing worse by the day. Not only had the enchantress successfully brought order to the city, but she had established a religion among her followers. Dalian was disgusted to learn that the worship of Jaa was slowly becoming illegal.

He spoke to the Fire Giant often, needing the fear of Jaa to drive him on, to keep his mind sharp and his hand swift. Unfortunately, as he looked over his kris blades to the armoured Ro guardsman in front of him, Dalian Thief Taker, greatest of the wind claws, wished only to be able to take off his boots and warm his sore feet by a roaring fire.

The Ro lunged forward. It was a restrained attack and he kept his longsword close to his body and his elbows tucked in, not allowing Dalian an opening to counter-attack. He was forced to back away to avoid the blade and found himself against a rickety wooden wall.

'Getting tired, grandpa?' The man's smile was filled with brown teeth and manic, staring eyes. 'Heard you were dangerous. I ain't impressed so far.'

Dalian leant against the wall and feigned fatigue, panting heavily and forcing himself to wheeze. He let his two kris knives drop slightly, opening up his guard, but keeping his arms taut for a quick strike. When the guardsman – young, arrogant and expecting a swift victory – moved to strike, Dalian darted to his left and opened the man's neck. Then he turned and drove his second blade into his ribs. Panting, the Thief Taker allowed the body to fall away from him and clatter against the wall.

'I think I should be allowed a glass of wine and a few hours sleep after I kill a man,' grumbled the tired wind claw as he bent over and surveyed the three dead bodies.

'If only we all had the gifts of Rham Jas Rami.' Dalian hoped that Jaa would hear him and assist him with some phenomenal new abilities, though he knew this was unlikely.

Exhaling deeply, he pulled himself upright and strolled out of the alley, making sure to stay away from the main streets. The sun was high above Ro Weir and the day was becoming hot and sticky. The main street, leading down towards the Kirin Ridge, was rippling in the heat – a visual distortion that made Dalian shield his eyes from the glare. He had little time. After weeks of spying on the comings and goings of Saara's minions, he had identified a Black cleric, Elihas of Du Ban, as her chief lieutenant. Dalian had followed the turncoat churchman for the last few days, staying in the shadows and witnessing Saara's new power base.

The Mistress of Pain had hundreds of followers, some from among the Karesian merchant princes and mobsters, and some from the noblest families of Weir. All served her willingly, under the illusion that their continued wealth and prosperity depended on submission to the Dead God. She offered base pleasures and Dalian hated how easily her seductive preaching had spread. He had expected it from the idiot Ro, but to see the faithful of Jaa so easily swayed was distressing for the old wind claw.

'For what it is worth,' said Dalian, addressing the Fire Giant, 'I am, as ever, your devoted servant. I will fear nothing but you.'

He caught his breath and started to walk off the bumps and bruises he'd collected from repeated combat. He had not had leisure to seek healing or to take any rest, and the Thief Taker was functioning on anger and devotion rather than energy. He needed to lean against a wall and take a few sharp intakes of breath before hastening down the street towards the small Black chapel. He knew that Saara had retreated to the catacombs a week ago – probably in consequence of Rham Jas having killed another of her sisters – but now the Thief Taker was faced with the challenge of locating the witch.

Dalian stayed off the main street, weaving between alleyways and sun-dappled yards. Ro Weir was always a hot city, but to a Karesian, used to the burning humidity of the south, it was rather pleasant. It was early morning and easy enough to stay hidden as the lethargic men of Ro did not rise early from their beds. Again the Thief Taker wondered how such a pathetic bunch of men had risen to such prominence.

'You look tired, Karesian man.'

Dalian looked up and saw the smiling face of Tyr Nanon. The strange forest-dweller was perched on a wall in the shadow of a large tree with a small sack tied across his back.

'Good morning, grey-skin,' he replied. 'Have you just arrived or did you watch me nearly get killed a minute ago?'

'You were better than him, I knew you'd win,' said Nanon, confirming that he'd witnessed the encounter.

'Better maybe, but I'm also older . . . and much more tired.'

Nanon smiled again and hopped down to stand next to Dalian in the quiet side street. They were about the same height, but the forest-dweller was thin and had an otherworldly glint in his dark eyes. He still carried a longsword and wore Ro clothing of common design. With his hood up, the Dokkalfar looked no different from a hundred other wanderers and brigands in the city of Weir.

He peered at the Thief Taker, inspecting his face, before his mouth curved into a frown. 'You do look tired. And . . . older than when I last saw you.'

'I've not been sleeping much,' replied Dalian, taking the opportunity to pause, leaning against a garden wall three streets from the main road. 'I was careless and let my face be seen by a wind claw. The enchantress has everyone she can spare out looking for me. Weir is a big city, but I can't stay hidden forever.'

'Indeed,' replied the Dokkalfar. 'I've seen a few gangs of mercenaries wandering around this morning. Watchmen, too. They have a Wanted poster. I don't think they captured your stare.'

Dalian coughed and slumped down the wall to sit in the dusty side street. His feet hurt, his back was sore and his arms were stiff. If he had to fight a bunch of swordsmen every time he turned a corner, the Thief Taker doubted he'd make it to the Black chapel. He glanced up at the sky and guessed that Elihas of Du Ban would be leaving his austere quarters within the hour.

'Well, I can spare a few minutes' rest,' he wheezed.

Nanon joined him, sitting on the ground and looking up at the sky. 'Killing yourself won't please Jaa,' he said. 'The Fire Giant likes living people.'

Dalian snorted with amusement. 'If I was less tired, I'd hurt you for being disrespectful.'

The forest-dweller tilted his head ever so slightly and his eyes narrowed. 'I've been a respectful admirer of your god for many years, Karesian man. The Dokkalfar and Jaa are old friends.'

'So you say,' he replied. 'How fares your forest?'

'Poorly. We are holding them, but . . . the iron of my people begins to fade.'

'All things eventually turn to sand, knife-ears,' said Dalian.

A clatter of metal sounded from nearby and they both looked up sharply to see four men strolling into the side street. They were Ro guardsmen, city officials of some kind, and though they were armed and armoured none of them looked ready for a fight. Dalian guessed they were on a random patrol and had struck lucky.

'Back to work,' muttered the Thief Taker, beginning the process of pulling himself back on to his feet.

The guardsmen were startled for a moment at coming face to face with the notorious wind claw, but quickly drew their swords and stood at the ready.

'You're to come with us, old man,' barked one of the men.

'Fuck off,' muttered Dalian, not having the energy to argue.

Nanon chuckled. 'That's what Rham Jas would say.' The forest-dweller sprang quickly to his feet and stepped into the middle of the side street. 'My friend Dalian is a little tired currently, so if you don't mind, I'll be killing you,' he said, sounding sympathetic towards the guardsmen. 'Though I suppose you could run away.'

Dalian managed to get to his feet. 'They can't run away. They need to die,' he offered, drawing his kris knives.

'Oh, sorry, apparently you need to die,' said Nanon. A moment later he had his longsword drawn and a broad smile on his grey features.

The Ro hadn't registered that their opponent wasn't human and Dalian realized how skilled Nanon was at blending in. His height and the cloak he usually wore, along with a habit of staying in the shadows, made him appear no more than a grey-skinned man.

The leading Ro lunged first, extending his sword arm well away from his body, aiming at Nanon's stomach. The Dokkalfar parried swiftly and offered a skilful riposte, shifting position and driving his own blade through the watchman's chest. It was a smooth motion and the blade emerged through the man's back, making blood spray from his mouth. Nanon then raised a leg and kicked out, sending the dead body to the floor.

'Next,' he said.

'Just kill them, Nanon,' snapped Dalian, worried that the men would get away.

'All right, don't get annoyed,' replied the forest-dweller, advancing on the three remaining Ro.

Luckily, none of them seemed about to run. The next attack came quickly. A high strike launched at Nanon's head. He sidestepped the blow and sliced open the Ro's stomach, advancing again to meet an incoming lunge. The Dokkalfar twirled with inhuman skill and slapped away the blade, disarming the man and cleaving in his head with a downward swing. The last Ro stood in awe for a moment, before raising his sword and attempting to stop the forest-dweller. Nanon simply directed a feint at the man's side and spun round, then decapitated the guardsman with a graceful swing of his longsword.

'See, they're dead. There was no reason to get annoyed.' He moved over to Dalian and helped him upright.

The Thief Taker shook his head, but laughed at the Dokkalfar's manner.

'I hesitate to say this, but thank you,' muttered Dalian, reluctantly conceding that he probably couldn't have bested the four men of Ro in his current condition.

'You don't need to thank me. We're friends, remember.'

Another snort of amusement and Dalian replied, 'Yes, I suppose we are, grey-skin.'

Nanon helped Dalian out of the street and in moments they were skulking through a multi-levelled garden, well away from the main street of Weir. He could hear raised voices behind them, muffled by intervening buildings, but unmistakably the sounds of men discovering the guardsmen they had recently killed.

'We should hurry up and find somewhere to skulk,' Dalian muttered, brushing away Nanon's help and standing more easily on his own.

'I think I'm quite good at skulking. If that means being quiet and stealthy,' replied the forest-dweller.

'Precisely,' confirmed Dalian, pointing to a wide street that led away from the central road.

Their pace quickened. Within a minute they were bounding across the garden and down wide steps. Dalian's boots struck cobbles and they turned sharply away from the port side of Ro Weir. A few locals – men of Ro up and about their business at an early hour – were startled by the two running figures, but the blood on their clothing and weapons at their sides made the common folk turn away and pretend they hadn't seen anything. There were no sounds of pursuit and the Thief Taker slowed down, preserving his energy and looking for a place to stop.

The street climbed ahead of them at a steep incline and was flanked by low stone buildings, windowless and in bad repair. They were far from the port here, the populace were mostly destitute and, it appeared, largely foreign. Kirin and Karesian faces regarded them as they stopped running, but no one looked too closely or with any suspicion.

'Now we skulk,' Dalian said, wrapping his cloak around the two sheathed kris knives in his belt.

Nanon ducked into a narrow alley beside a crumbling and empty stable. He made sure no one saw him and then drew his sword and began to clean the blood from the blade. 'We should probably skulk over here. Out of the way.'

Dalian joined him and took up a watchful position just inside the alley, though his breath was coming fast and his limbs ached. A few minutes of running, it would seem, was too much now for the greatest of the wind claws.

'Relax,' offered Nanon, sitting down on a barrel well away from prying eyes. 'You work better when you're in control.'

'And how would you know that, risen man?' The response was barbed and tinged with irritation.

Nanon chuckled. 'A minute ago I was your friend and now I'm a risen man. That kind of attitude shift is the sign of a man not in control.'

Dalian glared at the forest-dweller – a dark-eyed stare that had made men cry in the past. However, his companion's reaction was one of laughter. It seemed Nanon was both difficult to kill and difficult to scare.

'We have half an hour until my quarry leaves his chamber,' said Dalian through gritted teeth.

'And who are we following?'

'A Black cleric, he's the Mistress of Pain's creature and he should lead us to the witch herself.'

'She's gone to ground?' Nanon had only recently arrived in Weir and was not abreast of the situation.

'I suspect that the Kirin executed another of her sisters,' replied the Thief Taker, smirking at the thought of Saara in distress. 'Their deaths seem to affect her. All I know is she's somewhere in the catacombs. I need the cleric to lead me to her if I'm to help Rham Jas do his work.'

Nanon finished cleaning his sword and stood up, stepping close to Dalian and inspecting his face. 'You need to rest, Karesian man.'

'While I can walk, I serve Jaa. I don't need rest, food, sleep or any help from you. I fear nothing but Jaa.'

'That's admirable, but you are a man of flesh and blood. Flesh and blood needs rest . . . and all that other stuff you mentioned.'

He puffed out his cheeks and looked around for somewhere to sit. Seeing only dirty barrels and refuse, Dalian decided to lean against the wall.

'I am tired, grey-skin. I'm tired of fighting and killing. I want a beach, several glasses of wine and a woman to massage my feet. Unfortunately, none of this can happen until my people are freed from the Seven Sisters, who have made the worship of my god illegal.' He almost shouted the last few words, but maintained sufficient control to realize that stealth was still important.

The forest-dweller paused before responding. He tilted his head and searched for something in Dalian's face. His eyes had no pupils and resembled deep wells of multilayered black.

'I like you, Karesian man. I hope you survive this and get to your beach and your wine.'

'I intend to,' he replied. 'But first I need to follow Elihas of Du Ban.'

Nanon smiled suddenly – a toothy grimace that would have been comical if it had come from a less dangerous creature. 'So, let's get moving,' he said.

Dalian shook his head at Nanon's manner and rocked back on to his feet. Testing each leg, he thought he could probably manage a few more minutes of running, though he had to concede that a good night's sleep in a warm bed would do his body no end of good. 'Okay, the Black chapel is off the main street, if we cut across we can get there in a few minutes. Stay hidden when we get near.'

The forest-dweller nodded and sheathed his longsword. 'Lead the way.'

They left the alley and, with cloaks obscuring their weapons, made their way back towards the port side of Ro Weir and the Black chapel. They were just two more anonymous travellers in the crowded city.

Once they had crossed the border back into the old town, Dalian grew more wary. The steep road that ran the length of Weir would be filled with watchmen and wind claws looking for the Thief Taker and he was not eager to engage in any more fighting. Gaining his bearings from the knight marshal's office in the distance, he led Nanon towards the tidal channels that littered the city. A dozen small bridges and outlet pipes dotted the area and made it easy for them to keep off the main roads. Many of the channels were used by Kirin smugglers and they were notoriously difficult to police.

'Why does a cleric of the One God follow the Seven Sisters? From what Rham Jas said, the man's not even enchanted,' asked Nanon, as they neared the Black chapel, nestled in a small courtyard in a quiet area of the old town.

'From what I hear, the man's insane. The common folk of Weir say he's obsessed with death . . . I know all Black clerics are, but Elihas of Du Ban apparently takes it to extremes.'

'Doesn't explain it,' replied the grey-skin.

'Maybe you should ask him once the Kirin has killed Saara.'

'Maybe I will.' Nanon had a vacuous but maddening smile on his face.

They crossed a street and emerged in a small blacksmith's yard. On the other side of the yard, Dalian could see the black spire of the chapel thrusting above the adjoining buildings and displaying the sign of a skeletal hand holding a goblet. There was a line of stone buildings blocking their way and the easiest, stealthiest route would take them over several rooftops.

Unfortunately, lounging around on barrels and passing a bottle of wine between them, was a squad of watchmen. The five men were presumably on duty, but they looked relaxed and only rose slowly when Dalian and Nanon entered the yard.

'Are these people a problem?' asked Nanon.

'I would think so, yes,' replied the Thief Taker, frowning at the forest-dweller's strange manner.

The five men of Ro stopped talking and gathered into a small group, facing the two intruders. They were watchful and confused, but they could not see Dalian's face and so they had no immediate reason to attack.

'Walk on, lads,' said one of the Ro.

Nanon leaned in to his companion and whispered, 'Shall we kill these ones?'

Dalian smiled slightly. 'So sorry, sirs,' he muttered to the watchmen, 'we'll move on.'

The men of Ro were suspicious, but they allowed the two strangers to move hurriedly out of the yard and into a side street. Dalian made sure they were not being followed before he stopped and skulked against a wall.

'We don't need to kill everyone,' he said to Nanon. 'I could really do with a fight-free morning from this point.'

'Thought I should ask before they attacked us,' replied the forest-dweller, looking up at the buildings that flanked them. 'I think we can still get to the chapel over the rooftops. Do you need a hand?'

'I'm fine,' grunted the Thief Taker, rubbing his sore back and flexing his arms. 'We should move, Elihas is nothing but punctual.'

* * *

Elihas of Du Ban slept on a stone bed under a narrow window scarcely big enough to see out of. He had no items of fabric or wood in his quarters and his personal belongings, what few he had, were kept on stone shelves by the door. The only possession he cared for was his armour and this was stowed on a metal mannequin, along with his Black tabard and longsword.

He rose at dawn each day and ran for an hour. He was at his most relaxed during this time and it reminded him that peace could still be achieved, despite the other demands on his time. After his run, he donned his clerical armour and attended the duke's residence and the Mistress of Pain. Each day he had to remind himself that his alliance with the Seven Sisters was a necessary evil in his austere life and that service to the One God was not as simple as his Purple and Gold brothers believed.

He was not her thrall, nor her servant, her lover or her friend. Elihas of Du Ban was her ally, nothing more, and this would last only as long as their goals coincided. With the betrayal of Utha the Ghost and the death of Roderick of the Falls of Arnon, Elihas believed himself to be the senior Black cleric in Tor Funweir, and his duties had of late required making some hard decisions. He'd tortured the Kirin apostate, Rham Jas Rami, assisted the enchantresses in annexing the south of his country, and helped in any way he could to exterminate the risen men and to birth more Dark Young.

He knew that his assistance confused Saara. He had done everything asked of him without the need for enchantment, and he had continually expressed his devotion to the One even while betraying his people and his church.

Elihas knew his mind was difficult to penetrate and secretly he believed that Saara enjoyed having an ally who did not need sorcery to make him compliant. He had not attempted to explain his actions, considering her understanding too limited for her to comprehend why he was willing to assist her. It was only in his quiet moments of prayer that he doubted this conviction.

As a cleric of the Black, Elihas was infused at all times with death. Long ago he had apprehended the divine nature of death and had realized it was a state to be aspired to, rather than feared. His life had been devoted to assisting the common folk of Tor Funweir to ascend to a divine death through the worship of the One. He had been called deranged, unstable and, on numerous occasions, insane, but Elihas heard the voice and will of the One and he was sure that his actions were right. If assisting Saara the Mistress of Pain to raise her Dead God would hasten the death of the Ro, he would remain her ally until his god told him to desist.

He took in the morning air and checked that his armour was spotless and his sword properly sheathed. Elihas liked to appear correctly attired at all times and he disliked slovenliness in others. Unfortunately, as he was currently resident in Ro Weir, he was surrounded by unwashed and degenerate scum – people who deserved more pain than a divine death offered.

Leaving his quarters, he quickly ascended the stone steps that led outside and left the small Black chapel. The building was deserted, the other clerics having been purged already, and as quiet as the tomb it resembled. Duke Lyam was not a pious man and permitted only unremarkable chapels in his city. Even the Purple church was small and easy to overlook.

He turned sharp left and looked down the steep road that bisected the centre of the city. From the gates to the harbour, the citizens of Ro Weir had to look down towards the Kirin Ridge. It was a large city, but filled with narrow streets and slum areas. The inlets that lanced through the old town held small, self-contained worlds populated by criminals of every kind. Many Kirin rainbow merchants plied their trade around the harbour, and hundreds of Karesian smugglers used the secret waterways and private docks that littered the old town. Even with the presence of so many Hounds, the city was still lawless. If anything, the foreign criminals had become emboldened. With few watchmen and even fewer clerics, the Kirin and Karesians controlled half the city. Many of the Ro had left already and the remainder huddled in the merchants' quarter, surrounded by paid guards, hoping that the Hounds would leave them alone so long as they caused no problem.

Elihas made no effort to disguise his clerical office, for he knew that he was feared by the common folk, who would not bother him. The only exception was the large presence of wind claws. The faithful of Jaa were Saara's closest followers. Many of them had willingly given themselves to her cause and now followed the Dead God, defying the Fire Giant and turning their back on the religion of Karesia. These men sickened Elihas and he refused to have anything to do with them. This went doubly for the ranks of merchant princes and mobsters who had come to Weir from Kessia and had begun to follow a perverted religion of which Saara was the high priestess. Much of the Mistress of Pain's time was spent leading bizarre ceremonies in worship of the Dead God – ceremonies that Elihas had glimpsed out of the corner of his eye and which seemed to involve a lot of nudity and self-mutilation. When she was occupied, Elihas found himself the leader of their cause. He met with their spies, directed the Hounds around Tor Funweir, and managed the day-to-day duties of intimidation and death that the annexation of Ro Weir required.

Next to the duke's residence were many large manor houses, newly occupied by rich Karesian followers of the Mistress of Pain. They had killed the Ro nobles who owned the dwellings and appropriated their wealth for the cause, adding it to the funds that had been gained from the razing of Cozz. Elihas sneered at the buildings as he made his way round the cloistered yard between the duke's residence and the huge harbour. The lowest levels of Weir were better maintained and the freshness coming from the sea even made the area seem pleasant.

'My lord Elihas,' said a Karesian accent from the yard.

The cleric turned to see a group of wind claws at attention behind several wide pillars. They wore billowing black robes and wielded scimitars and wavy-bladed kris knives.

'What?' he replied.

'You are asked to accompany us.'

Elihas slowly walked over to them, keeping his eyes on the Karesian. He said nothing in response and the wind claw began to look nervous after a few seconds of silence.

'My lord?' prompted the man.

'Where are we going?' asked the cleric after another moment.

'The mistress is still in prayer and asks that you attend her in the chapel.'

The chapel was the quaint and inappropriate name for the cavernous vaults under the knight marshal's office. It had formerly been used as Weir's grain silo, but had been cleared and was now the centre of Saara's new flock, the place where her debased followers met to worship the Dead God. It was also the place where the darkwood trees had been placed – those that had not already been shipped to other parts of the world.

There were three Karesians, each man off guard and not expecting trouble. Elihas thought for a moment and tried to hide the anger he felt at being spoken to by lesser men. He decided to remind them that they were not to speak to him.

He stepped closer to the wind claw and drew the punch-dagger he kept on his right forearm. The steel was a foot long and deadly sharp. It slid smoothly into the Karesian's neck and his expression moved through the stages of death while Elihas watched him. The cleric enjoyed seeing the light disappear from the eyes of men and he savoured the feeling, not wrenching out the blade so as to kill him quickly. The other wind claws instinctively moved their hands to their scimitars, but as Elihas withdrew his bloodstained dagger and stepped over the slumped body in front of him they held up their hands in submission.

'You are not to talk to me,' snarled the cleric.

The Karesians exchanged a worried glance. After a moment, one of them pointed towards the catacombs and the two men parted to allow Elihas to lead the way. Neither spoke again as the cleric cleaned his punch-dagger and placed it back along his forearm.

The cloistered yard was one of the oldest parts of Ro Weir and contained dozens of low entries leading into the vast tunnels beneath the city. When Saara was not seeing to her administrative duties in the duke's office, she would be in the catacombs practising her perverse religion in hedonistic isolation. Of late, since her latest sister had been killed, she had spent more and more time in the chapel, leaving the city in the hands of wind claws and her Ro thralls. Elihas did not fully understand why Saara became increasingly unhinged each time she lost a sister, but he had counted several dozen unfortunate men who had encountered her during such moments of madness and had been viciously killed. He had challenged her about it and had been told simply that she needed their energy to quieten her mind. He snorted with contempt at this answer, but did not care enough to press the issue.

The stone passageway became dark within a few strides, with no windows to allow in the morning light. It led downwards, though the stone ceiling stayed at the same height and contained a number of small balconies from which prisoners used to be thrown from the dungeons above. The catacombs had seen no use for centuries, until Saara had developed her liking for dark, underground places in which to worship her god.

'Good morning, Elihas,' a young woman's voice spoke from an adjoining chamber.

'Good morning, Keisha,' he replied, nodding his head at Saara's Kirin body-slave.

She was around eighteen years of age and a compliant young lady. 'The mistress asked me to escort you to the chapel,' she said, with a flirtatious curtsy. It was a habit she had presumably developed during her years as a pleasure-slave, and she had not yet broken the habit despite the cleric's failure to respond. 'She's been in a better mood this morning. Apparently we have an ally against the dark-blood.'

Elihas looked at her. 'Your mistress doesn't keep many secrets from you.'

'A body-slave should know all of her mistress's business. The better to assist her every need.'

Keisha led him to the huge central chamber, deep under the knight marshal's office. It was barely lit and the high ceiling was domed and filled with dancing shadows. Balconies were dimly visible around the dome. The central platform, raised, with steps at the corners, was adorned with a macabre altar of twisted tentacles. The statue's construction had driven three stonemasons insane. Its angles were strange and caused the light to play off it in bizarre patterns.

'I see her altar is finished,' said Elihas as they approached the platform.

'Vile, isn't it?' replied Keisha. 'I try not to look at it.'

Beyond the stone tentacles he could see a number of darkwood trees, sitting in the shadowy expanse of the catacombs. They were each surrounded by a small patch of earth and looked like nothing so much as a thinly spaced forest. A dozen or so could be seen, but the darkness beyond suggested that many more hid in the catacombs beneath Ro Weir. The trees were smaller than others he'd seen and Elihas surmised that they were not fully grown, having only recently sprouted from dead forest-dwellers.

Seated on the platform, Saara the Mistress of Pain was flanked by robed fanatics – men and women of Ro with wild eyes, fidgeting manically. The enchantress, with deep bags under her eyes and pallid skin, beckoned Elihas forward.

'If you'll excuse me,' said Keisha with a bow.

She broke off and walked towards her new quarters – a large side room with several adjoining chambers, which she shared with her mistress.

* * *

Dalian crouched in darkness, his form hidden behind the balcony's edge. Nanon skulked next to him and the two companions looked down into the catacombs of Ro Weir. They had followed Elihas of Du Ban to the cloistered yard and, thinking it suicide to follow him down, had found another means of entry. Through the bottom level of the knight marshal's office were empty dungeons – no bars or doors remained, merely rusted chains hanging from mossy and rotten brickwork – and they had managed to keep track of the cleric below them by poking their heads over the many balconies that looked down. They were too far above him to be seen, but Dalian was irritated that he couldn't hear what was being said or see much past the grotesque altar in the centre.

'Who's the girl?' he asked the Dokkalfar next to him.

'At a guess, I'd say that is Keisha of Oslan.' He smiled. 'Rham Jas's daughter.'

He frowned at this news. 'That will be a distraction for the Kirin. Perhaps we shouldn't tell him.'

Nanon tilted his head. 'That seems a little . . . cold-hearted.'

'Killing the enchantress will be hard enough,' replied Dalian, 'without worrying about rescuing the girl.'

'But she is a dark-blood,' said Nanon. 'Perhaps it's sensible to see her safe.'

The wind claw thought for a moment. Keisha would have been born after Rham Jas had gained his unnatural abilities, making it possible that his gifts had been passed on.

'Does it work like that?' he asked.

'I believe so,' replied the forest-dweller.

'So we should encourage the Kirin to father many children . . . just to have spares.'

Nanon again tilted his head. 'You are strange, Karesian man.'

Dalian nearly laughed at the irony, but kept himself under control and tried to focus down into the catacombs.

He could see the bulky black-armoured form of Elihas standing before the twisted altar and the Kirin girl walking towards the side door. In front of the cleric, seated and flanked by robed devotees, was a slim Karesian woman with flowing black hair. This was Saara the Mistress of Pain, a woman Dalian had not seen since he left Kessia months ago. She was too distant for them to discern her facial expression, but the leader of the Seven Sisters was resting her head on her hands and her body shape – slumped over and undignified – indicated that she was either tired or in some kind of distress.

'Would something simple like a rope work?' asked Nanon. 'Rham Jas is pretty nimble.'

'He is,' agreed Dalian, 'but he'd never get back up the rope.'

'So one of us stays up here and helps him. He's not very heavy.'

'It's a shame there isn't a clear shot. The Kirin is good with that Dokkalfar bow,' said the Thief Taker.

'Impossible shot, even for him.'

Dalian scanned the catacombs. They were mostly hidden in darkness and the entrance, leading up towards the cloistered yard, was well guarded by wind claws and Ro flunkies. To fight their way in, with or without Rham Jas, would be difficult. Dalian and Nanon were both fearsome killers but superior numbers could still overwhelm them and to die this close to their quarry would serve no purpose.

'We need a viable way in,' said the Thief Taker.

'I'm still supporting the rope idea,' replied Nanon.

'It's a stupid idea.'

'You're stupid,' replied the forest-dweller.

'Is petulance a common failing among your people?' Dalian asked. 'I thought you were all calm and stoic.'

'You're being mean,' stated Nanon. 'I thought we were friends.'

'Just shut up. I'm trying to think.'

Far below them, casting multiple shadows on the stone floor, Elihas and Saara were deep in conversation. The cleric was impassive and was listening to the animated enchantress, fidgeting in her chair and scratching her head in agitation. The Seven Sisters were known for always being in control, never letting stress or anger intrude upon their serenity, but to watch Saara now, even from afar, was to watch a woman at the edge of her sanity. By Dalian's count she'd lost four of her sisters, and through some connection unknown to him she was feeling their loss deeply.

'I have an idea,' he said after a minute of looking into the dark catacombs. 'A distraction.'

Nanon tilted his head again. 'Now, that's a good idea.'

CHAPTER TEN

LORD BROMVY BLACK GUARD
IN THE CITY OF CANARN

H IS DREAMS WERE never simple, even after boring days
spent talking to fools. Seeing the faces of noblemen turn
into braying donkeys was a particular favourite during
the hours of darkness. How much these dreams reflected Brom's
subconscious was unclear, but it made a nice change to wake up
smiling rather than sweating.

There were no braying donkeys on this occasion. He was
standing in a dense and snowy wood with the cawing of a raven
for company. It was in the north, cold and windswept. Somewhere
in the Freelands. The trees were swaying in the wind, shaking a
thin mist of snow into the air.

Shadowy figures surrounded him. Some were dressed as Red
knights, some as Free Company men and Fjorlan battle-brothers.
A few black-armoured Hounds mixed with others covered in blue
markings and carrying wooden weapons. Standing close to him
were Hawks, the warriors of Ro Haran, with short swords and
heavy shields. No more than a handful of each force, standing
impassively in the snow.

Only the raven showed signs of life, hopping from one branch
to another above the heads of the frozen warriors. Behind it,
silhouetted against the trees, was another force of warriors. They
were mounted and dressed in dark blue leather coats.

'I wish you could talk,' said Brom, smiling weakly at the bird.

It stopped hopping and pointed its large, black beak at him.

'I know who you are, but I don't know what you want,' he said, not sure if he was really dreaming.

'Brom!' sounded a familiar voice.

He spun round, looking past a group of motionless Fjorlanders. Through the snowy trees, he could see Magnus Forkbeard. His old friend was armoured in chain mail, with Skeld hanging from his belt. His beard and hair were golden and his eyes a sparkling blue.

The lord of Canarn smiled. He had missed the stubborn Ranen priest.

'You look the same, friend,' said Brom.

'You look ill,' replied the smiling priest. 'Are you eating properly?'

They both laughed. The raven cawed as if it understood their humour.

'I know you're not real,' said Brom. 'I saw you die. But it's still good to see you.'

'Death, it seems, is little impediment to conversation,' said Magnus in his deep, rumbling voice. 'But, you're right, I'm not real.'

'Is the raven?' asked Brom.

The bird flapped awkwardly to the ground, flaring its wings and snapping its beak.

'Few of our gods can truly perceive the lands of men. We move and grow too quickly for them,' said Magnus, smiling at the agitated raven. 'Only Brytag has the wit to reach from the halls without an old-blood.'

'And he doesn't speak Ro,' said Brom. 'Tricky.'

The frozen warriors around him began to move. Each one raised a weapon and sneered: axes, swords, bows and scimitars in the snowy forest.

Brom jumped in surprise as the figures swung their weapons. They ignored him and quickly created a chaotic melee of blood and steel. The Ranen attacked the knights, the Hounds attacked the Hawks. Each man fought with no sense for self-preservation and all of them died brutally, hacked to pieces. The last man standing was a young Red knight who died slowly from an arrow wound to the neck. The force of blue-clad riders did not take part. They stayed back, observing the carnage.

The raven cawed angrily.

'I don't understand you,' shouted Brom. 'I've seen you when I've slept ever since I was a boy. So has Bronwyn. But we've never been able to understand you.'

'You have gifts you don't appreciate, you and your sister,' said Magnus. 'Noble twins are a rare thing. Bullvy and Brunhilde, Bromvy and Bronwyn. The World Raven likes twins. Somehow he can see you more clearly than others.'

The dead bodies disappeared. The forest shook with a strong wind, shaking ice and snow into his face. Cold was cold, whether he was asleep or not. It was both a dream and more than a dream.

'You've shared dreams with Bronwyn, haven't you?' asked Magnus. 'When Canarn fell?'

His shivering increased, his teeth chattered and his hands shook.

'I'm Ro, why does a Ranen god care?' he asked, his breath appearing as a cloud of steam.

'You were born on the earth of Rowanoco, across the sea from your Tor Funweir.'

'I'm a traitor to my own people, I have no allegiance there. But he needs to tell me what he wants.'

Magnus strode over the hard snow and beckoned to the raven. His thick beard was flecked with glittering snowflakes and his eyes narrowed against the white glare.

The raven flapped its wings. In an ungainly flutter, it hopped from the grass to perch on Magnus's forearm. The force of riders, shadowy and opaque, was still in the distance. Their standard showed a raven flying over a half-moon.

'The World Raven doesn't like what is happening to the lands of men,' said Magnus.

'I didn't think the gods truly cared,' replied Brom.

'Do you care about rats, goats, sheep and cows?'

Brom smirked and shook his head. 'Why is Brytag different?'

The raven cawed, hopping on Magnus's forearm.

'He was never a Giant. He ascended with his friend and became a god, but he is just a raven.'

A shrill caw.

'Sorry,' said Magnus, 'he was just a raven.'

Brom approached the bird and tentatively stroked its glossy head. Was this actually Brytag the World Raven, or just a vivid dream?

Another caw and the raven pulled back its head, snapping at Brom's hand. Its eyes were black, but they conveyed more emotion than they should. What did it want him to know?

'Do you understand it?' he asked Magnus.

'After a fashion. I can see what he wants to show you.' His old friend narrowed his eyes.

He was so real, Brom felt sad. He hadn't realized how much he had valued Magnus until he saw him, bloodied and cloven on the floor of his great hall.

'Did he send you?' he asked.

'Rowanoco did,' replied Magnus, as if it were the simplest thing in the world. 'The gods have their own reasons for the things they do. They scheme and twist in ways we can't understand.'

'So they're allies? Rowanoco and Brytag?'

'They're friends,' he replied. 'In the lands of men, all that requires is a few drinks and shared interest in whoring.' He grinned, and Brom recalled a hundred debauched nights they'd spent together. 'But in the halls beyond the world it's a deeper understanding. Imagine being friends for a few thousand years.'

Brom blinked. 'I can't really imagine a thousand years. Only in stories.'

'That's what this is,' he replied. 'It's an old, old story. Happens to be true. They call it the Long War. In the end, it's the only story that matters, the only one that never ends.' He bowed his head, his broad forehead creasing in concern.

'Tell me what you see?' asked Brom. 'What does he want to show me?'

'Fire,' he replied. 'And pain.'

'My end?'

'Your beginning,' he answered. 'But he wants to say sorry.'

* * *

Winter was slowly fading away and the citadel of Canarn was no longer enveloped in endless storms. The sheer drop from the highest tower, down a wall of stone and another of cliffs and rock, was clearer in the daytime, with less snow and fewer ferocious waves. The way down was a greater distance than Brom could imagine falling, and to look down at the sea for too long brought him headaches and dizziness, though he still came to the tower and he still looked down.

Brom had become a more thoughtful man of late, less reckless and impulsive, more willing to consider his actions and to avoid conflict. He had successfully rebuilt his city, brought back some of its previous joy, replanted the crops, rebuilt the farms and returned life to the duchy of Canarn. He had even managed to keep the humans and Dokkalfar integrated to some extent. The forest-dwellers had begun to socialize more outside of their species and a few had become watchmen, lending their leaf-blades to the defence of the city. Many farmers and non-military men had also volunteered and were being trained in an informal barracks to the north. After the occupation, the populace had developed a stern determination never to be subjugated people again. An already strong-willed people had become even more so.

As for their lord, he played the part of duke while not being one and tried his best to project confidence and optimism about the future. In reality, Brom was frustrated and becoming more impatient with each passing day. He knew that the Freelands were under attack and that Tor Funweir was under the sway of the Seven Sisters. Canarn was in the middle of the two conflicts. Not currently engaged in hostilities, it was a bastion of peace in the lands of men. Brom enjoyed the peace, but his sword hand twitched whenever he received a report from Tiris or the Freelands.

Rham Jas was off killing enchantresses, Nanon was defending the Fell, Al-Hasim was fighting Red knights. Brom was holding meetings with landowners and watchmen. He doubted his skills were being used appropriately.

A sound behind him drew the young lord's attention away from the rocks. He stepped away from the battlements and saw two of his personal guardsmen approaching from the keep. Auker and Sigurd – one a man, one a forest-dweller – were charged with guarding the lord of Canarn and they took their work seriously. Brom had many enemies, both in Tor Funweir and beyond, and the landowners and merchants of the duchy had insisted he be protected from assassins and hidden enemies.

Vithar Joror, the eldest and wisest of the Dokkalfar, had started spending more time in the city and had, in the absence of Nanon, taken over diplomatic duties. He had suggested that a Tyr join Brom's guard and Sigurd had volunteered enthusiastically.

'My lord,' greeted Auker with a casual salute. 'Have the waves changed?'

'Still wet, still loud,' replied Brom. 'Less snow.'

Tyr Sigurd moved gracefully to the battlements and looked down. 'Why do you stand here each day?' he asked, his sonorous voice carrying far in the open air. 'It is cold and the wind is strong.' The Dokkalfar's words were plain and without irony or humour.

'It helps me think.'

Auker shivered and stepped back towards the sturdy wooden door. 'My lord, you have dozens of men just waiting to be appointed to your court, or whatever you call it. Hannah's father keeps dropping hints that he'd be a good knight marshal. Maybe he'd help you think.'

'I don't need a knight marshal,' replied Brom. 'Lord Justin can get rich without me giving him a position.' He'd so far managed to keep his court relatively clear of hangers-on and sycophants, and he was not eager to delegate authority.

'Well, at least deal with the prisoner.' Auker was talking about the single occupant of the dungeon – a turncoat Red knight with a mangled hand. He'd been shot as he fled south from his house, a fugitive from the king's army. 'He's still asking for you.'

'I have too many other idiots to deal with before I can get to William of Verellian,' stated the lord of Canarn.

'He is not giving us any trouble. I think he just likes being indoors,' said Sigurd. 'Though he has repeatedly asked for you.'

Brom glared at him. 'I know. Auker just said that.'

'I was just making sure you had heard. You have been unfocused of late,' replied the forest-dweller. Sigurd was close to seven foot in height and, though he was more considered and calm than most of the Tyr, he was still an intimidating presence. 'Perhaps you should listen to counsel.'

'I don't need counsel,' he replied.

'Yes, you do.' The Tyr had tilted his head, though Brom was still bad at reading the head movements of the forest-dwellers.

'I suppose you think I'm being very arrogant, Sigurd?'

'Not at all, Bromvy,' replied the Dokkalfar, and Auker baulked at his familiarity. 'I merely state that you cannot do everything yourself.'

The young lord of Canarn smiled, realizing how useful was the blunt appraisal of the forest-dwellers to his duchy. They were not subject to the whims and peculiarities of personality that made the humans such a chaotic bunch.

'Maybe I should go and speak to Verellian,' he said, glancing back out to sea and letting the breeze blow over his bearded face. 'He was part of the invasion of our fair city, was he not?'

'That he was, my lord,' replied Auker. 'His unit was sent north after your sister. Most of them apparently died in Ro Hail, but we still don't know why he fled south.'

'Bring him up to the hall,' said Brom.

'With chains or without?'

The young lord considered it. Verellian was, by reputation, an honourable man, but he had still been a part of the assault on Canarn. The man was, at least formerly, a knight of the Red and those men were dangerous even when alone. 'With. And you two stay with him.'

'Aye, my lord,' replied Auker.

The two guards saluted – the human respectfully and the Dokkalfar awkwardly – before they turned and left the high tower of Canarn.

If dealing with the knight would assuage the monotony for a few moments, Brom was prepared to see him. He doubted that Verellian had anything to say beyond a woeful tale of being drunk on duty and deserting his post, but at least it would be a change from dealing with farmers and hangers-on.

He lingered outside for another minute, breathing in the air, before closing the door to the high tower and returning to his duties.

The halls were cluttered, with servants running around and guardsmen patrolling. Everyone saluted or bowed as Brom walked back to the staircase that led to the great hall. He enjoyed the bustle as it reminded him that his city was free again, but the constant attention bothered him. Two more of his personal guard fell in step behind him as he entered the cavernous great hall.

This room had special significance for Brom. It was here that his father had died. It was here that Magnus had fallen, and it was here that Canarn had been freed. The blood had long been cleaned up, the feast tables repaired and the hall returned to its former warmth, but the room still rang with the sounds of battle each time Brom entered. He had killed Sir Rillion just in front of his ducal chair and he often found himself absently looking at the spot when he had to endure a tedious meeting.

He did not want to forget what had happened here. The young lord smiled to himself as he realized that he was also worried that he could never forget.

'My lord,' said a guardsman named Hawkin. 'There are several men waiting to talk to you.' He pointed to the central doors of the great hall, where stood a handful of well-dressed citizens. Brom recognized a few faces as landowners and merchants, including

Lord Justin, men who curried his favour while trying to secure more influence for themselves.

'I'm dealing with the prisoner. Have the noblemen return tomorrow,' muttered Brom.

Hawkin smiled, unsurprised by his lord's reluctance to deal with administrative tasks.

'At once.' He casually saluted and strode across the hall, between long feast tables and empty fire-pits, to the lords of the duchy. Words were exchanged and Brom enjoyed the look of exasperation on Justin's face as they were asked to leave. Hawkin returned and Brom took his seat on the raised dais at the far end of the hall.

The hall had five exits, the main door and four smaller entrances that led into the keep, and the area was used as a thoroughfare by Brom's household guards and servants. They cleaned, tidied and went about Canarn's business with vigour, but their tasks made their lord weary and he could wish for other surroundings.

He sat there, quietly musing on his life for a few minutes, until Auker and Sigurd arrived with the prisoner.

William of Verellian did not look his best. He was unkempt and his clothing was of common design, homespun and filthy. He looked rather like a bird of prey, with his sharp nose and angular face. He had a thin growth of hair and had not been allowed a razor to shave his head. Most notable, thought Brom, was the man's hand. He was missing two fingers – a career-ending injury for a knight of the Red – but his bearing was still noble and he stood upright and defiant as he was led in.

'My Lord Bromvy,' said the knight. 'I have been asking to see you for weeks.'

'And I have been ignoring you for weeks,' replied Brom. 'I'm only seeing you now to avoid dealing with idiot courtiers.'

Auker chuckled and led Verellian to a stop in front of the raised dais. 'Still in chains, my lord,' he offered casually.

The knight didn't look impressed. 'Though they are not strictly necessary. Ro Canarn was my destination. Why would I want to run?'

Brom sat forward on his chair. 'The last Red knight to come here had an army with him.'

Verellian laughed in frustration. 'I'm no longer a knight, my lord. I fell at Ro Hail and spent two months living as a prisoner in South Warden.' He smiled, largely to himself, shaking his head and tugging on the restraining chains. 'These are not the first chains I've worn recently . . . but I'm tired and I don't want to be a prisoner any more.'

'So far you've not said anything that makes me want to remove your chains,' replied Brom, curious as to why the knight was still alive. Neither the Free Companies nor the knights of the Red were renowned for their mercy.

Verellian was silent. He locked eyes with the young lord of Canarn, giving a world-weary smile and showing no fear for his current predicament.

'I'm just a man, now,' he said quietly. 'Not a knight, a lord or anyone of significance. Just a man. Deal with me as you see fit.'

Brom was about to reply when a horn sounded from the outer walls. The sound was a single deep note, rumbling and prolonged, indicating a ship approaching from the south. The harbour of Canarn was closed to ships and no sails had appeared since the city had been retaken. Silence fell at the sound. As it stretched and deepened, everyone present in the great hall of Canarn raised their heads and froze in place.

'Auker, check that,' he ordered, his eyes narrowed.

'My lord,' replied the guardsman, turning quickly and rushing from the hall.

Verellian, still unmoved by his surroundings, smirked at Brom. 'Want me to come back later?'

'Stay where you are,' he replied, looking over the knight's shoulder to watch Auker leave by the main door.

More horns sounded and Brom grew concerned. The others in the hall – guardsmen and servants – were now chattering among themselves, reliving the last time the warning horns had been blown. Brom had not been in Canarn when the Red fleet arrived, but a shiver travelled up his spine as he imagined how his father would have felt.

'Do you know anything about this?' he asked Verellian.

A shake of the head from the former knight. 'They won't be men of the Red. They're all either in Ranen or on their way to Ranen. Maybe a few are dotted around in barracks, but no battle force.'

'Bring him,' Brom said to Tyr Sigurd as he rose from his chair and hurried towards a side entrance.

Hawkin ushered the common folk out of the way and followed, overtaking his lord and opening the door before Brom reached it. 'To the forward battlements, my lord?' he asked.

Brom nodded and rushed through the door. The wooden-vaulted corridor was empty and they hurried over dark green carpets and past closed doors and narrow windows. The inner keep of Canarn was a maze to those who did not know its twists and turns, and the warning horn echoed through the endless corridors as they walked quickly on. These walls had recently been repaired and were freshly painted a muted shade of brown.

At the end of the corridor a spiral staircase made of stone led up to the battlements. Brom kept his eyes to the front and tried not to imagine what he might see on the southern horizon. Multiple ships were approaching, judging by the repeated horns, and there were few such fleets left in Tor Funweir. It was unlikely that merchants would approach the city, let alone in force, and Brom could think of no explanation for the warning horn.

At the top of the stone steps, several storeys above the great hall, was a wooden door which he flung outwards. Beyond, the gentle wind blew north across the stone walkway that ran atop the battlements, and the sound of the horns was louder. Brom rushed to the fortifications and leant out over the stone wall of his keep, peering across the sea. Those with him took their own places between stone castellations – all except Verellian, who stood back, unconcerned by the approaching ships.

Across the horizon, lined up in close formation, were twenty sails, each one a troop transport with forward catapults and laden with armoured men. All present held their breath for a moment as they made out the ships' red insignia.

'My lord,' said Hawkin, panting in relief. 'Those are the banners of Ro Haran.' He pointed to the red hawk emblazoned on the sails.

The lord of Canarn relaxed as the ships slowed and a white signal arrow was fired, indicating they wished for peaceful contact. Sails were lowered and the transports held a line off the coast of Canarn.

'Why do the bastards have to use the colour red?' replied Brom. 'It's very confusing.'

Tyr Sigurd, the Dokkalfar warrior, looked at the approaching ships and asked, 'Are we not to prepare for battle, Lord Bromvy?'

'I don't think so, but keep alert,' replied Brom, unsure why the army of Haran should come to Canarn in force. 'Hawkin, signal to them. Let's keep it simple, one ship can approach.'

The guardsman marched off down the battlements towards the inner courtyard. Tyr Sigurd took up Verellian's chains and stood in close guard, glaring down at the prisoner.

'If Alexander Tiris wants to chat, who am I to argue,' mused Brom, largely to himself.

* * *

Lord Bromvy Black Guard of Canarn waited. He sat in his father's chair, flanked by his guardsmen and behind fifty armed men of his city. William of Verellian was still chained and held by Hawkin to the side of the raised dais, and the hall was well lit by the fire-pits that ran the length of the huge space. A contingent of guardsmen, numbering several Dokkalfar, were escorting the visitors to the great hall. Brom was nervous. He didn't know why the Hawks had come, but he couldn't think of a reason that was in any way good.

The doors were opened and they entered. The guardsmen of Canarn stood, in organized columns, either side of the red-clad soldiers. These were the Hawks of Ro, wearing the insignia of their city and striding with a strength of purpose that was impressive to behold. At their front was a muscular, armoured man with a shaved head and an oversized bastard sword at his side. Brom recognized Alexander Tiris and, at his side, Gwendolyn of Hunter's Cross, his intense wife.

'Lord Bromvy,' bellowed Xander, 'your hall returns to something of its previous warmth.'

'Fewer people,' replied Brom.

The Hawks strode forward until they stood in tight lines before the raised dais. Xander had a Blue cleric with him, an older man armed with a heavy mace and a small steel buckler, reminding the lord of Canarn that he no longer had a cleric as a confessor.

'Sorry to bring another army here,' said Xander with a smile. 'It was not my intention to scare your people.'

'Red is clearly a popular colour in Tor Funweir,' replied Brom, feeling small in the company of the Red Prince. 'But you are welcome here.'

'Make no mistake, we do not come here under the banner of the One God.'

The lord of Ro Haran was renowned as a rebellious man, unlike the others of his family. He was the king's younger brother and the only man to have left the knights of the Red – though William of Verellian claimed otherwise.

'Then why do you come here?' he asked. 'Tor Funweir could use you elsewhere.'

'I came here seeking an ally. Though I'd prefer to talk over a drink . . . with fewer soldiers.'

Brom glanced at his guardsmen. If Xander was here to kill him, he'd have done so already. As long as his fleet of ships remained at anchor in the bay, there was no immediate danger. The men and forest-dwellers of Canarn were a tough bunch, dedicated to protecting the city and keeping its people free.

'Of course,' replied Brom. 'Auker, have the Hawks picketed in the courtyard.'

The guardsman nodded and left, taking several more men with him.

'My lord Tiris, come with me.' The lord of Canarn stood and motioned for Tyr Sigurd to accompany him to the adjoining antechamber.

The newcomers showed no signs of surprise at the Dokkalfar present in the great hall and Brom was glad that he didn't have to explain their presence.

He stepped down on to the carpeted floor and walked to the back of his hall. The room, formerly used as his father's study, and more recently by Mortimer Rillion, was a cosy office, adorned with the heraldry of Canarn. The black raven in flight, rising over a longsword, a leaf-blade and an axe, carried a special significance for the citizens of the duchy. It symbolized those who had lost their lives defending Canarn and retaking the city from the Red knights.

'You've changed your banner,' observed Xander as he entered the antechamber, followed by his wife and the Blue cleric. 'That's Brytag, isn't it?'

Brom nodded. 'That bit hasn't changed.'

'And I hear you've removed the word Ro from your city,' said the cleric, though his tone was not disapproving.

'It's just Canarn now,' said Brom. 'I don't think we count as part of Tor Funweir any more.'

The duke of Haran took a seat opposite Brom and frowned. 'The banner and name are both your business, my friend, but I have to correct you on something.'

'Please do,' he said, gesturing for Sigurd to bring a decanter of wine from a side table.

'You are still a lord of Ro,' said Xander.

Brom chuckled, pouring two glasses of wine.

'Do I not get one?' asked the cleric. 'Oh, don't worry about it, I'll pour my own.' He sat next to the Red Prince and took a large glass of wine. Turning back to Gwendolyn, he asked, 'Want one?'

She shook her head and remained standing. 'Maybe one of us should not drink.'

'Suit yourself,' replied the cleric, gulping down a mouthful of wine.

'If we all have suitable refreshment,' began Brom, 'you can explain why I should give a shit about Tor Funweir or your idiot brother.'

Xander did not change his expression. 'Do you want me to say it again?' he asked.

'Say what?'

'You are a lord of Ro. Like it or not, your blood is noble, your name is noble, you are the duke of Canarn and I need your help to save Tor Funweir.'

Brom began to reply, but Gwendolyn interrupted him. 'Before you speak, Lord Bromvy, please consider the situation. I have a feeling that you often act through passion and instinct. I implore you to try considered reason on this occasion.'

He looked at her with suspicious eyes, wondering exactly what they wanted from him. He didn't have much of an army or any real desire to assist Tor Funweir. As a Black Guard, he was technically an outlaw.

'What do you want me to do?' he asked. 'I can offer you hospitality, but little else.'

Xander slammed his fist on the table. 'You are a lord of Ro!' he repeated, this time virtually shouting. 'You have a duty to your people. You can hide in your keep or you can ride with me.'

'To what end?' demanded Brom, also raising his voice. 'You can't win against people who can control your mind.'

The Red Prince leant back, letting the corner of his mouth curl into a smile. 'Your friend, the Kirin assassin, claims he's killed four of the Seven Sisters . . . I can vouch for one at least. That leaves only three women who can control our minds.'

Brom smiled at the mention of Rham Jas. He had heard nothing about his friend's progress and was happy to hear that he was alive and still successfully killing enchantresses. 'You've spoken to him?'

'He said he was bound for Ro Weir,' replied Xander. 'All we need to worry about are the Hounds.'

'Of which there are likely to be a lot,' interjected the Blue cleric.

'But just men . . . who die at the edge of a blade,' offered Gwendolyn.

Brom sipped at his wine, considering their words. He had been waiting in Canarn for months with an itchy sword hand, hoping for an enemy to fight or a battle to join. Now that he had the opportunity to take up arms, he found himself hesitant. He was no coward, but the lord of Canarn doubted that a frontal assault would be the answer.

'We can win, Brom,' said Xander.

'How many Hawks do you have?'

'Five thousand,' he replied. 'Plus any men you can bring. The barracks in Tiris are mostly empty, but once we retake the city there'll be another five thousand at least – guardsmen and knights. I can send to Leith and Arnon for allies as well, once Ro Tiris is ours. The White Knights of the Dawn from Arnon haven't taken the field yet. Markos of Rayne commands five thousand knights.'

Brom puffed out his cheeks. 'And your brother?'

'He'll be busy in Ranen for months. The people of Rowanoco won't fall easily and the king won't know what we're doing until we've done it.'

'Come with us, Lord Bromvy,' said Gwendolyn.

'I think you should go with them, my lord,' said Sigurd, tilting his head at Gwendolyn.

'You are welcome as well, Tyr,' said Xander, showing an awareness of Dokkalfar names. 'And any forest-dweller who will stand against the Seven Sisters and their Dead God.'

'There are many who will come . . . humans, too,' replied Sigurd. 'But only if our lord leads us.' He looked at Brom, displaying his loyalty to Canarn for perhaps the first time.

Brom looked down, muddling through his options. To leave Canarn with a skeletal force to protect it would be asking for trouble, but Xander was right about the king. He would be unlikely to turn away from his Ranen campaign. The lord of Canarn could muster two thousand good men and, depending on Vithar

Joror, another hundred or so Dokkalfar. If the forest-dwellers were feeling particularly active, they might even come in force.

'Okay,' he said quietly, still looking down.

'Okay, what?' asked Xander.

'Okay, I'll come.' He paused, standing up and puffing out his chest. 'You can count on the forces of Canarn, and her lord.'

The Red Prince also stood, extending his hand to Brom. 'We are glad to have you, my lord.'

They shook hands, maintaining eye contact, and Brom felt he was entering into a pact from which he would not be able to withdraw. 'Is there a plan?' he asked, resuming his seat.

'There is,' replied Xander. 'Archibald will defend Tiris, throwing guardsmen at us, but once we breach the city walls they'll likely surrender.'

'Likely?' queried Brom.

'We'll march straight for the knight marshal's office and the Spire of the King. My cousin will surrender or lose his head.'

'Even if they surrender, we'll need to get past catapults and the sea wall first,' offered Daganay. 'Make no mistake, they won't give it to us, we'll have to take it. If we just sail through the shipping channels, they'll bombard us to wooden splinters.'

'Black wart,' said Gwen, smiling at Sigurd. 'If we can procure enough and chain the explosions – boom.'

'Vithar Joror will provide us with all we need,' replied the Dokkalfar guardsman. 'Enough for any sea wall.'

'Do you know what it's like there?' asked Brom. 'Since the Sisters took control?'

Xander shook his head. 'No, but we should have at least one friend there. The Brown cardinal is not an easy target for enchantment and he's still at the Low Cathedral.'

'Cerro?' queried Brom, who had met the chief Brown cleric when he was a young man.

Daganay nodded. 'I know the man, he's one of two cardinals in the city. The other is a Purple bastard called Severen. Of the two, I'd say the Brown is more likely to be a friend . . . he's a good man, respected by the populace. He's got one of our men with him, a young Blue acolyte of mine. We sent him before we retook Haran. If Cerro's faith is still strong, we'll have an ally.'

'Sooner or later you'll have to deal with the Purple,' said Brom. 'Attacking Tiris will piss them off.'

Xander's expression showed how little he cared about the clerics of nobility. 'They'll do what they're fucking told.'

Daganay chuckled and Gwendolyn rolled her eyes. The Red Prince was an intimidating presence, especially so when angry, and Brom found himself wishing he had a witty response or a way to impose his own presence. After a moment's thought, he said, 'You're very confident.'

'It helps to remove doubt,' replied Xander. 'Win or lose, doubt does not help a man.'

'Or a woman,' interjected Gwen.

'Or a Dokkalfar,' said Tyr Sigurd.

'Good, so none of us have doubts,' said Daganay. 'An excellent start.'

CHAPTER ELEVEN

KALE GLENWOOD IN
THE CITY OF RO WEIR

IT DIDN'T FEEL like lying. Each time he told Rham Jas he was okay, each smile he faked when the insufferable Kirin cracked a joke, every minute and every day he pretended to be something he wasn't. It was easy to simulate friendship. Up until recently it had been genuine. Now he employed it as a front while he played a part for his mistress. He was not to kill his companion, though he wanted to. He was to stay close to him, to wait until the Mistress of Pain sought an advantage. When he was awake, his mind was clear, as if nothing had happened. But when he slept, she called to him, directing his actions.

I am concerned by the forest-dweller, she said.

'Surely he is insignificant beside your power, mistress.'

Do not underestimate Tyr Nanon, he has been fighting longer than I.

'Shall I kill him when we meet in Ro Weir?'

No . . . we will remain quiet a while longer. Though I will soften my hold on your mind, removing knowledge of the beautiful gift I have given you. The forest-dweller will not sense anything.

'I don't want to go back to my pointless life, mistress. I want to hear your voice in my head until the day I die.'

You will. I will always be in your mind, sweet Kale. I will just allow you to act . . . normally, as if you had never had your mind caressed by my enduring love. You will forget until I need you to remember.

'And when can I sit at your side?'
When the dark-blood is dead.

* * *

They had moved quickly away from Haran and now, within sight of Ro Weir, Rham Jas was irritated by his companion's constant worrying. Glenwood felt strange and, try as he might, he could not shake off the feeling that something was wrong. Even the thought of meeting up with Dalian Thief Taker and Tyr Nanon proved insufficient distraction for the tired forger, who felt as if he were merely being dragged along. He had become more and more involved with the Kirin's plans over the past year, to the point where their goals appeared the same. But now, as they neared Saara the Mistress of Pain, Glenwood once again felt like an outsider.

'You'll feel better when we're actually in the city, Kale,' said the Kirin. 'It's all this sleeping rough, I don't think it agrees with you.'

'Getting hit on the head with a metal torch-holder probably didn't help.'

Ro Weir was an unpleasant place at the best of times, but now it was even worse. Law and order – an almost religious concept for the Ro – was being implemented with the unusual brutality that marked the rule of the Seven Sisters throughout Tor Funweir. Glenwood wondered if life was in any way sacred to the Karesian witches. They had let the citizens of Haran wallow in pestilence and, judging by the lines of headless bodies that flanked the main gate of Weir, things were even worse in the south.

'Not trying to rule with benevolence then?' joked Rham Jas, as they rode past the main gate and headed for a low trench through which water was flowing.

'True to form,' muttered Glenwood.

The northern muster fields of Weir were empty, though a huge military camp, flying a twisted tree banner, could be seen to the east. The sprawling Hound encampment was almost as big as the city and Glenwood couldn't imagine how many soldiers it would take to fill the place. The northern farms were full of camp followers and huge carts, from which the Hounds' drugs were distributed. They took a potent cocktail of Karesian black, a sticky, pungent substance which, when smoked, made them both violent and compliant. The entire duchy was caught up in preparations for war, making travel surprisingly easy. The Karesians cared about armies, not individual men.

'So, it's a full-on invasion now,' he said, largely to himself. 'That Red Prince fellow had better be as dangerous as he appears or Tor Funweir is in big trouble.'

'Let's just see how much of an invasion they can muster once I've killed their mistress,' replied the Kirin, with a confident grin.

'We need to get inside the city first,' Glenwood said, scanning the trench for any signs left by Nanon or Dalian.

When they had parted ways in the Fell, with a vague plan of action, the idea had been for those already in Weir to find a way through which Rham Jas and Glenwood could sneak in unobserved. Attempting to ride through any one of the official gates would likely be suicide, but the assassin was sure there must be numerous other entrances.

Weir had many gates, catering to many different groups of people. The Warder's Gate, facing north, was for officials and urban soldiers. The Leith Gate, leading to the port side, was barely guarded and the road beyond plunged into the poorest area of the city. The Hawkwood Gate, to the east, was for traders and led to the Grand Market. The only entrance to the old town was through the King's Gate, a huge bulwark, generally kept closed, through which the lords of Weir travelled.

'There,' said Rham Jas, pointing to a collection of loose rocks at the base of the wall. 'See the mark?'

Glenwood peered into the low trench and could see several parallel cuts just above the pile of rocks.

'That's Karesian trail script. They use it in the deserts to help people stay on the safe road.' He grinned. 'Dalian's being funny . . . it means Kirin only.'

'Does that mean I can stay outside?' asked the forger, without any real attempt at humour.

'No, it does not. I need your assistance once we're inside. It's a four-man job – one to rescue my daughter, two to kill the enchantress, and one to get us out of the city once it's done.'

'And which of those will I be trusted with?' he asked.

'We'll see,' replied Rham Jas. 'Think you'll be any good in a massive fight?'

'Er, no,' he replied.

Rham Jas rode towards the trench. The stone walls were hundreds of years old and solidly built, though at their base there were several low trenches through which slow-running water flowed from the city. They looked to have been formerly part of a moat and, though no longer used defensively, Glenwood could still see the outlet pipes that used to pump water into the gullies. The one Dalian had marked had no water flowing from it. Rham Jas dismounted as he approached. They were close to the Leith Gate and clear of wall guards and patrols.

'It's a bit disturbing that this won't be my first time trudging through other people's shit and piss,' said Glenwood, joining his companion on the ground.

Rham Jas looked at him. 'That sewage pipe in Arnon was mostly water . . . just a little bit of shit and piss.'

'And this one, what's the ratio this time?'

The Kirin peered down, leading his horse into the shallow trench. 'Looks empty. Rusty if anything.' He grinned mischievously. 'I could find one with some shit and piss in it if you'd prefer.'

'Fuck you, Rham Jas. Let's just get this over with,' Glenwood replied, following the assassin.

They quickly tied their horses to rusted steel pipes and stood side by side, looking into the dark passage. Visibility was minimal, but Glenwood could just about make out a broken section a few feet in. It would be tight, but they could probably squeeze through the pipe and drop down into whatever lay under the old outlet.

'Any idea what's on the other side of that?' he asked.

'Not a clue,' replied Rham Jas, 'but I'm sure Dalian wouldn't lead us into a watch barracks.'

'And once we're in?'

'There's a tavern I used to work at – not behind the bar, incidentally – called the Dirty Beggar. Dalian knows it and we'll meet there. Hopefully he'll have some information for us.'

'Hopefully,' agreed Glenwood.

It took a few minutes for them to haul themselves up into the outlet pipe and, with muttered swearing, Rham Jas started to squeeze through the broken section.

'Putting on weight?' quipped Glenwood, as the assassin inched his way through the gap, taking care not to wound himself on the jagged metal.

He received a glare in return. Then Rham Jas suddenly grinned and let go of the outlet pipe, dropping down into darkness. Glenwood crawled slowly up to the hole and, placing his hands carefully on the rusted metal, peered after his companion.

'You alive down there?'

'Yup,' replied Rham Jas. 'It's just an old warehouse.'

A few sparks of light appeared as the Kirin coaxed a torch into life and illuminated the stone room. It was ridden with cobwebs and rats scattered away from the light. Rham Jas moved away, blowing on the small flame and casting light over the floor. A door came into view, fused to its frame with rust.

'So Dalian has led us into a room with no way out?' asked Glenwood, still crouched in the outlet pipe above. 'That was nice of him.'

'Stop whingeing, Kale, and get down here. I think there are some loose bricks, should lead us out into the city, north of King's Folly.'

Glenwood pursed his lips and nodded before starting to negotiate the rusted opening beneath him. 'Tally ho,' he muttered.

It took them a few minutes to move the loose bricks and find their way out of the abandoned warehouse. They were nestled against the city walls and surrounded by rusted pipes, snaking up the brickwork and depositing brown water on the cobbles below. A few deserted back roads to the south and they emerged on the northern road, within sight of the watch barracks.

Ro Weir was a mess of a city. Buildings were boarded up, streets were devoid of life, shops were forced to employ armed guards, and Glenwood was startled to see Karesian wind claws and Ro watchmen working side by side. Wooden stocks lined the streets near the Warder's Gate, the majority occupied by terrified and malnourished Ro, their heads and hands poking through the wood and covered with vegetable matter and excrement.

'I like a bit of dirt on the street, but this is ridiculous,' he said, joining Rham Jas as they walked away from the barracks and towards the main bridge that led to the old town. 'Where's this tavern of yours?'

'Near the eastern harbour. Past the market,' replied the Kirin, making sure his hood was up and his face obscured. His Dokkalfar war-bow was wrapped in a bedroll and his katana was inside his cloak.

'Try not to look at any wind claws. We don't want a street fight.'

'Good plan, I'll . . . I'll do that.'

The street was wide, with shallow trenches indicating cart tracks and cobbled stones marking the walkways either side. Compared with Ro Tiris, where Glenwood had lived for many years, Weir had always been dirty and overcrowded but had made up for those shortcomings by being colourful and full of life. These advantages had disappeared now and all that was left was the dirt.

'They've sucked the life out of two cities,' said Glenwood, feeling a little patriotic for a change. 'I'm suddenly glad we helped out in Tiris and Arnon before it got this bad.'

'We?' queried Rham Jas, with a smug grin.

'I helped,' replied the forger. 'You couldn't have got close to either of them without me. Katja the . . . whatever, and the bitch of death.'

'You ran off in Leith,' joked the assassin, gently prodding his companion in the ribs, 'like the coward you are.'

'If I'd helped, I'd be dead. They don't care about me, remember.'

'Just pointing out that there are still enchantresses to be killed when we're done in Weir,' replied Rham Jas. 'The one in Leith slipped through my tenacious fingers.'

'One enchantress at a time,' said Glenwood.

The Kirin nodded towards a side street, leading south past the Grand Market. Though Weir was a wide sprawl of a place, it was filled with narrow alleys and labyrinthine streets, making it a paradise for men who lived on the wrong side of the law.

The two of them cut through the port side, trusting in the Kirin's sense of direction and staying away from patrolled areas. It felt strange to Glenwood that he had learned to trust in Rham Jas's abilities over the last few months – from his knack of staying alive to his skill at killing. Even the infuriating man's quick wits and guile had proven invaluable since they left Ro Tiris all those months ago.

'Just where I left it,' said Rham Jas, pointing to a scummy shithouse of a tavern. 'Ah, it's good to be back.'

'Places like this only exist in Weir,' replied Glenwood, not finding the Dirty Beggar a particularly welcoming establishment.

* * *

The four of them sat in a shady booth in a dark corner. The three men held glasses of wine – a cheap red – and the forest-dweller sipped from a cup of milk. Dalian and Rham Jas were both on edge, furtively looking round the tavern and taking note of patrons who might be enemies. Luckily, they didn't see anyone who aroused their suspicion. Within a few minutes they had relaxed ever so slightly.

'I like taverns,' said Nanon, breaking the silence. 'Men are funny when they drink.'

'I think the point is that other people are funnier when you're drunk,' replied Glenwood. 'It's a shit world, booze makes it slightly less shit.'

'Profound,' said Rham Jas, grinning.

'I believe the intention was to be humorous,' said Dalian Thief

Taker. 'However, I found it neither profound nor humorous.' He was just as miserable as Glenwood remembered. 'Please remain professional.'

'Sorry, Dalian,' said Rham Jas, showing his curiously immature fear of the Karesian.

'Yeah, sorry,' repeated Glenwood, who did not share his companion's fear of the man.

'Can we just discuss the business at hand? Time is important,' said Dalian.

Nanon was glancing from one to the other as each of his companions spoke. His eyes were narrow and his lips pursed – an expression that might seem gormless on a man, but the forest-dweller looked confused more than anything. 'See, we're having fun already,' he said with a broad smile.

Dalian glared, Glenwood chuckled and Rham Jas patted Nanon on the shoulder. The comment might have been a little naive but it had cut through the tension.

The four of them were in Ro Weir to kill the leader of the Seven Sisters. They were in enemy territory and hunted by people who would think nothing of torturing them to death if they were caught. Rham Jas risked the most, but then he was also the most capable. If his daughter were truly in the city, he also had the greatest motivation. For Dalian, it was a religious matter, a calling from his god, to be treated not as a joke or an adventure but as an essential crusade. Nanon and Glenwood had the least invested in Saara's death, but Glenwood at least felt bound to this strangest of causes. He had seen enough of the Seven Sisters' reign in Tor Funweir to know that he didn't want them entrenched in the lands of Ro. But, try as he might, he couldn't help but feel he was the weak link among them.

'If we can begin,' said Dalian. 'This will be difficult and each man must know his job. Let us remember what is at stake.' His eyes were hard and serious.

'We know what's at stake,' replied Rham Jas, averting his eyes from the Thief Taker's stare.

'Very good.' Dalian sat upright and shot a final glance round the tavern. 'Now, this is what we know. The enchantress resides in the catacombs beneath the knight marshal's office. Multiple wind claws and Ro guardsmen guard her. She has formed a steadily growing religion based on her Dead God and is frequently surrounded by her devotees.'

'Not fighters, I would guess?' asked Rham Jas.

The Thief Taker shook his head. 'Ro nobles and Karesian merchant princes. They spend their time fucking, taking drugs and cavorting. Saara has dozens of chambers down there in which orgies take place.'

'I've seen one of those orgies,' interrupted Glenwood. 'It did not look like the fun kind.'

'I was speaking,' snapped Dalian.

'So how do I get to her? And where's my daughter?' asked Rham Jas.

Nanon and Dalian exchanged a glance.

'The girl is not our priority,' said the Karesian.

'She is to me,' replied Rham Jas.

Dalian was about to reply, a pursed expression of frustration appearing on his face, but Nanon interrupted. 'She stays with the witch. Getting her out will be difficult.'

'Is she in the catacombs, too?' asked the Kirin.

'Saara's personal chambers are on the left side of the main room – high-domed and mostly dark. Her body-slave rarely leaves the room.'

'So we should be able to get to her without running into the enchantress.'

Another look passed between Nanon and Dalian.

'Stop being furtive,' snapped Rham Jas. 'I'm only here if Keisha is part of the plan. If not, you two are welcome to kill the witch without me.'

'Grow up, Kirin,' said Dalian. 'The world is of more importance than your child.'

Rham Jas snarled. He brought himself under control quickly,

but for a moment Glenwood saw distress in his eyes.

'What if I rescue the girl?' offered the forger. He didn't know where his sudden courage had come from, just that he should take responsibility for Keisha.

They all looked at him.

'I mean, I won't be much use in a drawn-out fight.'

'Hopefully we can avoid a drawn-out fight,' replied Nanon, 'but you are probably best suited for the rescue element of the . . . plan.'

Dalian shook his head. 'This is a distraction.'

'Take it or leave it,' replied Rham Jas, crossing his arms to make it clear that he'd made up his mind.

The Thief Taker puffed out his cheeks. 'I suppose it doesn't make a lot of difference to the plan. And I seem to have little choice.'

The assassin smiled. 'So, you have a plan?'

Nanon pointed to his bag. 'In there I have enough black wart to make the city think it's under serious attack. I can stay hidden better than any of you, so I'll start blowing stuff up around the duke's harbour – troop transports, wooden jetties and the like – drawing off as many wind claws and guardsmen as I can. They need the docks to keep their reinforcements rolling in so they should move to protect it. There are also a few hundred Hounds stationed there – I'll take them out first.'

Dalian took over. 'The three of us will take up position in the cloistered yard that leads to the catacombs. Once we're sure most of the fighters have left, we will move in. Rham Jas and I should be a match for any stragglers.'

'And how do we get out?' asked Glenwood, imagining he was the only one among them concerned with their escape.

'There are balconies in the domed ceiling. I tied a rope up there a week ago. I was going to suggest that Glenwood remain up there to throw the rope down for us to escape, but if you want him in the catacombs with us, we will have to rethink.'

'We get out the way we came in,' offered Rham Jas.

'That's risky,' replied Nanon. 'We don't know how much

connection Saara has to her thralls. You may find an army coming the other way to help their mistress. I can only keep them busy for so long once they know she's in danger.'

'So we'll be quick,' said the assassin. 'Kale breaks off as soon as we enter. He goes straight to Keisha while Dalian and I get to the enchantress.'

Nanon considered it, narrowing his eyes and scratching at his chin. 'It's still risky, but, if you're quick . . .'

'Very quick,' said Dalian. 'How long will it take to despatch the Mistress of Pain?'

Rham Jas shrugged. 'She's just a woman, she can die in a second like anyone . . . except maybe me.' These last words were delivered with a grin.

Dalian's patience was evidently being stretched and his mouth curled up into an expression of restrained anger. The old wind claw – who claimed to be the greatest of his order – leant in towards the Kirin. 'If your ego, sense of humour or heathen lack of faith causes this mission to fail, I will inch you up to your shoulders and then immolate the rest.'

Rham Jas actually looked afraid for a moment, and Glenwood chuckled at the childish reverence his companion showed Dalian.

'Look, the threats don't help,' said the forger. 'Nanon, be the voice of reason.'

'Me?' replied the forest-dweller. 'I try and stay away from reason. I don't think he means it, he just likes to be scary . . . probably a defence mechanism of some kind.'

This comment made all three men look at him.

'Why do you let him get away with comments like that?' asked Rham Jas. 'You don't threaten to cut his arms off.'

'The fate of my god does not rest on his shoulders,' countered the Thief Taker. 'He is no dark-blood.'

'And what if it goes wrong?' asked Glenwood. 'The plan.'

Nanon chuckled. 'In that case, I expect we'll all be dead within a few hours.'

Dalian banged his fist on the table. 'Number one – she doesn't know we're coming,' he announced. 'Number two – the Kirin is probably the best assassin in the lands of men, and number three – Jaa wills it.'

Rham Jas blushed slightly. 'Thanks,' he muttered.

The Thief Taker glanced out of the window. 'It's approaching twilight. I propose that Nanon leaves us soon and gives us enough time to get to the knight marshal's office. Then he begins his campaign of terror.'

Rham Jas laughed at Dalian's phrasing. 'I think we should call it that from now on. Nanon the Terrible has a certain ring to it . . . suits you.'

'Is that an insult?' asked the forest-dweller.

'A friendly jibe, maybe,' replied Rham Jas.

Dalian rubbed his eyes and sighed loudly. 'I am tired and I am too old to be constantly reminding you three of your importance. Please confirm that you understand the plan.'

'Yup,' said Glenwood. 'Good plan.'

'Agreed,' said Nanon.

Rham Jas merely gave a thumbs-up and the four of them sat in silence for a moment, with shallow nods and forced expressions of encouragement. Again, Glenwood felt out of place. His companions were a superhuman killer, an ancient Dokkalfar and a highly skilled warrior of Jaa. In comparison, the forger from Ro Leith was just a common criminal, a man with no special skills beyond a talent for art and fakery, and he doubted that a dodgy church seal or an attractive charcoal sketch would be much use now.

'You okay?' asked Nanon, placing a hand on Glenwood's shoulder.

'Yeah . . . mostly. I suppose I'm afraid,' he replied.

'He got hit on the head a week ago,' said Rham Jas. 'Helping me get past the naked noble folk.'

Glenwood scratched at the rough section of tender flesh just above his right ear. The bump had disappeared but a scar was visible through his hair. Maybe it was just the blow to his head.

He'd been afraid in Tiris, Arnon, Leith and Haran, but he'd coped. He'd cope in Weir, too.

You're doing well, said a voice in his head. Not long now, sweet Kale.

* * *

The cloistered yard had many exits, narrow passages that led out on to the port side of Ro Weir. It was old and the pillars were covered in moss and lichen, and wild bramble bushes lined the yard. Dalian had led them to the narrowest of the entrances and they had been skulking in darkness on the edge of the yard for half an hour. Beyond the bushes, flanking the way down, were four wind claws.

They had not spoken since Nanon had left, and even Rham Jas had been enveloped in the nervous silence. All three had their weapons drawn – Dalian's kris knives, the Kirin's katana and Glenwood's old longsword.

Then an explosion sounded in the distance and they jumped in surprise. The sound was a deep, rumbling crash, and a plume of smoke rose from the harbour, indicating that the Dokkalfar had begun his campaign of terror.

'That black wart is a dangerous substance,' whispered Dalian drily. 'Let us hope Nanon has more.'

'Trust me, a little goes a long way,' replied Rham Jas, inching his way towards the yard.

They stayed in shadows, close to the bushes and out of sight of the wind claws on guard. The Karesian warriors were startled, pulled out of the tedium of late-night guard duty by the sudden explosion. With animated arm movements they shouted back through the huge door where running feet could be heard.

'Come on, come on,' muttered Dalian impatiently, padding his feet.

Activity increased around the entrance. Glenwood's view was blocked, but he could hear several men shouting at each other and several more running.

'Silence!' shouted an unseen man of Ro. 'Your mistress orders you to investigate. Quickly now.'

'Who the fuck was that?' asked Rham Jas, staying low to the ground and trying to peer into the yard.

'Elihas of Du Ban,' replied Dalian. 'He is dangerous, watch for him.'

Several dozen armoured Karesians rushed past them. None looked in their direction and the wind claws quickly left the cloistered area and moved out into the old town of Weir.

'You two, stay on guard,' ordered Elihas, as more men emerged into the yard.

'Wait!' muttered Dalian. 'There are more.'

Ro guardsmen now emerged and joined the wind claws to form a large patrol to investigate the explosion, just as another plume of fire rose into the air from the harbour.

'That's it, let's move,' said the Karesian.

A cat-like flash of brutal violence removed the two guards. Dalian and Rham Jas moved so quickly that Glenwood had barely stood upright by the time the two men had fallen. They didn't look back and rushed towards the archway leading downwards. Glenwood nervously left the foliage, feeling like a tourist as he followed them into the catacombs. The stone passageway was dimly lit by torch emplacements and sloped gradually down.

'How many more?' asked the assassin.

'Maybe five, not including the cleric,' replied Dalian. 'They'll be in the main chamber.'

Glenwood was making far too much noise. The unnatural stealth of the Kirin and the light feet of the Karesian made him feel like a heavy-footed fat man in comparison. With weapons drawn, they continued until the entrance was no longer visible behind them and side rooms with closed doors lined the passageway. It was deathly quiet and Glenwood became aware of each breath and footstep, as if each sound would give away their location. The hard, grey stone was unadorned, though smells of incense and blood drifted down the cavernous emptiness.

Dalian signalled a halt and the three men hugged the walls. Ahead of them, at a crossroads in the passage, two figures stood guard. Their silhouettes showed scimitars and black armour, but the weapons were sheathed and the men were clearly not expecting trouble.

'I think this is where we part ways, Glenwood,' said Dalian. 'You want to take the left passage up ahead. Keep going straight on and you'll reach the girl's quarters.'

'And you're sure her mistress won't be there?' asked the forger nervously.

'As sure as I can be,' was the response. 'She spends her evenings cavorting with her flock.'

Glenwood puffed out his cheeks. 'Okay, then. I assume you'll deal with those two?'

His two companions nodded. 'Kale, she's my daughter,' said Rham Jas, without a grin. 'Get her out of here and we'll meet by the wall. That disused warehouse.'

Dalian and the Kirin shared a look and advanced towards the two guards. Glenwood stayed out of the way, ready to move quickly to the left once the wind claws were dealt with. Staying in the shadows, they got as close as possible before making their presence known. Rham Jas silenced one man with a measured thrust through his neck, while Dalian wrapped an arm round the other and drove his kris knife upwards through his back.

'Kale, go!' snapped the Kirin, already moving forward.

Glenwood backed away down the left corridor for a few paces and then began to speak. He was going to offer some words of encouragement, or at the very least to wish them good luck, but his words were cut off by the sudden emergence of more guards from the passageway ahead. Dalian had underestimated and the forger counted ten, emerging fully armed and ready from the darkness. He paused for a further second, then left the fighting to the two warriors and sped away to rescue the

Kirin's daughter. Strangely, in that moment, running down a dark corridor with the sounds of violence behind him, Glenwood's mind turned to the face of Shilpa the Shadow of Lies.

It is almost time, said the voice in his head.

* * *

Dalian prayed as he fought. Ro guardsmen emerged from side doors and passageways and were crippled or killed by the Karesian and his Kirin companion. More men than they could best, more men than should have been here.

'Jaa, strengthen my arm.'

He ducked under a clumsy longsword and opened the man's groin.

'Fill my heart with your fire.'

He headbutted a young Ro and kicked him back down the passage.

'I am your instrument.'

He saw Rham Jas roll forward, barrelling three men to the ground and killing a fourth as he rose to his feet.

'I am your servant.'

He received a deep cut to his leg.

From the central chamber, now agonizingly close, he could hear a woman's laughter. The sound was lyrical and had a note of sorcery in it that made him feel sick.

The Kirin was now a little way ahead and Dalian had to acknowledge that without Rham Jas he would have been overwhelmed. It was only the whirling katana and the narrowness of the passage that prevented the guardsmen from surrounding them. He'd lost count of the men arrayed against them, and he was too concerned with staying alive to worry about how their plan had been discovered.

More laughter as Saara the Mistress of Pain made her presence known. 'You are brave, but your bodies will soon be mine.'

Driving forward, Rham Jas reached the end of the passageway.

He paused at the opening, killing two more men with a graceful twirl.

'Dalian, come on!' he shouted, beckoning for the old Karesian to hurry up. 'We're almost there.'

Quickening his pace and concentrating on keeping the attackers back, the Thief Taker advanced towards his companion. With sweat and blood clouding his vision, he felt a sudden burning in his side and looked down to see a wide tear in his flesh. It was a bad wound, but not enough to make him drop his kris knives. He mustered enough strength to jump at the Ro who had stabbed him and drive a knife into the man's neck, cutting out his throat with a savage growl.

Rham Jas tried to get to him, but his path was now blocked. Ahead, the central chamber beckoned and no guards stood in his way.

Through bloodied teeth, Dalian spat out the words, 'Move, you Kirin scum.' He pressed at the wound in his side, blood flowing out from between his fingers. Nausea enveloped him and he had to use the wall in order to keep moving. 'Kill her, Rham Jas!'

The assassin nodded and bounded into the central chamber. Dalian tackled a man and stabbed him in the head, then flailed to his left and killed another. If he could just reach the central chamber, he'd be able to stay alive. If Rham Jas could kill the enchantress, they might yet escape.

I will fear nothing but Jaa. I will fear nothing but Jaa.

He gritted his teeth and kept moving. The last man was a lesser wind claw, a traitor to his god and his people. Dalian let his rage consume him and he savagely crushed the man's skull against the wall. With blood on his hands, his chest and seeping from his mouth, the greatest of the wind claws followed into the wide-open catacombs.

Rham Jas had advanced quickly and was now in front of the raised platform and the seated enchantress. Wind claws guarded Saara but they stood back, merely blocking the Kirin's advance. The enchantress herself appeared euphoric and her body swayed in a sensual dance, though she also looked unwashed and had deep shadows under her eyes. To the left stood Elihas of Du Ban, looking impassively past the Kirin to where Dalian was entering the chamber.

'Time to die, bitch,' spat the assassin, holding his blood-covered katana in both hands and running at the wind claws.

'I don't think so,' she replied in a girlish chuckle.

Men of Ro emerged from the passageway behind and took up position blocking the exit. There were dozens of them.

'Do not kill the old man,' ordered Saara. 'He is now harmless.'

'Harmless!' he roared. 'I am Dalian Thief Taker, the greatest of the wind claws.'

'Then die as a man,' replied Elihas, lunging forward.

Dalian parried with both his knives and spun the cleric round, kicking him hard in the groin. His armour bore the blow and he turned quickly, holding his longsword at arm's length.

Rham Jas, roaring with anger, was duelling four wind claws and trying to reach the enchantress. They were highly trained and even the unnaturally skilled Kirin was hard-pressed. More treacherous warriors now stood with Saara, guarding her closely. Her laughter rose in volume and echoed around the huge chamber.

'You're wounded, old man,' said Elihas. 'But I will give you the gift of death.'

Dalian tried to slow his breathing, but he felt cold and his skin crackled with pain. 'I will fear nothing but Jaa,' he stated.

'Fear me!' shouted the cleric, swinging his sword.

Dalian had to use both blades to parry the heavy blows and each time he deflected the longsword his strength waned a little more. Elihas was strong and his technique was brutal. But I'm quicker than you, he thought, drawing the cleric forwards and overbalancing him. The longsword hit the stone floor and Dalian, fighting against pain and loss of blood, stepped past the blade and stabbed at the man's face. The cut glanced off Elihas's cheek and Dalian discarded his other knife, wrapping himself round the cleric's neck and forcing him to drop his sword.

As the two men wrestled to the ground, with Dalian's blade inches from the Ro's face, Rham Jas could be heard screaming curses at the men who stood before him.

'I will fear . . . nothing . . . but . . . Jaa,' growled the Thief Taker, using the last of his strength to press down on the hilt of his knife.

Elihas was on his back, grasping Dalian's wrists and preventing the kris blade from entering his forehead. Then the Black cleric smiled. From his forearm, a punch-dagger sprung out, piercing Dalian's hand through the palm. He flew back in sharp pain and surprise, all the strength now fled from his bloodied body.

'Jaa . . .'

'Dalian, get up,' screamed Rham Jas. 'You don't die before me.'

Men rushed in and the greatest of the wind claws was surrounded. He was kicked and punched until his vision grew cloudy and he felt the beckoning of the fire halls beyond the world.

'Rham Jas!' shouted a familiar voice from the side of the chamber.

The men surrounding Dalian stopped attacking him and roughly pulled him to his feet, holding him in mid-air. Rham Jas stood over five dead wind claws, but now he paused, looking in astonishment at the man who had spoken. Entering the light in the centre of the chamber, Kale Glenwood came forward with a young Kirin girl in front of him. The man of Leith had a euphoric look in his eyes.

'Kale . . .' spluttered the Kirin. 'What . . .?'

'A glance from one of the Seven Sisters is sufficient, my dear Rham Jas,' said Saara mockingly.

Glenwood, staring at the enchantress with hollow eyes, placed his longsword across Keisha's neck and held her head back. The girl looked confused and scared, but nothing in her demeanour suggested that she knew her father.

'Stop!' roared Rham Jas.

'Drop your sword,' demanded Elihas, getting to his feet and clutching his wounded face. He retrieved his longsword and flashed a sneer at the Thief Taker.

'Kill her!' implored Dalian, blood spewing from his mouth.

'You are a worm of a man,' said Glenwood. 'It made me choke to follow you this last week. Now drop your sword or I'll slit the girl's throat.'

Rham Jas Rami, dark-blood and Kirin assassin, started to cry. His eyes turned red with anguish and his legs began to wobble beneath him. He looked at Dalian, and then at Glenwood. A weak smile appeared as he saw his daughter's face for the first time in more than ten years. Finally, with a deep breath, he dropped his katana.

'You look like your mother,' he said, as Elihas swung at his neck.

'No!' roared Dalian as he saw the Kirin's head severed and his body crumple to the floor. 'I . . . Jaa, please . . .' His last words were directed skywards. Then he was beaten into unconsciousness.

* * *

Saara stepped from her throne. For a moment her mind was quiet, with no background voices calling to her and no phantom thralls causing her pain. All was peaceful, all was serene. She didn't see the blood, the bodies, the Thief Taker or her minions. She only saw the dark-blood. His body was sprawled on the floor, his head had rolled to a stop near her and his katana had skittered away. Blood dripped from the blade, the head and the body, but they were all motionless.

He didn't look dangerous any more. His power had left the world, his will and his strength eclipsed by the might of Shub-Nillurath.

Then the body moved. It was a violent twitch that sent it into the air before it slumped back to the stone. From the severed neck, splitting the flesh, came a black tentacle. It grew, flailing from the corpse and writhing in the air, spraying out blood and black ichor.

Elihas, panicked by the monstrosity, hacked at the tentacle, slicing at its base. His face, cut and bloodied, screwed up in revulsion, but he kept striking until the tentacle was severed and the body again lay motionless. Then another tentacle followed it, then another, and another, until a flailing mass grew from the neck.

'Elihas, step back,' said Saara. 'No one approach it.'

There were dozens of men in the catacombs now and all of them backed away, terrified of what was taking form in front of them.

'Kale, take the girl away,' she commanded.

The tentacles slowed. Now they vibrated sensually in the air, lifting the corpse from the stone. One tentacle grasped the severed head and pulled it back to the body. The clothes split and the trunk was now black and bark-like, but it was not a Dark Young.

'Everyone leave!' she shouted. 'Take the Thief Taker to a cell and make sure he doesn't die.'

The chamber cleared of men in seconds. Elihas remained, but even he was showing his fear of the thing that had been Rham Jas Rami.

'Come to me, creature,' she said, beckoning it towards her.

Its body was pulsing and the head was jammed back on to the neck to form a bizarre contortion of man and monster, which rocked slowly forwards. More tentacles had burst from the limbs and it steadied itself, the face twisting into a human scream of unimaginable terror.

'Don't be afraid, creature,' she said, smiling. 'You can join your brothers in service.'

The thing scuttled across the floor. It stopped before her, facing the twisted statue on the raised platform, its tentacles feeling at the surroundings. They caressed the bloody floor, the statue, and then they reached for Saara. She flinched from the black appendages as the grotesque face snapped at her. In death, Rham Jas's face was pallid and twisted but the teeth were bared and the unseeing eyes were filled with anger. For an instant, Saara was afraid of the creature, then its tentacles returned to the statue.

She took a step back and the beast left her, moving into the darkness beyond the raised platform. There, in the catacombs of Weir, the creature that had been Rham Jas Rami joined the growing horde of Dark Young.

'What is it?' asked Elihas.

'I don't know. I read about something in Ar Kral Desh Jek . . . the blood has made aberrations before. It joins the thousand young of Shub-Nillurath.'

If only I'd known this before I had Zeldantor dissolved, she thought. If she had cut off the boy's head, she would now have two aberrations. Perhaps she would execute Keisha in the morning.

Then her headache returned and Saara the Mistress of Pain left the catacombs in search of rest.

EPILOGUE

THE BROWN CATHEDRAL of Ro Tiris had many names. To the common populace, who relied on it for food and healing, it was the House of the Kind. To the nobles, men and women who thought it beneath them, it was Old Gerard's. To the other churchmen, arrogant in their sensed of superiority, it was the Low Cathedral.

To Cardinal Cerro of Darkwald, it was home. He had lived there through thick and thin, through invasions and wars, peacetime and famine. As long as there were people in need of care, he would stay in Ro Tiris until the One claimed him.

'You can't just stick your head in the earth and hope the world doesn't notice you, my lord,' said Brother Artus, the Blue cleric, recently arrived from Ro Haran.

Cerro looked at him, absently stroking his grey beard. 'I wasn't aware that I was doing that,' replied the cardinal. 'Simply because I don't wish to see an invasion fleet appear over the horizon . . . that does not make me naive.'

Artus was in the city in secret. He had prevailed upon Cerro's goodwill and his friendship with Brother Daganay to keep his presence from the Purple clerics. They were short of allies. Cardinal Severen and Lord Markos of Rayne were both senior to him but unlikely to help Prince Alexander.

Cerro didn't like conspiracies. He didn't like complications, difficulties or surprises. What he liked was peace. Hearing Brother Artus talk of invasion and the Hawks of Ro was not conducive to peace.

'He's starting a civil war,' said the cardinal, closing his chamber windows to keep out the nightly chill.

'No, he's liberating Tor Funweir,' replied Artus.

Cerro frowned at him. 'The one does not necessarily exclude the other.'

'What would you do? If your arm was stronger and you had fewer years behind you?'

'Would I fight, do you mean?' asked Cerro. 'And don't try to turn this into a matter of patriotism.'

Artus was young, barely twenty, but he had a stern certitude in his manner.

'These are the lands of Ro, my lord, we have a duty to the One,' said the cleric stubbornly. 'I am not a warrior, but if I were, I would fight these traitors.'

'These traitors . . . being?' prompted Cerro. 'You mean the guardsmen of Tiris? Men of Ro. Soldiers whose only crime is to obey Lord Archibald.'

The cardinal sat in his rocking chair and poured them a cup of tea from an old teapot. Despite the tension in their conversation, he was nothing if not hospitable.

'I have honey if you prefer sweet tea.'

'What?' stuttered Artus, taken aback by the sudden change of topic.

'I could probably rustle up some food if you're hungry,' said Cerro. 'It's a long way from Ro Haran. I don't know what the roadside taverns are like, but . . .'

The young Blue cleric was open-mouthed. His eyes narrowed and he peered at the cardinal. 'I'm not hungry, my lord. I'm eager to get things in place for the general's arrival.'

'Hmm,' replied Cerro sceptically. 'The term "arrival" has acres of implied meaning. I think I'd prefer to just drink tea . . . for now.'

'This city flies a banner not of Ro,' said Artus, banging his hand on the table.

'Hmm,' Cerro replied again, crossing to the window and parting the simple, woven curtains.

He looked out over Ro Tiris. The Brown church was in Stone Town, a small section of the city inhabited by the poor and destitute. Flying over inner walls and the House of Tiris, he could see the new banner. A black design with a twisted tree hung from the Spire of the King.

Archibald and Cardinal Severen had enacted martial law. The terrified populace, fresh from a rash of public executions, would obey rather than argue. The city guard of watchmen were loyal to whoever occupied the palace and had, so far, proved compliant. With Purple clerics and Karesian warriors implementing Archibald's whims, the city had been reduced to a mockery of order – a strange, nihilistic new world where it was becoming dangerous to mention the One. Only Lord Markos of the White, newly arrived, spoke out against the new regime, but his knights of the dawn were in Arnon and he had to tread a fine line.

Cerro, on the other hand, had worked hard at remaining invisible to those to whom status meant everything, and he was sufficiently beloved by the populace that to kill him would cause unnecessary trouble. He kept the soup kitchens open, healed the sick, delivered last rites, and kept his preaching to a minimum. So far, he'd been ignored.

'I don't like the banner,' he said. 'But I'm not sure that's enough. Men die for all sorts of reasons . . . I think patriotism is the worst. The virtue of the vicious. We're all the same really, even the Karesians and the Kirin. Our blood is red.'

'I hear the Hounds bleed black,' replied Artus.

'Do you now? I'm sure some Ranen eat babies as well. Perhaps we can discount random gossip, young man.'

Artus sipped at his tea. 'My lord cardinal, we need your help.'

'I know. Attacking a city is not the same as securing a city,' replied Cerro.

'Liberating,' corrected Artus. 'And the population respect you. They will need your wisdom after the battle.'

'The battle,' mused Cerro. 'Yes, after the battle.'

'Unless, of course, you can open the gate or kill Lord Archibald,' quipped the young cleric.

'Hmm . . . you are aware that the purpose of humour is to make people laugh, or at least smile?'

He turned back to the window, leaving Artus feeling awkward for a moment.

What was he going to do? Drink tea until things were back to normal? Sit in his chapel and watch Prince Alexander destroy the sea wall and assault the king's dock? Two hundred thousand people lived in Ro Tiris. Hardly any of them cared who was in charge, so long as they still had food, money and their loved ones. One overly fed, pampered leader was as bad as another. Would the Red Prince be any different? Cerro wanted to believe so. He followed the One, at least nominally. He was a former knight, a hard, honourable man. He'd pull down that bloody banner and get rid of the Karesian wind claws. But how many men would he kill? How many innocent guardsmen and civilians?

Cerro puffed out his cheeks and took a sip of tea. It was refreshing and sweet, and the aroma filled his nostrils. Closing his eyes, he imagined a more peaceful time. A time of plenty and sunshine, when the winds were gentle and the tides low.

'I'll help you,' he said, his eyes still closed.

'I knew you would,' replied Artus. 'Daganay respects you . . . he wouldn't have sent me otherwise.'

'What is Prince Alexander's plan?' asked Cerro. 'And does he need me to do more than care for thousands of dying men after the battle?'

Artus joined him by the window. The young man was muscular for a Blue cleric, with a wide neck and calloused hands. 'General Tiris will be here in a week. He'll have seven thousand warriors on . . . I don't know how many ships. They'll destroy the sea wall. If they were to sail through the channels, they'd be cut to pieces by catapults. Once inside the city... well, the guardsmen would do well to surrender.'

Seven thousand warriors? Cerro didn't know that many soldiers were left in Tor Funweir . . . not outside the control of the Seven Sisters. As for destroying the sea wall, it was inconceivable.

'And afterwards?' he asked.

'We need you to assemble those still loyal to the One, to Tor Funweir, and to the family of Tiris, for the battles ahead.'

Cerro shook his head, fighting the urge to fall asleep and only wake again when everything was at peace. 'Once I've ministered to the dead and dying, I will be at Prince Alexander's disposal.'

BOOK TWO

THE GREY KNIGHT

THE TALE OF JAA

T HE FIRE BURNED and the Giant felt stronger. As each lick of flame caressed his scaly hide, Jaa looked upon the world and felt that fire no longer hurt, that cold no longer froze, that rock no longer wounded, that shadow no longer obscured.

The flames danced and formed shapes. He looked upon the fire and built himself a hall of flame and fear. All lesser beings would fear nothing but him. He had harnessed fire and bent it to his will. He had risen from the world to his hall beyond.

He had betrayed all of his allies, used and discarded them to increase his power. He had woven treachery and avarice into the world, and his followers would wield them as Rowanoco's followers wielded their axes.

He breathed fire upon the world and formed the southern deserts. He flapped his huge wings and caused great sandstorms. He roared dominance and suppression, fear and pain. He decried the older Giants and made war upon their followers, for the Long War was his to win.

PROLOGUE

DALIAN WAS STILL alive. He had received just enough healing aid to prevent his death, but not so much as to enable him to stand unaided. His wounded hand was twisted into a claw and wrapped tightly in bandages. Another bandage was secured around his midriff, preventing his lifeblood from leaking from the sword wound in his side. He slumped against steel, surrounded by bars. He could not focus sufficiently to see his cage or think clearly enough to remember his coming into it. All he could do was pray.

His journey was coming to an end. He had no doubt. Death would soon rise to envelop him, and his faith was all he had left.

'I am not afraid, my lord.' He rasped the words out of a dry mouth. 'I have always done what I believed was right. What I believed you wanted.'

He wanted no reward. He just wanted Jaa to blink at his death. To acknowledge that the greatest of the wind claws would be missed.

'I know I have failed.'

It was a hard admission. Dalian would have casually killed any subordinate who had miscalculated as badly as he had. To expect mercy from the Fire Giant was foolish, but death had a way of providing clarity.

'I can fight anything but failure, my lord. That enemy I cannot defeat.'

He heard a response. Or maybe his mind conjured one.

'Failure is of the moment, Dalian,' the voice said. 'Your life has been in service. One moment versus a thousand.'

He laughed. His face hurt, but he still laughed. He didn't care if the voice was real.

The cold steel of the cell offered no warmth. The wind, lancing through the catacombs, pierced his skin and left him numb.

'I don't know what's real any more,' he said to the darkness. 'Is even death real?'

'The end of one journey,' replied the voice. 'But there is another to begin. Your service will not end in death.'

He thought of his past. The dark cloisters of Jaa in Kessia. The beautiful fear he embraced as a blanket. A life, or a series of moments, spent in certitude. No doubt, no hesitation, only Jaa.

'I will fear nothing but Jaa.' The words were warm in his mouth. 'I will die. But not in fear.'

He thought of his son. What kind of man was he? Dalian had never cared. Was he strong and honourable, or weak and craven? The thoughts were undoubtedly the product of the cage and his wounds, but maybe Al-Hasim had deserved more of a father. Would he have been the Prince of the Wastes if Dalian had offered him moral guidance? Whoring and villainy had their place, but not to the extent enjoyed by his son. He should have been a wind claw. He should have stayed in Karesia and embraced the fear. As his father had done.

'He lives still. He fights the Long War, though he does not know it,' said the voice.

'Is he strong?'

'He has killed many men for a cause not his own. He loves a woman he can never truly have. He has friends, enemies, and he is in need of rest.'

Dalian laughed again. This time, he winced in pain. His chest felt heavy, as if he carried a great weight. His eyes could discern the bars now. Looking up, he could see a heavy chain connected to the ceiling. Looking down, only darkness. Somewhere down there the catacombs loomed, momentarily appearing out of the gloom when his mind cleared.

'I am glad he lives.'

A tear appeared. Emotions were dangerous, a hindrance to his work. He had always suppressed them. Or maybe he had never felt them. It had been so long that he couldn't be sure.

'Allow the tears,' said the voice. 'Let them flow. You must not fear them.'

'I fear nothing but Jaa.' The words were spoken quickly. He didn't want to forget them. His mind was so foggy, so uncertain, maybe his emotions were unreal.

He roared. A primal snarl, pulled from the depths of his stomach and thrown into the black air. It was a roar of anger, of frustration, but mostly of defeat. He had failed. He was slumped, near to death, in a cage. The greatest of the wind claws would not die in a great battle. His end would be a whimper, a murmur in deep time. Maybe not even that. He cried.

'Why?' he roared through the tears. 'Why now, when I am old?'

He didn't want answers, he just wanted to shout. If he shouted loud enough, he would be heard. If he ripped his lungs to pieces and bellowed his last into the air, his voice would travel beyond the world and echo through the fire halls.

'If you had died in youth, you would not have become the greatest of the wind claws,' replied the voice. 'And your service would have ended in death.'

He began to recognize the voice. Each word grew clearer and its edges sharper, revealing a deep Karesian accent. 'Tell me who you are?' asked Dalian.

'You know who I am.'

'Tell me!' he snapped.

'I am the shade of Dalian Thief Taker, greatest of the wind claws. I am you . . . in death.'

'I am not dead yet,' he replied.

'Your journey ends. You know this. I am what you will become. Even now, your mind sends pieces beyond and I slowly take shape from all that you were . . . from all that you have done. I am the memory of you.'

Dalian's mind softened. For an instant, just an instant, he was at peace. His death, when it came, held no fear. But he was not ready to stop fighting. If the lands of men were to fall to a Dead God, if Jaa were to be supplanted, then Dalian, dead or alive, would stand at his side.

PART ONE

CHAPTER ONE

FALLON THE GREY
IN THE REALM OF SCARLET

H E HAD BEEN functioning in a strange, twilight world for months. An in-between that didn't allow for doubt or rest. He was kept alert by conviction, laid low by tiredness, strengthened by his friends, but weakened by his guilt. Maybe he was being tested. Maybe the One was trying to see into his heart. Was he a servant of a god or was he a brutal killer? Was the one exclusive of the other?

'Wake up, Fallon,' he said to himself. 'Just wake up.'

The city of South Warden was the first thing he saw when he rose from his tent each morning. Right now he didn't want to see it. The second thing was the sprawling camp of yeomanry. They were good men and loyal soldiers, but determination would only take them so far if they were forced to fight the knights of the Red.

The Red banners were a daily reminder that Fallon was a traitor. A traitor whose situation would get an awful lot worse before it would get any better. Although he had good counsel – Sir Theron, Vladimir, Brother Lanry and Major Dimitri – he still bore many burdens himself.

'Captain,' said Theron, by way of greeting, as Fallon stepped on to the grass for another tense day.

'Anything new?' he asked.

His adjutant shook his head. 'Normal stuff. The knights keep sending detachments to ride in full-dress uniform across the plains . . . just waving their cocks at us.'

Fallon chuckled. 'Informal language this morning?'

'Sorry, sir, the situation of late has loosened my tongue a little.'

'It's okay, Theron. Hopefully, you'll stop calling me "sir" in the next month.'

He strode away from his tent towards the eastern fortifications of the camp. They had built a wooden stockade and a wide moat, behind which sat their artillery – huge trebuchets armed and sighted at the distant city. Vladimir had overseen the work and the Lord of Mud was a surprisingly effective motivator when he was not drunk.

'How are the troops?' asked Fallon.

'Tense. Nervous. Brother Lanry is doing his best, but ministering to seven thousand men is tricky.'

The Brown cleric was a good man and he would go without sleep if Fallon would let him, but the army needed more than a single churchman.

'Oh, there is one thing,' said Theron. 'They were setting up some wooden contraption in front of the gates. Not a catapult. No idea what it is.'

'Let's go and have a look,' replied the former knight of the Red.

They walked to a nearby ladder and, a moment later, stood on raised wooden planks looking eastwards across the barricade. The plain was largely empty, although small patrols rode back and forth in front of them. Cardinal Mobius and the king didn't trust Fallon's word, it seemed. The Red knights were not at rest and small figures strode along the distant stockade, as if they were waiting for something. He couldn't see crossbows or loaded catapults.

'There,' said Theron, pointing to the newly repaired gateway. 'Looks like a wooden cross of some kind.'

Fallon peered at a squad of knights busily erecting the wooden frame. Behind them, arrayed in the open gateway of South Warden, were a dozen Purple clerics. He couldn't see Mobius or Jakan, but they would be there, skulking out of sight, directing their minions.

'I think they want to show us something,' said Fallon. 'Maybe they're growing impatient.'

Before Theron could answer, a deep bugle sounded from the city. Three long blasts, indicating a parlay. Fallon and his adjutant shared a look of confusion. This was the first time the knights had attempted to communicate since they had escaped from the city. It gave him a sinking feeling.

'Muster a company of men. Ohms and twenty others,' ordered Fallon. 'Let's go and see what they want . . . and sight the trebuchets, just in case they forget we've got them.'

'Aye, sir,' responded Theron with a salute.

Fallon stayed on the raised platform as his adjutant left. He felt the telltale headache that indicated he was not alone. To his left, standing proud in ethereal purple armour, was Torian's shade. The apparition was looking towards South Warden.

'Steady yourself, exemplar,' said the shade. 'You are about to be tested by unworthy men.'

'Can you be more specific?' he asked. 'There are many such men over there.'

'Keep your sword arm loose,' replied Torian.

'I always do.'

* * *

They lined up, mounted and fully armoured, before a vastly superior force. Vladimir and Lanry had insisted on accompanying them, leaving Major Dimitri in charge of their camp. The small company of men, with the loaded and sighted trebuchets behind them, faced a guard of two hundred knights of the Red and a dozen Purple clerics. Fallon had taken his men to the mid-point between the two forces and waited. The wooden frame was braced in front of the opposing force, and Red knights, wearing the black aprons common to torturers, stood nearby.

'Oh dear,' offered Brother Lanry. 'I never understood why torture is necessary. Good men don't treat their fellows in such a fashion.'

'Cunts do,' replied Vladimir with venom.

'My lord!' exclaimed the cleric, blushing at the Lord of Mud's language.

'The word seems to apply,' said Fallon. He scanned the knights. 'I don't see Tristram.'

'Perhaps he feels the same about torture as you and I,' said Vladimir.

'Maybe. But why isn't he here?'

A single blast from the bugle and a guard of Purple clerics parted to allow a small group to march forward. Brother Jakan and Cardinal Mobius, mounted and armoured, rode in front of three men dragging a chained figure. The two senior clerics wore burnished breastplates with the Purple sceptre of nobility prominently displayed.

'I know that man,' gasped Brother Lanry, flapping his hands at the chained figure. 'That's Horrock Green Blade, the captain of Wraith Company.'

'Thought he died at the breach,' said Fallon, resting his hand on his sword hilt.

'He was definitely wounded,' replied the cleric. 'He fought Brother Jakan.'

The Ranen chieftain was barely clothed, his bloodied body clad only in rags, and his long, wild hair was matted and stained red. He was chained at the hands and feet and was being carried as a dead weight by three bound knights.

He was taken to the wooden frame and given to the torturers in full view. The Darkwald yeomanry were also watching – crammed on to the raised stockade or peering through the wooden gates.

'Behold the justice of Tor Funweir,' announced Mobius, riding to the front of the assembled knights. 'All traitors will meet the same fate if they do not surrender to our will. It is our right, our duty to rule these lands. Peasants and lesser men will be treated as they deserve.'

Jakan directed the torturers to tie Horrock to the frame, which was now lying flat on the grass. His arms and legs were spread wide and tied to the four points of the cross, leaving his head to hang limply. He was still alive, though his movements, limited by his restraints, were jerky and hesitant. He was dazed and barely conscious.

'This lesser man will be an example to you all,' bellowed Mobius, wheeling his horse theatrically in front of his men.

Jakan stayed close to Horrock and was giving the orders. 'Cripple him,' he commanded.

Four torturers were positioned at the Ranen's extremities, hefting small hatchets and sneering at the captive. With a wave of the cleric's hand, they swung. With deft skill, they removed Horrock's hands and feet. It was a grisly sight and a worse sound.

Brother Lanry vomited from his horse, and several other men baulked and turned away.

Horrock wailed in pain, but he was a broken man with little awareness of where he was or what had been done to him. The torturers flung the man's severed parts into a bucket and used burning torches to seal the wounds. The smell travelled far.

Fallon saw red. This wanton cruelty was as far from an honourable death as he could imagine. Jakan's indifference, Mobius's arrogance, the knights' compliance. The exemplar of the One was angry. He clenched his fists and panted heavily, curling his mouth into a snarl.

'Look upon this man, Fallon,' screamed Jakan. 'Look upon his broken body.'

Horrock was no longer moving and the Grey Knight lost control. He kicked his horse forward. Those around him, still stunned by the Ranen's mutilation, didn't react, only registering surprise and then words of alarm once Fallon was plunging over the grass towards the Red knights. He wasn't thinking. All he could see was Brother Jakan, standing with his sword raised and a smirk on his face. This man must die, he thought, over and over.

'With me,' roared Theron, kicking his own horse into motion and following. 'Fallon . . .'

The exemplar could hear his cries but didn't turn away or slow his charge. He heard a distant bugle from the camp of the yeomanry. The rest of the army knew something was wrong.

Ahead of him, two hundred knights of the Red were looking at their commanders, hesitantly drawing swords as the lone rider approached. The few Purple clerics were forming up round Mobius, protecting their cardinal, and Jakan stood awaiting Fallon, with the torturers at his back. Horrock was spreadeagled behind them, the smouldering stumps of his limbs filling the air with a foul stench.

'You are a coward,' bellowed the exemplar, clamping his legs to the saddle and keeping his sword close to his body. He didn't care about the men before him, the two hundred knights, the armed clerics – or about his chances of survival. He only cared about killing Jakan.

'Breath slowly, exemplar,' whispered Torian, 'The One protects you. Your sword will be as lightning, your strength as mountains, your mind as stone.'

Fallon saw things in slow motion. The ground beneath him, eaten up by his charge, flowed and contorted, and the men before him moved as flickering echoes. Each one, a trained soldier and skilled fighter, was hesitant, taken completely by surprise.

He rode closer to Jakan, passing the forward ranks of their army.

'Hold your ground. He is but one man,' ordered Mobius. 'Jakan, deal with him.'

'Crossbows,' commanded Jakan, directing a squad of bound men to load their weapons and stand to.

The strings flexed and the bolts flew, all in slow motion, as Fallon neared the Purple cleric. They should have hit him but he jumped from his horse at the last moment. He didn't know how, how he was fast enough, but he was. His senses were heightened and the crossbow bolts passed harmlessly over him. He felt both serenity and anger as he rolled forward on to the grass.

'Fallon of Leith . . . time to die,' challenged Jakan, running at the lone figure.

The crossbowmen stood in close guard but held their position, watching their commander advance as they began to reload. The other two hundred knights, uncertain what to do, began to encircle the two swordsmen, creating an open area with the mutilated Ranen chieftain in the centre. Fallon stood, surrounded by a wall of steel and red, facing Brother Jakan.

Behind him, he could hear Theron, Ohms and the others riding hard to join him, but knights blocked their path and to continue would have meant their death. In the distance he could hear horses returning to their stockade and guessed that Vladimir and Lanry were not accompanying the former knights.

'You have betrayed the One,' said Fallon, sidestepping a measured opening thrust from the Purple cleric. 'And now you will die for it.'

He was aware that he stood alone, within an overwhelming force of knights, but all he felt was the strength of his god and all he saw was the loathsome Purple cleric before him.

Jakan attacked again, but his overhead swing was easily deflected. Fallon took a step back and allowed the cleric to advance.

'Behold, the finest swordsmen in Tor Funweir,' barked Jakan. 'He will fall before a nobleman of the One God.'

The exemplar smiled. He saw the warrior opposite him for what he was – a small-minded bully with no might beyond his station.

'I'm going to use you,' whispered Fallon. 'I'm going to kill you in increments so all can see.'

'So kill me, you turncoat bastard.'

Fallon attacked and their swords clashed. He used minimal strength, swinging in tight circles and keeping the cleric from countering. He was faster than Jakan and their audience held its collective breath.

'You delegate too much of your swordplay . . . you're out of practice,' mocked the exemplar, delivering a feint to the cleric's side. Jakan tried to block it, but couldn't move quickly enough to deflect the follow-up attack. Fallon's blade swung low, delivering a deep cut to the man's unprotected thigh.

'One cut for your dishonour,' shouted Fallon, kicking Jakan to the ground.

The cleric rolled backwards skilfully, wincing as blood seeped from his leg. He got back to his feet and looked around. He saw hundreds of his men, all standing off and allowing them to fight. Now he looked afraid. He was close to the wooden frame and Horrock's broken body, and the obstacle would make retreat difficult.

Fallon stepped forward, nimbly crossing the grass and forcing Jakan on to the defensive. Their swords clashed repeatedly as combinations were delivered and parried. Fallon conserved his strength. He was the better swordsman – taller, stronger and faster, with battle-tested skill. He used the wooden frame to keep Jakan off guard and never felt as if the cleric was his match. His sword felt weightless and his movements were smooth, flowing from one into the next, almost before Jakan could react.

An opening appeared and the exemplar swung a light cut at Jakan's neck.

'Two cuts for the battle of South Warden,' he roared, again kicking the Purple cleric to the grass.

His opponent grabbed at the wound and blood snaked out from between his fingers. It was enough to show that the cleric was outmatched. He shuffled backwards, keeping his sword up, but he didn't stand up.

Cardinal Mobius, still mounted and remaining behind his troops, shouted over the sound of combat. 'Jakan, kill him.'

He gestured to the surrounding knights and each man of the Red drew his blade and made the circle of combat shrink.

Fallon readied to defend himself when another bugle sounded from the yeomanry camp. He turned back to the west, as did many of the opposing knights, and Mobius flashed a grimace of anger.

'Let them fight,' commanded a familiar voice from behind the knights. Fallon couldn't see him, but recognized Theron's voice. As the knights slowly parted, he saw a line of yeomanry approaching with Vladimir at the head. Over their shoulders, loaded and ready, poking out from the stockade, were four huge trebuchets. Theron, Ohms and the rest of Fallon's former unit were lined up just beyond the Red knights with swords raised.

'If that fight becomes anything other than one on one we will bombard you until you cry,' shouted Theron. 'It's a duel. Jakan started it, Fallon will finish it.'

'How dare you!' Mobius's voice was shrill and tinged with indignation. 'Traitors will never prevail.'

'Fuck you and fuck your words!' replied Theron, shouting across the assembled knights of the Red. 'We are the true servants of the One . . . now, let them fight.'

Mobius was wrestling with his desire to kill them all, but the cardinal wouldn't risk losing his force to sustained artillery fire. The trebuchets would cripple any advance before it could reach the yeomanry's stockade. They equalized the odds against the greater skill of the Red knights.

'Knights, stand to,' ordered Mobius reluctantly.

Fallon turned back to Jakan. 'Stand!'

All those assembled watched the two warriors and the circle grew again to give them room to fight. The wounded cleric stood and took his hand from his neck. The cut was not deep but looked ugly and continued to bleed. The leg wound was more of an impediment to movement and he approached gingerly.

'Are you ready to die, cleric?' asked Fallon.

'Killing me will only prove your dishonour,' he replied.

Torian's shade, hovering next to the exemplar, let out a muted laugh – the first expression of this kind Fallon had heard from him. The apparition transferred a stoical resolve that strengthened the former knight. As he attacked Jakan, he felt more righteous than he had ever done.

The duel was now one-sided, with Fallon slowly dissecting Jakan's flawed technique, made worse by his wounds.

'Three cuts for the One God,' said Fallon as he opened up the cleric's shoulder, cutting to the bone.

A swift pivot, a braced forearm, and the exemplar severed Jakan's head. 'Four cuts for me,' he said in a throaty growl.

Fallon looked down at the pool of blood spreading from the neck and again he felt serene. Torian was next to him, showing a more expressive face than usual. A look passed between the exemplar and the shade conveyed that the One God was pleased with the Grey Knight's resolve.

He turned his attention to the encircling soldiers. 'Any man who doubts my faith, let him step forward,' he challenged. 'I am Fallon the Grey and I speak for the One God.'

Silence. More than two hundred eyes regarded him, some in shock, but most in fear. Brother Jakan was renowned as a cleric of the sword and an accomplished warrior, and he had just been killed with ease. The knights were helpless, unable to move for fear of the trebuchets. Vladimir had assembled five hundred men and the yeomanry were fast approaching, causing Cardinal Mobius to wheel his horse back towards South Warden and order a garbled withdrawal.

Fallon didn't move as the knights of the Red enacted an orderly retreat back through the gates of the Ranen city. Most averted their eyes from the exemplar, keeping them focused on the men in front of them and trying to find solace in their knightly training. He allowed himself a smile as he strolled casually back to his own troops.

'What are you doing, Fallon?' screamed Vladimir. 'You made me shit myself . . . and puke . . . and I really need a fucking drink.'

* * *

Moving Horrock Green Blade back to the camp of the yeomanry was a grisly process. The poor man was alive but had been beaten so severely that, even before his mutilation, he would have been unlikely to recover fully. Brother Lanry was the only man among them who knew him, but all of Fallon's unit felt responsible for his fate. The Brown cleric, ushering away anyone who enquired as to the Ranen's condition, stood over him the entire way back, whispering kind words into the unconscious man's ear.

Horrock was moved to a quiet tent where Lanry and several of the camp physicians saw to his wounds, while Fallon joined Vladimir, Theron and Major Dimitri in the command tent.

'Do you mind telling me why you did that?' demanded the Lord of Mud, swigging from a bottle of Darkwald red. 'It's only a chance in a million that you're still alive.'

'He had his reasons,' replied Theron, looking at his commander with pride.

'My arse,' spat Vladimir. 'Something happened there. What? Fallon, what?'

The exemplar was seated with his sword still belted around his waist. He'd not seen or heard from Torian since Jakan died, but he could still feel the shade's presence. Fallon was clear of mind and hoped those with him could understand, or at least trust him.

'I got angry,' he replied.

'My arse . . . again,' said Vladimir. 'Come on, talk to us. We're all traitors, remember.'

'I knew I wouldn't die,' said Fallon, knowing how cryptic it sounded. 'We're doing the right thing. It's not the safe thing or the easy thing, but it is what the One God wants. If we act with honour . . .' he smiled, 'we will always be doing the right thing.'

Major Dimitri, a wine-maker who was not used to combat, let alone facing off against an army of Red knights, looked especially confused by this answer. 'I'm not sure it's my place to say, but I think I trust Sir Fallon,' he said.

'As do I,' agreed Theron quickly.

'You're too earnest for your own good,' snapped Vladimir, 'and I'm too sober to worry about this . . . we're alive, Jakan is dead, the stand-off remains.' He paused. 'Just warn me when you're going to do shit like that, Fallon.'

'But Jakan is dead,' replied the exemplar with a smile. 'And the man was a pig.'

The Lord of Mud shook his head, wrestling with his growing helplessness. 'You're not just a swordsman, are you?' He paused. 'I like you, Fallon, but I'm taking a lot on trust here.'

'Are you? The king threw your men away at the breach of South Warden. As far as I can tell, I'm your only way of getting home.' Fallon spoke calmly, before standing up and offering his hand to the lord of Darkwald. 'I can't promise you a happy ending, my friend, but I can promise you that I speak for the One. Please trust me.'

Vladimir was not a coward but he had already lost half his force in Ranen and was primarily concerned with keeping the rest of them alive. For a change, his mind was not addled with drink and his intelligence shone through.

'Put your hand down, man, we're beyond handshakes.' He tried to smile, though the expression was weak and tired. 'Share a drink with me . . . and promise me you will try your utmost to keep my men alive.'

'Agreed,' replied Fallon, lowering his hand and returning to his seat.

Vladimir rubbed his eyes and plonked himself down on a second chair. He puffed out his cheeks and reached for the bottle of wine, waving for Dimitri to join him. 'Theron, will you share a drink with us?'

The former knight had not yet broken his vows. Unlike Fallon, he was reluctant to do so. 'I've not tasted alcohol for . . . maybe seven years,' said Theron.

'Perfect, consider me your spiritual father, then,' joked Vladimir, grabbing some extra goblets and pouring out four large measures.

Dimitri and Theron sat down and the four men leant in, each holding a brass goblet of red wine.

'I would like to propose a toast,' said the Lord of Mud. 'To Fallon the Grey and the continued survival of our little rebellion.'

A muffled laugh came from Fallon and was quickly shared by the others. They all drank deeply and shared a moment of quiet reflection, glancing at one another and hoping they were not being foolish in maintaining the stand-off. Win or lose, they were on the right side. Fallon was sure that he acted with the blessing of the One God, but he did not know if that would mean their survival.

They sat in silence for another minute as Vladimir refilled their goblets and each man drank. Then, pushing the tent flap inwards, Brother Lanry entered the command pavilion. The Brown cleric was flushed and a residue of blood was on his hands.

'Sir Fallon,' he said, 'I think Captain Horrock wants to speak to you. He is awake and talking, but his mind and body are broken.'

The exemplar bowed his head, placing his goblet on the floor. Lanry realized that he'd interrupted something and frowned. 'Alcohol, Sir Fallon? So, our vows mean nothing now?'

'My vows, not yours . . . each to their own, brother.'

'Hmm,' replied Lanry. 'I'll try not to judge . . . but I think we should honour Captain Horrock.'

'The only time I saw the Ranen before today was when he fought Verellian in Ro Hail,' Fallon replied. 'And I was his enemy that day.'

'Please come with me, Sir Fallon,' implored the old cleric.

He bore no ill will towards the chieftain of Wraith Company, but he had no words of comfort for the man. His people were probably all dead and his land was being ridden over by knights of the Red. That was the reality and Fallon was not able to soften it, not even for a mutilated man.

'What does he want from me?' he asked, already standing and preparing to accompany Lanry.

'He wants to know what happened to the Free Companies. I don't think he's up to date with current events. The poor man barely remembers fighting at the breach of South Warden.'

'Okay, I can spare the time. He's lost more than any of us.'

Fallon left the others sitting quietly and continuing to drink as he accompanied Lanry out of the command pavilion. Outside, their men had rapidly returned to their positions at ease around cook fires and between their tents. The trebuchet crews were still on duty, as was a single company patrolling the palisade above.

A quick glance to the east showed that South Warden was once again locked up tight. The Plains of Scarlet were clear of knights. For a change, the situation looked stable.

'May I be impertinent?' asked Lanry, once they were alone.

'Of course,' he replied. 'I like impertinence.'

'That's what I thought, Sir Fallon, but one likes to be sure.'

'What is it, brother?' he prompted, facing the old cleric.

'Well, you see, I'm not a soldier,' he said, stating the obvious. 'Nor am I a commander, a diplomat or a cardinal. What I am is a cleric of the One. I have not turned from my god, my country or my vows.'

'Granted,' said Fallon. 'Please, get to your point.'

Lanry frowned, his grey eyebrows wrinkling up in consternation. 'I'll get to my point in my own time. A cleric of the Brown I may be, but I'm a good deal older and wiser than you, young man.'

Fallon chuckled. 'I'm sorry. Please continue, brother.'

'Apology accepted,' he replied. 'Now, if you'll allow me to continue. I know what you are, Sir Fallon, even if the others do not.'

The former knight smiled, looking at Lanry with friendly suspicion. 'You know what I am?'

'I do, I do. I've known all along and, unless I'm mistaken, an exemplar needs a confessor as much as a duke.'

This made Fallon laugh. His head went back with involuntary amusement at the old man's words.

'For months I've been wrestling with this. It's turned my head inside out . . . and you knew all along?'

'Well, I had to make sure that you were suitable. I served under Cardinal Cerro. It's unlikely a knight of the Red would know, but we of the Brown church are given certain . . . knowledge, that the other orders of churchmen are not privy to. We seek neither power nor glory and the One sees our worth.'

Fallon had never been particularly pious, even when he was supposed to be. His time in the Red cathedral had been spent yawning and pulling strange faces at William of Verellian. It was no surprise to him that the other orders had secrets that they did not share with the aspect of war.

'How am I doing so far?' he asked. 'As exemplar?'

'Admirably,' replied Lanry, with a warm smile. 'Overwhelming odds are a good way to ascertain a man's worth. I must say, you have been most honourable and strong. As your confessor, I am to assist with wisdom and . . . other less violent elements.'

Fallon put his hand on the cleric's shoulder. 'I would welcome a confessor, brother. My time as exemplar has been rather . . . lonely.'

'Oh, my dear boy, for that I apologize.' The Brown cleric gave the tall swordsman a fatherly smile. 'Shall we go and talk to Captain Horrock?'

'Let's,' agreed Fallon.

They walked along the line of tents, receiving salutes and nods of greeting from a dozen or more men of Darkwald. At the end of the row was Lanry's pavilion, an informal chapel that the Brown cleric had claimed. He didn't preach or deliver sermons, but the old man was available for any who wished for counsel or meditation. He was also very skilled at making tea and had, on more than one occasion, calmed Fallon's nerves with a pot of steaming liquid. He sweetened it with honey and seemed to have an inexhaustible supply.

At the end of the line of tents they entered the makeshift chapel. Within, the stench of death was all-pervasive. The smell was familiar to Fallon. It had hung over every battlefield he'd ever seen. On this occasion it emanated from the mutilated body of the Ranen chieftain. He was still, except for a slight movement in his chest, and bloodied bandages held the stumps of his arms and legs. He lay on a waist-high table in the centre of the tent, with bowls of bloody water and bandages all around him.

'It's not a pleasant sight,' said Lanry, moving to inspect the Ranen's wounds.

'Haffen!' screamed Horrock suddenly. 'We need to defend the courtyard.'

'Easy, master Green Blade,' said Lanry softly. 'Breathe slowly.'

'Has he ranted much?' asked Fallon.

The cleric nodded. 'Since he woke up, he's jumped in and out of lucidity. I think a bit of him is still defending Ro Hail.'

'You're not in Tor Fuck-Weir any more,' growled Horrock, beginning to thrash around. 'We are men of Wraith!'

'He was tortured . . . badly. Even before they crippled him,' said Lanry. 'He'll think clearly again, I'm sure.'

The cleric placed a hand on Horrock's forehead. 'Be at peace, warrior of Rowanoco,' he said. 'Your fighting is done. You can rest.'

The Ranen began to sob. His body shivered and curled up into a ball.

'Captain Horrock,' said Fallon, stepping forward. 'I wish you would hear me.'

'I hear you,' he replied, choking the words out through tears. He turned over, directing his bright green eyes at Fallon. 'Am I alive?'

'You are,' he replied. 'Though your body is broken.'

Lanry frowned at the exemplar. 'That's not much of a bedside manner.'

'Is that what you think he needs, brother?' asked Fallon. 'A kind word? A pat on the shoulder? He's a true fighting man, I won't patronize him.'

Horrock tried to sit up. Lanry quickly moved to assist him, providing support for his neck.

'Up we go,' said the cleric.

The Ranen's eyes were more aware now. He bit his lip and twitched, but his mind worked. For the moment at least.

'You're Fallon of Leith,' said Horrock, peering at the tall swordsman.

'I am. We met once as enemies.'

'I knew William of Verellian. He was an honourable man,' replied the Ranen, grimacing in pain as Lanry started to change his bandages.

'He was. And is,' said Fallon.

'Master Green Blade, you really should lie down,' said Lanry, lowering Horrock back to the table.

'I can't feel anything,' said the wounded man.

'You have endured more than any man should,' said Fallon. 'I can offer you a peaceful death, but little else.'

'Please!' said Lanry. 'Can we not talk of death?'

'I know what I'd want if Jakan had crippled me,' replied Fallon.

'I have failed to defend the Freelands,' said Horrock, sobbing once again.

Lanry tried to calm him, using his healing skills to deaden the pain and enable the man to breathe easier. The magic was subtle, causing only a slight distortion around his hands.

Fallon moved closer, leaning over the Ranen captain.

'Horrock. I can't undo what has happened to your lands. I can't bring back your people or rebuild your cities. But I will fight till I die to free your land of the One God's armies.'

The Ranen barely moved. His eyes were open, the deep green stained red.

'Can he hear me, brother?' asked Fallon.

'I don't know,' replied Lanry. 'His mind is . . . as broken as his body.'

'I can hear!' snapped Horrock. 'I just can't feel.'

Silence. Lanry continued to care for the wounded Ranen while Fallon searched for words to say. The healing powers of the Brown church were not powerful enough to help someone as badly wounded as Horrock. He had been torn apart, mentally and physically, reduced to a broken warrior.

All the exemplar felt was anger. No sympathy or guilt, just rage at the men who had mutilated Horrock, claiming to serve the One.

'Just talk to him, dear boy. Not about death and war, just talk. Calm him, occupy his mind.' Lanry narrowed his eyes and concentrated on his work, wrapping bandages and soaking fresh towels.

'Okay,' replied Fallon uncomfortably.

How do you calm a dying man? He'd never had to do so. Battle chaplains had always done such things. The White healed the wounded and the Black sped the dying on their way.

Something occurred to him. A question to which he didn't know the answer.

'Horrock! Horrock, look at me.'

The chieftain's face was taut and covered in veins.

'The Free Companies, how do they get their names? Why are you Wraith Company?'

Horrock pursed his lips and screwed up his face. He winced whenever Lanry touched him, as if every inch of his flesh was causing him pain.

'Horrock Green Blade!' snapped Fallon. 'How did Wraith Company get its name?'

The Ranen coughed and stared at the exemplar.

'It means "ghost" in Old Gar. It's a very old Ranen word,' he replied in a raspy voice. 'It's why we never rebuilt Hail. We are ghosts protecting a land of dead men. Dead men killed by the One God.'

Fallon nodded. 'And Scarlet Company? Something to do with blood, I expect.'

The chieftain tried to curl up into a ball but Lanry stopped him. The cleric was wiping dried blood from the stump of his leg and causing him much pain.

'Horrock, listen,' said the exemplar. 'Scarlet Company, how did they get their name?'

He tried to compose himself again, to pull forth a moment of clarity and shut out the pain. 'A Volk . . . from the north. Called Orrin Scarlet Beard. He freed the first men of Scarlet Company from their Ro masters. Named in his honour.'

'I've never met a Volk,' replied Fallon, almost in tears at the sight of the dying man.

Horrock lay back down. He stopped twitching and his eyes flickered from tiredness to serenity.

'I don't think he'll feel any more pain . . . death rises to embrace him,' said Lanry.

'No more wars, Horrock,' said Fallon. 'No more fighting, no more death. Rise to meet your Ice Giant.'

He had seen men die at the edge of a thousand swords, under hundreds of boulders and pierced by countless crossbow bolts. Seeing Horrock Green Blade die quietly in a tent was by far the most powerful moment.

CHAPTER TWO

BRONWYN OF CANARN
IN THE MOON WOODS

S HE HADN'T EVEN said hello or asked how he was. As soon
as Al-Hasim had appeared, led through the trees by Dawn
Sun Runner, she'd run at him and planted a kiss on his lips.
She didn't care how he came to be in the Moon Woods, or how
he was still alive. His face, stern, dusky, with constantly moving
eyes, was like a glimpse of a former life. A life she had almost
forgotten. The kiss lingered until her tears made him pull back
and gently stroke her face.

Federick had allowed them time together, guarded at a distance,
while Hasim told her all that had happened since she had left
South Warden. She'd wept, gritted her teeth, punched the earth
and not let go of his hands.

Scarlet and Wraith were both smashed. The women and children
of South Warden were corralled like sheep and the strong were
again slaves to the Ro. Their axes had been taken and they were
reduced to beasts of burden.

'There's still hope, Bronwyn,' said Hasim. 'Fallon is a cunning
bastard. And we still have work to do. We need these Crescent
men to ride south.'

'Not likely,' she replied, wiping a tear from her eye and
resting her head on his shoulder. 'Two Hearts is stubborn. It
was only Warm Heart that made him call for the other Moon
clan chieftains.'

'Warm Heart?' he asked. 'Bit of a strange name for a Ranen.'

284

Bronwyn sniffed, with little elegance, and rubbed her nose. As she was about to speak, the war-hound appeared from a low bramble thicket. He'd been silent up to that point and caused Hasim to leap to his feet.

'Jaa's balls! You again,' he exclaimed, stumbling backwards.

Bronwyn petted the hound, scratching him behind the ears. 'This is Warm Heart. I understand he's a Volk war-hound of the white pack, whatever that means.'

'Yeah, I know,' replied the Karesian. 'I think he saved my life, but he really shouldn't sneak up on people. Seeing them is a lot scarier than reading about them.'

'You've heard of them? How does a man of the sun know of such things?'

'Algenon had a collection of books written by a Volk. The Nine Tomes of Higher Xar, something like that. I read a few when I was in Fredericksand. There wasn't much else to do in the evenings, and a man can only drink so much mead.'

'So?' she prompted. 'They're not just big dogs, are they?'

'Er, no. From what I remember they were called forth when the Volk were at war with their cousins . . . the Dvergar.' He didn't know how to pronounce the word properly. 'They asked Rowanoco for help and he sent the hounds, allowing the Volk warriors to ride them into battle.' Warm Heart whined, hunkering down to the ground. His front paws patted the ground in front of Hasim. 'But we're a long way from Volkast . . . tenacious little bastard must have run the whole way.'

If it weren't for the Volk war-hound, Bronwyn's time among the Moon clans would have been much less comfortable. As it was, whenever a man or woman of the Crescent began a tirade against her people or thought to make an off-colour comment, Warm Heart was quick to growl at them. The huge dog was affectionate and had no idea of its own strength. It jumped at her, nudged her and found a hundred creative ways to slobber on her. The beast rarely strayed from her side and she had to concede that his presence had become comforting.

'I hear you've met before,' said Bronwyn, glad to have something to smile about.

'Yeah, I saw him half-eat a Red knight. Glad he likes you.'

'So, what do we do?' she asked, reaching for his hand and pulling him back to sit next to her.

'Since when did you ask my advice?' He stroked her hair.

'Since everything changed . . . whenever that was. It kind of sneaked up on me. One minute I knew something, then I didn't.'

Hasim raised his eyebrows.

'So to speak,' she said, realizing how tired and vague she must seem.

He faced her, his lips parting slightly and his eyes narrowing.

'You and I are still alive,' he said. 'So is Micah and that bird man, and the dog.'

A weary smile. 'Yes, we're still alive,' she agreed. 'For now, at least.'

They shared the silence. Their hands were locked together, giving her more physical security than she'd felt for months. She hated the way he made he feel, and loved it at the same time, as she hated and loved her entire situation. But in that moment she needed him. That was it, that was all, and that was enough. Warm Heart snuffled and backed away, sensing their intimacy.

'Still want my advice?' Hasim asked gently, looking down at their intertwined fingers.

She nodded, a tear appearing in her eye.

'We could just stay here. It's not so bad. The trees are nice, there are no Red knights attacking us. We could light a fire, get comfy, and see what happens. Stone Dog could be our personal servant.'

She knew she couldn't stay here. But, sitting there with Al-Hasim, she wished that she could. That her responsibilities belonged to someone else, that war had never come to Ranen and that she had never had to leave Ro Canarn.

'I know what you're thinking,' he said, kissing her slowly. 'You're screaming silently at the world. In Karesia, we call that "fighting the sand".'

'You can read me now?'

'You're only this affectionate when you're miserable,' he replied, backing away.

Suddenly, Bronwyn felt bad. He was right, she was using him. Maybe they were using each other. But it only took a second for reality to return. They were still in the snowy forest and they were still in danger.

'So, what do we do?' she asked again.

'That's my girl.' He chuckled. 'We wait, I suppose. How long until the other chieftains arrive?'

'They don't tell me anything,' she replied. 'It had better be soon. To look at Two Hearts, you'd think we have all the time in the world. He hasn't stopped smoking since I arrived.'

'Ground rowan oak mushrooms,' said Hasim. 'Better than Karesian rainbow smoke, and they're free.'

'It doesn't stop time,' she replied, glaring at him.

'Well, what time we have depends on Fallon of Leith. If these wood-wielders don't march south, he's going to die and the knights are going to burn down the Moon Woods. Simple, really.'

'What a lovely appraisal of the situation.'

'Funny, really. You and I are going to have to persuade more Ranen that the knights are a threat. Feels like we've been doing that since Ro Hail. A Karesian and a Ro . . . who would have predicted that?'

'Do you think these ones will listen?' she asked wearily.

Warm Heart growled from the trees. The hound had returned silently and Bronwyn jumped at its reappearance. The growl was deep and rumbling, and the hound nuzzled between the two of them.

'What do you want, dog?' asked Al-Hasim, hesitantly stroking it.

Warm Heart licked Hasim's face and the Karesian was too intimidated to resist. He groaned and screwed up his face. Bronwyn laughed and pulled the hound away.

'He wants us to go with him,' she said.

He wiped his face, scrubbing his slobbery cheeks with the hem of his cloak.

'How the fuck do you know that?'

'Language, man of the sun,' she replied, smiling.

* * *

The grove of the rowan oak tree was a huge, open clearing. A snowy amphitheatre, set in a weather-beaten river bed, with a ring of lesser oak trees surrounding it. The tree itself was a spectacle of white, a dense canopy of branches, dripping with ice and snow. Around the base, wooden scaffolding ringed the huge trunk, allowing the Ranen to collect the sap and any wood it offered them. The mushrooms, blue and growing in clusters, sprouted from the branches in their hundreds. The tree was the centre of their culture and gave them almost everything of value they had.

It had been an interesting day up to this point. Their intimacy had been fleeting and was now a world away as the chieftains, bearded, tattooed, armed to the teeth and angry, assembled in front of their battle-brothers. Five clans had answered the summons issued by Federick Two Hearts, but until he silenced them they had appeared more interested in fighting each other.

More sombre were the wise women, and the men of the Earth Shaker, led by Barron Crow Friend. They stood in reverence, evoking the spirits of earth and rock to bless the gathering. Lastly, they called on the Earth Shaker himself. They asked Rowanoco to protect their woods, to protect their families and their way of life. Their chanted words were humble, bringing a tear of devotion to the eyes of several Ranen.

Once the prayers were finished, Federick Two Hearts and his drug-fuelled cohorts returned to their loafing about, and the visiting Moon clans reverted to aggressive posturing. It became clear that Magnar Rock Skin had killed Theen Burnt Face's son a few years ago. The father demanded satisfaction, eliciting a dozen screamed challenges from other warriors.

'I told you it was pointless,' Two Hearts had repeated several times since the first chieftains arrived. 'They shut up for the Earth Shaker, but nothing else.'

He grinned at her as the clans commenced duels and screamed declarations of eternal hatred at the sky. It took hours for old rivalries to be settled and new ones to be formed. Several times Warm Heart had defended her and her friends from angry warriors, displeased with the presence of foreigners under the Moon, until, finally, they stood in silence round the rowan oak tree.

She stood at the edge of the clearing. To her left was Micah Stone Dog, leaning heavily on a crutch, stubbornly clutching his locaber axe. Hasim was to her right, his hood partially covering his face. Dragneel was back at the camp. The priest of Brytag was still unconscious and Aesyr Two Hearts had declared that he'd be dead within a day. Both Bronwyn and Micah had been sad at this news, but had quickly accepted that there were more pressing matters at hand.

'I call upon the faithful of Rowanoco,' bellowed Barron Crow Friend from the base of the huge tree. 'We have fought and come to a peace. Grievances have been settled and now we keep our axes sheathed in this hallowed place.'

A hundred Ranen warriors bowed their heads. Only the chieftains, their lieutenants, sons, axe-maidens and priests were permitted in the grove. Roughly twenty were present from each of the five clans.

'What the fuck are we doin' 'ere?' shouted Theen Burnt Face. 'I don't wanna look at Two Hearts' ugly fucking face any longer than I have to.'

'Watch your tongue, maggot cock,' replied Dawn Sun Runner.

The insults flew like poorly aimed arrows. Bronwyn listened, weathering sardonic quips from Stone Dog and Hasim, as the men and women of the Crescent shouted until they started to repeat themselves.

'They're stupid. This does not bode well,' said Stone Dog.

'They're stupid and they've got axes. Just point them in the right direction,' replied Hasim.

'Hmm, tricky,' said Micah. 'I'm not good with stupid people.'

'You could fight them.'

'I might.'

The exchange was dry and delivered with little humour. Bronwyn barely registered their words, trying to focus on the chieftains. She was growing tired of listening to their tedious threats. They jumped around on the spot, waving their axes in impotent rage. Their complaints were petty and mostly generations old, being pulled out like an ailing relative to challenge their enemies. Even Barron rolled his eyes. He shrugged at Federick, as if to say *I'm trying*.

'Where's the hound?' asked Hasim.

She looked around the clearing. 'I haven't seen him since he led us here.'

'How can such a big dog be so stealthy?'

A fresh round of threats from the Ranen muffled his words. They'd moved on to accusations of treachery, flinging half-remembered tales at each other as if they were absolute truth.

Two Hearts was now engaged in a small party off to the side. He and his followers were ignoring the other clans and throwing mushroom smoke and alcohol down their necks. Whatever seniority he had, he was choosing not to use it. His deep voice was easy to identify, but it emerged as laughter, rippling across the clearing. It was a bizarre accompaniment to the arguing. It would have been funny, were Bronwyn not so tightly wound up.

A sound of horses suddenly rang around the clearing. From the north, shaking snow from the high branches, multiple riders approached. Warning arrows, buzzing loudly through the air, were fired by men of the Crescent. The chieftains were startled out of threatening one another and turned to face the oncoming horses.

She was amazed that riders could get so close to the rowan oak without being attacked by men of the Crescent. The sound of hooves had appeared out of nowhere, rising suddenly in volume from a murmur to a roar.

Hasim drew his scimitar smoothly. 'Wrong direction for the knights.'

Micah tried to heft his axe, but his strength would not allow him to hold the weapon above his waist. Bronwyn looked around, unsure how to react. The warriors guarding the clearing had fired the warning arrows and they now flooded in to protect their leaders.

Men on horseback appeared. They pulled up on the edge of the clearing and fanned out. They were men of Ranen, dressed in chain mail with dark blue leather coats. They each had thick-bladed swords and steel helmets. Their standard was carried by the leader and bore the insignia of a raven, flying over a half-moon.

'I've never seen Ranen dressed like that,' said Hasim. 'They've actually got uniforms.'

'That's a Free Company from the north. Don't know which one,' offered Micah, discarding his walking stick.

'Explain yourselves!' bellowed Theen Burnt Face.

The standard-bearer trotted forward from his men. He held up a hand and more riders appeared through the trees. Fifty men or more, arrayed in an orderly line, formed a semicircle at the edge of the clearing.

Theen shook his axe angrily. 'Answer me, shit-head!'

The leader passed the banner to another man and removed his helmet. He was young, with a thin face and closely cut black hair. Bronwyn looked again and thought that he might be older after all. He had a wildness in his eyes and his glare was not that of a young man. He smiled at Theen, a broad, toothy expression that split his face.

'We are Twilight Company. Tell me where Dragneel Dark Crest is or I'll tear out your liver.'

Angry shouts came from the men of the Crescent. They swung their axes menacingly, throwing out guttural insults at the Free Company.

'Get off your fucking horse and say that again, boy,' snarled Theen.

The riders didn't react. Neither the leader nor his men responded to the threats. They sat, impassively scanning the clearing.

'Are things about to get nasty?' Hasim asked Micah.

'Only if the men of the Crescent are even more stupid than we thought,' replied the young axe-man. 'This lot are from Ranen Gar, they don't fuck around.'

The lead rider nudged his horse forward and slowly dismounted. He ignored Theen and flexed his back, groaning contentedly. He was tall and lean, with boyish looks but dark, penetrating eyes. He discarded his helmet and strolled towards Theen, stopping barely a foot from the chieftain.

'Do you know what the last thing I killed was?' asked the Free Company man in a precise and clear voice.

The men of the Crescent were silent now, waiting to see how Theen would react.

'It was a troll,' continued the leader. 'I lured it into a cave and burned it alive. Have you ever heard a burning troll keen? It's beautiful.'

The silence was total. Theen tried to stare the man down but his eyes flickered nervously until he turned away.

'Where is Dragneel Dark Crest?' repeated the strange man.

'You want something here, you talk to me,' bellowed Federick Two Hearts from across the clearing. 'The piss-stain you're staring at is an idiot.'

Tattooed night-raiders had silently appeared behind Two Hearts. They nocked arrows and stood ready. Their chieftain pulled himself upright, rolling on to his feet and coughing.

'You'll have to excuse me, Free Company man, I'm utterly fucked.' He grinned manically. 'I didn't expect anyone important actually to turn up.'

'You!' he shouted at Bronwyn, taking her completely by surprise. 'You're with me.'

She looked around. First at Hasim, then at Micah. Neither offered any reassurance. In fact, they looked as surprised as she was. After a few moments, stuttering and wishing the earth would envelop her whole, she followed the Ranen chieftain.

It was strange that she was more concerned about losing her footing on the snowy ground and falling over in front of a hundred men than about meeting the strange visitor.

Federick slowed and slung a muscular arm round her shoulder. He was bare-chested and emitted a fearful stench of drugs, alcohol and sweat.

'Don't worry, love, I can barely stand up. If it becomes a fight, it'll be over pretty quick.' He guffawed at his own comment, spluttering and pinching her cheek.

She slapped his arm away and shot a helpless look over her shoulder at Hasim. The Karesian spread his arms wide and frowned.

The two of the them crossed the clearing. They circled round the huge tree trunk, receiving a light shower of fine snowflakes. The night-raiders followed and a hundred warriors watched.

'Right, you,' he said cheerfully to the stranger, 'what d'you want with the bird man?'

Twilight Company had barely shifted position since they had arrived in the clearing. Only their leader had spoken.

'Introductions,' stated the stranger, his face contorting into a wild grin.

'What did he say?' Federick muttered to Bronwyn in a deep whisper.

'He wants to know who you are.' She turned to the smiling man. 'Sorry, my lord Ranen, this man is overly fond of narcotics. May I introduce myself?'

He looked her up and down, but didn't stop grinning. 'You may.'

'I am Lady Bronwyn of Canarn,' she said, bowing her head. 'I travelled from South Warden with Dragneel. He is wounded.'

There was no response. The man just looked at her and his smile turned sinister.

'And you are?' she prompted.

'Fynius Black Claw,' he said after a further moment of silence. 'Captain Fynius Black Claw. I come from Old Gar following a raven, seeking a priest of Brytag. What are you looking for, Lady Bronwyn?'

In the deep recesses of her mind, she heard cawing.

'You're Dominic Black Claw's brother?' asked Two Hearts, taking a step backwards.

Other men reacted to the name. Some lowered their weapons in fear, others snarled angrily. Theen was wild-eyed, ignorant of whom he had been insulting.

Bronwyn had heard of Dominic Black Claw. He was the master of Ranen Gar and the captain of Greywood Company. She knew nothing of his brother.

'I'm here seeking allies,' she said. 'Originally for South Warden, now for all of Ranen. The king of Tor Funweir is camped on the Plains of Scarlet.'

'What of the men of Wraith and Scarlet?' asked Fynius, ceasing to smile.

She shook her head, looking across the clearing at Micah Stone Dog. 'The young axe-man over there may be the last member of Wraith Company.'

Fynius paced back and forth in front of them. He was agitated, muttering to himself. He argued into the air, gesticulating wildly.

'Right!' he exclaimed after a moment. 'You, fat man.' He pointed to Two Hearts. 'See to my men. I have five hundred. They need food and the horses need water. You.' He point to Bronwyn. 'Take me to Dragneel.'

* * *

Twilight Company were as stealthy as they were numerous. Hundreds of riders, clad in dark blue, appeared from nowhere and took up residence in Federick's camp. They responded to aggression with indifference, refusing to answer challenges. Once their numbers were apparent, the other Moon clans kept their distance, whispering about Fynius.

Rumours of Dominic Black Claw's brother were numerous. Most told of his madness. Bronwyn heard variously that he was touched with visions by Brytag, that he had been struck on the head by his brother, that he had spent ten years living with berserkers in the Low Kast. She asked him, but he just ignored her. Even Two Hearts, striding through his drugged oblivion, was wary of Fynius and his men.

Bronwyn didn't understand. The Ranen were a strange bunch at the best of times – violent, stubborn, short-sighted – but with the appearance of the men from Ranen Gar they were reduced to fearful barbarians. Their axes, their rage, their allegiance – all were dissipated when faced with a company of true fighting men.

'He's fucking mental, y'know?' said Two Hearts, slumped on a cushion below the tree house.

'He's an ally,' replied Bronwyn.

Fynius had been with Dragneel for nearly an hour. They had talked quietly but had not conveyed anything to those who waited below.

'They follow Brytag,' offered Micah, resting his wounded leg on a tree stump. 'That makes them unpredictable.'

'He's got a lot of men,' said Hasim, swigging from a bottle of Ranen mead.

The four of them sat near a fire. The sun had disappeared and the cold whipped through the forest and made everyone sluggish.

'Five hundred won't scratch the surface, I'm afraid,' said Bronwyn, remembering the swarm of Red knights that had attacked Ro Hail.

'Things changed after you left,' said Hasim. 'But, you're right, five hundred is a lot for the Ranen . . . it's barely an army for the Ro. If you want to stop the king marching north, you'll need to equal his numbers, at the very least.'

Two Hearts laughed. A deep rumble that was barely recognizable as humour. His drug and alcohol intake had not slowed since Twilight Company had arrived.

'You've never met anyone from Old Gar, have you?' asked the chieftain.

'If you'd like to patronize the foreigners, be my guest,' said Micah, leaning forward. 'But I'm a man of Wraith.' He glared at Two Hearts.

The chieftain maintained eye contact for a second, assessing the young man.

'Fair enough,' he said. 'Why don't you educate these foreigners about Old Gar.'

'Why don't you shut up,' replied Micah, 'your voice grates.'

Two Hearts flopped forward on his cushion, blinking in order to focus clearly on Stone Dog.

'Do you want a slap, son?'

'From you? You can barely stand up,' replied Micah, showing no fear of the chieftain. 'Go and get half a dozen of your tattooed bastards, make it a fair fight.'

Bronwyn chuckled and they both looked at her.

'Micah, you're full of arrows. Federick, you're in another world. I could probably best either of you.'

Both the Ranen warriors looked wounded at the comment. Two Hearts pouted like a scolded child and Stone Dog sat open-mouthed.

'She's right,' offered Hasim, stamping his feet and rubbing his hands together. 'About more than you two.'

'When did I stop getting respect from visitors in my own woods?' asked Two Hearts. 'First, this madman from Gar, now a Ro bitch and her pet Karesian.'

Hasim, the only one of them standing up, casually strolled towards Two Hearts. 'You don't know me,' he said quietly. 'And you don't know Bronwyn. We are trying to help you, but you've got to earn respect.' He smiled. 'Call her a bitch or me a pet again, and we'll have a falling-out.'

It wasn't clear whether the Ranen chieftain heard the words. His eyes glazed over and with a vacuous smile he fell unconscious.

'Shame,' said Micah. 'I'd have liked to see his reaction to that. He might have cut your balls off.'

'He's an idiot,' replied Hasim.

'An idiot with a clan of nutcases fully prepared to cut your balls off,' said Stone Dog.

Without Two Hearts, their conversation became more friendly. Micah and Hasim bonded over a mutual dislike of the Moon clans. They told stories of what had happened since they were last together. Hasim had been wounded at the breach of South Warden, and Micah had been wounded fighting the people of the Crescent. They shared scars, told of individual opponents and no doubt made up all sorts of finer details. She had been with Micah during his fight and she didn't remember him besting ten men while defending Bronwyn and Dragneel. But she let it pass.

The three of them had travelled far together. From Canarn and Ro Hail. They'd fought in battles and they were still alive. She took a moment to appreciate that, listening to them chat and laugh, as if imagining a more peaceful time.

But still the raven cawed in the depths of her mind. It still wanted her to know something, to direct her in some way, but she couldn't understand it.

'It's funny watching you try to understand him,' said Fynius Black Claw, emerging from the tree house. 'Not everything can use words and meanings in the way you expect. Conversations are a decidedly human occupation.'

The captain of Twilight Company swung himself on to the ladder and slid to the ground. Hasim and Micah stopped chatting and both stood up.

'Are you seeing my thoughts?' asked Bronwyn. The possibility bothered her less than she might have expected.

'Only when Brytag tries to speak to you,' he replied, his sinister smile returning. 'Things are stranger than either of us realized, Lady Bronwyn of Canarn.'

'I don't understand him.'

'I know. So does he,' replied Fynius. 'Don't worry, he'll keep trying.'

'Please stop smiling, it's quite unnerving,' she said, looking away.

'Do I bother you?'

'Yes, you do.'

Hasim raised his hand. 'You bother me, too. If you care,' he said.

'I don't.' He turned his thin face towards the Karesian. 'What are you doing here, man of the sun? You're a long way from the lands of Jaa.'

'Circumstances have conspired against me,' replied Hasim.

Fynius looked at each of them in turn. He frowned at the unconscious body of Two Hearts, but smiled at the others. His manner was twitchy and she could see a barely contained mania in his eyes.

'How many Ro are on the Plains of Scarlet?' he asked.

'Friends or foes?' said Hasim.

'They are Ro, there is no difference,' replied the Ranen.

Hasim chuckled and drank some more mead. 'Well, there are five thousand knights that want to subjugate your land, and there are six thousand yeomanry that don't want to subjugate your land. So, I suppose there are eleven thousand Ro on the Plains of Scarlet.'

Fynius stopped smiling. His face assumed a grimace and he narrowed his eyes at Hasim. 'That's a lot of men.'

'Fallon of Leith commands the yeomanry and he is not your enemy,' said the Karesian.

'Who the fuck is Fally of Leith?' asked Fynius.

'Fallon. He's a knight of Ro,' answered Bronwyn. 'Apparently he is an enemy of the king.'

'Trust me, he's an enemy of the king,' offered Hasim. 'The bad news, if eleven thousand isn't bad enough, is that the Red general is on his way. That's another ten thousand knights at least.'

Fynius began to pace in front of them. His eyes darted from side to side and his arms wove strange patterns in the freezing air. His blue-stained leather coat dragged on the snowy ground and his broadsword swung as he walked.

'Eleven thousand, ten thousand,' he muttered. 'Five thousand, six thousand, the king, the knight, the general.'

He twitched, kicking his feet through the snow. He mumbled about Ro, Ranen, Twilight Company, Red knights. He acted as if he were speaking to someone, or something, throwing incomprehensible questions into the air.

They all looked at him. Superimposed across his back, she thought she saw black wings. For an instant they flared and disappeared.

'I think I will go to South Warden,' he said. 'Yes, that is my road.'

The others exchanged looks. Micah frowned, Hasim raised his eyebrows, only Bronwyn spoke. 'That is good to hear,' she said, 'but you are outnumbered.'

'So?' he replied, screwing his face up. 'I have the men I have.'

She smiled. The man from Ranen Gar was unstable but he was an ally. He was a Ranen and he was a follower of Brytag. Perhaps he was just what was needed.

'Could you get your brother to bring Greywood Company?' asked Micah. 'Just in case they're needed.'

Fynius smiled again. The expression covered half his face. 'Nah,' he said after a moment. 'I'll tell him what happened after it happens.'

'So, your plan?' she asked, hoping for a semblance of wisdom.

'Well, South Warden makes nice cheese, doesn't it?' he replied.

Hasim shrugged, shaking his head at Bronwyn.

'Yes, I believe it does,' offered Micah. 'Well, it used to. Hungry, are we?'

'Nope,' replied Fynius. 'Just thinking about things that the Red men wouldn't know. If they don't know about the cheese, it's unlikely they'd know about the massive tunnels used to mature the cheese.'

He's clever, she thought. Mad, but clever.

He ignored them and carried on talking to the air. Occasionally he'd laugh, chuckling at a joke only he could hear. He didn't leave them, or show any awareness that they were listening.

'Right!' he said suddenly. 'We have lots to do. You most of all, Lady Bronwyn of Canarn. Come with me.' He left, heading back to the ladder and Dragneel's deathbed.

CHAPTER THREE

HALLA SUMMER WOLF
AT THE BEAR'S MOUTH

F JORLAN WAS A realm at war. The Freelands of Ranen were being torn apart by foreign invaders and an alien god. Halla was a warrior, a follower of Rowanoco, and she was becoming a fine leader, but she could not predict what would happen to her homeland.

More than anything, she wanted to tell her men that they would win – that Alahan Teardrop would be a triumphant high thain, that Rulag Ursa would be killed, and that Fjorlan would remain free. In her quieter moments, with no one for company and the freezing air turning her thoughts dark, she wondered whether there was any point in fighting. Halla would never admit it, but she was afraid for Fjorlan. She was worried that spirit and honour were not sufficient and that Rulag Ursa's forces were too strong.

Even if they did win and all their hopes of freedom were achieved, she would still be faced with a young thain whose father had killed her father. The family of Teardrop had done little to secure the loyalty of Summer Wolf, but they were the best option available to a warrior with blood on her hands and with no end to the slaughter in sight. That her battle-brothers obeyed her without question almost made the situation worse. Only Rorg the Defiler questioned her and even he did so politely.

The Low Kast berserkers and their family of trolls had made no effort to integrate. They kept to themselves at the front of the company. When the day ended and they had found rocky ledges on which to sleep, Rorg kept his men active, sleeping only for an hour or two and scouting ahead. The troll's constant keening had not bothered Halla. Once she had grown used to it, the sound was almost calming. Only Lullaby spent time with the Ice Men and the strange old woman deflected a hundred questions from Wulfrick about the beasts. Falling Cloud and Oleff had taken to teasing the huge axe-master about his fear of trolls and it was only Halla's interference that had stopped her lieutenants coming to blows.

'It's not natural,' said Wulfrick.

They were nestled in a ravine less than a day's march from the Bear's Mouth. They had lit no fires and pitched no tents, hoping not to give away their position to the forces of Grammah Black Eyes.

'What's not natural?' asked Halla.

'Trolls eat men and men hunt trolls. They keep to the ice and we keep to the towns. It's just the way it is.'

Her company were picketed close together, with the men and beasts of the Low Kast a short distance away. The sun had disappeared and only stars illuminated the plateaus of Ursa. Anya Lullaby and Falling Cloud joined them, while Oleff and Heinrich saw to the nightly guard duty.

'Things are not always so absolute, young man,' offered Lullaby. 'The Ice Men have ways of talking to Rowanoco that we could never understand.'

'If they fight for Fjorlan, they stay,' said Halla, growing tired of Wulfrick's whingeing.

'For a big man, you're a proper little girl,' said Oleff, grinning like a fool.

'I don't see you making friends with them,' replied Wulfrick.

'Just shut up!' said Halla. 'I'm trying to think.'

'What have you got to think about?' asked Wulfrick. 'We kill any men of Ursa that don't get out of the way.'

'And we clear the Bear's Mouth . . . simple,' offered Falling Cloud.

'You worry too much, Halla,' said Wulfrick.

'And you two are dim-witted axe-hurlers who should leave the thinking to me,' she replied, smiling at them.

The two men looked at each other.

'It's a fair point,' said Falling Cloud. 'Okay, my lady, what are you thinking about?'

'The Bear's Mouth, the Wolf Wood, trolls, axes, Tiergarten – everything.'

'Why don't you turn your tactical genius to the subject of sleep,' said Wulfrick. 'We'll need it tomorrow, it should be well rested.'

* * *

The Bear's Mouth was an old fortress of rock and ice. In ancient tales, the Ice Giants carved it out of the bedrock of Fjorlan. The lords of Hammerfall looked to it as their deepest connection to Rowanoco, and no oppressor had ever used it before.

The deep fissure that ran from Hammerfall to Jarvik was a natural highway, largely free of trolls and bandits. This made the Bear's Mouth an ideal place for Grammah Black Eyes to base his brutal rule over the region. It was impassable, unless you wanted to traverse the spider tunnels beneath.

'I wish we had some more cloud-men,' murmured Falling Cloud, crouched next to Halla within sight of the fortress. 'Your lot don't know this ground.'

'You do,' replied Halla. 'You're my adviser, remember.'

He looked unimpressed.

'Tell me what I'm looking at, Rexel.'

He poked his head over a rock and surveyed the snowy ground ahead of them. The Mouth was arrayed on five levels, forming natural galleries in the rocky fissure. They were narrow and treacherous at the top, but wide and easily defensible at the base. The frozen river at the bottom was narrow and free-flowing only for a couple of months of the year, making travel by boat a risky endeavour.

'He's got a lot of men,' said Rexel, ducking back behind the rock. 'Wooden palisades, axe-hurlers.'

'Is there good news?' she asked.

'Of course.'

He craned his neck up again and peered further down the fissure.

'They're all looking in the other direction.' He smiled wickedly. 'They're expecting trouble from Hammerfall, not Jarvik.'

Halla joined him. She had to shield her eye from the glare, but she could see dark shapes moving across the stark white ground. The bottom level was a wooden fort of sorts, comprising a stockade and gate. Further up the fissure, axe-hurlers patrolled smaller wooden walls. Ladders and walkways, with a few solid structures, linked the levels. All of the fortifications pointed westwards, towards the Wolf Wood.

'That's a lot of men,' she said, losing count of the warriors below.

'We need to take the top levels,' he replied.

'Maybe a landslide,' mused Halla. 'They won't see us coming, so confusion could be an ally.'

'The Low Kasters and their pets could make an awful mess down there. So, send them in first?'

Halla considered it. 'Get Wulfrick up here,' she ordered.

Rexel nodded and skulked backwards. Behind them, waiting on the low ground, were five hundred battle-brothers. Lean and ready, they sat poised, weapons in hand, waiting for the word to attack. Hulking off to the side were the Low Kasters and the family of trolls. Even now they stayed away from the bulk of the forces, grunting to each other in their strange language.

'How's it looking?' asked Wulfrick, coming to join them.

The axe-master had to crawl to stay behind the rocks. He was not built for stealth, as he frequently told her.

'Have a look,' replied Halla. 'How outnumbered are we?'

He hefted his huge body along the ground until his head was poking up above the rocks. His bearded face contorted with surprise as he looked at the fortress in their way.

'Hard to tell how many are on the lowest level,' said Wulfrick. 'I think we can take them.'

Falling Cloud chuckled. 'If we're quiet, we can get men down to the top few levels. The fort at the bottom is the problem. Anyone approaching will be seen along the eastern gully.'

Halla thought for a moment. Wulfrick and Rexel continued talking, musing on the battle to come, and she tuned out their voices. Below, scurrying across her field of vision, was a huge force of Ursa's men. At least double her numbers, spread out across the Bear's Mouth.

'This is what we're going to do,' she said quietly.

Both men looked at her.

'Wulfrick, you and I will take a hundred men each and attack at the highest levels.' She pointed to the narrow platforms at the top of the fissure. 'You take the north, I'll take the south. Then we fight our way down.'

He grinned, nodding his head.

'Rexel, you and Oleff take another hundred each and attack three levels down.'

'That will surprise the shit out of them,' replied Falling Cloud. 'You two fight your way to us and we'll all go for the fort.'

'No, that's not the plan,' she said. 'Rorg and Unrahgahr can have the fort. Tell them to charge the eastern gully when we give the signal.'

Wulfrick snorted in surprise, coughing a gobbet of phlegm on to the snow.

'Perhaps we could do it without them, Halla,' he said.

'No. Whether you like it or not, they're part of the company,' she replied.

Slow nods from both men. Falling Cloud clenched his fists and Wulfrick gritted his teeth.

'Grammah Black Eyes will be in the fort. What do we know about him?' asked Wulfrick.

Rexel shook his head. 'He's a pig-fucking troll cunt.'

'It was a serious question,' snapped Halla.

'Sorry,' replied Rexel with a grin. 'Don't know much about him. One of Rulag's axe-masters. He used to raid the Wolf Wood and steal deep ice.'

'Well, hopefully, a troll will be gnawing on his skull in half an hour,' said Wulfrick.

Halla motioned for them to back away and return to the company. 'Get to it. Assemble with light armour only. And no shouting.'

'Aye, my lady,' they said in unison.

'Let's liberate Hammerfall, shall we?'

* * *

She crouched, using a slight overhang as cover. In front, warming their hands round flaming barrels, were battle-brothers of Ursa. The highest level of the Bear's Mouth was poorly guarded, with barely twenty men behind a low wooden wall. Across the chasm, Wulfrick faced a similar force.

The levels below, easily accessible from wide, sloping platforms, were more heavily guarded. Halla and Wulfrick's forces would have to kill several hundred men each before they reached Oleff and Rexel.

A deep breath, a growled command to charge, and they attacked. She glanced to her left and saw the huge axe-master of Fredericksand breaking cover with a dramatic swing of his axe. Below, more of her company appeared from behind rocks and hidden gullies, rushing the defenders in a sudden flood of sound and movement.

The Bear's Mouth was a defensive position, rather than a castle, and they attacked through no stockade or perimeter. The men of Ursa were unprepared and most were neither armed nor armoured. Halla killed three before any could raise a blade to parry her axe. The hundred men at her back swept across the top platform, meeting little resistance.

Blood and steel filled her field of vision. Across the fissure, Wulfrick barrelled men from the platform, sending them to a gruesome death on the rocks below.

The men of Ursa were driven back and killed, clearing the top level of the fortress. She reached the wooden stockade and paused, seeing no one left to kill and with blood in her eye. It had all happened quickly. Men had died and confused shouting had filled the air.

'The top levels are ours, my lady,' stated Heinrich Blood, the novice of the Order of the Hammer.

'Move down to the next level,' she commanded, rubbing her eye.

Her men were still fresh, their faces dripping with blood and conviction, as they ran for the sloping walkway leading downwards.

The Bear's Mouth was now alive with combat. On multiple levels men and axes clashed at close quarters, sending ice and snow across the chasm. Their flanking attack had taken a brutal toll and the men of Ursa struggled to hold their ground.

On the second level, though, the men were prepared. She still had the advantage of surprise but now the killing began in earnest.

'To arms,' roared a man of Ursa.

'Drive them back,' yelled another.

Halla grunted and swung for a man's neck. She turned quickly and sliced another across the chest. An arrow flew over her shoulder, then another lodged in a man's stomach to her left, as Heinrich joined her. Although they were armed, most of their opponents wore no armour. They were skilled and they did not give away their lives easily, but without steel to protect them their mistakes were fatal.

The ground was being churned up. The more they fought, the more snow and ice ran down the platforms and filled the Bear's Mouth. She couldn't see beyond the platform she was on and the snow now sent a spray across her field of vision.

A glaive appeared in front of her, held by a screaming man of Ursa. The jagged blade sawed downwards, narrowly missing her head but biting deeply into her left arm. She screamed in pain and crouched, swinging her axe upwards one-handed. The blade struck him between his legs and caused a spray of blood to erupt from his mouth.

She fell to the ground and grabbed her arm. 'Fuck!' she shouted, in annoyance more than pain.

Heinrich ran to her side and stood protectively with his bow drawn. 'You alive?' he asked.

'He mangled my arm. Bastard!' She gritted her teeth.

'Get up, we need to keep moving.'

She nodded and leant heavily on her good arm, passing Heinrich her axe. Blood smeared across the snow as she stood. The pain was sharp and biting, but she clenched her fists and shut it out. She grabbed her axe back and clutched her wounded arm to her chest. She'd been sliced across the biceps and could feel little strength in her hand.

'I can heal it when we're done,' said Heinrich. 'Just stay alive for now.'

Beneath her was Oleff Hard Head, one level down. He was at the front of his men, pushing the defenders back against their own wall. Hung from his belt was a curved horn.

'Oleff,' she shouted, 'signal Rorg!'

'Let's make a mess,' he bellowed in response.

The old chain-master disengaged, turning sharply and moving back along the platform. He wiped blood from his brow and placed the horn to his mouth. With a wink to Halla, he released a single, resonating note.

The horn rose above the sound of men fighting and dying. Halla leant against the rock, breathing heavily. Her men were still fighting on the second level and, like the defenders, they were too distracted to register the horn. They were dark shapes, flailing their arms and axes through the sheet of white. Across the chasm, when the wind cleared the snow, she could see the rest of her company. They had advanced deep into the Bear's Mouth and now held the upper levels.

The fort, at the base of the wide fissure, was alive with activity. Hundreds of men moved over wooden platforms and between large structures, running to reinforce their lines. All of their defences were pointed the other way and their artillery – ballistae and catapults – were too cumbersome to move quickly.

Everything changed when the keening started. Echoing along

the eastern gully, bouncing off the icy walls and displacing the
fog of snow, the sound of the trolls reached every ear. The noise
impinged on the minds of every man and woman of Fjorlan. It
was a noise they had been taught to fear.

'Varorg!'

The bellowed voice was a grunting snarl creating a harmony
with the keening. It was chased up the gully by the roar of the
berserker warriors. The defenders had time to see the Low Kasters
and their trolls but they spent most of that time staring in terrified
disbelief.

Halla's men were as dumbfounded as those of Ursa. They
paused, letting their axes fall, as the huge hairy shapes bounded
towards the fort.

'What are you looking at?' shouted Halla. 'You have killing
to do.'

She was impressed at the volume she could manage when
she meant it. Her words reached the two nearest levels and was
immediately obeyed. The defenders were now on the back foot.
They couldn't tear their eyes from the Ice Men and they died
quickly, their half-hearted parrying easily deflected.

'Hold this platform,' commanded Halla. 'Oleff! Don't get in
their way.'

He looked up at her and nodded, braining a man of Ursa with
the hilt of his axe. He blew a softer note on his horn, signalling
to Rexel and Wulfrick to hold their ground. The top platforms
were now theirs.

The pause allowed Halla and her men to observe the charge
along the eastern gully. The Ice Men, leaping over the snow on
all-fours, continued their keening. They moved as a dozen mounds
of dark fur, springing across rocks and clawing at the gully walls.
Unrahgahr was at the front, his tusks dripping with slobber, as he
plunged towards the unprepared men of Ursa. Several hundred
defenders were in the fort. Hundreds more swarmed across the
lower levels. They moved slowly, their bodies hesitant.

'Axes!' screamed a man of Ursa.

Axe-hurlers, standing ready on wooden platforms, shook their heads in confusion and amazement. They had armed themselves but their feet were unsteady.

'The ice halls beckon, lads,' shouted the same man, a rotund warrior in a fur-trimmed cloak.

Their survival instincts returned just in time. The trolls were close when the first volley of axes hit them. They bounced off their dense muscle or embedded into shallow cuts, but none of the Ice Men slowed. Unrahgahr received an axe to the chest which lodged in his fur, but he contemptuously plucked it from his body and threw it aside. Blades did not scare them.

'Again,' commanded the rotund man of Ursa, but his men didn't react quickly enough.

The trolls had reached the outer platforms, dragging axe-hurlers to the ground with their huge, bulbous limbs. The men were battered against rock, sending pulpy red body parts into the air. The next line of men tried to brace themselves behind spears but the charge didn't slow. Unrahgahr ignored two spear thrusts to his face, splintering the wooden shafts with minimal effort and clubbing the spearmen to death. He struck them as a smith would strike an anvil, flattening them against the snow and leaving their bodies a broken mass of red.

The fort was of solid construction and forced the Ice Men to slow down. A mass of warriors stood, a sea of armour and steel, ready for the trolls. Axes were thrown and groups of men gathered to surround the beasts.

'Halla, they're turning their ballistae,' said Heinrich.

She sheltered her eye from the glare. Men of Ursa were hurriedly manoeuvring huge wooden frameworks, sighting the thick arrows along the eastern gully.

'Let's get down there.'

She waved to the nearest men and word spread quickly. They formed up in a loose column and moved down the sloping platform towards Oleff Hard Head.

Beneath them, Rorg and his berserkers had reached the fort.

The howling madmen of Varorg leapt at the defenders with suicidal ferocity, biting, kicking and headbutting. Their powerful axes, made of deep ice, sliced through armour with ease, leaving jagged, smouldering cuts. Their broken skulls pulsed and split, their faces covered with a mantle of bloody insanity. There were few of them, but, like the trolls, they made an almighty mess.

'To the ballistae, my lady?' asked Oleff.

The two warriors met on the third platform, halfway down the fissure. All around them lay bodies, bloodied and cleaved. A handful of their men had died but they were few compared with the lifeless forms of the defenders.

'Aye,' she replied, hugging her wounded arm to her chest.

'You okay?' asked Oleff. 'That looks nasty.'

'To the ballistae,' she said, ignoring his question.

Across the Bear's Mouth, Wulfrick waved his axe high above his head, signalling that their side was clear. So far, the plan was working.

Below, the trolls were now tearing their way through wooden walls and butting into structures. They reached within, grabbing men as if they were dolls and pulling them into the open to be eaten or hacked apart by the Low Kasters.

One of the smaller Ice Men was surrounded, penned in by spears and distracted by heavy rocks thrown from above. If Halla didn't get to the artillery, the trolls would begin to falter. On open ground they were unstoppable, but within wooden structures and narrow quarters they were easily distracted. Already one of them had lost his bearings and run back along the gully, confused as to where he was.

Oleff stayed close to her as they led their men down to a solid wall of defenders. Wulfrick and Falling Cloud did the same and the two forces now flanked the bottom levels.

The rotund man, commanding his troops, locked eyes with Halla. Across dead bodies and broken wood she saw a pair of black eyes.

'Easy, lads,' shouted Grammah Black Eyes. 'We can hold them.'

He didn't turn his gaze from Halla as he spoke. 'Ballistae! Bring the trolls down.'

The huge, wooden frames flexed. Three artillery pieces fired, one after the other, sending massive arrows along the gully. They flew over the fort and found their mark. One troll was barrelled backwards with a shaft clean through his chest. Another went flying into the rocky wall of the gully as his leg was torn apart. The third killed one of Rorg's men, cutting him in two.

Neither of the trolls was dead. They sat on the ground, looking in surprise at the huge arrows stuck in their bodies, but they were no longer mobile.

'Move,' commanded Halla, pushing her men forward.

They hit a wall of circular shields and were stopped. The defenders were too many. The initial assault had caught them by surprise but they had not panicked at the sight of the charging Ice Men and they now held their ground. Getting to the fort would take time and Rorg's company was now dangerously isolated.

The trolls had faltered. Some appeared lost, others sat on the ground, grabbing any men that came close, but not advancing. More ballistae bolts hit them. The huge arrows weren't designed to kill the beasts, just to slow them down and cause confusion. Some had bells attached, others trailed wire nets. The men of Ursa were skilled at dealing with the Ice Men. Unrahgahr, more aware than his family, was crouched behind a wall. He surveyed the scene and bellowed.

Halla ignored the pain in her arm and redoubled her efforts, joining Oleff and flinging herself at the shield wall in front of them. She rammed her shoulder into a braced shield and swung her axe under it, severing the man's foot and creating an opening. Spears cut her in the shoulder, neck and across her legs, but she grunted and kept going.

'With me!' she shouted.

Oleff dived through the opening behind her, hacking at the shield-bearers and entering a dense melee of defenders. He pulled

Halla away from a dozen spear thrusts and kept them at bay with wide swings of his battleaxe. He cut at wood and flesh, and was cut badly in turn.

Heinrich joined them as more of their company pushed into the gap. Halla stood, blood flowing over her body, sticking to her hands and dripping into her eye. But she didn't stop.

'Fight for Fjorlan! For Teardrop and Summer Wolf!' Her words were primal.

Men died, body parts flew and blood flowed. She was at the front of a wedge of men, splintering the shield wall and driving towards the fort. Her axe felt light and she swung it easily with one hand, making circles in the air. There were too many men to engage individuals and her company could only hack at passing targets and hope their advance would continue. To stop amidst so many enemies would mean certain death.

She couldn't see beyond the men in front of her. Bearded faces came and went in a blur of shouting and dying. She felt blood and pain, but they didn't slow her.

Then her boots struck wood and they had reached the fort, penetrating the dense mass of defenders. Over her shoulder she saw the broken shield wall fleeing west down the gully. They had routed several hundred men of Ursa with the sheer suicidal aggression of their attack.

With no one in front of her, she allowed Oleff to drag her behind a splintered wooden wall. She caught her breath.

'Look at this,' panted Oleff, pointing over the barricades at the fleeing men.

Halla saw axes fly from cover, killing the men of Ursa as they retreated. She couldn't see who threw them, but they came from dozens of places at once. Behind rocks, within caves, filling the air with whirling blades.

'For Hammerfall!' The voice was guttural and carried down the gully.

From the direction of the Wolf Wood, cloud-men appeared, hundreds of them.

'Reinforce the walls,' commanded Grammah Black Eyes, as the men of Hammerfall charged the wooden stockade.

The artillery was pointed the other way and few men remained on the defensive wall, allowing the cloud-men to swarm the defences. Like Falling Cloud, they wielded small axes and relied on speed as much as on strength, severing arteries and limbs.

'You're outflanked,' shouted Wulfrick from the second level. 'Surrender!'

Grammah and his men were now isolated inside the fort. Either side of them, Halla's battle-brothers held the lower platforms. To the east, trolls slumped in the snow, pulling arrows from their bodies and annihilating anyone who approached. To the west, over their defences, cloud-men pushed them back. It was a hopeless fight now and Grammah knew it.

'Enough,' shouted the thain of Hammerfall. 'Enough, we surrender.'

Halla slumped to the ground and let her head rock back against the wooden wall. She heard shouting, fighting, axes thrown to the ground and the pained keening of wounded trolls. Even with the surrender, the combat ended slowly. Men filled with bloodlust did not back down easily.

'I think we won,' said Oleff, slumped next to Halla. 'And I think I need a rest.'

She smiled and rocked her head to the side, looking at her friend. She stopped smiling when she saw his wounds. His chest was a canvas of red, with blood seeping from every gap in his chain mail.

'Don't rest here,' she said, turning to cradle his head as he lolled forward. 'You can't rest here. We need to stay awake.'

'I don't think I can,' he replied, a peaceful smile coming over his grizzled face.

'Heinrich!' she shouted, her voice cracking with emotion. 'I need help.'

She held Oleff's hand. It was clammy and stained a muddy

red. She tried to unbuckle his chain mail but the blood made everything stick together.

Heinrich appeared. He stood over them, breathing rapidly. 'I . . . I don't think I can help,' whispered the young novice.

'What? No, you must be able to. Help me get his chain mail off.'

'Halla,' said Oleff, grasping her hand firmly. 'Let me go. I could do with a drink and they say the ice halls have the best ale . . .'

With a serene expression on his face, Oleff Hard Head, chain-master of Fredericksand, left to join the Ice Giants in their halls beyond the world.

* * *

She had lost a hundred and twenty-three men. Her company was battered and exhausted, but they couldn't rest. They had four hundred prisoners to secure and Halla had a deposed thain to deal with. Dozens of wounded men on both sides needed attention, and Lullaby and Heinrich were busy with their healing salves, bandages and their strange craft.

The trolls were having the huge ballistae bolts removed from their bodies, though they didn't stop keening and appeared not to care, or even notice, that they were wounded. Rorg and his berserkers had lost men, but they were highly exhilarated by the combat, screaming battle cries and declarations of glorious victory. Tending to their wounded would have to wait until they'd finished shouting.

Wulfrick was largely unhurt, but Rexel Falling Cloud had lost an ear and Halla needed bandages and a new walking stick. Her wounds had not been too deep but she had lost a lot of blood and found it difficult to stand. Heinrich had seen to her arm but she would be unlikely fully to recover its use.

'My Lady Summer Wolf, I thank you on behalf of Hammerfall.'

The cloud-man was called Moniac Dawn Cloud. He'd been scouting the Bear's Mouth, waiting for the right time to attack, when Halla's charge had given him his opportunity. With the artillery pointing the other way and the men of Ursa fully occupied, his force of three hundred had broken their lines. He was young, with delicate features, but lean and muscled. He held the rank of axe-master and had assembled a mixed company from handfuls of cloud-men who had not yet been cowed by Grammah and his men.

'I did it for Hammerfall, and I did it for Fjorlan,' she replied. 'And your help is appreciated.'

They were sitting in a long wooden hall in the centre of the fort. They had found food, ale, cold-weather clothing and all manner of essential supplies. Grammah Black Eyes was restrained against the far wall and Halla and her lieutenants were now to decide his fate.

'The bastard razed the Wolf Wood,' said Rexel, clutching a wadded bandage to his ear. 'For that alone he should die.'

'His men killed Oleff, that's enough for me,' offered Wulfrick.

'I claim his head for my people,' said Moniac, snarling at Grammah.

The man of Ursa was hugely overweight. His bear-skin cloak barely covered his belly and his black eyes conveyed no emotion.

'I served my thain,' said Grammah. 'I accept any justice the Ice Giant dispenses. But you have no priest.'

Halla stood up from the bench. Her arm was in a sling and her hand grasped a walking stick. Her right leg was numb and she winced each time she put weight on it.

'You are right,' she said, hobbling towards the thain. 'We have no priest. But you can't hide behind that.'

She endured the pain and discarded her walking stick. Drawing her axe, she stood close to Grammah.

'I'm going to kill you, thain of Hammerfall. Say your words.'

His face twisted into a defiant frown. 'I have lived well. I am strong and I served with honour. Let it be your axe that ends me, Daughter of the Wolf.'

She raised her weapon and bought it down on Grammah's neck. The blade sheared into his flesh and blood seeped from his mouth. His black eyes didn't flicker as he died.

'This isn't a victory,' she said to the others. 'It's just a step on the road. We have many leagues to travel and many battles to fight before this will be a victory.'

'So, let's raise a mug,' said Wulfrick, reaching for a bottle of mead. 'Let's raise a mug to the journey, the battles and the victory.'

'Aye,' agreed Falling Cloud.

'And to Oleff and the men we lost,' said Halla, taking a mug of mead.

With the drip of Grammah's blood in the background, they drank deeply.

'There are many halls in the Wolf Wood,' she said. 'Many men between here and Tiergarten. We will visit every hall and give every man the chance to join us.'

CHAPTER FOUR

GWENDOLYN OF HUNTER'S CROSS IN THE CITY OF RO TIRIS

THE SEA WALL of Ro Tiris was a marvel of engineering. Twelve huge stone pillars rose from the water, connected by heavy wooden beams, wrapped in chains. Daganay said that the wall took twenty years to build, with the greatest artisans of Ro working only at low tide. The wood rose and fell as the tide dictated, breaking the waves before they could disrupt the capital's shipping. The only routes in and out of the king's dock were two narrow channels either side of the wall, covered from above by catapults. The channels were big enough for large ships, but only in single file, and a wise captain knew to sail slowly to keep clear of the wall. Now they were going to blow it up and sail straight for the king's dock.

Their force had grown significantly since visiting Canarn, and Gwen was now part of an army of seven thousand men and Dokkalfar, spread across twenty ships. The *Wave Runner*, Xander's flagship, was at the front of a close formation that spread behind them to form an arrowhead pointing towards Ro Tiris. Brom was on the nearest escort ship, marshalling his own men and trying to convey his sympathy to the seasick forest-dwellers. They were not accustomed to sea travel and found the whole idea of boats bewildering.

Xander himself stood at the prow of their ship and, in consequence, at the head of the entire army. He grasped a wooden beam and stared at the rapidly approaching city. He had said little since they had left Canarn, confiding in Daganay alone. Even when he came to bed, husband and wife communicated only through their unspoken language. Looks, gestures and physical contact were enough to let Gwen know that he was tightly wound up. To sail a battle fleet into the harbour of Ro Tiris was to betray his family, his country and his god, but the Red Prince was stubborn. He had decided that if no one else was going to do it, then he must.

The city before them was as tall as it was wide, nestled in a shallow bay and defended by high battlements set back from the sea. Although most of the Red knights were in Ranen, Tiris was still filled to the rafters with guardsmen and watchmen, making it a difficult prize. She could see the white Spire of the King and the top of the Red cathedral. From both flew a new banner, of black with the image of a twisted tree.

'Captain Brennan!' shouted the lookout. 'We have a clear run to the sea wall.'

The wall loomed before them, a huge floating wooden barrier that arced round the city's two harbours.

'Artillery? Ships?' asked Brennan.

'Looks like . . . hmm, catapults on the channel defences, a few more overlooking the king's dock. Some ships at harbour in Northwind Bay. The main harbour's clear. Shit-loads of watchmen, sir.'

Brennan nodded. 'Well, they can see us coming, they know what we're coming to do, let's fucking do it!' He shouted a few commands and Sergeant Ashwyn rang a bell, alerting all the men to stand to. The bell was picked up and continued on the nearest ships and flowed across the fleet as a dull, echoing command.

Daganay appeared from below deck and, with a huge yawn, joined them. 'We there yet?' he asked, rubbing his eyes.

'Almost,' replied Gwen.

'You know, a Blue chaplain I once knew said that the sea wall of Tiris was the greatest wonder of the world. Engineering that showed the Ro were the finest craftsmen and artisans in the lands of men.'

'Well, we're going to blow it up,' offered Brennan.

Daganay frowned. 'No romance, that's the problem with soldiers nowadays.'

Gwen chuckled. 'Dag, go and make sure he hasn't fallen into a trance.'

'Yes, my lady.'

Daganay, almost as unsure on board the ship as the Dokkalfar, rolled forward, his arms spread wide to stabilize himself and his feet tentative. When he reached Xander, the general was shaken out of his contemplation and looked momentarily surprised at being addressed.

The forward catapults were being loaded and the Hawks on board were armed and ready for combat. They had not yet reconciled themselves to the fact that they would be fighting other men of Ro, and it showed in their faces. They were armed with heavy short swords and carried sturdy, rectangular shields. Each man had segmented steel armour, worn for its flexibility and lightness, and their greaves were of hardened leather.

After a moment of conversation between the two men, Xander pulled himself atop a catapult mount and turned back to address the crew.

'Brothers!' His words carried across the wooden deck. 'This city flies a banner not of Ro. These men will fight and they will die, but make no mistake, we are liberators, not conquerors.'

Salutes and shouts from the Hawks indicated that his words were needed.

'The faster we move, the faster the bloody work will be done,' he continued. 'Brennan, raise the forward ram and signal Brom to do the same. Ashwyn, sight the catapults at the sea wall. Tyr Sigurd, prepare to light your fuses.'

'Aye, sir,' shouted Brennan and Ashwyn in unison. Sigurd just tilted his head.

'And raise the hawk,' said Xander, indicating his banner, currently flying at half-mast.

With quick and practised movements the flag was raised and men began to winch the metal apparatus that raised the ram. Behind them, Brom received the signal and his men did the same, though their banner was of a raven in flight. The winch clicked into place and a huge iron protrusion now jutted from the *Wave Runner.*

Gwen imagined what the men and women of Tiris would see and how they would feel. Two banners of Ro, of Haran and Canarn, sailing towards them. A fleet of men, shouting and aiming catapults. Some would be glad, others angry . . . she doubted any would not be terrified.

'How long?' Brennan asked Tyr Sigurd, as he and his forest-dwellers touched flames to short fuses protruding from wax-sealed barrels of black wart. Two barrels sat in the cradle of each catapult and most of the men of Ro were afraid to approach them.

'You should use your contraptions straightaway,' replied the Dokkalfar, pointing at the catapults. 'Once the fuse is within the barrel they are watertight, and water will aid the explosion.'

'Whatever you say,' replied Brennan. 'General! Catapults ready, sir.'

Xander, still standing on the frame of a loaded catapult, turned back to the sea wall. They were close now. With a calm sea and a gentle following wind, they sailed between stone pillars and straight for the heavy wooden beams. 'Announce our presence, captain,' said the general.

'Fire!' commanded Brennan.

The artillery crews, wincing at the explosive barrels, gladly unloaded their catapults. The wooden frames jerked and Xander jumped to the deck as four barrels arced away from the *Wave Runner.* Thousands of men – warriors across twenty ships, and anyone watching from the city – saw the barrels fly. They flashed into clear blue sky before plummeting back into the shadow of Ro Tiris and towards the sea wall. They hit the water and lolled against heavy wood and chains.

'This will announce our presence,' stated Tyr Sigurd as all four barrels detonated.

It started as a crack and a flash of white light, erupting outwards in a dome. The water magnified the explosion and the two stone towers, anchoring the wooden wall, crumbled outwards in a spray of masonry and water. The wood was reduced to splinters in the centre and flying planks of flaming wood at the edges. When the smoke and debris had cleared an entire section of the sea wall, wider than either of the shipping channels, was reduced to burning wood and twisted metal. The greatest monument of Ro irreparably damaged in one moment of fire and noise.

The *Wave Runner* crested a rising swell as the shock wave reached them, flowing under the fleet as a breaking ripple. Bells were rung and the fleet redeployed, narrowing their formation to funnel into the king's dock.

'Give me some speed,' ordered Xander.

Brennan shouted orders and men scrambled to their places in the rigging, pulling ropes and unfurling sails, making the ship lurch towards the ruined sea wall. The ships behind followed suit and the fleet accelerated to ramming speed. Gwen held on to a taut rope as they approached the smoking ruin. The wood was burned to the water-line and their ram cleared any debris with ease, until they breached the wall and entered the king's dock.

This was her first close-up sight of Ro Tiris. It was huge compared with Haran, and sat behind high walls of grey stone and acres of wooden docks. The battlements above the main gate swarmed with watchmen and hundreds more ran from Northwind Bay, clattering across wooden platforms to a long barricade. The channel defences had been turned and the catapults now pointed towards the harbour. They were well out of range, but still their crews loaded and fired. Boulders splashed harmlessly into the bay as the rest of their ships passed the collapsing sea wall and into the huge harbour beyond.

'So far, so good, general,' shouted Brennan. 'Just walls and men to deal with now.'

'Reload those catapults,' ordered Xander. 'Sight them at the gates.'

Sigurd and his Dokkalfar left the catapults and Hawks of Ro reloaded with heavy boulders. They cranked the frames forward and sighted them along a level plane.

Once past the sea wall, the fleet spread out again, forming a fast-moving wedge, pointed at the huge wooden dock platforms. More bells rang as commands travelled across the ships and men prepared for combat.

'Barricade before the gate, general,' said Brennan. 'Few hundred men.'

'Pull in sails,' boomed Xander. 'Brace for impact.'

The dock snaked into the water, resting on solid wooden pillars. The stone waterfront began well back from the dock and, as the *Wave Runner* slowed, it ploughed into wooden planks. The ram sliced into the jetties, sending more splinters across the deck and gradually bringing the ship to a halt.

There was a moment of silence. Or maybe she just imagined it was silence. It was certainly stillness. A spray of wood and water had reduced her vision for a second and she could only see Daganay and a dozen Hawks. When the air cleared, she saw hundreds of faces – nervous men of Ro aiming crossbows with shaking hands. They crouched behind a barricade on the stone waterfront, guarding the gates of their city. Then more ships smashed into the wooden platforms, bringing back chaos and noise. Twenty ships laden with warriors, weapons, catapults and supplies stopped before the walls of Ro Tiris.

'To arms!' Xander drew Peacekeeper and was the first to leap from the ship. He landed on hardened wood and was followed by two hundred Hawks from the *Wave Runner*. They slid down broken planks and flooded on to the dock, their voices rising in primal roars of challenge.

Gwendolyn and Daganay looked at each other and joined them, vaulting from the ship. Bells sounded all around – from their ships, indicating the attack, and from the city, signalling the defence.

Crossbow bolts flew from the barricade and men fell, but the Hawks kept moving. From other ships more feet hit the wood and the attack began. They swarmed the barricade from all sides, meeting little resistance. Xander leapt at a guardsman, cleaving in his skull with a powerful downward stroke. Brennan kicked a crossbow from a man's hand and ran him through. Gwen and Daganay, a little way behind the others, engaged a small group of armoured men. Even as the white eagle of Tiris fronting their chain mail turned blood red, the battle had a sour note to it. Ro fought Ro and, however just their cause, their enemies were not the men before them. Their enemies were skulking behind high walls and letting common folk do their fighting.

The barricade was overturned by the Hawks and those guardsmen not already dead ran for the city walls. Over their heads, the *Wave Runner* launched two boulders at the city gates, firing horizontally. The gates were solid and reinforced with metal but they had not been tested by catapults for hundreds of years.

The initial surge was too much for the guardsmen. Once the Hawks had fought beyond the barricade and on to the wooden dock, the defenders were completely routed. Thousands of warriors – Hawks of Ro, men of Tiris, and Dokkalfar – now formed up and advanced.

Once again, she felt for the citizens of Ro Tiris. Not the watchmen or the clerics, but the ordinary folk, huddling behind shutters, seeing an army arrive at their city gates.

'Lock shields and advance,' commanded Xander, pulling Brennan over the barricade to join him on the dock.

Just behind, Bromvy and Tyr Sigurd had caught up with them. The Dokkalfar of Canarn did not mingle with the Hawks but were formed into a tight mob, each Tyr wielding two heavy leaf-blades.

'Smooth,' said Brom to Gwen. 'I think they call that a frontal assault.' The young lord had his sword in hand and blood dripped from the blade, showing that he had not been too late to join the initial attack.

'Your general is direct,' offered Sigurd, 'but effective.'

'He's angry,' replied Gwen. 'He can be very direct when he's angry.'

'Maybe we should take cover,' said Daganay, as crossbow bolts began to thud into the wooden dock around them.

Joining the advancing army, they caught up with Xander and ran to reach the walls. Men fell from rocks and crossbow bolts, but the armies of Haran and Canarn were too many and reached the walls of Tiris in quick time. The shield formation moved to cover them and they spread out along the base of the wall either side of the huge gates.

The catapult crews aboard the *Wave Runner* had stopped firing for a moment, allowing the army to reach the walls, but now they aimed and sighted with care. Both catapults fired together, sending huge boulders over the dock and into the gates of Ro Tiris.

'Again,' roared Xander, waving Peacekeeper at the catapult crews.

Another volley. The gates creaked and wooden splinters went flying, but the metal struts held firm, barring their passage. Two flanking ships aimed their catapults and the additional support – six large stone boulders in total – smashed the top half of the wooden gates to pieces. The metal bands kept the wood intact and there was no viable breach.

'Hold, lads,' commanded Brennan. 'Keep those shields up.' His words were punctuated by the thud of rocks thrown from above and impacting on the raised shields.

'We can't stay here long,' said Brom, hugging the wall next to Gwendolyn. 'They'll have hot oil and pitch.'

'The gates will give,' replied Xander stubbornly. 'Again!' he shouted.

Just as Gwen was beginning to doubt the wisdom of their frontal assault, the catapults fired again. They were well aimed and caused a huge cloud of dust and splinters to fly up, and there was a thud as the boulders landed in the stone street beyond.

Her ears rang. Once the dust had cleared, the gates were gone. The metal had buckled and skeletal remnants of wood hung limply either side of the stone gateway.

'Brennan, lock shields and advance. I want to know what's inside,' ordered the general.

'Tight formation!' shouted the captain, and a hundred men of the first cohort assumed a defensive posture, locking their rectangular shields into a solid protective block. Rocks were still being thrown down from above and crossbow bolts fired, but they only struck the raised shields as Brennan moved the cohort towards the open gateway.

'Steady!' he commanded from within the tight formation.

The shell of Hawks advanced and halted, slamming their shields to the ground and maintaining their defensive position. Xander motioned for men to follow and moved quickly behind the formation, keeping his head low and Peacekeeper high. Brom joined him and the two lords of Tor Funweir peered through the open gateway.

'Sigurd,' said Brom. 'Think you can get up to the battlements?'

'Most definitely,' replied the Dokkalfar, thrusting out his chin.

Gwen stayed back, hugging the wall with Daganay under a ceiling of interlocked shields. She could not see any defensive assault from within the walls, and Brennan's advance cohort had not been attacked with either blades or bows. Whoever was guarding the inner courtyard had allowed the formation to advance into the gateway.

'I am the Red Prince of Ro Haran,' shouted Xander, addressing whoever was there. 'We are the Hawks of Ro. Stand down and you will not be harmed. The city that bears my name is now under my protection.'

'Prince Alexander!' came a response. 'This is Cardinal Severen. By what right do you sail an army into the king's dock?'

Daganay spat at the man's name. 'I hate Purple clerics,' he said through gritted teeth.

Gwen moved forwards, motioning for the Blue cleric to follow, and the two of them crouched behind the advance cohort. Beyond the shattered gates, wooden barricades circled the inner courtyard, blocking their passage into the city streets. Overhead the white Spire of the King and the clenched fist of the Red cathedral competed to dominate of the skyline. Hundreds of steel and leather helmets poked above the barricades and many more men skulked on rooftops and battlements. Some aimed crossbows, some brandished blades and spears. The urban warriors of Tiris were professionals, but they were not an army.

'Where's the cardinal hiding?' mused Daganay, pointing to a statue. 'I think I see purple over there.'

The statue was of a Gold cleric, gleefully hefting bags of coin.

'We are not here to sack the city, cardinal,' replied Xander in a shout. 'We are here to liberate it from the Seven Sisters.'

Severen's response was a virtual shriek. 'Lord Archibald Tiris commands here. Your actions mark you as a traitor, Prince Alexander. We will never betray our beloved allies.'

Gwen followed his voice and saw a small group of purple-clad warriors behind the statue. They were beyond the barricades, protected by lesser clerics, with their backs to the knight marshal's office.

'General!' she shouted to her husband. 'The cleric speaks from the gold statue.'

'Advance!' commanded Xander, without replying.

The first cohort, still locked in tightly behind their shields, spread out and covered the entranceway as two more cohorts moved to join them. Behind, the army had moved on to the stone waterfront and was holding position behind shield walls. Tyr Sigurd and two dozen forest-dwellers of Canarn had disappeared along the outer wall.

'Keep it tight,' shouted Brennan, as the first few hundred Hawks cleared the gateway and entered Ro Tiris.

'This advance stops when you surrender,' said Xander. 'Don't make us kill any more men of Ro. And don't make me kill you.'

They were now within the courtyard, their steel-shod boots clattering on the cobbled ground.

Shouting from the guardsmen. Orders were passed and men moved quickly to strengthen the barricades. Those on high ground fired crossbows against the shield wall and others prepared cauldrons of boiling oil.

A scream came from above and a guardsman fell to the cobbles, his head severed from his body. More bodies fell as Tyr Sigurd and the Dokkalfar swept across the battlements.

'Risen men!' screamed a man of Ro. 'Monsters, risen to haunt us.'

The forest-dwellers made no noise and Gwen had to crane her neck to see them. They whirled and cartwheeled across the stone, killing men with inhuman efficiency.

'Kill the creatures,' ordered Severen, emerging from cover with his fellow clerics.

The first cohort sped up. With no more crossbow bolts or pitch to concern them, they quickly reached the far barricade. In front, the main road led away from the harbour, past the knight marshal's office, to the white Spire of the King and the House of Tiris.

'Last chance,' roared Xander, as the first cohort halted.

'We will fight to the last man,' replied Severen, making himself visible for the first time.

The Purple cardinal of Ro Tiris, second only to Mobius of the Falls, was a tall man, well armoured in gold and steel, with a broken nose and a lame right arm.

'Don't be a fucking fool,' shouted Daganay, unleashing his frustration. 'Don't die for an enchantress.'

'She loves us!' shrieked the cardinal. 'Kill them all.'

Many guardsmen were hesitant, seeing the Hawks flooding into their city, but a few of the most loyal and committed followed the cardinal's orders. The flanking barricades burst open and the warriors of Ro Tiris rushed the attackers.

'Break into wings!' ordered Xander.

The first cohort parted, forming two wings, spreading either side of the general in a V shape. They met the oncoming guardsmen with locked shields and thrusting swords, dropping a dozen men in the first clash. Behind, more Hawks advanced to cover their flanks, driving their opponents back. The defenders screamed orders as they tried to fight back, but the Hawks methodically blunted their efforts.

Hundreds of men of Tiris were running, abandoning their posts and fleeing from the attackers. The Purple clerics shouted at those who were retreating, threatening a gruesome death for all deserters, but their words were not heard.

Gwen stood with Xander and Brom at the front. The Purple clerics had advanced, with only men and a low wooden barricade between them.

'Clear the front,' shouted Xander.

The Hawks holding the point rushed forward, parting to allow their general to advance. Brennan leapt atop the wood, slamming back a guardsman with a heavy bash of his shield. Brom went the other way, shoulder-charging a man off the barricade.

Things became chaotic. They were at the front of the attack now, fighting a solid block of men. Gwen, Daganay and the others fought either side of Xander, helping him push towards the clerics. Their advance was measured, with attacks coming from between shields. Only Brom and Xander fought in the open, sweeping across the wooden barricade towards the gold statue.

She ducked a spear thrust and saw the defender killed by a Hawk to her left. She returned the favour a moment later, slicing the neck of a man attacking Daganay. They fought as one, each man defending those around him.

'Prince Alexander!' shouted Severen. 'You will die for this.'

The cardinal was holding a jewelled longsword in his left hand. It was evident that the man was incapable of fighting effectively with a lame sword arm.

Xander broke the line of guardsmen and engaged a Purple cleric, grasping Peacekeeper in both hands and thrusting it through the man's chest. Behind him, the wedge of Hawks had smashed their way through the defences and most of the guardsmen were now retreating.

'Fight, you cowards,' screamed Severen. 'Fight for our beloved allies.'

Gwen paused, watching the cardinal through the melee. She was protected by a shield to her left and took aim carefully. Her leaf-blade cut the air between them, over Xander's shoulder, to lodge in Severen's neck. He fell, clutching at the blade and flapping his arms.

'We are the Hawks of Ro. Stand down or die,' bellowed Captain Brennan.

Xander and Brom reached the clear street. Hundreds of Hawks followed, their interlocked shields covering any possibility of the defenders rallying for a counter-attack.

'Stand down!' repeated Xander.

Spears and swords were thrown to the ground. Men dropped to their knees and begged for mercy. It was a disordered surrender, but it was enough. The Hawks held position, a line of shields creating a semicircle round the gateway. The ground had been taken and the soldiers of Haran and Canarn now flooded into the city and on to the battlements.

'Secure the gate, Brennan,' ordered Xander, more calmly now. 'And gather those that surrendered.'

He stepped over a dead cleric and approached Cardinal Severen, sprawled on the road.

'Brom, Daganay, you're with me,' said Xander. He turned to his wife and smiled thinly. With a gentle beckoning gesture, he motioned her to come to him.

Gwen tuned out the sounds of dying men and metal-clad soldiers. She stood face to face with Xander, inspecting a deep cut to his cheek.

'Still alive, my love?' she asked.

'Tired, but alive,' he replied. 'Give me a kiss.'

She held his head gently and planted a deep kiss on his mouth.

Closing her eyes, she tasted blood on his lips and salty sweat.

'That was a good throw,' he said, turning towards Severen.

Their moment of calm passed and they returned to the bloody cobblestones of Ro Tiris. Brom and Daganay were with them, both cleaning blood from their weapons. The four warriors stood round Cardinal Severen. He was alive, but gasping for breath, with Gwen's leaf-blade lodged deeply in his neck.

'I did my duty,' spluttered Severen. 'I did only what she wanted.' His eyes were wide and manic. 'She loves us and we love her.'

'It's not your fault, brother,' said Daganay, kneeling down next to his fellow cleric. 'Your mind is not your own. We follow the One . . . as you once did.'

There was conflict in the dying man's eyes.

'Die easy, Cardinal Severen of Tiris,' said Daganay, closing the man's eyes as he stopped breathing.

* * *

Gwen stood behind Xander and Brom as the two lords of Tor Funweir flung open the doors to the House of Tiris. Gold-armoured king's men guarded the royal compound. They did not throw down their swords, but backed away and allowed the first cohort of Ro Haran to advance without a fight. Within, they strode across carpeted floors, trailing blood and dirt into the opulent building.

'Cousin!' shouted Xander. 'Do you want me to drag you out from under your bed or will you come and stand before me?'

They fanned out, creating alarm among the household servants, who dropped whatever they were doing and fled into the palace, hiding behind doors and cowering under furniture.

Brom puffed out his cheeks and sank into a padded chair, cocking a leg over the arm. 'Can't he hurry up, we've been on our feet for a while?'

'Is there any wine?' asked Daganay, looking at a gold-inlayed table.

'Er, yes,' replied Brom, reaching for a crystal decanter.

The lord of Canarn winced, rubbing his chest where a glancing sword blow had split his armour. He loosened the shoulder strap and pulled away a broken metal section.

Daganay strolled over to him and assisted in pouring two glasses of wine. 'Anyone else?' asked the cleric.

A few Hawks smiled and looked hopefully at their general.

'Sorry, lads, 'tis the privilege of clerics and lords,' joked Gwen, waving away an offered glass.

A sound from above drew all their eyes. From the top of a sweeping staircase strode a group of men. At the fore was a Karesian man in black armour. His scimitar was sheathed, but he stood protectively in front of Archibald Tiris. Xander's cousin was a thin man, with receding hair and sickly yellow skin. His eyes were unfocused and he appeared enchanted. Behind, among the guardsmen, was a striking figure in silvery plate armour. His cloak was white and he wore a greatsword across his back.

'Good day, cousin,' said Xander, slowly drawing his bastard sword. 'Step forward and be judged.'

'Blasphemer,' slurred the Karesian. 'The Seven Sisters hold sway here.'

Xander threw his head back in laughter. He rested Peacekeeper across his shoulders and ambled forward, placing a foot on the bottom step.

'The harbour, the walls and the streets are ours. The people have no desire to die.' He smiled viciously. 'And this is Tor Funweir, this is my land. Fuck off back to Karesia. I hold sway here.'

The Karesian drew a wavy-bladed knife and passed it to Archibald. The regent of Ro Tiris glared at Xander.

'I will not die at your hand, Prince Alexander,' cackled Archibald. 'I will show you how little death means to the faithful.' He thrust the knife into his own stomach, wrenching it sideways and disembowelling himself. 'I will always love her,' he muttered.

Xander strode up the stairs, closely followed by men-at-arms. He flung a gauntleted fist at the Karesian, smashing into his jaw.

He grabbed the man by the throat and drove Peacekeeper into his chest.

'This is my land,' he repeated, emphasizing each word.

The Karesian fell off the blade, blood oozing from his mouth. Xander then levelled his bastard sword at the man in silver armour. He held it in one hand and the blade was still, not wavering an inch. 'And you are?' he asked.

The man, a lump of steel and muscle, bowed his head. 'Lord Markos of Rayne, knight of the White church. I greet you, Prince Alexander.'

* * *

Reports flooded in from all over the city. Although pockets of resistance did spring up, the word on the street was of liberation, not of conquest. From the balcony high in the House of Tiris, Gwen saw celebrations in the square. Cheering citizens praised the duke of Haran and decried the despotic rule of Archibald. Captain Brennan and a squad of men hauled down the new banner and raised the white eagle, signalling the end of the Seven Sisters' brief dominion.

She was extremely tired, but adrenaline kept her awake to enjoy the spectacle. They had rounded up hundreds of Karesians and dozens of clerics who were still deeply in thrall to the Mistress of Pain. The Purple cathedral was under close guard but had, so far, remained compliant. As had the defeated ranks of watchmen and the city guard. The soldiers now helped to settle a liberated population, taking their orders from senior Hawks. Gwen was glad they carried out their new duties happily. She had not heard a single word of support for the deposed regent, and Archibald's death was being celebrated rather than mourned.

She swayed against the railing, letting the gentle wind take her. She could feel a skin of blood and grime on her face. It was dried and cracked as her mouth contorted into a yawn. Tendrils of hair irritated her eyes, falling from her tangled topknot and sticking to her flesh.

Maybe a bath, the first one for weeks. The thought was like a warm blanket, cutting through the chill of the wind and the stench of blood and death. But that would have to wait. Her counsel was still needed. Xander needed a calm voice, Daganay needed someone with common sense and Brom needed reassurance. She played her roles well, and with sincerity. Her own needs, a bath, a change of clothes and a little peace, were not a priority.

She flexed her hands, stained red and tender. Broken and dead skin peeled from her fingertips and her palms were calloused and bruised. She didn't wear gloves to fight and the criss-cross pattern of her blade handles was imbedded in her skin.

Her blades. That was another need that would have to wait. They needed sharpening and the nicks needed repairing. Leaf-blades were more precise than longswords and required constant care. She couldn't remember where her whetstone was. Or her belongings. Lennifer would have entered the city by now, escorted in with the rest of the servants. Gwen's belongings were packed in travelling sacks, squeezed between barrels of grain and spare weapons. Lennifer would be standing guard over them, ensuring her lady's clothes were cared for. The young servant could be ferocious where clothes were concerned.

The thought made Gwen smile. That normality could exist in the midst of so much death and chaos. That someone, somewhere, still cared about the state of their clothes.

She heard an irritated voice behind her. Xander, Brom and Daganay had been interrogating Cardinal Cerro of the Brown and Lord Markos of the White for nearly an hour, ascertaining precisely where their loyalties lay. Their interrogations had not, so far, led to summary executions. She hoped that both the clerics would remain polite.

Through the open doors and billowing red curtains, the balcony was connected to an upper state room. From it strode a large, robed man, scratching his balding head and pursing his lips. He ignored Gwen and took a deep breath of fresh air.

'Cardinal Cerro,' said Gwen. 'Meeting not going as planned?'

The Brown cleric composed himself.

'It is the way of soldiers to see things as simply as possible. It is the way of nobility to be confident and stubborn. Your husband has the worst traits of both.'

'I won't disagree,' replied Gwen. 'He's simple and stubborn.'

'You know what he plans to do? And that Markos of bloody Rayne agrees with him?'

'Aye. The broad strokes at least,' she replied.

'And you don't think he's mad?'

She shrugged. 'Mad or not, I agree with him. He's backed into a corner. A dangerous place to put him.'

'But he's barely secured Tiris. He's taking that impulsive young idiot from Canarn, the Black Guard, whatever his name is. They're going to ride for Cozz, in the morning. They're going to ride for Cozz in the morning!'

'I know,' she replied.

'And that doesn't bother you?'

She stepped closer to him. 'It does. It bothers him, too. Which is why he's leaving you in charge.'

He banged his chubby fist on the railing. Deep breaths and closed eyes, the Brown cleric was frustrated and angry.

'Do any of you people from Haran actually listen?'

'I'm from Hunter's Cross,' she replied. 'And no, we don't listen either.'

'I would have expected a bit more sense from you, my lady,' said the cardinal, puffing out his cheeks. 'You're not burdened with nobility.'

'But I am a soldier. By your rationale I should be simple, but not arrogant.'

He flushed a little with embarrassment. 'Er, yes, sorry about that. Anger sometimes loosens a man's tongue.'

'I've been called worse, brother.'

From within, raised voices carried out on to the balcony. Lord Markos, Xander and Brom were arguing about who was to stay behind and who was to ride hard for Cozz.

'I just want . . . maybe some considered wisdom,' said Cerro. 'All of this is happening too fast.'

'Not fast enough, according to some.'

'How many men is he taking?' asked the cardinal. 'You don't have that many to begin with.'

She laughed. 'Skill and loyalty are as important as numbers. The Hounds in Cozz are poorly trained and disorganized. They're a mob, not an army.'

He placed both palms on his forehead and dragged them down his face. It was a gesture of internal anger and external frustration. The cardinal was a good man, but a pacifist.

'When will this end?' he asked.

'Interesting question. I'd say it's up for debate,' she replied.

'Being glib does not help, my lady.'

She breathed in some cool air. She should be exhausted, but her mind was racing and wouldn't let her be tired. In fact, she felt more awake than she had in years. The rush of combat, the thrill of survival. Even the ride for Cozz was filling her with adrenaline.

She chuckled. 'I think I've been married to Xander for too long.'

He looked confused. Poor Cerro, she thought. He was not cut out for the sort of excitement they had thrust upon him. She didn't know what his average day entailed, but doubted it involved anything particularly interesting.

Gwen smiled and put her hand across Cerro's shoulders, leading him from the balcony back into the state room. Within, Xander, Brom and Daganay were sprawled on wide couches surrounding a circular meeting table. Markos of the Knights of the Dawn was still standing, his white cloak still tied around his neck. He was tall and his face, unadorned with any hair, was smooth and angular. He wore burnished white armour, decorated with gold and silver, with a greatsword across his back.

'I will leave for Ro Arnon tonight,' said Lord Markos. 'I will meet you in Cozz at the head of five thousand knights.'

Xander frowned. His eyes drooped and he was fighting tiredness. 'Why? Why do you so readily pledge your support?'

'We answer only to the king and to the realm,' replied the White cleric. 'The king is not here. His son is dead. The realm is in need of purification. So we act to purify it. We will follow you, Prince Alexander . . . until you prove yourself unworthy.'

* * *

'Do we have to use them?' sneered Daganay.

'Got something against knights that wear white rather than red?' she demanded.

'Men of peace clad in death? Yes, I have something against them. Markos of Rayne is a puritanical autocrat of the worse kind. A battle chaplain who let men die because they weren't worthy of the One God's love. I have no respect for White clerics who don armour.'

'Even when he has five thousand clerics in armour?' asked Xander, finishing his wine.

Daganay took offence. 'They're not clerics. Not really. They're paladins. They don't heal men or lead worship. They heal the land and enforce worship.'

'We won. It's not important right now,' said Gwen. 'We're sitting in the House of Tiris . . . we have wine, I'm not wearing armour . . . and for now, we're at peace.'

'For now,' replied Xander. 'In the morning, our armour will be back on and we'll be riding south.'

'Then I'll worry about that when the time comes,' she said, smiling at her husband.

CHAPTER FIVE

RANDALL OF DARKWALD
IN THE CITY OF THRAKKA

RANDALL HAD IDENTIFIED twelve different kinds of dust and sand since he had left Kessia. The Long Mark, spoken of as if it were a road, was nothing more than a dusty track heading south. He'd seen mountains, skeletal trees, muddy rivers, but few people. Those he had seen were riding in caravans, mostly moving north, transporting what appeared to be their entire worldly goods along the barren trail.

Whatever trade existed in Karesia was clearly located within the walls of its cities and did not involve much import or export. They'd travelled past numerous small encampments of semi-permanent tents and picketed camels, comprised of stoical men and women with no conception of hospitality.

Voon of Rikara, the exemplar of Jaa and the newest member of their strange travelling group, had tried his best to explain the nature of his land to the men of Ro, but his accounts had not been overly helpful. The Karesians were not interested in friendly contact with their northern neighbours and the few who travelled to Tor Funweir were there to plough an illegal trade.

Jaa taught fear above all other virtues and did not care for the children of other gods, preferring to keep his people under his control. The recent rise of the Dead God had not reversed this state of affairs and his people remained as xenophobic as ever.

More opulent covered wagons plunged past them every few hours, with billowing black canvas over wooden platforms, pulled by muscular white horses and flanked by armed Karesian riders. Those within were obscured and Voon had told them that travelling mobsters and merchant princes would never let their faces be seen by lesser men for fear of assassination.

Randall worried that the preponderance of anonymous travellers, moving much faster than they were, could mean their pursuers would pass them and reach Thrakka first. Voon, stating that it would draw too much attention to them, had vetoed his suggestion that they use horses to speed up their travel.

'Foreigners don't ride horses. They don't travel the Long Mark and they don't visit Thrakka,' said the exemplar of Jaa. 'Any one of those factors could get your master killed, so why add to the risks?'

'So we get there ahead of the enchantress,' replied Randall.

Voon was expressionless. 'You are a good squire, young man. You care for your master. From what I have seen, you represent Utha's rational side, but you must defer to me on all matters related to Karesia. This land will bite you if you let it.'

'Is Thrakka any different from Kessia?' asked Utha, as they sat beneath a rocky overhang out of the midday sun.

'Yes,' replied Voon, taking a deep drink of water from a large flask. 'The viziers live in high towers. The architecture may seem . . . wondrous to your eyes.'

'I thought you were a vizier,' interjected Randall. 'The high vizier in fact.'

Voon looked at him for a moment before passing the water flask. 'I was. I am now a traitor in the new Karesia. My tower has fallen and my friends curse my name.'

'Do we need to stop there?' asked Ruth, sitting demurely on a rock, unconcerned by the dust and heat. 'We could simply bypass the city.'

'We could,' said Voon with a nod, 'but we need food, water, supplies.'

They had been eating salted meat and porridge for the past week, supplemented by foraging trips and the occasion Gorlan.

Strangely, Ruth cared nothing for her human companions eating spiders and had even eaten a little of the stew they'd made from her distant brethren.

'You said you have a friend there,' said Utha. 'I assume he can provide such supplies.'

'If he is still alive,' replied Voon. 'The Dead God has had influence in Thrakka for many years. Shadaran is a sharp old goat, but the Sisters will certainly have tried to silence him.'

'He's loyal to Jaa?' asked Utha.

'If he is still alive,' repeated Voon.

Utha shook his head in evident frustration. The exemplar and the old-blood had not bonded on their journey. Voon was calm, Utha was passionate. Randall often felt the need to interject or change the subject, delaying the inevitable punch in the face from the caustic albino.

'How close are we?' asked Randall.

'Close,' replied Voon. 'You will see the spires over the next rise.'

* * *

Beyond the line of craggy rocks, poking out from the shimmer of the baking hot sands, Randall could see spires, hundreds of them. Each one was different, with no consistent design or architecture. Some were topped with garish minarets, others held jewel-encrusted statues or carried bizarre symbols, but all were wondrous to his eyes.

'How tall are those towers?' he asked.

'As tall as the egos of their masters,' replied Voon. 'Mine was relatively modest in comparison.'

'Jekkan magic,' offered Ruth, peering at the glittering spires in the distance. 'The stones of Thrakka were not planted by Karesians. They merely stole what was already there and twisted it for their own ends.'

Utha and Randall shared a look. Both master and squire were practical men of Ro, unused to overt displays of magic. They preferred buildings and cities to be built of stone and wood, with proper engineering. To see Karesian craft based on sorcery was startling to them.

'The men of Ro have never really understood their southern neighbours,' said Voon, noting their reaction.

'Could you define Jekkan magic for me?' asked Randall, knowing nothing about the semi-mythical Jekkans.

'These lands have only belonged to the Karesians for a few millennia,' answered Ruth. 'Before that they were part of the Jekkan caliphate.'

Voon looked at her. 'This is Jaa's land.'

'It is . . . now,' replied the Gorlan mother. 'But the magic your viziers twist into their own forms was not originally theirs to command.'

He was silent for a moment. 'You are right,' he said. 'It is just strange to hear someone put it in those terms.'

'Your kind have difficulty understanding time. It is a gift of your people,' replied Ruth.

'Yes, yes, very profound,' grumbled Utha. 'Just tell me what we have to worry about here.'

Voon turned away from Ruth only slowly. His eyes were narrow and suspicious. 'You trouble me, sister,' said the exemplar.

'Is anyone listening to me?' asked Utha.

Voon walked away without replying.

'Let's just keep walking,' said Randall. 'And cover our faces.'

Thrakka had no encircling wall or defensive perimeter. The dusty track simply plunged out of the desert and into the forest of towers. At ground level the city was covered in a thick smog, reminiscent of winter mist, but with more unpleasant smells and an acrid sting that hit the back of the throat.

The Thrakkans wore facial coverings of dark colours. Slaves wafted away the smog with elaborate fans or carried their masters in discreet litters. It was eerily quiet, with no chatter or vibrancy in the streets. When he looked upwards, Randall felt that the city itself was made up of the towers.

Now he was closer, the true wonder of the place was evident.

The viziers' towers had no logical construction, no regularity to their design and, in several cases, no obvious means of staying upright. Each was a reflection of the mind of its custodian, magically reinforced by whatever Jekkan magic existed in the city, kept aloft by unknown means. Walkways and huge domed structures acted as a web between the towers. On the lowest platforms, above the mist, men and women wore brightly coloured clothes and walked in clear air.

Utha kept stopping to stare incredulously at the mile-high towers. Few men of Ro had ever been this far south. To see magic displayed in such a fashion was jarring to both of them.

'I don't believe what I'm seeing,' said Utha. 'Is this shit even possible? The Spire of the King in Tiris is the tallest thing I'd seen before today.'

'I've seen taller mountains,' replied Randall, 'but not many.'

Utha tore his eyes from the towers and looked at his squire. 'It's important we stick together, my dear boy. We're surrounded by Karesians, spiders and god knows what else.'

Randall chuckled. 'Is that concern I hear, master?'

'No, it's fear. But close enough.' He frowned. 'I do understand, you know.'

Randall slowed down and screwed up his eyes. 'Understand what?'

'I understand that I've asked a lot of you,' he replied.

'You didn't ask.'

'You know what I mean, you cheeky bastard.'

Randall coughed as the dust caught the back of his throat. 'Is it always this dusty?'

'Never been here before,' replied Utha. He glanced up again. 'Maybe we should try for higher ground. Some of those walkways look clear.'

Voon and Ruth, sauntering a little way ahead of them, stopped and pointed to an open doorway at the top of a set of wide steps. The door was at the base of one of the smaller towers. From the mid-point upwards the tower was in ruins, with only a single walkway leading to the rest of the web.

'Just thinking we should get out of the dust,' said Utha, joining the others.

'Indeed,' replied Voon. 'It is not wise to remain on the streets of Thrakka for too long. People watch. And they whisper.'

Randall glanced around. 'There's no one here. Who's watching us?'

'The viziers will have noted our presence,' said Voon. 'They are lethargic and decadent, but they will eventually become concerned.'

'Where's your friend's tower?' asked Utha.

'Not far. But let us be rested before we approach. I fear that he may be watched.'

Ruth gathered the hem of her dress and walked up the steps. She peered through the open doorway, slowly scanning whatever was inside. Then she waved for the others to follow.

Through the door, the bottom level of the ruined tower was wide and tall, with no internal walls and dusty detritus covering the floor. A staircase snaked its way round the circular walls, leading to the upper levels high above. The steps were broken in places and showed no signs of recent use.

'We've stayed in worse,' joked Randal. 'Do we rest here or go further up?'

Without replying, Voon walked to the staircase and mounted higher up the tower. Randall scoffed at his rudeness, shaking his head at Utha.

'He only answers questions he believes need answers,' said Ruth, following the exemplar up the stairs. 'He desires rest before we move on.'

'He's a contrary bastard,' said Utha, slapping Randall on the shoulder. 'Come on, let's get up out of the dust.'

The stairs had no railing and completed two full circles of the tower before they reached the second floor. Randall was puffing by the end, leaning on his knees for the last few steps. He glanced down and wished that he hadn't.

'All right, lad?' asked Utha.

'Heights,' replied Randall. 'I'm not too good with them.'

The old-blood chuckled. 'This place is full of towers, my dear boy. Heights and towers go hand in hand.'

The young squire felt nauseous. The ground below caused a distortion that made his head hurt.

'Sorry I teased you for being seasick,' he said, without looking at his master.

Utha pulled Randall away from the top of the stairs. 'Come on, lad.'

The second floor of the ruined tower was bizarre. Sounds began as soon as they left the staircase, as if they had been masked up to that point: the babble of water, the rustling of foliage, the whistle of wind. The second floor was an overgrown garden, its roots delving into the stone of the tower. The walls were coated with creeping vines and from the ceiling dropped gnarly wooden tendrils. A small rock pool sat in the middle of the circular space, with an elegant waterfall dribbling murky water into it. The garden had not been tended for some time, but it had a soporific quality that made a tingle travel up his spine.

Voon was already reclining on the vibrant green grass, leaving Utha and Randall to look at each other in amazement. The wide, open chamber was at least two storeys high, with several crumbling archways providing exits from the garden into thin air.

'Who owned this tower?' asked Utha.

Voon shrugged. 'Many viziers like gardens. It takes magic to make anything grow in this dust and heat.' He flexed his back and placed his spear on the grass. 'As for who owned it . . . I neither know nor care.'

Randall reached out and ran his hand through the grass, half expecting it to be fake. 'How does it grow halfway up a tower on cold stone?'

'Magic,' repeated Voon, shaking off his travelling cloak and closing his eyes.

'I don't like this tower,' muttered Ruth, looking out of an archway to the dusty street below. 'Something isn't right.'

Randall dumped his backpack on the grass and sat down with a grunt of tired exertion. Utha followed, unbuckling his sword belt and making himself comfortable against a thick vine.

'Can we talk about it after we've slept for a few hours,' said Utha, rubbing his eyes. 'I think I might even take my boots off.'

'I'm not tired,' replied Ruth. 'I may go for a walk.'

'Be safe,' slurred Randall, feeling his eyelids droop.

* * *

Sasha the Illusionist smiled. She slowly opened her eyes and surveyed her design. The tower was perfect. Ruined, discrete and strangely desirable. Exactly the refuge a man such as Voon would seek. The garden, modelled after a similar one in Oron Kaa, was a personal touch. She enjoyed gardens and thought it a kindness to give her victims a sense of peace before she sliced off their skin.

It was a simple matter to pass Utha on the road. They had purchased a covered litter and paid for the strongest slaves. She estimated that they had arrived a day before their quarry.

Voon's friend, Shadaran Bakara, had been taken into custody and Sasha had prepared a meticulous trap for the Ghost and his retinue. They now waited on a higher balcony, looking down from Bakara's tower.

'Who's the woman?' asked Pevain, licking his lips.

'I don't know,' she replied. 'She has a highly trained mind.'

Sasha narrowed her eyes and followed the movements of the dark woman. She had not fallen asleep and was strolling along a nearby walkway. Something about her was confusing, as if her mind was not open. The illusion affected the exemplar and the old-blood, but not the woman. She was neither Karesian nor Ro. She glided across the walkway, taking note of people and structures. Her eyes were never still, but her movements were slow and precise, suggesting a stalking animal. She moved away from the illusion, disappearing among Thrakkans.

'No, I don't know who she is,' Sasha repeated. 'But she is not our concern. Let her walk.'

'We can deal with her later,' replied the knight. 'That vizier has got men round the tower, ready to move in. I'll escort you over when it's done.'

'No,' replied Sasha. 'I will be there when they are subdued. I want to see their faces.'

'Whatever you want,' grunted Pevain, 'so long as I get to fuck the boy and kill the Ghost.'

Sasha tried to ignore the man's mutterings. She had wondered about this moment, played it through in her mind. Since her beloved sister had tasked her with finding the Ghost, she had imagined his face. Would he beg or cry? Surely not. The famous Utha the Ghost was a true fighting man, strong and resolute. He would fight until the end. It would take much torture to break him. Perhaps he would never break. What a wondrous thought. She smiled, feeling warmth run through her body.

'Whenever you're ready,' bleated Pevain.

'I am ready,' she replied.

He flashed her a sneering grin and drew his Ranen war-hammer. Behind them, standing ready in the smashed remnants of Bakara's tower, were a dozen men of Ro. Pevain's bastards were swarthy and wore the masks of men who enjoyed the baser things in life. She'd largely ignored them during their journey, accepted their deference and tuned out their ignorance.

'Tell the Karesians to wait for us,' commanded Pevain, sending a flunky scurrying for the stairs.

The rest of them followed, sharing a collective sense of anticipation. The men grunted and growled, like beasts preparing for the hunt. Their words were mumbled and unintelligible, conveying primal desires for death and defilement. Sasha had nothing but contempt for their shallow, empty lives.

She followed quietly, letting her mind focus on the Ghost. She could see his pale face, his pink eyes and his bone-white hair. She desired him in many ways. To see him, touch him, experience him. She longed for him as a spider longs for a fly.

They left the tower via a long walkway above the dust of the street. Poised and ready for combat were twenty templars of Thrakka and their vizier master. Sanaa Law Keeper approached her and spread his arms wide in an unnecessarily florid greeting. He wore yellow and red robes, with garish jewellery on his hands and around his neck.

'Most beautiful mistress,' said the vizier. 'We await your well-considered word.'

'Let's just kill 'em,' offered Pevain.

'Please be silent,' replied Sasha. 'Master vizier, have your men surround the ruined tower.'

Sanaa looked up at the crumbling stone. Sasha had built her illusion atop an existing structure. Utha rested, not on grass surrounded by shrubbery, but on cold stone, with the open air for company.

'Where does the real tower end, my lady?' asked Sanaa.

'The bottom level is real,' she replied. 'My craft starts at the top of the stairs.'

'Very well, we will stop the criminals from escaping. Though I would enjoy the opportunity to immolate them, mistress. Or perhaps inch them . . .'

Sasha had no stomach for the whims of lesser beings. She scowled at the vizier. 'Just do as you're told. Your desires have no place here.'

'Your will, mistress,' replied Sanaa, bowing again.

She dismissed him and glided to the ruined tower. Pevain and his mercenaries followed, drawing their uncouth weapons and exchanging vile expressions of intent, none of which she would allow them to indulge.

She could still feel the mind of the old-blood, calling to her like a flower to a bee. To taste his death would be to taste the purest of nectar, the sweetest of fruit. She would do what her sisters could not, what the armies of Tor Funweir could not. She would enslave Utha the Ghost.

347

Within, the tower was a broken stone shell. A whistle of wind swirled downwards from the open level above, agitating the detritus. Sweat and travel dust marked the stairs. Voon had led them into her trap. The exemplar was foolish to return. If he had stayed in the deserts, they might have ignored him, for without an old-blood he was harmless. But he had reared his head and become an enemy worth killing. He was almost as rich a prize as the old-blood himself.

'Let me go first and subdue the Ghost,' offered Pevain, hefting his war-hammer.

'Have I ordered you to do that?' countered Sasha, reluctantly leaving her thoughts.

'No,' he replied, scratching his scarred neck. 'I was just—'

'Confine yourself to things I have ordered you to do,' she interrupted. 'You are to accompany me and fight when I tell you to fight. You are not to talk to me. Understood?'

'Your sister was more agreeable,' replied the knight of Ro.

Sasha stopped walking. She took a moment to compose herself and faced Pevain. 'Do I need to do something unpleasant? Something to impress my dominance upon you? Hurt you or enchant you?'

He sneered, but didn't say anything unwise. 'I apologize, my lady. Lead the way.'

She smiled. 'That is a good attitude, please maintain it.'

Keeping a tight rein on her irritation, Sasha advanced into the tower. She breathed slowly, tuning out the inane babble of the men. Her thoughts returned to the old-blood. She could feel his breathing, his heartbeat, the cool touch of his skin, the soft white of his hair. He was beautifully unique.

She walked up the encircling stairs and entered her own illusion. The babble of water and rustling of trees aided her calm, bringing a serene smile to her face. Behind, Pevain's men stayed on the stairs, allowing her to enter and survey her design.

'There you are,' she breathed, fixing her eyes on the sleeping old-blood.

Voon, Utha, and the young squire slumped against trees and on the grass, sleeping deeply. All three looked so peaceful she almost didn't want to wake them.

The squire was closest. He was a strapping young man, tightly muscled and lean. She crouched next to him and ran her hands across his bare shoulders and down his arms. His skin was smooth, with few scars. He was handsome in a boyish way, with a thin beard and light brown hair.

'The boy's more dangerous than he looks,' whispered Pevain.

She fought the urge to hurt the ignorant mercenary.

'What is his name?' she asked.

'Randall of . . . somewhere. Darkwald, I think.'

She leant over the young man, placing her mouth next to his. She kissed him gently, savouring the taste. 'We will start with you,' she murmured, feeling her body sway with pleasure.

'Pevain, stand your men on guard. Secure the other two, but do not wake them.'

He grinned and positioned his men in the garden, standing over Voon and Utha. Even the uncivilized mercenaries were lulled into tranquillity by her illusion. She did not make them sleep but her design halted their banter.

'Wake up, Randall,' she said, gently weaving an enchantment into his young mind.

His eyes opened slowly and a childlike smile appeared. His will was stronger than his years would suggest, but Sasha enjoyed grasping his mind. He was now hers. For this moment and forever.

'Who are you?' he whispered breathlessly.

'I am your life . . . from now on, I am all you will love, all you will care for.'

He nodded, his eyes wide and euphoric.

'I am yours,' said Randall of Darkwald, caressing her cheek with rough hands.

'You may stand, sweet Randall,' she said, beckoning him to his feet.

Pevain nodded approvingly as the young squire stood up.

Randall drew his sword and adopted a protective pose behind his mistress.

'That is good, my love,' she said, transferring waves of pleasure to the young man. 'You will enjoy being in my service.'

'He's not so tough now,' guffawed Pevain.

'Silence when the mistress is talking,' barked Randall, levelling his longsword at the mercenary knight.

Sasha gasped with pleasure. 'Not now, my dear, we have work to do,' she said. 'Let us rouse the old-blood.'

She waved the mercenaries to the perimeter of the garden. Her illusion was masterfully constructed and now that they were all within it the space was indistinguishable from reality. The men with her leant against the illusory walls, feeling their solidity with no fear of falling to the street below.

Sasha strolled across the garden, taking Randall with her. Then she stopped. Something was wrong. A nagging tickle developed at the back of her mind, a persistent irritation made her eyes twitch.

She stopped walking in the centre of the garden and looked up. Her illusion formed a dome above, with knitted vines and grasses criss-crossing the ceiling.

'What's the matter?' asked Pevain, swinging his hammer over Utha's head in a threatening manner. He looked up. 'What are you looking at?'

'I see web,' she replied.

Gaps were appearing in the ceiling, small patches where the illusion had broken. In the spaces Sasha could see dense web, and it was spreading, each patch of web growing like a fungus and eating into her design.

'That is not possible,' she said.

Then pain. A biting surge of unknowable power as her illusion was shattered. Above and all around them was web, a dome of dense, white fibre encompassing the ruined second floor of the tower.

'Fuck me!' exclaimed Pevain. 'Where did that come from?'

Utha and Voon awoke. Both men opened their eyes and stood up suddenly, the soporific illusion disappearing in an instant.

'You!' roared Voon, locking eyes with Sasha. 'Utha, we must leave . . . now.'

The old-blood took in his surroundings quickly. Taking advantage of Pevain's shock, he punched the mercenary in the face and floored him. The two men grabbed their weapons while Sasha still stood in awe of the huge black shape moving across the web.

Fighting began, but for the enchantress it all happened in slow motion. Pevain's men rushed Utha and Voon, but Randall remained guarding his mistress.

'My lady, we must leave,' said the squire, gesturing to the huge shape beginning to delve downwards through its web.

'Randall, what the fuck are you doing?' roared Utha.

'He's gone,' replied Voon. 'He's hers now.'

The albino attacked with ferocity, hacking at the mercenaries, trying to reach his squire.

'I'll tear your fucking face off, bitch!' he screamed at Sasha.

Sanaa Law Keeper rang an alarm bell and Karesian warriors entered the bottom level. She heard them and she saw the fight out of the corner of her eye, but she kept looking upwards.

She knew what it was, but she barely believed it. They were extinct, surely they were extinct. The Seven Sisters had searched the lands of men looking for them, hoping to harness their ancient power. They had found nothing.

'Utha, he's gone,' repeated the exemplar of Jaa.

She didn't turn away from the shape, even as Voon tackled Utha and pulled him away.

The Karesians flooded into the webbed dome. Too many to fight, and Voon knew it. Sasha remained transfixed as the exemplar ran for a gap in the web, an opening that led to the single walkway from the tower. The old-blood reluctantly followed, throwing a pained grimace towards his squire as he ran for safety.

'Get after them,' ordered Pevain, groggily getting to his feet.

The Karesians flooded past her towards the gap. There was no grass now, only cold stone, and she began to shiver with fear. She had never felt it, it was alien and unwelcome.

Her prey had gone, fled beyond her sight. She could no longer feel the old-blood. She should pursue, but she couldn't move. She couldn't move and she couldn't turn away.

The shape plunged downwards, its thick legs displacing the web. It darted across the dome, gracefully sliding into the path of the running Karesians. They stopped, and then began to flee, dropping their weapons in panic. Pevain and his remaining mercenaries screamed with primal terror and flung themselves away from the creature.

It was a Gorlan mother, a legendary beast, pulled from the depths of deep time. Myths and fables were told about them in Oron Kaa. Of their father, the old one Atlach-Nacha, of their offspring, the bloated spiders of Leng. But they were all dead, surely they were all dead. Even as it began killing her soldiers, Sasha didn't believe what she was seeing.

It crushed some men and ate others, ignoring their feeble attempts to resist. Its beautiful abdomen, hairy and mottled red, twitched upwards, shrugging fine hairs into the air. They formed a mist, sticking foot-long shards into the men's faces. Screams filled the ruined tower. Men ran and men died. But still she didn't turn away.

'We must leave, mistress,' said Randall, clinging to her arm.

The Gorlan flexed its huge bulk and scuttled towards her, baring its fangs. It reared up and blocked out the light of the sun that seeped through the web. She didn't move or turn away even as the fangs plunged downwards and entered her chest.

She was of the Seven Sisters of Shub-Nillurath. She was an ageless enchantress whom no man could attack, but Sasha the Illusionist felt like a terrified child as the Gorlan mother injected her venom and tore out her life.

* * *

Randall was confused. He thought he was awake, but he wasn't sure. Maybe he had seen a fight, maybe he hadn't. Strange memories filled his head. He wasn't sure if they were his, but they felt real. Was it a fight? Or was it something else? A woman's face, a lot of blood, a lot of death. A mosaic of things, real and unreal.

He had fallen asleep on grass. That much was certain. Everything beyond that was up for debate.

'Hello!' he said.

He didn't know if he had said it aloud or just in his mind, but it had seemed the thing to say.

'My name's Randall. Is anyone there?'

'I see you, young man,' said a female voice, sensual and husky.

'Where am I? Who are you? Am I alive? Why can't I feel or see anything?'

It must be a dream. It must be. It couldn't be anything else.

'You are not dreaming,' replied the woman. 'You belong to me now. If seeing and feeling are important to you, we will adjourn to somewhere more familiar.'

He was suddenly in a village of thatch and wood. Smoking chimneys above flaming hearths. Trees and narrow streams bisected the village and the rich smell of red wine filled the air. The weather was fine. Sunny with a chill of cool air. It was autumn and textures of brown and green carpeted the ground. It was the Darkwald, a village near where he had grown up.

Randall was not tired and his limbs were not sore. His sword was clean and his cloak smelled of lavender as if recently washed.

'A pleasant village,' said the woman. 'A good place to grow up.'

She appeared in front of him. A beautiful, tall woman in a figure-hugging black dress. Her hair was lustrous and rippled gently in the wind.

'I find your memories calming,' she said.

'You're an enchantress!'

353

'Yes, Randall, I am. My name is Saara the Mistress of Pain.'

He gulped and averted his eyes.

She laughed. 'My sweet boy, you are already enthralled. There is no further benefit to resistance.'

'We have never met,' he replied. 'Though you're almost identical to Katja the Hand of Despair. I saw her in Ro Tiris. But how can I be enchanted by you?'

'So full of questions,' replied Saara. 'I suppose there is no harm, we have all the time in the world.' She looked around at the village, taking in the clean air. 'Your mind is a peaceful place. Much nicer than some I have been forced to endure of late.'

'But . . . how?' he repeated.

Saara rubbed the sides of her head. She was intoxicating to look at, but her brow was troubled. 'Can we not just enjoy the peace? Before we must return to the whirlwind of real life.'

'Sorry,' he mumbled. 'I'm just a bit confused. Well, a lot confused. Where's Utha? Is he dead?'

She frowned. 'I'm sorry, I do not know, sweet boy.'

'We were in Thrakka . . . actually, I probably shouldn't talk to you.'

Another laugh, though it was pained. 'I am in your mind, Randall. You are my phantom thrall. Your thoughts and memories are mine to view and manipulate as I wish.'

'I . . . we . . . shit.' They had lost. He remembered nothing after falling asleep in the ruined tower. Nothing of Utha, Voon or Ruth. He couldn't see how they could be alive if he had been enchanted. His master would not abandon him easily. He'd likely die, foolishly fighting to help his squire, although Voon was less passionate. Hopefully, he would have saved the miserable old albino from a pointless death.

'You have much love in your heart, sweet Randall. But you may relax now, your struggles are over. You are no longer burdened with having to think for yourself.'

'I quite like thinking for myself,' he replied.

She cradled his cheek. 'All men do. Until they experience the clarity of servitude.' She frowned suddenly. 'Wait . . . who is the woman?'

Randall felt the enchantress delve further into his memories. She watched him mating with Ruth on the floor of Captain Makad's ship, and then to an isolated clearing, deep in the Fell. He stood next to her, watching Utha and his younger self approach Ryuthula's cave.

When the Gorlan appeared, Saara gasped.

'So, the mother comes out of hibernation. I always knew they couldn't be extinct.'

She watched and listened, re-reading the conversation. She saw Randall cowering behind his master and she heard Ryuthula offer to be Utha's guide. She heard of the staircase, the labyrinth and the guardian.

'You killed my sister,' she mused, watching the Gorlan transform into a woman. 'I kill one assassin and another appears.'

Randall's head felt heavy. The enchantress was becoming agitated and it was affecting him. He didn't understand sorcery or any of the weird craft he'd seen over the past year. He was uncomfortable that it existed. Tor Funweir was clear of strange magic and he didn't like having to endure things he didn't understand.

Saara looked at him. 'You retain freedom of thought,' she said. 'That is unexpected.'

'Er, sorry,' he replied. 'I didn't mean to have freedom of thought.'

They left the clearing and returned to the small village nestled on the edge of the Darkwald.

'The Gorlan mother has touched your mind,' said Saara.

'I advise you to leave the young man alone,' said Ruth in the depths of his mind.

She was unseen, but Randall could feel the warmth of her touch and the heat of her breath. Unlike the enchantress, he didn't feel as if she was manipulating him. Saara's distortions of his memories made of him a cipher, a window through which to view reality. He was barely involved in the process, whereas the Gorlan mother caressed his mind as if asking to be allowed in.

'How is this possible?' said Saara, hearing the voice and looking around her. 'This is not possible. His thoughts are mine.'

'No, they are not,' was the reply. 'They are his.'

Saara sneered. 'Am I addressing the creature that killed my sister?'

'Ate is a more appropriate term, but yes, you are.'

The enchantress closed her eyes. The corners of her mouth twitched as if she were experiencing sporadic pain.

Randall's mind was clearer now and he thought he remembered what had happened in Thrakka. Sasha the Illusionist had enchanted him. He wrestled with vague memories, trying to locate Utha and Voon, but he couldn't place them. Were they alive? Or enchanted like he was?

'I wish no conflict with you,' said Saara, opening her eyes and revealing tears in them. 'Our goals do not collide. Let us keep it that way.'

'You were right,' replied Ruth. 'I care nothing for these lands of men and their inhabitants. But now you manipulate one I do care for. Leave his mind, now!'

'If you were truly so powerful you would have simply dismissed me,' said Saara, her eyes darting from side to side. 'I believe you have no power here. This is my territory, not yours.'

'Yes and no,' replied Ruth. 'I have no power in the mind of another. It is the height of bad manners to enter another's mind unbidden. Walking through thoughts and dreams without being invited is mental rape. You are a rapist, Mistress of Pain.'

The enchantress laughed, twisting Randall's memories into something else. She took them to a high tower overlooking the city of Kessia. It was a tall minaret in the centre of the sprawl.

'Step to the edge, Randall,' she said.

He did as she asked, unable to resist. Beneath him a sheer drop loomed. He saw smoke rising from buildings, he smelled leather, meat and fish. To the north, the Kirin Ridge rippled across the horizon.

'I could command him to jump and he would do so gladly,' she said. 'I could turn his waking body into a mindless shell if I willed it.'

Ruth didn't answer.

'Do you hear me, spider?'

'Er, she's a Gorlan, not a spider,' corrected Randall. 'She doesn't like being called a spider.'

Saara glared at him through narrow eyes. 'How is it you are able to talk to me thus?' she asked. 'You should be grovelling in the corners of your mind, begging for my favour. You are my phantom thrall.'

He shrugged. 'Don't know. I don't really like being on the edge of this tower, though. It's a long way down.'

Her glare grew deeper, pushing further into his mind. He felt her anchor herself to pieces of him, hooking her sorcery into his thoughts. It hurt.

'Do you have to do that?' he asked, wincing.

'I will not give up so keen a weapon,' she replied. 'You will be a valuable asset against the Ghost.'

She delved into his past, seeing Sir Leon Great Claw, Brother Torian of Arnon, the encounter in the oubliette of Tiris. It was an open tapestry upon which she could paint anything she wanted, anything she could imagine.

'Please don't make me betray him,' he pleaded, wishing he could cry.

'My dear Randall, you have already betrayed him. I know he is bound for Oron Kaa. That is all the information I need. He knows not what power lies in wait there . . . the City of Insects and the footprint of the Forest Giant.'

Then Ruth laughed. It was not the velvety and seductive sound made by the Seven Sisters, it was a laugh of malevolence.

'What do you know of power?' asked the disembodied voice.

'How are you still here?' demanded Saara. 'I don't care what you are, you are not welcome.'

'I tell you again, leave his mind.'

'I will destroy his consciousness,' screamed Saara. 'Do not test me.'

'You cannot have him,' replied Ruth, her voice calm.

Randall nearly fell forwards, toppling into thin air. Saara was using all her concentration trying to dismiss Ruth and he felt her exertion. Her mind surged in huge waves of power, each wave making Randall gasp with pleasure and pain.

'What are you trying to do, little girl?' asked Ruth.

'Leave!' roared Saara, throwing a wall of raw energy into Randall's mind.

'No!' replied Ruth.

His surroundings became unrecognizable. He flew through unformed realities, following the chaos of Saara's struggle. He felt drunk, but not lost.

'Can I speak?' he slurred.

The chaos halted and he returned to the high minaret. Saara was flushed and her tears were constant now.

'I just wanted to ask Ruth something,' he said feebly. 'If it's impolite to enter another's mind unbidden, why can't I invite you in? Because I'd like to, if it would help.'

'No!' muttered the enchantress.

'Yes, Randall, you can. It would have defeated the object to have suggested such a thing,' replied Ruth calmly.

'You can come in. Really, you can come in.'

Everything changed. His mind unravelled and came together again. He felt a cool breeze, a clear head, fresh air. He still felt powerless but at least it was within Ruth's embrace and not Saara's. The Darkwald village and the Karesian minaret were both unreal but the blue sky above him appeared different. Maybe it was real, or maybe he was dead and all this was the last surge of the power of his mind.

'Can I go home? I'm fed up of magic.'

'But your journey has only just begun,' answered Ruth.

He wanted to believe that he was actually resting in her arms, looking up at the blue sky, but he couldn't trust his senses.

'Look at me, Randall!'

He craned his neck up and saw her face. She was cradling him in her arms. He could feel his body again. He wiggled his toes and felt the leather of his boots. He scratched at his neck and relieved an itch. It was real.

'Where are we?' he asked, feeling like a poorly child.

She stroked his hair out of his eyes. 'We are sitting on top of a vizier's tower. Many people are looking for me.'

'Are we safe?'

'We are safer up here than anywhere else. No one saw me climb the tower with you encased in a web.'

He screwed up his face. 'I'm not sure how I feel about that. I periodically forget what you really are.'

'Relax, Randall, you need rest. Your mind has been assaulted. It will take time for you to recover.'

'Where's Utha?' Once the thought had entered his head, it was all he could think about. 'Please tell me I didn't get him killed. I don't think I could live with that.'

'The old-blood and the exemplar escaped,' she replied. 'I killed the enchantress before she could pursue them.'

Randall smiled. He felt like an idiot, but he smiled anyway. His head was heavy, though the sensation was not unpleasant. His fingertips were sensitive and the wind crackled across his skin. Somewhere, beyond the stress of enchantment, the fatigue of travel and the fear of the unknown, he felt happy.

CHAPTER SIX

FYNIUS BLACK CLAW IN THE CITY OF SOUTH WARDEN

T HE KNIGHTS OF Ro were stupid. They were arrogant, short-sighted, ordered and easy to trick. They made war in organized lines and became confused whenever their enemy was not right in front of them. He thought it little challenge to outwit them, but with Brytag's wisdom he was going to do it anyway. He was going to do it with five hundred men of Twilight Company and six hundred idiots of the Crescent. As long as everyone shut up and let him think, Fynius was confident they would take South Warden back from the bastards of Ro.

He smiled, looking from the tree line towards the northern wall of the city. The Red men were distracted, with plenty of interesting things to look at on the Plains of Scarlet. The Karesian's estimate of their numbers had been wildly inaccurate, or maybe things had changed since he left. Fynius didn't care. Either way, there were three distinct armies within sight of South Warden.

'What do those banners mean?' he asked the man of the sun, crouching next to him on the edge of the Moon Woods.

'Which ones?' asked Hasim.

Fynius didn't answer.

'Hey, which ones?' repeated the man of the sun.

'The red ones.'

'They're all red. Be more specific.'

Fynius guessed that the king was in South Warden and that Lallon of Feith, or whatever his name was, had the wooden stockade to the west. It was the mass of armour and horses to the south that he was worried about.

Hasim waved a hand in front of the captain's face. 'Are you listening to me?'

'On occasion,' replied Fynius. 'Those banners.' He pointed to the huge southern camp.

'I don't know what they all mean, but the main one – the crossed swords and clenched fist – that's the banner of the Red cardinal, Malaki Frith. He wasn't here when I left.'

Fynius turned to him and smiled. 'So, how many Ro are on the Plains of Scarlet now?'

Hasim frowned. 'You're a disagreeable bastard, you know that?'

'Answer the fucking question.' He was still smiling.

The Karesian maintained eye contact and Fynius studied his face. Hasim wasn't easy to scare. He was also lucky, and that was a worthy trait.

'Maybe twenty thousand . . . and change,' he replied.

'And that Lallon fellow, where's he?'

'Fallon, his name's Fallon. He's in the yeomanry's camp. The one place with no red banners.'

Fynius turned back to South Warden. The Red cardinal's camp was newly constructed, suggesting he had only recently arrived. The camp of the yeomanry was locked up tight, indicating that Sir Fallon of Leith had not yet ventured forth to speak to the general. The city itself was more or less intact, suggesting there would be plenty of Ranen prisoners.

Interesting. Perhaps a plan was forming. Perhaps the Ro were about to get a lesson in how not to fuck with Fynius Black Claw and the Freelands of Ranen. Either way, he knew something was going to happen. He wasn't sure what, but whatever it was, it was definitely going to happen.

'You have some kind of idea?' asked Hasim. 'Or some magic power to turn your five hundred men into twenty thousand?'

Fynius ignored him, formulating his plan.

'Maybe we should find a way to approach Fallon.' The Karesian was clearly uncomfortable with silence. 'Or send Bronwyn.'

The walls of South Warden were well defended on the western side, but the rest were largely empty. Few chimneys produced smoke and only the centre looked to be inhabited, though Rowanoco's Stone was in ruins. His eyes twitched as he thought quickly.

Hasim didn't ask any more questions and instead muttered swear words under his breath. He wasn't a complete fool, so Fynius chose not to be too mean to him.

'I am thinking,' said the Ranen captain. 'Your incessant prattling does not help.'

'Incessant prattling? Big words,' replied Hasim. 'Not particularly polite, however.'

Fynius dropped his smile. He rubbed his hands together and spoke to the air. 'I know he's a friend, but if he doesn't shut up, I'm going to hurt him.'

Hasim twisted his face upwards in confusion. 'Who the fuck are you talking to?'

'See what I mean?' he demanded of Brytag. 'Just because he's lucky, doesn't mean he's helpful.'

'Are you talking about me?' asked the Karesian.

'Don't interrupt,' snapped Fynius. 'I'm talking to someone worth talking to.'

Hasim began to respond, but stopped before he could say anything unwise.

'Look, man of the sun, I am formulating a plan. This plan does not involve much fighting, so the numbers . . . they're irrelevant. I plan to talk to Fallon of Leith if and when I have to, not before. Any more questions?'

He raised his eyebrows. 'Just one,' he said. 'Are you really mad, or is this all an act?'

Fynius didn't respond. He sprang to his feet and darted forward through the trees. He waved his hand behind and the line of blue-clad warriors followed. They moved silently over uneven ground, their swords sheathed.

Twilight Company were the misfits, the younger brothers, the short in statue but quick of mind. They were called the rogues, the raven men, the blue twilight and Brytag's wing. They were Fynius's men, an extension of his will, and they were lucky and wise, blessed by the World Raven.

'Vincent, with me,' he whispered, coming to a stop at the last line of cover before the plains.

Vincent Hundred Howl, his cousin, ghosted next to him. Hasim followed, a look of exasperation on his dusky face,

'The old cheese cellars?' asked Vincent.

'I think so, certainly,' replied Fynius.

'The what?' interjected Hasim.

'South Warden used to be famed for its cheese, man of the sun,' answered Fynius. 'I doubt you got much of it in Karesia.'

'How does that help?'

Fynius breathed in deeply, fighting the urge to slap the slow-witted Karesian.

'I wasn't aware I had to tell you everything, Hasim. You had your chance to ask questions.'

'Okay, just tell me . . . do you have a way into South Warden?'

'I do. It doesn't smell terribly nice, but I do,' he replied.

* * *

Fynius didn't like cheese. The soft, goat's stuff you got in Old Gar was normally served on toast and tended to ruin the toast. The harder southern stuff smelled less, but its chewy texture made him retch.

South Warden made a tangy, red cheese that was matured in large underground cellars. He doubted that knights of the Red would deign to eat any cheese not blessed by the righteous piss of the One God, so they wouldn't think to look for the wooden hatches to the north of the city, used to air the cheese.

Twilight Company was arrayed across the northern plains, crouched in the low ground. Everything was pointed away from them and it was easier to stay hidden than he had anticipated. Even the man of the sun was stealthy enough to avoid the occasional glare of a Red knight.

They approached a natural gully with circular wooden hatches at every ten paces. The grass half covered them and Fynius signalled to his men. They clustered, gathering in front of the hatches.

He paused, taking in the surroundings. The wooden walls of South Warden were close, barely a hundred feet away. The yeomanry's stockade was just visible, its trebuchets poking above the foreground. To the south, the Red general's camp was obscured. Fynius knew something was going to happen, but he wasn't sure where. If he was honest with himself, he wasn't sure what either. Brytag didn't give his wisdom in clear, concise lines. His visions came as snippets of mist, floating across his eyes. If he grabbed one, it became an idea. When it became an idea, he trusted it. He was still alive, so he must be doing something right.

'South Warden is a Ranen city,' he muttered. 'It must not be in the hands of the Ro. We will take it back.'

With a quick movement he drew his sword. It was called Leg Biter, a gift from his big brother. The hatch was rusted shut from years of neglect and needed considerable leverage to open it. The smell was disgusting – unless you liked mouldy cheese, in which case it was probably quite nice.

Once open, a dark tunnel plunged away from him. Cobwebs and dust covered the smooth wood but the unmistakable smell of cheese carried from the underground cellars.

'I like dark tunnels,' he whispered to Vincent. 'Let's see where it leads.'

A wave of his hand and Twilight Company opened the other hatches. It would take time to move everyone into the tunnels and Fynius thought he should scout ahead.

'I'll get the men assembled in the cellars,' said Vincent, picking up on his captain's intentions.

'Hasim, come with me,' said Fynius, darting into the tunnel as the Karesian spluttered a whingeing reply.

The wooden planks were treated and bent into a perfect circle. Tufts of weed sprang up from splintered gaps, and the smell grew stronger. Within ten feet he had covered his nose. The cellars had not been used for some time and whatever remained had been left to fester. Hopefully, the knights hadn't investigated the smell of over-ripe cheese. It was worse than the pungent mushrooms smoked by the Moon clans.

'How did you know about this place?' asked Hasim in his annoying, whining accent.

'My mum loved the cheese from South Warden. She always said we'd go and visit the cheese-makers one day. We never did, but I remembered the cellars.'

The Karesian looked doubtful.

'Okay, maybe Brytag told me,' said Fynius. 'What difference does it make?'

'None. I'm just trying to figure you out. You're either full of shit or you know something I don't.'

Fynius ignored him and moved further along the tunnel. He had to crouch, but not so much that he couldn't walk quickly. He knew the tunnels led to large cellars, but not much after that. He'd see something when he got there, he was sure.

The cramped, wooden passageway opened up and the two of them hopped down into a dark silo. Shafts of light spread downwards from broken planks, illuminating old tables and cheese-making equipment. From the angle of the light, he estimated that they were just inside the walls of South Warden.

'Right, things to do, things to do,' he muttered. 'The king of Ro, the Purple man, the Red knights, Scarlet Company, the wise woman, Lilon of Foth.'

'His name's Fallon of Leith,' interrupted Hasim.

'What?'

'It's not that difficult a name to remember,' said the Karesian.

Fynius ignored him. He walked to the middle of the cellar and looked at the ceiling. They weren't under a building, which was useful, but he needed to get to Long Shadow's hall. It was quite a way. Luckily, there were more tunnels leading away from the cellar.

'We're going to do some exploring,' he said. 'That way, I think.'

He picked a tunnel leading into the city and proceeded along it.

'Seriously, are you full of shit?' asked Hasim, grudgingly following the Ranen.

The tunnels leading away from the cellar were of cyclopean stone blocks, forced together with dusty grey mortar. Old wheels of cheese sat in wooden frames, gathering moisture and mould from the humid cellars. The floor dust was undisturbed and the torch emplacements rusted into odd shapes.

'There's nothing like an invasion to halt cheese-making,' remarked Hasim.

'Stopped before that,' Fynius replied. 'They've made normal, everyday cheese for years. These cellars are an expensive luxury when you're short on funds and trying to feed a growing population.'

He paused, listening to the wind. It blew from several directions, swirling gently through the tunnels.

'Shut up now, I'm thinking again,' said Fynius, creeping slowly past the cheese racks.

They were under the city, moving towards the mount and Rowanoco's Stone. Light was sporadic, appearing from small, angled holes every few paces. On the outside, the tunnels poked above the ground as semicircles of moss-covered stone. The Ranen of South Warden had abandoned them, so why would the Red knights think to look?

'Find a loose stone, I need to see where we are,' he said, testing the blocks with his foot.

Hasim joined him, using a knife to chip away at rotten mortar. He was crouched and foolishly trying to loosen the lower bricks.

'Perhaps you should try higher up,' said Fynius. 'Try not to be too much of an idiot.'

He glared, looking like a sinister gremlin in the dark tunnel. But he seemed to accept his idiocy and moved to a brick that might lead outside.

Together they found a small section where the blocks of stone had crumbled. There was not much of a gap on the outside, but within, a solid shove would cause the stone shell to break. Fynius pulled away chunks of masonry and allowed a thick stream of morning sunshine to flood over his face. The gap was still small, but big enough to allow him to orient himself.

They were between an empty stable and a wooden house, nestled in dead ground. Looming over nearby houses was Long Shadow's hall, a wooden long house with a sloping roof, thatched with golden straw. Beyond that, the crumbling dome of Rowanoco's Stone.

'The Red bastards,' grumbled Fynius. 'Is nothing sacred?'

'This isn't Tor Funweir,' replied Hasim. 'Nothing is sacred outside Tor Funweir. To the knights you're just peasants and lesser men.'

'Is that how they won?'

Hasim nodded. 'They couldn't take the breach, so they bombarded the assembly and drove the Ranen to frenzy.'

'Stupid, rage-filled, hairy, southern, Free Company idiots.'

'That's a bit strong. They fought like the Ice Giant himself to defend their ground.'

'They lost . . . bravery means fuck all if you lose,' replied Fynius.

The Karesian snorted and shook his head. He cared for these southern Ranen. It was all over his face. He'd fought to defend this city and stayed alive. That put him a little way above Scarlet Company.

'Why do you care?' he asked Hasim. 'This isn't your land or your god.'

'My god's a vicious tyrant . . . if I'm going to fight for something, it might as well be a god that gives a shit about his followers.'

'Good attitude,' he replied.

The opening was in a disused corner of South Warden and moving the crumbling stone to poke his head out was free of risk. Fynius gained his bearings quickly. The tunnel travelled under the hall and snaked its way across the town. It poked above the ground at irregular intervals, forming mounds of grass and brick.

There were few knights in evidence. They appeared between buildings and disappeared again, making their way towards the main gate. Small patrols were far off, keeping their eyes on the western defences. They had hubris enough to ignore the peasants and lesser men of Ranen skulking to the north. The bulk of the king's forces were in here somewhere, but not looking for a couple of men in a cheese cellar.

He left the spy-hole and carried on along the tunnel, moving quickly again. He counted his strides, judging when he was below Long Shadow's hall. There was little light now and Fynius narrowed his eyes and trusted in his night vision. The ceiling was flat and the tunnel angled downwards.

'Are you going to tell me your plan yet?' asked Hasim.

'Something's going to happen,' he replied.

'What?'

'Not sure, but we need to be ready when it does,' stated Fynius.

The Karesian puffed out his cheeks. He was impatient and needed to relax. Fynius wondered why people were so reluctant to trust him.

'Are we going to have a problem?' he asked Hasim. 'So far you've only been slightly stupid. Much more, and we may fall out.'

'You're taking all this very lightly,' replied the man of the sun. 'People have died. Lots of people. And, unless you're cleverer than you appear, many more are going to die before this is done.'

'Don't worry, I am much cleverer than I appear,' replied Fynius.

Hasim chuckled. At least he had a sense of humour. 'You're funny, man of Gar. But I'm taking a lot on trust.'

Fynius was confused. He didn't really feel the need or the inclination to explain himself. He was following Brytag and he trusted the World Raven with his life. Why did others not just keep out of his way?

'Answer me this, man of the sun – what choice do you have?'

He didn't wait for an answer.

The tunnel had opened into a basement, a cube of grey, mouldy stone. Old doors hung limply on broken hinges, turning a dark green in the musty air. Above, a long-sealed trapdoor and a few slivers of light.

'Right, first things first,' he said. 'I need to see the king.'

'Er, what?' asked Hasim.

Fynius smiled, splitting his mouth into a broad grin. 'I don't plan to have a drink with him. I just need to see him. Then I can think about Scarlet Company and the wise woman.'

He moved a heavy barrel to the centre of the basement and vaulted on top of it. At full stretch he could reach the trapdoor.

'Do you know where that leads?' asked Hasim.

'Nope. Well, yes . . . it leads up.'

He grabbed a rusted semicircle of metal that used to be a handle and used his weight as leverage. A few seconds of creaking and falling dust, and the trapdoor buckled downwards. Fynius let go and fell to the stone floor, covered in wooden splinters and thick dust. Two white fabric sacks fell down from above and bounced off his head, eliciting grunts of annoyance.

When the dust had cleared there was an open hatchway leading up.

Fynius coughed and rubbed the grime and dirt from his face, kicking the sacks out of the way.

'Up we go then,' he said, getting back on the barrel.

He leapt up and got a good hold on the lip of the opening, pulling himself up into musty darkness. It was another basement, built on top of the cheese tunnels. This one was full, with sacks and barrels in disorganized lines across the slotted wooden floor. Fynius had emerged in the middle of forgotten supplies and under a low ceiling. The wood above was poorly maintained and each floorboard had gaps. The light was flickering, coming from fire-pits in the long hall. Best of all, he could hear muffled voices.

Hasim hauled himself up into the basement of Long Shadow's hall, crouching amidst the barrels.

'What are you doing?' asked Fynius.

'I'm hiding,' whispered Hasim in response.

'From what? There's no one here.'

The Karesian pointed upwards. 'There are people up there.'

'They're not looking for two sneaky rodents in their basement, though, are they?'

'Rodents? Fuck off,' replied Hasim.

Fynius moved across the discarded barrels to the corner of the basement. The gaps between the floorboards were wider here and larger blades of light illuminated his face. The voices were still too far away. He needed to get closer. He tested the floorboards and found them loose. With a lift and a slide, he moved a plank of wood out of the way and poked his head up through the floor.

It was a small room, filled with food and bottles of mead. A door at each end, both latched from the outside. Sides of salted pork, baskets of apples, oranges and rounds of hard bread. The larder of the long hall was well used, with little dust and multiple footprints.

'Stay down there, man of the sun. Your big, heavy feet will give us away.'

He ignored the grumbled reply and hefted himself into the larder. Voices, footsteps, the clank of armour, all were clear and alarmingly close. The knights and clerics occupying the hall appeared to be flustered. Their voices were raised and their movements quick.

'The king, the Purple man, the king, the Purple man, the enchantress, the wise woman. What to do, what to do?'

With the tip of Leg Biter, he gently raised the latch on the left-hand door. Glancing into the hall, he saw light, natural and unnatural. Torches in the corridors, fire-pits in the long hall, and the silvery glow of dawn from the windows.

He darted across the corridor to an adjacent room. Two Purple clerics clanked across the carpet a second later, talking about the Red cardinal. They were encased in ornate armour, looking like mobile fortresses of interlocked metal and leather strapping. They hadn't seen or heard him.

His new location was a bedroom, perhaps formerly belonging to a cook or a kitchen servant. There was blood on the white sheets and sword marks on the wall. Someone had died there. Bastard knights.

'Up or along, up or along?' he muttered, hoping for an answer. 'Up is safer, along is quicker.'

'Up it is!'

Above the room, a dense criss-cross of interlocked wooden beams held up the thatched roof. There was no lower ceiling and a sufficiently nimble man could traverse the length of Long Shadow's hall in the rafters.

'I'm sufficiently nimble. Let's go and see the king,' he said to Brytag, making sure the World Raven was still with him.

He put a chair on top of the bed and climbed up. It was tricky to reach the rafters, though the lack of light helped conceal him. Within a few minutes he was hanging in the middle of the small bedroom, clinging to the horizontal wooden beams. He strained with exertion and flexed his forearms, pulling his lean body into the dark rafters.

'Much better, I can see where I'm going.'

Perched on a beam in darkness, Fynius could see a lot of men. A dozen small bedrooms were occupied by clerics. Ranen prisoners were held in a dozen more storerooms. Ranen women were cleaning the corridors and the long hall was flanked by Purple clerics. The hierarchy was obvious. The Purple men were in charge and the Red men were the muscle. What a strange way to organize an army. What gave them the right to rule? And Purple was a stupid colour.

He moved through the rafters, silently edging his way towards the hall. Raised voices and the crackle of a fire greeted him. South Warden was warm compared with Old Gar, but cold for these men of Ro, and they kept the fire-pits burning.

'Will the king tell me what's going to happen?' he asked Brytag. 'Hmm, let's see.'

At the far end of the hall, seated in Long Shadow's chair and surrounded by men of the Purple, was the king of Tor Funweir.

371

Fynius didn't know his name but he looked like a manic child.

'There you are,' he whispered.

A cleric, older and haughtier-looking than the rest, was at the king's side, arguing with him.

'And you're the Purple man.'

He moved closer, trusting in shadow and stealth, until he could hear what they were talking about.

'I know what she wants, my king,' said the Purple cardinal. 'She has touched me with her love and blessed me with conviction.'

'Be silent, Mobius,' said the king. 'Saara is my love, my life, and I feel her needs better than you.'

The cardinal grimaced, as if he were fighting the urge to do or say something unwise. The seated man was his king, but some other influence was causing a rift. Was this what Fynius needed to see?

'Educate me, my king . . . what does she need?' asked Mobius, containing his anger.

'She needs her king to act with strength and certitude. I have been idle and weak. This Fallon of Leith needs to be taught not to defy his king. The Red general must annihilate the peasants of Darkwald.'

The king was flapping his hands in the air. He twitched and contorted, moving his body into strange angles. Whatever else he was, the king of Tor Funweir was clearly under the influence of sorcery.

'This is wrong,' muttered Fynius. 'This is very, very wrong.'

'My king!' snapped the Purple cardinal. 'Please listen to counsel. I know her heart and I know what she wants.'

The king widened his eyes and his face flushed red. 'You claim to know her better than me? Insolence!'

Mobius put a hand on the hilt of his sword. The other clerics did the same, indicating that they were loyal to their cardinal before their king.

'Be careful, my king,' said the cardinal. 'I spoke to our beloved allies before you'd even heard of them. Don't make the mistake of thinking I am your servant.'

The king, oblivious to the armed men all around him, raised his chin. 'I do not like the knights of the Red meeting without me. When they parlay, I will attend.'

Mobius motioned for his men to stand at their ease and they withdrew their hands from their swords. Fynius didn't understand these men. Even taking into account the sorcery, they were strange creatures. The king was in charge, but not really. The cardinal maintained a strange deceit that he obeyed his monarch, while flexing his muscles and reminding the king how tenuous his power was.

'The situation needs the leadership of nobility, my king. Let your clerics lead.' The cardinal stepped close to the king. 'Stay in the hall, be quiet, know your place. Saara has tasked me with keeping you in line.'

The king began to stand, but was shoved back into his seat by Mobius. He curled up in a mockery of childish emotion, clutching his knees to his chest and crying.

'If you insist on attending the parlay, my men will accompany you and they will be in charge. You will do as you are told.'

'I just want her to love me,' he wailed.

'We all do, my king, but she only truly loves me,' replied Mobius, the mania of enchantment bringing a glint to the corner of his eyes.

'So you're both enchanted,' said Fynius. 'Lovely.'

Around the hall, slouching on chairs and round tables were a dozen men of the Purple. A further squad stood behind Mobius. Fynius had expected the Red men to be in charge, but none of them were in Long Shadow's hall.

'Right, I know what's going to happen,' he told Brytag. 'And I know how we can help. Excellent.'

With a jaunty spring in his step, Fynius hopped back across the rafters to the cook's bedroom.

* * *

Five cheese cellars were now full of blue-jacketed men of Twilight Company. Vincent Hundred Howl had moved everyone under the city and they had spread out through the first few tunnels. When it happened, they would be ready, but Fynius had one more thing to do. He had to find the wise woman.

'What about Two Hearts?' asked Hasim. 'He's got a lot of men.'

'He'll just get in the way,' replied Fynius. 'Your lover will be useful, though.'

The man of the sun chuckled, slumped against the wooden floor of the cellar.

'She'd hate you calling her that.'

'Don't care,' replied Fynius. 'The World Raven likes her, which means I trust her.'

'You trust her, a lady of Ro, and not me?'

'I'd forgotten she was Ro,' he responded. 'Gods come before countries. She can speak on my behalf to this Fallon of Leith.'

'You got his name right . . . well done!'

Fynius ignored him and again left the bulk of his men. He didn't need Hasim to accompany him this time and he knew exactly where he was going. He took the same tunnel, ignoring the trapdoor that led up to Long Shadow's hall, and continuing as far as Rowanoco's Stone. He could feel the wise woman, huddled under the ruined chapel. At least some of Scarlet Company had not felt the need to die foolishly in the breach.

The cheese tunnels ended in a central stone chamber. Wooden framing lined the circular walls from the floor to the ceiling twenty feet above. Mouldy wheels of cheese and forgotten cheese-making equipment sat on broken wooden shelves. A sufficiently foolhardy man could use the frames as a ladder to reach the hatch in the centre of the ceiling.

'I'm sufficiently foolhardy,' he announced, beginning to climb.

The frame was rickety, but the upright supports were solid enough and Fynius was freakishly dextrous. He reached the central hatch. It was a dirty glass window set in the floor of whatever was up there. There was no way to open it without breaking the glass.

'Hmm, let's trust to luck, shall we?'

He knocked on the glass and waited, wedged between an upright wooden beam and the wall. After a minute, dark silhouettes moved across the glass.

'Hello!' he said, speaking as loudly as he dared. 'I'm not a Red knight, or a Purple cleric.'

Whispered voices from above. A man and a woman. The man was suspicious and the woman wanted to open the glass hatch.

'Brytag sent me,' he said more quietly.

The silhouettes stopped talking. The larger of the two shapes knelt down and prized away the rusty metal latch. The glass was pulled upwards and Fynius smiled at the two Ranen above.

'Who the fuck are you?' asked the man, a corpulent warrior in middle age with a short black beard.

Fynius ignored him and stretched to reach the lip of the hatch. He got a good hold and pulled himself through. The man stepped back and hefted an old-looking axe. The woman stayed put and smiled at him. Elsewhere in the stone chamber were dozens of men, women and children. Some wore the crimson of South Warden, others the blue of Hail. Many were wounded and many more were starving.

He felt the man deserved an answer. 'I'm Fynius Black Claw. I come from Old Gar, following a raven.'

The man slowly lowered his axe and a tired smile flowed across his face. His wrinkles showed and there were shadows under his eyes.

'Mathias Flame Tooth, axe-master of South Warden. This is Freya Cold Eyes of Hail. Welcome, man of Gar.'

* * *

Fynius was pleased with himself. He'd found two more groups of survivors huddled in basements and cheese cellars, trying to stay alive by eating what they could steal and drinking rainwater. Flame Tooth was in charge, and in remarkably good health considering he'd sustained a dozen separate wounds fighting in the breach. He had managed to remain jovial and keep their spirits up as they waited for rescue or death.

The prisoners had stayed in their sanctuaries, joined by groups of Twilight Company who cared for their wounds and prepared them for what was to come. This proved tricky, as Fynius hadn't felt the need to explain what was going to happen, even to Mathias Flame Tooth or the wise woman, Freya.

He'd found caches of weapons, taken by the Ro following the battle, and the bundles of axes, hammers, knives and bows were again in the hands of the Ranen.

'We can't fight, Fynius,' said Flame Tooth. 'It's nice for the lads to have their weapons back, but we can't fight them.'

'We won't have to,' he replied. 'Not all of them, anyway.'

They were in a forgotten basement of the chapel, sealed from Rowanoco's Stone above and accessed through a hidden passageway behind the assembly steps. Freya and Mathias had escaped the knights and had slowly rescued others until several hundred men, women and children were out of the knights' clutches. It didn't surprise him that the Ro hadn't noticed. They had apparently only taken notice of the captive Ranen when they had needed to assemble a work-gang or had wanted to beat someone up.

'I trust you, man of Gar,' said Freya. 'The World Raven will see us safe.'

He grinned in appreciation. It was the first time a southerner had shown any faith in him.

'The World Raven doesn't have an army,' countered Mathias.

'But he has me . . . that's almost as good,' replied Fynius, still smiling. 'Don't worry, axe-master, South Warden will be ours again, that's all you need to worry about. When the time comes, worry for South Warden. Worry not for the king, the knights or the yeomanry. Leave them to me, and to the World Raven.'

Mathias was a big man, barrel-chested, with a face covered in dense black hair. He was looking at Fynius as if the man of Gar was mad. Or maybe it was just the way he showed his appreciation. Probably the former.

'So what do we do? Wait?' asked Flame Tooth, cocking an eyebrow.

'You can wait, if you like,' he replied. 'Now, if you'd excuse me, axe-master, I have to go and talk to a woman of Ro.'

* * *

Gathered at the tree line, cowering behind wide tree trunks and dense bramble thickets, were the men and women of the Crescent. Federick Two Hearts had somehow managed to cajole or threaten the other chieftains into following him south.

Fynius had left South Warden, with the Karesian idiot trailing along behind, and had found Bronwyn in a small clearing behind Theen Burnt Face and his warriors. They all looked at him, glaring, turning away, or asking their companions who he was. Stories were circulated as the thuggish Moon clans shared their mutual hatred of anyone of culture or sophistication. He was amazed they hadn't been killed before now. Any idiot with an axe and an army could conquer these fools.

'Have they been treating you well?' he asked the sullen noblewoman.

She began to reply, standing up from the rock upon which she was sitting.

'Actually, don't tell me,' he interrupted. 'I don't care.'

The young axe-man, Bronwyn's loyal lapdog, snarled at Fynius. He had a big pointy axe and a generally bad attitude, but he had conviction and that was worth something.

'Don't bark at me, young man,' he said, trying to remember the Wraith man's name. 'I've had enough of bloody southerners and I have no particular desire to talk to you.'

The man of Wraith was wounded, but hefted his axe angrily all the same. 'We're on the same side, fuck-head,' said the young man. 'Try to remember that.'

'Fuck-head?' replied Fynius, filing the insult away for future use. 'Is that a Ro Hail thing? Some new curse?'

'Micah, he's not as much an arsehole as he appears,' said Al-Hasim. 'He's just . . . touched, in some way.'

Bronwyn shook her head, thinking herself better than the men around her. She was sweet in a naive Ro kind of way, but she was far more important than she knew and should probably grow up.

'You need to grow up, young lady,' he said.

'Er, what?' she replied, raising her eyebrow. 'I didn't say anything.'

'I didn't say you did.'

She opened her mouth, but didn't speak. She shook her head, grunted in bewilderment, and looked at Al-Hasim.

'Fynius, can you act like a human for a second?' asked the Karesian. 'You're not making any friends here.'

Why did people keep questioning him? If they would shut up and listen, things would go so much smoother. Hasim was ignorant, Bronwyn was childish and Micah was just some man of no importance. Together, they had somehow managed to stay alive and serve Brytag without knowing it.

'This will be so much easier when the World Raven deigns to give me a shade,' he said, not caring if they understood. 'Anyway, you, Lady Bronwyn of Canarn, have something to do.'

'What exactly do I have to do?' she asked sneeringly.

'Well, if you're going to be like that, I might not tell you.'

'Fynius!' snapped Hasim. 'Time is important here.'

'Yes, yes, whatever. Right, Lady Bronwyn of Canarn, you're going to be my intermediary with Fallon of Leith. Lots of stuff is going to happen in an hour or two. When it happens, people are going to be surprised. Your job is to tell the good guys that the bad guys are dealt with.'

'And who are the good guys?' she asked.

'Apparently this Fallon chap is on our side. For now, at least. Don't worry, Lady Bronwyn of Canarn, you're only responsible for

making sure there isn't a massive battle. A battle we won't win.'
He smiled. 'Now, if you'll excuse me, I'm going to find somewhere comfortable to watch the coming antics. And I should probably send a message to the One God. Brytag is nothing if not polite.'

'So, are you going to tell us what's going to happen?' asked Hasim.

Apparently these people weren't going to trust him. Telling them what the raven had told him would be an easy way to shut them up. They probably wouldn't believe him, but it would shut them up.

'Okay, I can pander to you lot for a little while longer. Have a seat and let me tell you a story.' He pointed at Micah. 'You too, fuck-head.'

PART TWO

FALLON THE GREY IN THE REALM OF SCARLET

A LARGE, BLACK raven flew across the Plains of Scarlet towards the yeomanry's camp. He followed its trajectory, drifting in decreasing circles, until it came to rest inside the camp.

The southern horizon was a rippling sea of red. Hundreds of banners hung from countless tents. Horses, carts and men covered the Plains of Scarlet. From the stockade of South Warden, across the yeomanry's defences, to the huge camp of Malaki Frith, the Freelands of Ranen were brimming with soldiers of Tor Funweir.

The Red cardinal had spent the morning establishing his camp, south of the city, and Fallon had remained impassive throughout their deployment. He had no idea how the confrontation would play out. He didn't let the slightest doubt appear in his words or on his face, but in his mind Fallon wanted to bite his lip and pray for a peaceful solution. Maybe Cardinal Frith was an honourable man. Maybe he loathed Mobius and had come to calm the situation, not to make it worse. Fallon was a realist, not a misty-eyed young knight, but he hated having to kill men and order men to their deaths.

'They're setting up a tent,' said Vladimir, supping from a brass goblet. 'In the middle of the field. What does that mean?'

'It means that he's not just going to attack us,' replied Fallon.

'Ah, a parlay,' guffawed the noble, slurring his words. 'I think I'd be good at parlaying. Never tried, but I'm eager to give it a go, dear chap.'

'How much have you drunk this morning?'

'Nowhere near enough,' replied Vladimir, draining his goblet. 'Want some?'

Fallon tried not to laugh but failed. 'I've not met Malaki Frith. Maybe I should make a good first impression.'

'Go on!' coaxed the nobleman, waving a half-empty bottle of wine.

'Vladimir, look over there. What do you see?'

He swayed forward against the wooden stockade. 'Is that a trick question?' he asked, belching into the cold morning air. 'Excuse me. Terrible manners, old boy.'

'What do you see?' Fallon repeated.

The drunken noble rubbed his eyes. 'I see a lot of knights. Five thousand with Tristram and the king. Another . . . maybe ten, with General Frith.'

He began to reply, but Vladimir belched again and interrupted him. 'Okay, Fallon, I know what you're saying. We have six thousand.'

'It's a blunt lesson, but one worth stating,' replied the exemplar. 'We can't win a fight. I need to find another solution, and I'm better at doing that when I'm sober.'

Vladimir pouted and looked down at his bottle of wine. 'Sorry, I must seem awfully naive to you. Here I am, losing men by the cartful, and all I can offer by way of help is drunken blathering.'

'You make me laugh, my lord. That counts for something.'

The Lord of Mud frowned, as if uncomfortable at being complimented.

'I just wish I could swing a sword or do something useful,' replied Vladimir, patting his ornamental longsword.

'You've had training,' said Fallon.

'A lord's training, it's not really the same thing. I've never fought to kill.'

'You're a lord of Ro,' countered Fallon. 'That matters more than a hundred knights. They can ignore me, they can't ignore you.'

Vladimir took a messy swig of wine. 'I've been ignored all my life,' he said, wiping his mouth. 'I'm not the lord of diamonds or gold, my dear chap.'

'You're the lord of wine,' Fallon replied.

'True enough.' Another, deeper, swig.

Fallon peered across the fields of Scarlet. The Red cardinal had half emptied the barracks of Arnon to reinforce the king. His forces displayed dozens of banners. Noble knights of Du Ban and the Falls of Arnon showed their personal standards alongside the clenched fist of the Red.

Maybe Frith knew about the enchantresses, maybe he didn't. Either way, he wanted to talk to Fallon before he attacked. Curiously, the tent they had erected had only the banner of the Red knights above it. No Purple sceptre or white eagle of the king. Strange. Frith should have clerics of nobility with him, not to mention the presence of Mobius in South Warden. It appeared that neither would be invited to the parlay.

Fallon had known the previous cardinal well. Jareth of Du Ban had named him the Grey Knight after a drunken indiscretion during his years as a trainee. He had been a fine man. Malaki Frith was an unknown. He had risen to the highest office of knights through loyalty and, by all accounts, an apathetic approach to politics.

Hundreds of possibilities flowed through Fallon's mind. He was pessimistic by nature and couldn't ignore the many ways he could get himself and his men killed. An ill-advised insult, a drunken comment from Vladimir. None of it mattered until he knew what kind of man the cardinal was.

The raven took flight again. It circled the camp above Fallon's head and glided across the trebuchets. Its cawing was the loudest noise he could hear, rising over the distant clatter of armour and the braying of horses.

'That's the symbol of Canarn isn't it?' slurred Vladimir. 'A raven in flight?'

'Used to be,' he replied, shielding his eyes from the morning sun and looking at the large bird. 'I hear the risen men are in charge there these days.'

Vladimir bit his thumb to ward off evil spirits and took another drink. 'I never met Lord Bromvy. Maybe he sent a raven to watch over us,' he said, spluttering out some wine.

The raven drifted to a halt nearby, resting on a barrel of crossbow bolts. To its left, the ghostly form of Torian's shade appeared. The Purple cleric approached the bird with interest and Fallon narrowed his eyes.

'Something wrong?' asked Vladimir, looking at the bird.

The bird flapped, but Fallon wasn't sure whether it flapped at the shade or not. They appeared to be looking at each other, but that could have been a trick of the dawn light.

'No,' replied Fallon, not wishing to confide in Vladimir. 'Just remembering Canarn.'

'Lots of people die?'

'Unnecessarily,' he replied. 'Same at Hail and South Warden. No one likes being conquered.'

The Lord of Mud didn't know how to respond. He opened his mouth a couple of times but no words came out. His lips were stained red from the wine and his eyes drooped. Fallon liked him, but occasionally he could wish for a more balanced confidant.

'Don't worry, my Lord Corkoson,' he said, turning from the raven as it took flight and soared away from the yeomanry's camp. 'You and I are going to make sure that no one else dies.'

'Or gets conquered,' said Vladimir.

They left the forward defences and went to prepare their men for whatever was going to happen. Arms and armour were cleaned, repaired and donned, horses were fed and saddled, trebuchets loaded and crewed. Once everything was in place and no word had arrived from the cardinal, Fallon returned to the forward palisade and waited.

* * *

Malaki Frith wore unadorned armour. His breastplate was polished steel and his tabard a dark red. Neither had any conspicuous insignia or marks of personal status. Even the cardinal's sword was a simple blade in a simple scabbard. He could have been mistaken for an ordinary knight if it weren't for the embroidery on his cloak and the high, white plume on his helmet.

Fallon took this as a good sign. The more ornate a man's attire, the more concerned he was likely to be with status and hierarchy. His own armour had been simple and patched together, and he'd not had a red cloak since Ro Canarn. Currently, he looked more like a mercenary than a former knight, with reinforced leather armour and heavy riding boots. Mud stains, rusted buckles and mottled leather had become his new uniform.

He scratched at his stubble and hoped the cardinal wasn't concerned with personal grooming. He chuckled to himself, realizing that his former life as a knight was hard to shake off. The mere sight of the Red cardinal had conjured images of midnight inspections and punishments for appearing slovenly on duty. Verellian would often chide him for his less than exemplary appearance, his missing cloak, his lackadaisical attitude to his uniform. None of it mattered now. At least, he hoped it didn't.

'He looks very serious,' said Vladimir, riding between Fallon and Theron towards the parlay table.

From the other direction, Knight Commander Tristram and his adjutant, Taufel, rode from South Warden to join the growing assembly of senior knights. The Red cardinal himself was accompanied by a single knight, a captain from the look of his armour, and several bound men standing as aides.

'He looks quite humble, though,' offered Theron. 'Look at his breastplate. No personal heraldry. That's rare for a senior knight.'

'Okay, serious but humble,' said the Lord of Mud. 'Is that good?'

'It's better than jovial but arrogant,' answered Fallon. 'Assuming he acts as his appearance would suggest.'

The raven cawed from above. The bird had been lingering around the camp most of the morning. Since it had first soared overhead from South Warden, Fallon had seen it flapping at Torian's shade, pecking at the yeomanry's defences, and shitting on Red knights. A few crossbow bolts had been loosed at it from Frith's camp, but the large, glossy black bird remained defiantly aloft.

'Is that thing an omen of some kind?' asked Vladimir, miming the pull of a bowstring at the raven.

'No idea. Omens, portents, visions, who needs them?' replied Fallon.

As if in answer to his question, Torian appeared, floating in the air before him. The apparition was transparent and more like a mist than usual. It said nothing, merely ghosting alongside them, moving as a wisp.

'Just so everyone's clear,' said Vladimir, 'I am absolutely terrified . . . and a little drunk.'

'Just don't puke on him,' replied Fallon.

The three of them rode slowly, as did Tristram and Taufel. Each group was giving the others the chance to see them. The Red knights assessed one another and Vladimir tried not to vomit.

The cardinal only looked at Fallon. He was inscrutable, showing no emotion, positive or negative, as he assessed the Grey Knight.

'Fallon of Leith, Tristram of the Cross, you are both welcome.' Sit in peace with your blades tied.' Frith stood as he spoke, holding his arms wide.

The riders all stopped and dismounted, handing their reins to the attentive bound men. The parlay table was a slab of oak on four squat pillars, with well-made armchairs all round it. The table was isolated, equidistant from South Warden, the camp of the yeomanry, and Frith's army. No men stood guard over them and no crossbows or artillery were aimed at them. For a change, Fallon didn't feel like a traitor or a criminal.

Tristram looked at him with a thin smile. The knight commander appeared unwell and peace-tied his sword with shaking hands. Captain Taufel saluted the cardinal enthusiastically with a ramrod-straight back and an imperious rise of his chin. The two knights then sat.

Fallon waited, motioning for Theron and Vladimir to sit before him.

'Hello,' said Vladimir, breaking the uncomfortable silence.

'May I present Lord Vladimir Corkoson, commander of the Darkwald yeomanry,' said Fallon.

Cardinal Frith nodded to the Lord of Mud, but said nothing, motioning for Fallon to sit. The two men stood, looking at each other, both remaining on their feet. Slowly, keeping his eyes on the knight general, Fallon sat down. Now that he was close to the man, he found him still inscrutable. His face was lined, but not harsh, and there was wisdom in his eyes. Or maybe it was something else, not wisdom. He still didn't know what kind of man he was.

Frith sat last, leaning forward and crossing his arms on the table.

'I am Knight General Malaki Frith. This is Knight Captain Dolf Halan.' He leant back, his face becoming harsher. 'Which of you is going to tell me what in the name of the One is going on here?'

Fallon chuckled, Tristram frowned and Vladimir smiled awkwardly.

'It's complicated, my lord cardinal,' said the Lord of Mud.

'Clearly,' replied Frith. 'I was summoned from Arnon to reinforce the king. Does he still need reinforcing? I can't tell from my current view. What I can tell is that we do not have a unified army on the Plains of Scarlet.'

'South Warden appears cowed,' said Captain Halan. 'Scarlet Company no longer a threat?'

'I would ask you to speak plainly, knight commander,' said the general, addressing Tristram. 'Whose orders do you follow?'

'That, too, is complicated, sir,' replied Tristram, coughing into his hand. 'Cardinal Mobius has taken day-to-day command.'

Frith snorted with humour and exchanged a glance with Halan. Fallon could tell that neither of the men liked the Purple cardinal.

'Please, Tristram, do you have any idea how long it takes ten thousand men to march here from Ro Arnon? We are tired, irritable, and we don't know why we're here. Speaking to other knights should have cleared this up . . . but so far it has not. Perhaps the Purple would be more talkative.'

'May I speak?' asked Fallon.

The cardinal bowed his head and screwed up his face. He didn't look at Fallon. 'I'm not sure. I'm actually questioning the wisdom of inviting you to parlay. Dolf wanted to clear your camp before we sat down.'

'I'm rather glad you didn't,' spluttered Vladimir. 'We really don't want to fight. We just want to go home.'

'Then you shouldn't have questioned your king,' replied Halan.

'Enough!' Frith said to his adjutant. 'We'll hear what Fallon of Leith has to say.'

Fallon leant back. 'I'll tell you the truth, my lord, but you won't like it.'

'Talk to me,' replied Frith. 'Your answer couldn't be worse than Tristram's.'

'The king is mad. A Karesian witch has enchanted him and the Purple cardinal. Mobius is a pig who does not speak for the One. You have been called to help them subjugate the Ranen because that's what the Seven Sisters want.'

It was a gamble to tell him this, to blurt it out as a man would describe movements on a battlefield, but he was fed up with uncertainty. The general could listen or he could kill him. Either way, the stalemate was over.

'Seeing conspiracies, captain?' said Dolf Halan. 'That is not your reputation.'

'I'm not a captain, not any more,' he replied.

'I could kill you just for that,' snapped Frith. 'I should kill you just for that.'

Each man reacted. Theron leant towards Fallon protectively. Vladimir backed away and held his hands up. Tristram and Taufel nodded in agreement. But Fallon laughed.

'I am Fallon the Grey, I serve the One God. That remains true whether you try to kill me or not . . . and I emphasize the word try.'

Frith didn't respond. He looked at the exemplar, neither blinking nor showing any sign of anger. His eyes were light green and his lined face had a day's growth of stubble. At least they agreed that shaving was to be done infrequently. Other than that, Fallon couldn't read him.

'This is a parlay, correct?' asked Vladimir, smiling pathetically. 'So we should all try to be friendly.'

A horn sounded from South Warden. They all looked up from the parlay table and saw the wooden gates open.

'My lord?' queried Dolf Halan, rising from his chair.

'Stand easy,' replied Frith.

The general stood and peered to the north. Fallon did the same, seeing ten mounted men riding fast towards them. Two banners were carried by a single man – a white eagle and a purple sceptre. Men watched from South Warden and the camp of the yeomanry, pointing with interest at horsemen coming from the city.

'The king approaches,' said Fallon drily. 'Perhaps he can clarify things.'

'Oh dear,' offered Vladimir, rubbing his face nervously.

Nine Purple clerics, fully armed and armoured, plunged noisily across the field. Cleon Montague, the king's bodyguard, bore their standards and rode at the front, his purple tabard spotlessly clean. The other clerics encircled the king, who cut an uninspiring figure. Thin, with poorly fitting armour and a lank, greasy ring of hair. His eyes were still manic and he appeared to twitch as he rode, finding it hard to control his horse.

Fallon strolled round the table, casually untying his sword. He stopped next to the knight general. 'You're about to see the evidence of madness and enchantment, my lord,' he said, taking no pleasure in being proved right.

'Peace-tie that sword, soldier,' replied Frith, not looking up from the approaching riders. 'And sit back down. I've known Sebastian Tiris since he was a boy, I'll know if anything is wrong.'

The clerics stopped, forming into a line with the king and Sir Montague at the front. Their swords were not peace-tied.

'My king,' said Knight General Frith, bowing respectfully. 'It has been too long. You are well?'

'How dare you meet without your king,' barked Montague. 'You of all people should know your place, my lord general.'

'Well, you're here now,' replied Frith, remaining cool.

King Sebastian did not take his eyes from Fallon. They were bloodshot and his red-veined cheeks gave him the appearance of a man the worse for drink. His golden robes were stained and he clutched them tightly around his shoulders, huddling up on his saddle. That did not make his glare any less sinister.

'We meant no disrespect, my king,' said Frith. 'Will you take a seat?'

The general was just as inscrutable when faced with the king. His face was like stone, hard and expressionless.

'I will sit when these traitors are dead,' whined Sebastian Tiris.

'This is a parlay table, my king.' Frith cast his eyes towards the nine clerics. 'You will notice that our weapons are tied.'

'We will not parlay with this peasant swordsman,' said Montague, pointing at Fallon.

'We will,' said Dolf Halan. 'As is our right as knights of the Red.'

'Your right?' bellowed the Purple cleric. 'You have the rights we give you and no more, soldier.'

Frith stepped towards the king's bodyguard. He looked up at the mounted man. Without changing expression, he pulled his saddle up from below, spilling the rider on to the grass. The horse reared up and the other clerics held their sword hilts. The knight general put his boot on Montague's throat, stopping the startled man from standing.

'I am Knight General Malaki Frith, cardinal of the Red. If you need more reason to treat me with respect, here's my boot.'

Fallon exchanged a look of amusement with Vladimir and Theron. The Lord of Mud, biting his lip and snorting, barely stopped himself from erupting into laughter.

'General!' shrieked the king. 'You insult a cleric of the sword.'

Frith removed his boot and stepped back. 'Of course, my king, I forget myself,' he said conversationally.

Cleon Montague stood and adjusted his tabard. He stared at the general but didn't answer the challenge. Picking up his fallen saddle, the cleric went to retrieve his horse. The rest of the Purple clerics dismounted and assisted the king as he clumsily tried to reach the ground.

'Are we going to die?' mumbled Vladimir. 'He looks angry.'

'He looks pathetic,' replied Theron.

'Both of you, shut up,' snapped Fallon. 'We're not going to die here.'

'I advise you to be silent,' whispered Dolf Halan sharply. 'Let us handle things and you and your men may survive.'

Frith approached Sebastian Tiris and dropped to one knee.

'My king, I report from Arnon as ordered,' he said, ignoring the armed Purple clerics glaring at him.

'I receive you gratefully,' slurred the king, offering his hand. 'I command that you place these criminals under arrest.'

The Red cardinal kissed the offered hand and stood up. His eyes were now narrow as he studied the king's face.

'As you say, my king. What is their crime?' asked Frith.

'Treason!' he shrieked.

'I see,' replied the general. 'And the details of this treason?'

Montague returned, leading his horse. His manner was more guarded now. Perhaps a boot to the throat was the best way to talk to a Purple cleric. 'The details are incidental, general,' said the king's bodyguard. 'You have been ordered to arrest them and arrest them you must.'

'I don't believe I was speaking to you, cleric,' replied Frith, dismissing the man with a wave of his hand.

The raven made its presence known with a caw. It had been there since the king had arrived, silently circling them, but now its shrill call signalled the appearance of Torian's shade. All eyes except Fallon's looked up. The Grey Knight studied the ghostly purple image that was facing the king, while the other men shouted curses at the bird.

Montague pointed at Dolf Halan. 'You, knight! Fetch me a crossbow. I'll deal with this winged harbinger.'

Halan looked unimpressed. He turned to his general for confirmation and Frith shook his head.

'Throw your sword at it,' said the knight general. 'And don't give my men orders.'

'Cardinal!' barked the king. 'I have given you an order. I trust I am permitted.'

The bird caught a downdraught and soared towards the ground. It flew over their heads and turned sharply, plunging directly at Torian's shade and the king. The raven was large and its glossy, black wings shone in the morning sun. It pulled up before the king and the others all followed its graceful flight. Fallon didn't look up. He looked at the ghostly raven that had sent its shade out towards Torian and the king. The form looked exactly like the raven, but was transparent and shimmering white.

Torian's shade held his arms wide and received the ghostly raven in its chest. The two apparitions fused and a bright blue light made Fallon wince. Then the bird emerged from the cleric's back and plunged at the king.

'For the One!' roared Torian in the depths of Fallon's mind.

The raven entered the king and the light disappeared. The other knights and clerics reacted only because Sebastian Tiris appeared to faint. They had not seen the ghostly raven and Fallon had kept his astonishment under control.

'My king,' spluttered Montague, moving to assist him.

394

Sebastian held his head while his clerics formed a circle round him. Fallon puffed out his cheeks and cocked an eyebrow. He found himself amused. He wasn't sure why, but so much time spent with Torian's shade had made him cynical, even about the supernatural. He was jaded about so much and this was just the latest thing to add to the list.

He nudged Vladimir. 'This should be interesting, my lord.'

'What? The king fell over. Fear of birds maybe,' replied the Lord of Mud.

'Just wait,' said Fallon. 'It would seem the gods are not above an alliance.'

Vladimir and Theron looked at him in confusion. He wished Lanry were here. The old cleric would have had wise counsel. He would probably also have seen the two shades meet. As it was, Fallon had to endure being an exemplar alone.

Captain Halan and General Frith did not go to the king. They left the clerics to flap around and help him stand up. Montague allowed Tiris to lean on him and the king was shaking his head and coughing.

'Perhaps you should return to the city and rest, my king,' said Frith. 'The winds of Scarlet seem not to agree with you.'

Sebastian Tiris was standing. His brow was creased and he pushed away the clerics. Montague sought to lead him away but was waved aside.

'What the devil is going on here?' he said, looking at himself as if he wanted a bath. 'I'm in a frightful state.'

'My king, we should return to Cardinal Mobius,' said Montague.

'Mobius? Where is he?' asked the king, his confused eyes darting from side to side. He noticed the Red cardinal. 'Malaki! Excellent, someone with sense. Now, tell me what's going on, old boy. I am in a field . . . it's cold . . . and there are a lot of warriors milling about. I say! A bloody awful lot of warriors.'

His manner had changed completely, as if a fog had lifted. Fallon took a gamble and spoke. 'What's the last thing you remember, my king?' he asked, raising his voice to be heard over the Purple clerics.

'You do not speak here,' commanded Montague.

The king frowned at his bodyguard. 'Er, there's no need for rudeness, Cleon. I'm sure we can sort this out in short order . . . obviously if someone tells me where I am.'

'You're in the Freelands, your grace,' said General Frith. 'And I think Fallon's question is a fair one. What's the last thing you remember?'

'Fallon, yes,' replied the king, smiling at the Grey Knight. 'Fallon of Leith, isn't it? The finest swordsman in Tor Funweir, by reputation. I'm honoured, Sir Fallon.'

Montague whispered in the ear of another cleric and two Purple men wheeled their horses swiftly, riding back to South Warden.

'Where are they going?' asked Frith.

'They are reporting in,' replied Montague. 'Lord Mobius will want to know what is happening here.' His voice was quiet and his tone worried. 'My king, we should leave. You're confused, these knights are not what you think. They are traitors.'

Frith and Halan began to respond, but were interrupted by the king. 'Nonsense!' snapped Sebastian Tiris. 'Malaki here is a dear old friend. Isn't that right, old boy?'

The Red general shoved two clerics out of the way and stood before his king. He smiled and offered his hand. 'It's good to see you again, Sebastian.'

They shook hands and the king leant in. 'I am awfully confused, though. What is going on here?'

'As Fallon asked, what is the last thing you remember, my king?'

His face screwed up and he chewed on his lower lip. 'Hmm, a party, I think. Well, a gathering, at the very least. Wine, food, music. My house in Ro Tiris.'

'You've been in Ranen for almost eight months, my king,' said Fallon. 'Ro Canarn, Ro Hail, South Warden, you've conquered the southern Ranen. Do you not remember?'

Sebastian Tiris studied himself. He looked at his tarnished

royal armour, his stained gold cloak. He scratched at his greasy hair and inspected his blackened fingernails. He frowned at what he saw.

'Have I been ill?' he asked. 'I remember nothing since . . . since meeting that Karesian woman. Cardinal Mobius introduced me to her.' He rubbed his face and Frith extended a hand to assist him.

'Thank you, old boy, you're a loyal servant.'

He leant forward and steadied himself against the Red cardinal. Montague and the Purple clerics stepped back and Dolf Halan joined Frith.

Torian's shade stood next to Fallon. The figure was brighter, the purple of his armour more vibrant and the sparkle in his eyes more penetrating. There was pride and conviction on his shimmering features, as if a plan had come to fruition.

Vladimir stood. 'I met him once before, years ago,' whispered the Lord of Mud. 'He was exactly like that.'

'What's happened?' asked Theron, less perceptive.

'The king regains his mind,' replied Fallon.

They both looked at him, keeping half an eye on the king leaning on Frith's shoulder. Neither man showed much faith, but they had not seen what he had seen.

'Right, let's sort this out,' announced the king. 'If Mobius is in South Warden, to South Warden we will go.'

His words were punctuated by the opening of the distant city gates. The two clerics rode inside and the gates closed. Whatever message they delivered to the Purple cardinal, Fallon guessed that the next hour would be rather interesting. But hopefully not terminal.

'As you say, my king,' replied Frith. 'We will accompany you.'

The Red cardinal signalled to his bound men and their horses were returned. Montague and the clerics had already wheeled their horses and left Sebastian Tiris with Frith. The king's eyes were brighter and he chatted with the general about the weather, the state of his clothes and a hundred other mundane things as they remounted.

'I hope the Ranen will allow me to have a bath, I smell frightful.'

'We don't know how many Ranen are left, my king,' replied Frith. 'Many were killed when your knights and yeomen took the city.'

Sebastian Tiris dropped his eyes to the grass. He had lived a sheltered life of power and nobility, but Fallon felt for him; he had woken from an enchanted sleep after many months to be told that he had started a war and killed thousands of men.

'Are we going with them?' asked Vladimir, pulling himself back into his saddle.

'Ask him,' replied Fallon. 'I doubt he'll kill you.'

'Reassuring. Thanks.'

The Lord of Mud nudged his horse close enough to be heard and coughed politely, interrupting the king's chatter.

'Lord Corkoson, isn't it? Of the Darkwald.'

'Yes, yes that's right,' replied Vladimir, smiling nervously. 'I don't know if you remember, but you sentenced me to hang, your grace.' The words were blurted out. 'Does that sentence no longer stand?'

'I should bloody well think not,' replied the king. 'Execute a lord of Tor Funweir? Such things should not be done. Well, not without due process and the necessary proof. What are you supposed to have done, my lord?'

The Lord of Mud tried to smile, but his nerves made it a strange mix of pain and fatigue. 'I disagreed with you on a matter of tactics, my king.'

'What matter of tactics?'

'Well, you and Mobius wanted to get all my men killed in the breach and I disagreed,' replied Vladimir, affecting his best upper-class accent.

Frith chuckled, though the Lord of Mud didn't relax.

'Don't you worry yourself,' said the king. 'You come with us, Sir Fallon too, and we'll sort this out. Lead the way, Malaki, old boy.'

Frith, Dolf Halan and five bound knights encircled the king and nudged their horses forward. Twelve riders left the parlay table with hundreds of eyes watching them from three separate military camps. Nothing had been conveyed to the camp of the yeomanry and Fallon knew that Major Dimitri and Brother Lanry would be exasperated.

Tristram and his adjutant were uncertain, but had said nothing to contradict either the general or the king. Now, as everyone rode towards the city gates, the knight commander fell in beside Fallon.

'The king regains his senses,' he said.

'I said that to Vladimir a minute ago,' replied Fallon. 'Good news for both of us.'

'Not for Mobius,' said Tristram. 'He will give up control reluctantly.'

'But you're with us, yes?' he asked, giving his former commander a chance to throw his lot in with the Red cardinal.

'I'm a knight of the Red, Fallon. I do what I'm told. As you once did.'

'After all of this we may eventually get to go home,' replied the Grey Knight, surprised at his brief feeling of optimism.

Vladimir interjected, 'That would be pleasant.'

'Best be quiet now,' said Tristram, as the city loomed before them.

Since he had escaped, Fallon had been looking at South Warden for weeks. Each morning and each night, he'd seen its repaired wooden walls and its red-armoured defenders. It was strange now to be at its gates. It was stranger still to be riding with Knight General Malaki Frith and King Sebastian Tiris. If only the One would inform him of a plan before it was enacted. He felt reactive and unprepared, as if something was yet to happen.

'That blasted raven,' said Vladimir, 'it's perched on the gate. Where they repaired it.'

The large bird was looking down at them, flaring its wings and emitting a mocking caw. Bound men, guarding the forward battlements, aimed crossbows, but could not get a clear shot.

'If it's an omen, it's a good one,' replied Fallon.

The Lord of Mud frowned at him. 'I was mostly worried about getting bird shit on my head.'

'Good omens can still shit on you,' he said, chuckling.

'Quiet,' repeated Tristram.

The riders stopped before the gates, allowing Frith and the king to advance. The men above were bound Red knights, staring at their king in confusion. Through the narrow gaps in the gate, purple tabards shone in the sun. No red could be seen, except on the walls. There were five thousand Red knights in South Warden, picketed somewhere beyond the entranceway.

'Where are your men?' he asked Commander Tristram.

'Mobius ordered us round the edge of the city, guarding the Ranen prisoners. The centre is just for the clerics, two hundred of them.'

'That's a lot of Purple,' he replied.

Fallon looked at the raven. It looked back, silently craning its neck forward. There was intelligence in the small, black eyes, and the bird managed to be more expressive up close.

'Open the gate!' commanded Frith in a deep, clear voice. 'The king returns.'

Men ran across the battlements, their steel-shod boots clattering on wood as they asked for orders. No one took charge and the gates remained closed, indicating a breakdown of command within. Whatever Mobius intended, he was taking his time.

'Don't make me ask again,' roared the Red cardinal.

Dolf Halan kicked his horse forward and banged on the wooden gate, the sound resonating along the walls.

'Commander Tristram, get your men to open this gate,' snapped the Red knight.

'The clerics control the gate, captain,' he replied. 'We await the Purple cardinal's pleasure.'

Fallon remained silent, allowing the situation to play out. The raven had freed the king, somehow removing the chains of enchantment, but Mobius remained an obstacle. If Brytag and the One had formed an alliance, they had done so only to free Sebastian Tiris.

Commands were shouted from within and men dressed in purple hurried to pull the gate inwards. Halan backed away and the riders reined in their horses, preparing to enter the city. Frith and Halan rode either side of the king, and the Red general's eyes were narrow and wary.

'What do we do, Fallon?' asked Vladimir, following the two Red knights through the gate.

'We let it play out,' he replied. 'Keep your eyes open and stay close to Theron.'

The twelve riders entered at a walk, taking in their surroundings as wooden buildings appeared behind ranks of Purple clerics. The inner courtyard, repaired by gangs of chained Ranen, was clear, and a horseshoe of armoured men encircled the riders. From the central mount, leading up towards the ruined assembly, approached the senior clerics, including Montague, just dismounting from his horse, and Cardinal Mobius. They were arriving along a winding road, lined with grass. The mount was steep and the road ended in steps, giving the Purple cardinal a high vantage point.

'Mobius, old fellow,' shouted the king, 'Malaki is here. I told him we'd sort out all this nonsense in short order.'

The Purple cardinal, his face sweaty and red, stopped on the steps, remaining behind his clerics. A quick scan round and Fallon saw over a hundred men guarding him, with more approaching from the Ranen assembly. There were no Red knights to be seen. The Purple cardinal had taken Tristram's command.

'How dare you enter here, Fallon of Leith?' Mobius croaked. 'You are a dead man, unaware of his own death.'

'What on earth are you going on about, old cock?' asked the king. 'Can't we dismount and dispense with the formalities? We are an awfully long way from home after all.'

'Silence, child!' shouted Mobius. 'The mistress gave me strict instructions on what to do should your conviction waver.'

Frith rode in front of Sebastian Tiris, waving for Dolf Halan to do the same.

'We should leave, my king,' he said quietly, not responding to Mobius's insult. 'It's not safe here.' He turned to Tristram. 'Commander, get your men down here and protect the king.'

Fallon saw a man level a crossbow. The Purple cleric stood next to Mobius and took aim. The Grey Knight kicked his horse forward.

'Crossbow!' he shouted, trying to get in front of the king.

He was too late. No one else had seen the weapon and the bolt was well aimed, striking Sebastian Tiris in the chest. His armour was poorly maintained and split loudly, buckling inwards. The king wailed in pain and blood spluttered from his mouth.

'Rally to me,' ordered Frith, causing Tristram, Theron and the rest of the knights to move forward and draw their swords. Vladimir stayed back, looking imploringly at the open gate behind them.

'Kill them all,' commanded Mobius.

More crossbows appeared and bolts flew. The riders were now alert, but the sheet of fire was hard to avoid. Fallon pushed his horse into Frith's and turned him back towards the gate as Theron took a bolt in the stomach.

'Fall back!' shouted Fallon. 'Ride for the gate.'

He kicked the king's horse, sending it towards the gate with Tiris slumped over the saddle.

Every man except Vladimir took a wound. Tristram received two bolts, one in the back and one in the ankle. Malaki Frith was shot in the shoulder and the neck, Dolf Halan was knocked from his horse with a wound in the side of his head. Fallon himself was shot in the side and in the thigh.

He kicked his horse, but couldn't see who was riding with him. Dolf and Theron had both fallen, but the others were just a mess of shouts and the braying of wounded horses. The Lord of Mud was ahead, wailing and flapping his reins, willing his horse to go faster. Behind, Purple clerics reloaded and screamed at the bound men to close the gates.

'Vladimir, move,' he roared. 'Don't look back, just ride.'

The Lord of Mud passed through the gate, his horse's hooves suddenly muffled on the grass of Scarlet. The raven cawed as Fallon reached the narrowing gateway and the men trying to close it. His horse barrelled into the wood and stopped abruptly, wedging the gate open. A swing of his sword struck a bound man in the skull and he kicked the gate backwards, creating a larger opening. More bolts hit his horse and Fallon was thrown to the grass beyond the gate, shattering the bolts sticking out of his side and thigh.

'Fallon!' shouted Frith, holding a bloodstained hand to the side of his neck. 'Reach.' He jumped over the dying horse and passed the gate.

The Grey Knight turned and flung his arms at the approaching Red general, pulling himself up on to the back of the horse. The gate stayed open just long enough for the riders to bolt. Dead and wounded men doubled over in their saddles and three riderless horses joined them.

Fallon sat behind the general, watching blood snake out from between his fingers as he clutched at his neck. They rode in chaotic lines, the horses wounded and overburdened.

'Make for the camp,' ordered Frith, choking on each word.

Fallon clamped his hands to the general's neck, stopping the blood. Frith allowed him to do so and clung on to his reins. The crossbow bolt was stopping the worst of the blood flow but the wound was bad.

'Just ride, my lord,' said the Grey Knight.

Vladimir was a good distance ahead. Tristram was hugging the neck of his horse and barely moving. Theron's horse was riderless and Dolf Halan was dead. The king's horse had taken Sebastian Tiris away from the city, but its rider wasn't moving.

Men from the general's camp were aware that something was wrong. They moved from between their tents and formed up to await the riders' return.

Frith swayed in his saddle and Fallon had to reach round him to grab the reins. 'Easy, general, nearly there,' he said, holding the man to stop him falling from his saddle.

They reached the edge of the camp and dozens of Red knights appeared to help the wounded down on to the grass.

'Fallon, are you alive?' shouted Vladimir, coming to join him.

'Just,' he replied, lowering Malaki Frith to a waiting White cleric.

The general was alive but losing blood. Tristram was helped out of his saddle and was barely conscious. The others were dead or missing. Fallon had two wounds and both of them hurt, but they were minor compared to the others'.

'What the fuck was that? Really, what the fuck was that?' demanded the Lord of Mud. 'He killed the fucking king.'

'Fallon!' roared General Frith, allowing the healer to clasp his neck and remove the crossbow bolt.

'Running every step,' he replied, pressing at his side.

A bound man assisted the Grey Knight and more White clerics appeared. Tristram was near to death with a bolt clean through his stomach. The king's horse had been grabbed and the motionless body was being bought into the camp. Theron and Dolf would see no more sunrises.

Fallon limped over to the general, feeling strange amid so many knights and clerics. At least a dozen men of the White and several of the Black mingled with the knights, angrily assessing the situation and shouting at their subordinates to stand ready.

Malaki Frith was pale and his hands shook. Two White clerics crouched over him and a third said prayers nearby. A chunk of his neck was missing and his words were gargled through his blood. His eyes were wide and flecked with red. His face was flushed and he gritted his teeth, vibrating with anger. 'Fallon!' he shouted again.

'I'm here, my lord, but you should stop talking until they've healed you.'

A White cleric nodded at him and tried to hold the general still. They could help, but Frith was trying to stand, relying on anger and adrenaline to keep him alive.

'Knight general, you need to lie still,' said a cleric. 'You are dying. Let us work.'

'See to the king before me,' choked Frith.

'He is being seen to,' replied the cleric. 'As is Commander Tristram.'

It began to snow, a steady and swirling mist of white coating hundreds of tents. The flurry was sudden and large flakes fell on Fallon's boots, mingling with the blood from his thigh.

'Move the wounded into the pavilions,' commanded a White cleric, waving to bound men to assist him.

Frith moved reluctantly, conceding only when loss of blood stopped him from standing upright. Tristram wasn't moving and was on a stretcher. The king was carried, his arms and legs dragging limply along the grass.

'I'm not wounded, but can I come too?' asked Vladimir.

'Just shut up and get over here,' replied Fallon.

Knights looked at them, whispering about who they were. Many knew Fallon of Leith and were confused by his lack of a uniform. Some knew the Lord of Mud and started gossiping about what had happened before the Red army arrived from Ro Arnon and why the Darkwald yeomanry were so few.

'Is the stand-off over?' asked Vladimir, wincing as Fallon's wounds were being cared for.

'I should imagine so,' he replied. 'Regicide has a way of galvanizing people.'

'Theron?' asked the Lord of Mud.

Fallon shook his head. 'Dead.'

'At least he didn't die on that bloody wooden stake.'

'Still dead.'

'And the king?' he looked at the motionless body being carried into a tent.

'Dead,' Fallon repeated. 'That's what regicide means.'

From his left, a triumphant caw signalled the return of the raven's shade. He turned to see Torian standing in the open, framed by curtains of falling snow. The ghostly bird sat on his shoulder and flapped its wings playfully. All around, knights and clerics of Tor Funweir moved past the apparition, ignorant of its presence, as they collected the riderless horses and assisted the wounded men.

'Fate is a strange thing, exemplar,' said Torian, the words echoing in Fallon's mind. 'For those who understand it, the future is irrelevant. For the gods, fate is all there is.' The shade smiled again. 'This is what you must do . . .'

CHAPTER EIGHT

TYR NANON IN THE CITY OF RO WEIR

H E WAS TIRED. His head hurt. He had not slept or rested for days. Even the slow meditation of the Dokkalfar did nothing to ease his mind and Nanon could not put into words how he felt. He had avoided the multitudes of men sent after him by taking the shape of a black hawk and nesting atop the small Brown chapel.

Rham Jas Rami was dead, Dalian was captive and undergoing torture, and Kale Glenwood was enchanted. By any measure, they had failed in spectacular fashion to kill the Mistress of Pain. As the only member of their group still free, Nanon was alarmed by the fact that he did not know what to do. He knew that he could not abandon Dalian, and that Rham Jas's daughter was still a dark-blood, but the old Tyr had been badly shaken by his friend's death and he couldn't think clearly. What to do?

Flying over the knight marshal's office, he had seen much of the enemy's movements during the past week. The endless procession of Hounds, the Ro nobles begging for the favour of the enchantress, none of it gave him any useful information. The idle chatter of the wind claws had told him of the Kirin's death and helped him fill in the blanks of what had happened in the catacombs, but he didn't know where they were holding Dalian or whether Keisha knew that the dead man was her father.

He flapped his wings and cawed in frustration. Time was running fast now. Somewhere to the east, in the depths of the

Fell, Vithar Loth was preparing his people for mass suicide. With no way to kill the enchantress, he felt defeated. He didn't like losing. It was a rare feeling, to have been out-thought and out-manoeuvred. If he were human, Nanon would have been swearing and pledging vengeance. As it was, he cawed. He could barely feel his brethren, they were so far away. All that remained of them was a dull thud in his mind, a suicidal impulse that was growing stronger.

It was twilight in Ro Weir. He had sat still, with barely a flap, for at least two hours. The fools that were searching for him had no idea that he could turn into a bird. A patrol of wind claws had now been circling the Brown chapel for a few minutes and Nanon decided to hop down from his perch and see what he could find out. They were nearing the end of their working day and they slumped around, throwing disinterested glances at anyone within view. Their talk was of bed and sleep, with occasional references to alcohol.

A gust of wind lifted him above the chapel and he angled his wings to catch a steady air current. The marshal's office was a huge building with many and varied structures jutting out from the central stone edifice. Nanon had little knowledge of human architecture and the strange logic that drove them to build in blocks and straight lines.

The building was an administrative centre – at least it used to be – as well as a home for affluent citizens, a store for Weir's winter needs and probably all sorts of other things. There was definitely a dungeon in there somewhere, but he couldn't identify where.

Castellations, walkways, balconies and exposed staircases dotted the stone, patrolled by guardsmen or Karesian flunkies. There were several dozen entrance points and hundreds of areas for exploration, but without a clear idea of where to go he would simply be trusting to luck. But Dalian's survival depended on him being lucky.

As frustration began to take hold and the wind picked up, Nanon glided to a low balcony protruding from a squat tower.

Two Karesians mounted a lacklustre guard, surveying the empty street below, but neither noticed the hawk. For a moment he remained still, letting the wind flow over his feathers.

A thought occurred. A strange thought of reclining on a beach with the waves lapping at his toes and his friends seated round him. Rham Jas sat to his left, Dalian to his right and Glenwood played happily in the water. The thought was not his own. Somewhere, deep within the stone of Weir, Dalian Thief Taker was dreaming. The world-weary Karesian had been healed and Nanon could sense a great internal peace, as if Dalian was praying. Being able to sense him in this way was unexpected. Although they had spent time together, his mind had always been hard and unyielding, not allowing Nanon to share his emotions. Perhaps impending death was softening the man's mind. Where are you, Karesian man? he thought.

Nanon hopped forward, landing on the balcony floor. The two Karesians, startled by the large bird, took a step back.

'Can you eat hawks?' asked one of them.

'Dunno,' replied the other. 'Not much meat on 'em.'

The door behind them was closed and the balcony relatively isolated. Nanon shifted back into his normal form and elbowed one of the men in the throat. The other gasped, fumbling for his sword, unable to comprehend what he was seeing. Nanon kicked him in the crotch and rammed his head into the stone wall.

He paused. The first man was alive but struggling to breathe through a crushed windpipe. Nanon crouched beside him.

'Somewhere beneath us is a Karesian man called Dalian. Where exactly is he?'

The man's eyes were bulging. His mouth was open and his tongue moved violently from side to side.

'Sorry, I seem to have hindered your ability to speak.'

He stood and glanced across at the second man. He was lying motionless on the floor of the balcony, a small pool of blood spreading from his skull.

'I forget my own strength,' he mused. 'Or maybe I forget the weakness of men. Or maybe I'm angry and you two are an outlet for my anger.'

He crouched down again.

'Just nod. Do you know where Dalian Thief Taker is?'

The man slowly stopped trying to breathe and his eyes relaxed. He was dead.

'Shit!' grumbled the forest-dweller.

He stepped to the edge of the balcony and looked down. He was at a corner of the knight marshal's office, two storeys up from the street. The front of the large building was a distance away and he couldn't see any more guards close by.

'Right, you're somewhere down there,' he stated, peering at the stone floor. 'Just soften your mind and I'll find you. I can't promise I'll rescue you, but I will find you.'

For the time being, though, Dalian's mind had hardened. There was a slight trail, a silvery path downwards through the stone, but not much to follow.

Nanon ghosted to the door and pressed his ear against the wood. Silence. The iron handle turned easily and he stepped into a dark corridor leading to a spiral staircase.

'Come on, Dalian, where are you? I can't just wander around in here.'

On light feet, he skulked to the stairs. A guard stood looking down at the stone, with his back to the forest-dweller. Nanon smiled at another opportunity to garner some information.

He wrapped an arm round the guard's neck and tensed, restricting the man's breathing. 'Hello,' he said, pulling the man's head back. 'I know you can't breathe, so don't try to talk. I need you to help me and I won't kill you if you do. Okay?'

The man spluttered against Nanon's arm, flapping his hands around in a feeble attempt to free himself.

'Listen!' he snapped, relaxing his arm slightly. 'I can be the worst thing you've ever met. Or I can be an interesting footnote to your day. Your choice.'

The man stopped spluttering. 'What do you want?' he whispered through a quivering mouth.

'Where's Dalian Thief Taker?'

The guardsman raised his arm and pointed a shaking hand down the spiral staircase.

'Yes, thank you, I already knew that,' said Nanon. 'Where precisely?'

'The hanging cells . . . above the catacombs.'

Nanon tried to smile but grimaced instead. He loosened his grip and punched the guardsman at the back of the neck, rendering him unconscious.

Flickering torchlight came from up and down the spiral staircase. The way up led to a higher balcony, the way down to the catacombs.

'Talk to me, Karesian man.'

He closed his eyes and let his mind drift downwards. He seeped into the brickwork, flowing through stone and mortar. Many guards stood below, casually patrolling the lower levels. Through chambers of rich hangings and corridors of carpeted opulence, he followed the echoes of Dalian's mind. He reached a sloping corridor, plunging into the catacombs. The bloody stone was being cleaned. Men of Ro scrubbed the floor and tried not to look into the darkness. He grimaced as a katana appeared. A pool of blood and torn clothing. The leather armour was in tatters, but there was no body. He felt great pain emanating from the stone. Rham Jas had died there. He had died looking at his daughter, but he had not been at peace. Something had happened to him in death, something vile.

He pulled his mind back, away from the central chamber. Back in the stairwell, Nanon dropped to his knees. The bastards had killed him and defiled his body. He deserved more. Or maybe he didn't. He was an assassin, a predator stalking other men. But he was Nanon's friend and he would be missed. He wanted to cry out and let the universe know that Rham Jas Rami was dead. The universe wouldn't care, but he felt it should know.

The Kirin had no gods, no Giants to miss them or priests to mourn their passing.

'Focus!' Dalian was still alive and needed his help, if only for a final conversation. Nanon liked talking to the Karesian man and he hoped they could at least say goodbye.

He let his mind drift again. He stayed clear of the Kirin's blood, delving into the rest of the catacombs. Chamber after chamber, down dark, forbidding corridors, he searched. The contortions of religion taking place in the bowels of Weir were jarring to his eyes, but he forced himself to continue. Hundreds of swaying sycophants danced to the Sisters' new song. They chanted and cavorted, pledging themselves to a new era of pleasure and blood, abandoning their morality and wilfully following an abomination.

He felt Dalian again. The Karesian man was slipping into a peaceful acceptance of death. Nanon doubted that he was conscious, but he was still alive and his mind still churned.

'There you are!' Nanon smiled.

He returned to his body and nimbly sprinted down the stairs, making no sound and letting Dalian's thoughts guide him. He ghosted past side passages and patrolling soldiers, sticking to the darkness, until he emerged on to another wide balcony. This one looked out over a large underground chamber, well below the city streets. Men and women writhed on the floor of the balcony, engaging in human coitus.

Nanon paused, tilting his head and watching the bizarre display. The sweaty ritual had no love or tenderness, just a euphoric repetition of movements, as if they were acting out of compliance. Saara kept her followers lost in shallow sensation, the better to control them.

It took a few moments for Nanon mentally to untangle the mound of naked bodies and count the participants. There were six of them, three men and three women, their blank, deathly eyes conveying pain and pleasure but no thought. There was no way stealthily to pass by the cavorting humans. Their addled minds had not registered his presence, but that would change if he advanced beyond the shadowy doorway.

He could still feel Dalian. He was close by, hanging in the cavern beyond. Chains slowly rippled in the black air, attached to cages, suspended over catacombs. Nanon wasn't close enough to see into the cages, but the Karesian man's thoughts were now more forceful. His mind had left the beach and his friends, and Dalian now wandered through fire. It was cleansing flame and Dalian believed it to be a gift of Jaa. A way of lulling him into peace before further torture and death. Nanon hoped he was right. That his Giant watched him, and that his thoughts were not merely illusions.

'Who are you?' snapped a voice from the stairs.

He swore under his breath. He had been foolish and dwelled too long in the doorway. He turned sharply and saw an armoured Ro guardsman with an ample belly and unfocused eyes. Nanon skipped forward, kicking the man in the face and sending him clattering into the solid stone wall.

The guard was unconscious but the commotion had alerted others from below. Mumbled words of alarm travelled up the stairs and the grunting of coitus from the balcony ceased.

Nanon reacted quickly, dancing through the doorway and on to the balcony. He kept his face low and sprinted past the naked worshippers, leaping over the railing and into the darkness beyond.

A surge of energy, a flap of his wings and he glided to a stop against the far wall. He could see further as a hawk, but fine detail was lost. The balcony opposite was now full of soldiers, waving away the participants in the orgy and scanning the catacombs. No one had seen his face or witnessed his transformation. They'd heard a commotion, and some had seen a running figure, but nothing clear or definite. The unconscious man would be out for hours and he had not clearly seen who had kicked him.

He clamped his talons against an empty torch emplacement and waited. Further along the cavern were the hanging cells. They stretched into shadows, creaking in the gentle wind that whistled past. The first few were empty. Only one cage was occupied.

When he judged that the guards had left and the orgy was back in full swing, he hopped from the wall and flew to the cage. He let the wind take him and tried not to flap his wings.

He was weary of being a hawk. Shape-taking was not to be undertaken lightly and the past few months had demanded much of him. Soon he would need to rest in his natural form. To push things too far could cause him to lose focus. But that didn't matter now.

He fluttered to a stop on top of the cage. Below, a bent figure sprawled across the steel bars, a mound of limbs and black fabric. Difficult to see where the head was. Nanon pulled in his wings and squeezed through the bars, dropping to the base of the cage. A gap in the blanket revealed a sliver of skin. A forehead, a nose and a mouth. Dark skin, mottled with blood. Dalian Thief Taker was a broken man. He had lost most of his strength. What age could not take from him, the Mistress of Pain had all but destroyed.

Nanon couldn't risk turning back into his normal form. The extra weight would create too much noise or cause the rickety cell to break and tumble down. Instead, he hopped across the cage and used his beak to pull back the blanket. The Karesian man underneath was unconscious, his chest barely moving.

Nanon tried to speak directly to Dalian's subconscious. The Thief Taker had briefly opened his mind before, unknowingly sharing a dream with his friend, and that was all Nanon needed.

'I'm sorry, Karesian man. I'm sorry we failed. I'm sorry Rham Jas is dead. I'm sorry Glenwood is enchanted. I'm sorry you're in a cage. I'm just sorry.'

'You have done nothing wrong,' came the reply.

'You're not Dalian!' said Nanon.

The voice was hollow, echoing with more powerful resonance than a human voice. 'And you should not be able to talk to me. That privilege belongs to one man.'

'I am not a man,' replied Nanon.

The strange voice didn't respond. It came from the Karesian man's mind, but it was not Dalian. It was not an unwelcome voice and he could sense that Dalian was comfortable with its presence.

'I'm Tyr Nanon of the Dokkalfar. I was Dalian's friend.'

'I am the shade of Dalian Thief Taker and you are not the exemplar of Jaa.'

He cawed quietly. The sound would have been a grunt of interest. As it was, it was a caw. Shades were known to him. In the oldest tales, the gods used them when their followers needed guidance. When their exemplars and their old bloods were not sufficient.

'Can we be friends?' he asked.

'No, but we are not enemies.'

He considered it. 'I can live with that. Just tell me . . . is Dalian at peace?'

'Not yet. His journey has one more turn before it ends, then he will be honoured in the fire halls beyond the world.'

Nanon slowly pulled back his mind. The shade had enveloped Dalian's mind within a blanket of serenity. It was a benevolent presence, gently lulling the man's mind into tranquillity and preparing him for death. Perhaps Jaa wasn't as helpless as the Seven Sisters believed.

He remained in the cage, peering at his friend through small, black eyes. He snapped his beak, padded his feet and flared his wings. He wanted to do more for Dalian.

'You have done all you can,' said the shade, appearing as a ghostly apparition in the cage. 'This one had fondness for you. You should return to safety.'

Nanon looked at it. He had travelled widely, lived many lives and seen many creatures, beasts and monsters, but he had never seen a shade. He had read tales in *The Edda* and other ancient texts, but had never spoken to one. It looked like Dalian, unhurt, wearing fine, black armour. The glare was the same, the dark eyes were the same, but something was missing, some depth of personality. It was a remnant of the Karesian man, but not all of him.

He slowly left the cage, backing away and squeezing through the rusted bars. He was humble enough to realize when he was out

415

of his depth. Whatever Jaa had in store for Dalian Thief Taker, it was outside Nanon's influence. Their journey together was over.

He fluttered from the cage and caught a breeze, gliding away through the cavernous catacombs of Weir. Red stone and moss-covered mortar wove away from the hanging cells. Arched entrances and shadowy alcoves plunged into darkness, spreading away from him like a honeycomb. It was mostly deserted, but balconies and flickering torch lights revealed more cavorting humans and a few guards. They ignored the hawk soaring gently through the wide stone passages.

He fluttered to the ground, flexing his large black wings. He was in a globe of light before Saara's throne. On the ground was a pool of dried blood and a katana. Beyond the throne, in the pitch black, swayed darkwood trees. A lot of darkwood trees. They were torpid, but their maddening presence infected the stone and Nanon could feel it more than most. It was a grimy itch in his wings, a tense need to snap his beak. He cawed quietly, feeling the aberration that had been Rham Jas vibrating in the darkness.

It was the worst kind of defilement. The defilement of a mortal by a god. It disgusted him. Saara had birthed the thousand young. She had tried to harness power that could destroy her. It would infect her in a way that no human, however powerful, could withstand for long. The madness of a god was the madness of chaos, of the void, of the halls beyond the world, and she was but a human.

But that didn't change anything. She could die tomorrow and there would still be a hundred thousand Hounds milling around in Tor Funweir. There would still be darkwood trees in every corner of the world, and the Giants would still need shades to talk to their followers. The world was already broken. Rham Jas was just the latest piece to break.

He returned to his normal form, crouched over the bloodstain. Looking around, the catacombs were empty. Nearby, he could sense Dalian lying on the floor. The Karesian man had watched

Rham Jas die. They had fought from the entrance to the catacombs and killed many warriors, but Saara had not revealed her plan until the last minute, when Kale Glenwood appeared. He felt dark and pessimistic, as if a piece of Nanon had died there.

He retrieved the katana, wiping blood from its blade and tucking it into his belt. It had been a gift from the Kirin's wife and it should not remain discarded on the cold stone.

He turned his back on the darkness. The walkway to the surface was bloodied and blades had cut chunks out of the walls. The silence was total. Even the wind that stroked his face made no sound. Off to the right, Nanon could sense Glenwood's confusion. When Saara had grasped his mind the Ro man had tried to fight it. He had not wanted to betray his friends. He was not to blame but, wherever he was, Nanon feared for his state of mind.

Further away, he could feel the girl, Keisha. By the sound of her mind, he guessed that she was asleep. She didn't know that her father was dead. He was just another victim of her mistress. One of hundreds, maybe thousands.

He could help Keisha. She might be the only person here that he could help. Rham Jas was dead, Dalian was on another journey, and Glenwood was with the enchantress.

He nimbly ran from the throne room, ducking into a side passage. Torches provided light but there was no warmth to the place. Once out of the huge catacombs, the stone corridors were carpeted red. Wooden doors, splashed with grotesque black designs of spirals and sharp lines. Each one was closed and no sounds came from within. The orgies were occurring elsewhere.

The further he walked from the catacombs, the stronger Keisha's mind became. She had the same edge as her father and it showed in her thoughts.

Round a corner two Karesian guards stood with their backs to him. Saara kept her servant under guard even when they were apart.

He wasn't in the mood to be gentle to the humans. He loved so much about their culture and their quirks, but he hated their servile nature. Independent thought was a luxury to these men, a burden they had gratefully discarded.

He drew the katana and his own longsword, making just enough noise to alert the two men. They turned round and exchanged a look of confusion at the strange being, wielding two swords, in the corridor.

'I'm afraid you don't get the chance to run,' said Nanon, dancing forward, whirling his blades.

He attacked both men at once, slicing the neck of the first and driving his longsword into the chest of the second. Fighting with two weapons came naturally to the Dokkalfar, though he'd never done it with such heavy blades.

The Karesians died with a muted clatter of armour on carpet and, though a slight echo travelled down the corridors, no one came running to investigate. He thought Saara must have mustered her followers elsewhere.

He sheathed both blades and approached a securely barred door. There were no symbols and it opened easily. Within was a comfortable sitting room and an adjoining bedroom. Red wall hangings of thick fabric masked the stone and free-standing braziers provided warmth. The chairs were unused and the space felt bare and unwelcoming.

He ghosted to the bedroom and moved the silk partition aside. 'Who are you?' asked Keisha.

The girl had heard him and was sitting up in her bed, clutching golden sheets to her terrified face.

He came in and looked at her. She was pretty but had a sadness in her eyes. Her dark hair was tangled and her bare shoulders bore a tapestry of whip marks.

'You have good ears,' he replied. 'Do you know how your senses came to be so sharp?'

She didn't answer. The girl played the part of a terrified youth but Nanon suspected that was not the whole story. Her hands were not shaking and her eyes remained still. Fear would have made her shake and blink.

'You are not afraid of me. Why?'

'I'm . . . I'm sorry, my lord . . . I am but a servant.'

Nanon chuckled. 'That's good, you didn't flinch. But you didn't answer my question either.' He stepped into the light and pushed back his hood, revealing his grey skin and pointed ears. 'Do you know where your power comes from?'

The revelation had the desired effect. Keisha showed genuine surprise and her mask of meekness cracked. She rolled to the side, sliding her hand under the pillow and producing a scimitar. Beneath the sheets she wore form-fitting clothing with the shoulders adjusted, mimicking the look of a nightgown.

'There we go,' said Nanon, tilting his head. 'You move well.'

She crouched like a cat and showed uncanny speed.

'Take another step, freak-face, and I'll cut something off you,' she barked.

He took another step. 'Go on, then. But when I take that weapon off you, you have to answer my question.'

She was not naive, nor was she impulsive. Her scimitar swayed in the air and she stepped slowly sideways. Nanon found her interesting. Then she attacked. It was an acrobatic leap, ending in a full stretch and a powerful lunge.

'You're quick, too,' he said, dancing backwards. 'Good ears and good reflexes. A mere quirk of fate?'

She pulled back and held her blade close.

'I knew your father, Kirin girl.'

'What? Who are you?' she asked, lowering her blade.

Nanon glanced behind him and listened. There was still no sound. Perhaps he had come down here to rescue the girl rather than Dalian. He couldn't be sure, but it was worth the gamble.

'I'm called Tyr Nanon. I'm not human.' He grinned.

'I see that,' she replied. 'You're a risen man.'

'A risen man who was a friend of your father's. Perhaps we should continue this conversation elsewhere.'

She was remarkably unemotional for a young girl. She had tight control over her emotions and even tighter control over her movements. It was obvious – even vulgar to think it – but she moved like Rham Jas.

'The mistress doesn't let me leave,' she replied.

'Feels good to break a rule now and then.'

Keisha became flustered. Her eyes shot around the room as she tried to weigh up the situation.

'What do you want with me?' she snapped. 'And don't say you knew my father. I never knew him, so you knowing him matters little.'

'You're not just a servant, Keisha, you're a dark-blood, like your father.'

She had heard the term, probably whispered in fear by Saara or Elihas. Though she had no reason to trust the strange forest-dweller standing in front of her.

Nanon liked her. For some reason he found her manner refreshing. She was barely eighteen years old but had lived a hard life of slavery and abuse. It had taught her to be wary and calculating. He enjoyed the sensation of being near her, feeling the sharp intellect that she tried to hide.

'That Kirin was called the Dark Blood. What does it mean?' she asked.

'It means a number of things. The main one being that that Kirin was your father.'

She barely reacted. Nanon could sense that Rham Jas had said something to her before he died and that it was preying on her mind.

'What did he say to you?' he asked.

Her mouth quivered at the corners and her forehead wrinkled up in agitation. 'He said that I looked like my mother,' she replied, a tear appearing. 'There was something in his face I recognized. I didn't allow myself to think about it. Thinking gets me in trouble. I do what I'm told and I don't think.'

Nanon stepped closer to her, sensing the young Kirin's barely contained anguish.

'He told me that you were four years old when you were taken

. . . when his wife, your mother, was killed. I know that you believe me.'

She dropped the scimitar and broke down on the floor. The tears now flowed and she wept frantically, her hands clasped to her face. Nanon could feel each tear as if it was his own. It took months, even years for him to read most people, but she was Rham Jas's daughter and the normal rules didn't apply. He saw a broken young girl, hanging on to life through stubbornness and intelligence. She smiled, nodded, did what she was told, all the while wishing a brutal death on those who harmed her. Above all, she was patient. She looked at the older men who used her and remained determined to outlive them. She looked at pampered nobles and bowed politely, while wishing she could be anywhere else in the world.

She raised her head. Her eyes were red and her cheeks flushed. 'What was his name?' she asked. 'I don't remember.'

'Rham Jas Rami,' replied Nanon. 'Your brother, Zeldantor, was killed by Saara the Mistress of Pain.'

Her thoughts now formed into spirals of anger. The tears continued, but now they flowed over a snarling face. Keisha was confused, tired, emotional and angry. Most of all, she was angry.

'I can offer you freedom,' he said. 'I can't bring back your parents or your brother, but if you come with me, you will never be a slave again. No man will use you, no man will harm you. No woman either.'

'Why do you care?' she asked, clenching her fists.

'I told you, he was my friend. I have few and he meant a great deal to me.'

'What's a dark-blood? What power do I have?' She was speaking quickly, her mind frantic.

He raised his hands and tried to soften his face. 'We have time, Keisha, but we cannot remain here.'

'What was your name again?' she asked, wiping tears from her red face.

'Nanon. I'm Dokkalfar. We won't be alone here for long.'

'Yes, we will,' she replied. 'The mistress has planned a huge celebration for the Thief Taker's death. The flock must be well rested. Only a few flesh addicts are still here. I don't think she cares about me any more.'

He smiled. The expression must have appeared strange because Keisha frowned with revulsion.

'Don't smile, it looks odd,' she said.

'Sorry. I try to blend in . . . humans smile, so I smile. It's a foolish habit.' He scanned the bedchamber. 'Do you have belongings, personal items? You should gather what you need.'

She peered at him, chewing her lower lip in thought. He could feel her anger and her distrust. It wasn't directed specifically at him. He thought that Keisha distrusted everything and everyone. It was a lonely way to live, but it had kept her alive.

'I have nothing I need. Except this,' she said, raising her scimitar. 'We can leave when you're ready.'

'You trust me?' He knew the answer.

'Do I need to trust you? You're offering me freedom. I've never had that, so I'm willing to gamble.'

He smiled again. This time, Keisha didn't grimace.

'But if you touch me, I'll kill you,' she said with a sweet smile.

Nanon frowned. 'I won't touch you. I'm not interested in touching you, I'm interested in helping you.'

'So, let's go.'

* * *

He liked her more and more as they skulked out of the catacombs and back to the northern wall. She wasn't shy and she liked to make comments as they hurried through the streets of Weir. Fat men, overdressed women, tough guardsmen, each group elicited a barbed witticism from the young Kirin girl.

'Grotesque stomachs must be a sign of virility around here,' she quipped, pointing out a rotund merchant surrounded by young women.

'I think it's the coin, not the stomach,' replied Nanon.

'Or maybe the sweat. I've been calling it Ro perfume. I'm surprised they don't sell it in shops – the underarm scent of fat bastards, guaranteed to make idiot women swoon.'

'Let's keep quiet and stay off the main streets for now.'

Any commotion he had caused by killing the guards had been drowned out by the noise of the evening festivities. Saara's flock was preparing for the death of Dalian Thief Taker.

They had reached the ruined drainage channel through which Glenwood and Rham Jas had entered the city and were close to the northern muster fields of Weir. As Keisha squeezed through the gap in the brickwork, he felt an itch at the back of his neck.

'What's the matter?' asked Keisha, as her new companion stopped by the wall.

It was hard to explain his intuition but he felt a great pain from his brethren, as if many Dokkalfar were being gravely hurt. There was a wave of pain, a surge of anger and a punctuation of despair. It was sudden and interrupted the excitement of his escape with Keisha.

'My people,' he replied. 'They are doing something very unwise.'

'They sound like every human I've ever met. I'm sure they'll get over it.'

She scuttled away, pulling herself up into the drainage tunnel that led from the city. Her nihilism was generally refreshing, but when applied to the Dokkalfar of the Fell the comment hurt.

What was Vithar Loth up to? Had he managed to coax life into the Shadow Flame?

'We need to hurry.'

'Where are we going?'

He followed her into the tunnel and crawled away from the abandoned warehouse.

'Your life is about to become very interesting, Kirin girl. We are bound for the Fell.'

'What's the Fell?'

He looked at her. 'It's a forest. A big one. Where the Dokkalfar live.'

CHAPTER NINE

BRONWYN OF CANARN
IN THE REALM OF SCARLET

T HE COLD MORNING brought a film of snow, framing the
ranks of Red knights assembled before the city. Malaki
Frith had cleared his camp and mustered ten thousand
armed men. They had formed up slowly, allowing the occupiers
of South Warden to see them. They didn't know it, but they were
also allowing the Moon clans and Twilight Company to assess
their strength.

Gleaming armour and high pennants, snapping in the snowy
breeze. Red knights, White clerics, nobleman of Tor Funweir.
Bound men, squires, blacksmiths and auxiliaries. There were a lot
of men on the Plains of Scarlet. In comparison, the few thousand
Ranen huddled at the tree line were no more than an armed mob.

Fynius Black Claw was somewhere in South Warden, watching
the drama play out. So far, he had been maddeningly right about
everything. The king was dead, the new army had sided with the
yeomanry and not with the clerics. If he were right about what
would happen next, Bronwyn would need to be ready.

He had been right about so much. Perhaps she was the only
person capable of diplomacy in this situation. Certainly Federick
Two Hearts and Theen Burnt Face were not suitable for the role.
One was permanently insensible, the other made a snowflake
seem intelligent.

At least they had a good vantage point, on rising ground beyond
the tree line, well hidden from the soldiers of Ro. No one was

looking north, the Red knights being far too arrogant to consider the Ranen a danger. Even the soldiers from Darkwald, assembled in front of their stockade and under the cover of trebuchets, were looking only to the east.

'Ten thousand men all told,' said Micah, finally able to walk unaided. 'Who's that at the front of the knights?'

'The tall one is Fallon of Leith,' she replied. 'I assume the Red cardinal is up there too.'

'Bloody bird man was right, this has not played out like I thought,' he said with a smile. 'There're still a shit-load of clerics and knights in South Warden, though.'

'It's not over yet. And you don't have any diplomatic duties.'

'I assumed I was coming with you,' replied Micah. 'I'll no doubt have to weather insults about my parentage or some such.'

'Is the Stone Dog family not well regarded?'

'Piss off . . . my lady,' he replied with a chuckle.

It was simple humour, but it was good to share a laugh.

'What are they waiting for?' asked Micah. 'They outnumber them by two to one, at least.'

'Red knights don't kill other Red knights,' she replied.

'And Purple clerics?'

She shrugged. 'Not sure. The relationship has always been a little . . . foggy.'

Shouts rose from the front rank of knights, ordering those behind to stand to attention. Their banners were held high and their shields locked in place. At the front, closest to the gates of South Warden, two riders broke away from the massed army. One wore a high-plumed helmet, glinting white in the snowy morning. The other, tall and black-haired, held himself ramrod straight.

'I saw him at Ro Hail,' said Micah. 'The tall one. That's Fallon, right?'

She nodded. 'Our ally, according to Hasim. I've not met the other one. The Red cardinal, I'd assume.'

She was amazed at how quiet ten thousand men could be. The army was motionless, stern-faced and looking to the front. Their armour rustled in the breeze and their horses whinnied, but the men were silent. From South Warden, keeping tight formation on the forward battlements, Purple clerics surveyed the knights before them.

'Brothers!' shouted the knight general towards the city. 'I do not address the nobles of the One. I do not address the Purple cardinal. I address the knights of the Red. I address my brothers.'

She couldn't see any knights in South Warden. There were five thousand of them, kept out of the way by Cardinal Mobius, prevented from seeing the massed army at their gate. How long they would remain loyal to the Purple once their general started to speak was open to debate.

'Brother knights, I am Knight General Malaki Frith. I come from Ro Arnon, answering the king's summons. The king who was murdered by Cardinal Mobius. I name him regicide and traitor to Tor Funweir.'

His voice was now a bellow, hoarse and emotional in the cold air of Scarlet.

'You must follow orders from the senior churchman. That churchman is now me. I will not order you to kill the clerics, I merely order you to stand down. Leave South Warden and muster on the fields of Scarlet. Enough men have died here.'

She frowned. Fynius was right again.

'Far be it from me to be optimistic,' said Micah, 'but this is looking good . . . well, for now.' He appeared embarrassed about his own assessment.

'Relax. I'm sure there is still plenty of time for things to go horribly wrong.'

She enjoyed the look on his face, but not as much as she enjoyed the stark fear she saw among the Purple clerics. They stood behind the wooden battlements, trying to keep their heads back and their chins forward. Some stepped back, fighting their fear and only kept at their posts by angry glares.

'No man will be held responsible for his actions here,' shouted Frith. 'If he stands down.'

A moment of silence. Sir Fallon of Leith rode forward. He exchanged words with the general and then his voice was directed at the city.

'Brothers! It's time to go home. Mobius can rant and rave, but let him do it alone.'

These men had been in the Freelands of Ranen for a long time. Bronwyn had seen the army move from Canarn, across the Grass Sea to Hail, and then over the Plains of Scarlet to South Warden. She wanted to hate them for all the deaths they had caused, but she couldn't bring herself to do it. Were they really to blame? Following orders to a fault made them servile, but it didn't make them evil.

'Perhaps the death ends here,' she muttered.

'Or perhaps the bird man will get something wrong,' replied Micah.

She raised her eyebrow at him.

'Okay,' he conceded, 'it's unlikely.'

Shouting from the city. Clerics turned from the battlements and waved their hands at those within. The clank of metal echoed through the snowy fields as Red knights made their way through the narrow streets of South Warden.

Frith's army was still silent, allowing their brothers in the city to act as they saw fit. They didn't gossip or whisper, nor did they smile or show agreement with their commander's words.

'Are you ready?' asked Micah. 'It's almost time.'

A sudden wave of fear hit her. 'What if they just attack us?'

He smirked. 'Well, I suppose in that case, we'll probably die.'

She puffed out her cheeks. 'Thank you, Micah, helpful as always.'

'What, you think we should fight them? Two against ten thousand? Yeah, I'll give that a go.'

'Shut up!' she snapped. 'Go and make sure Federick has the white flag ready.'

He backed away from the tree line and made his way towards the men of the crescent skulking nearby. Two Hearts and Theen

Burnt Face were just sufficiently afraid of the Red army to keep their boisterous arguing in check. Their warriors still drank their liquor and smoked their drugs, waiting for Fynius Black Claw's plan to advance. They were more trusting of the man of Gar than Bronwyn or Micah, but they were still afraid.

Fynius had suggested to her – well, demanded of her – that she not listen to the Moon clans and that she approach the Red knights of Ro on her own. Stone Dog would not be told what to do and would accompany her. His presence would prove scant comfort when ten thousand warriors turned to look at her, and his sardonic comments might hinder rather than help the negotiations. Somewhere in the trees behind her, Warm Heart also waited. She could hear the growls of the hound's breathing.

The gates of South Warden opened and she experienced another wave of apprehension. The entranceway was obscured but she could hear the shouts of Purple clerics and the clank of Red knights. After a moment a column of men marched forth through the crisp snow. The green Plains of Scarlet were steadily turning white and the veil of snow was heavier as the Red army left South Warden.

A single voice rose above the others. The screech of Cardinal Mobius, echoing around the wooden city, chasing the Red knights out of the gate, was pitiable. She could not see him, but he sounded desperate, on the edge of mania. He was ignored.

Frith didn't laugh or crow. Even from a distance, Bronwyn saw only an impassive face taking no pleasure in his victory. The tall swordsman next to him appeared less stoical, and Fallon of Leith greeted his brother knights as they filed out of South Warden. The column was narrow and it took time for them to squeeze through the gates, walking slowly of necessity, as the Purple cardinal's voice cracked and trailed away.

The knights were dirty, bearded and battle-worn. Their armour was dented and tarnished, in sharp contrast to the shiny mass of General Frith's army. They snaked through the waiting ranks of warriors, their backs bent and their eyes down, until the last dribble of men, most of them wounded, were helped from the city.

'How long have they been away from home?' asked Micah, reappearing silently and making her jump. 'They're a mess.'

She shoved him, grunting in her surprise.

'Almost a year . . . and don't sneak up on me, I'm twitchy enough.'

'What, you didn't smell me? I must stink to your noble nostrils.'

She ignored him. Looking back at the city, the gates were now being closed and the huge southern camp was receiving the Red knights who had withdrawn.

'Bronwyn, it's time.'

Overhead, a large raven flew from the trees. It glided from a high branch and soared over the army, cawing loudly. Over her shoulder, Warm Heart appeared, nuzzling her forwards.

She looked along the tree line. Federick Two Hearts and his night-raiders were camouflaged in a bramble thicket, nervously quaffing ale and gesturing at the fields of Scarlet. They had fashioned a large white square from an awning and attached it to a long branch.

With the deep note of a horn, the flag was extended and waved from side to side, catching the snow as it moved.

Tension grew to anguish as thousands of armoured men drew their swords and turned towards the Moon Woods. She nearly fell over under the weight of their hard stares. Even Micah gulped with fear as Malaki Frith's army spied the Ranen warriors. Their movements were quick and controlled, acting as a single unit to defend themselves against an unseen foe.

'Fuck me!' exclaimed Stone Dog. 'For the first time I actually understand how the Ro managed to conquer half the world.'

She composed herself and stood up. With small steps, she walked forward from the obscuring tree line. Micah and Warm Heart followed her and, further along, at the edge of the Moon Woods, Federick and his night-raiders emerged with Theen's warriors close behind.

Dawn Sun Runner held the white flag high. Even under the influence of their drugs, the warriors of the Crescent were hesitant.

'Identify yourself!' bellowed a knight of Ro.

The Ranen all turned to Bronwyn.

She breathed in deeply and a shiver lanced down her spine. The cold air made her throat dry. 'I am Lady Bronwyn of Canarn. We seek parlay.' She tried to shout but her voice came out as a cracked wheeze.

Ranks of crossbowmen moved skilfully through the Red army, taking up position. Hundreds of bolts pointed at the tree line.

'Bronwyn,' muttered Micah, 'they're pointing crossbows at us . . . shout louder!'

'I am Lady Bronwyn of Canarn,' she shouted, finding her voice. 'We seek parlay.' Warm Heart barked, drawing the aim of a hundred crossbowmen.

Men on horseback approached, churning up the snow in a steady canter. Officers by the look of them, they wore mottled red tabards over breastplates and flowing cloaks of the same blood-red.

'Step forward,' commanded the lead rider.

She gulped again. Making sure Micah and Warm Heart were with her, she did as she was told. 'I wish to speak to the knight general,' she said. 'I represent the Moon clans of Ranen.'

'Who the fuck are the Moon clans of Ranen?' responded the rider, wheeling his horse behind the crossbowmen.

Federick Two Hearts looked hurt. The large, drug-addled chieftain held his arms wide and gestured to the men and women skulking behind him. 'What do we look like? Fucking sheep-herders?' spat Federick. 'You cheeky Ro bastard.'

The Red knights looked at each other, their professionalism cracking ever so slightly. They remained silent, directing their attention from Bronwyn to Federick, then to the huge Volk hound.

'And the dog?'

'Hey, I ain't done with you, red man,' interrupted Two Hearts.

'I said, I speak for the Moon clans,' she repeated, emptying her lungs to be heard. 'And this is why. Be silent, Federick. You, sir knight, I am a noble of Ro and I demand to be taken to the Red general.'

The men on horseback conversed quietly. They directed men to form up and allow a narrow channel to appear, leading from the Moon Woods, plunging deep into the Red army.

'Lady Bronwyn, you say? Of Canarn? Long way from home . . . with a dishonourable name.'

She clenched her fists but diplomacy forced her to remain silent.

'You and one other,' said the knight. 'These Moon clans can remain in their woods for now.'

'Very well. Lead on,' she replied. 'But the hound comes too. He's no threat to you.' Warm Heart looked at her and she hoped she was right.

'As you say, Lady Bronwyn. Dogs get shot as easily as men.'

They left the safety of the trees and walked across the deepening snow. They were isolated and alone, moving across open ground from one group of warriors to another. Micah leant on his axe, gripping the shaft for comfort. Bronwyn was unarmed and aware of her appearance. Greasy hair, dirty hands, grubby fingernails. Her feet were calloused and sore, her face scratched and pale. But she was a diplomat of sorts, in a land where appearances meant nothing. Only Warm Heart gave her comfort, loping along next to her, his huge muzzle held upright.

They were led into the mass of soldiers, down an aisle between interlocked shields and hard faces. The riders trotted along on either side of them, providing escort. Within moments the aisle had closed behind them and she felt herself lost in a maze of steel and leather figures, stretching away from her in every direction. South Warden was a sliver of wood in the distance, the camp of the yeomanry was completely obscured, and the northern tree line was just a texture, barely visible through the snow.

They walked across uneven ground towards the front of the army. The city grew larger and larger, looming over the snow-capped knights, as they neared the gates of South Warden. The Red warriors broke their silence only to whisper about the huge dog.

'Lady Bronwyn! I did not expect to see you here,' said Fallon of Leith, dismounting. 'Who are your friends?'

'This is Micah Stone Dog of Wraith. This is Warm Heart, he's a Volk war-hound. Who's your friend?'

Fallon paused, looking at the hound, but he was not a man to be scared by a big dog. 'May I present Knight General Malaki Frith. My general, this is the young lady who escaped Canarn, Hail and, it seems, South Warden.'

'A pleasure, my lady,' said Frith with a bow. 'Lord Bromvy's sister, what are you doing here?'

'I am functioning as a go-between currently, speaking on behalf of the Moon clans and the remaining Free Company men. In fact, probably best to think of me as a diplomat.'

Fallon was tall and his back was straight. He wore no uniform or indication of rank. Again, Fynius was right, the swordsman was no longer a knight of the Red. Malaki Frith was shorter and wore a burnished breastplate across an ample chest.

'Well,' began the general, 'as long as your friends in the trees . . .' he turned to another officer. 'How many are there?'

'A few hundred. At most,' replied the knight.

The general nodded. 'Well, as long as your friends in the trees behave themselves, I see no reason not to parlay. Our mandate in the Freelands is open to change at this moment.'

'I'm sure Vladimir would relish another parlay,' said Fallon. 'He thinks he's getting good at them.' The tall swordsman noted the look of confusion on Bronwyn's face. 'That's Vladimir Corkoson, commander of the Darkwald yeomanry. Don't worry, he just wants to go home.'

'At least he's still got a home,' replied Micah, glaring at Fallon. 'I remember you from Ro Hail. You killed a priest of the Order of the Hammer. Our healer.'

'Now is not the time,' interjected Bronwyn, aware that Stone Dog's temper often overrode his reason.

'It's okay,' said Fallon. 'What was his name, your priest?'

'Dorron Moon Eye,' replied Micah. 'Miserable old bastard. You split his head open.'

'I'm sorry.'

It was a simple apology, said with a genuine smile, and it surprised them both. Red knights didn't apologize. They didn't show guilt or contrition, they merely implemented the will of the One with swift, often brutal, efficiency. They were barely human. 'You really have left the Red, haven't you?' she asked. 'I didn't believe it.'

'Let's not be hasty,' said Malaki Frith. 'The situation here is still uncertain. Sir Fallon has, as far as is clear, acted with honour. And one does not leave the Red, dear lady.'

The tall swordsman's face was open and light-hearted. He shook his head in amusement but didn't correct either Bronwyn or the Red general. Whatever had happened to him had had a profound effect on his demeanour.

'What do the Ranen want?' asked Frith.

Micah snorted. The answer would be obvious to anyone other than a Red knight.

'What do you think they want?' she responded. 'What would you want? If the situation was reversed. If that was Ro Tiris instead of South Warden?' She wiped snow from her hair. 'Can we continue this under cover?

'Of course, Lady Bronwyn, where are my manners?' said Frith with a forced smile. 'But your . . . dog is not welcome in my command tent.'

Warm Heart whined, wagging his tale at the Red general.

* * *

She had never known so many men bow to her. Every knight and bound man showed his respect. Breastplates were struck, helmets removed. No one questioned them as they were escorted through the vast military camp.

At the centre, covered with a thick layer of pristine white snow, sat Malaki Frith's command pavilion. The Red banner swayed from side to side, snapping against the flagpole, but it was the only heraldry on display. There was no Purple sceptre. That was a good sign.

'What the fuck am I doing here?' asked Stone Dog, not addressing anyone in particular.

'You insisted on coming with me,' she replied.

'I did? Didn't you try to talk me out of it?' He smiled politely at a grizzled Red knight moving a stack of swords from one tent to another.

'Are you scared, young Micah?'

'Piss off . . . my lady. I'm just having a lot of new experiences recently.' He grinned. 'Still alive. though.'

Warm Heart bounded along in front, excitedly sticking his nose into anything the Red knights were doing. They frowned and flapped at him, their fear quickly turning to confusion as the huge hound acted like a playful puppy.

'Stay!' commanded Bronwyn, as Frith and Fallon disappeared inside the command tent.

Warm Heart hunkered down and his tongue lolled out over a mass of slobbery teeth. He remained still, lying on the snowy grass outside the tent.

'Can he understand you?' asked Micah.

'Well . . . if he doesn't, I expect he'll get shot.'

The hound whined and pulled in his muscular forelegs, lying as flat as he could to the ground.

They turned their backs on Warm Heart and were led inside the large tent. The temperature rose instantly. The pavilion was divided into several sections, each warmed from a central brazier. Everything was red – the fabrics, the hangings, the furniture. It was a little piece of Tor Funweir and the closest she'd been to home in many months.

'Take a seat,' said the general. 'It's not a palace, but it's warm.'

Five senior knights entered with them, standing on guard round the central chamber. Each man was at least a captain. They eyed up Micah's axe but did not move to disarm him.

She sat in a comfortable chair and her feet rested on thick carpet. 'It's strange how nice it feels to sit in a chair,' she said, smiling.

'Not strange,' replied Fallon. 'I haven't seen a proper bed in almost a year.'

'I don't think I've ever seen a proper bed,' said Micah. 'Bet you have four posts and paid servants.'

'You forget the silk sheets,' quipped Malaki Frith. 'Look, I've heard the put-upon barbarian routine. Yes, we have killed a lot of Ranen. Clearly you hate us. Get over it.'

'Fuck you, Red man,' spat Micah. 'Knowledge of your sins does not absolve you of them.'

'Please, young man. Did your mother not teach you to respect your elders . . . and men with an army. A fucking big army.'

The young axe-man wrestled with his temper. 'My mother's dead. My father too.'

'So we have something in common. But you don't see me being disrespectful,' replied the general.

Fallon of Leith was smiling at her. His expression appeared genuine, as if he shared her frustration at the bickering.

'No one else needs to die. In a tent or on a battlefield,' said Fallon. 'You can hate us . . . sorry, what was your name?'

'Stone Dog,' he replied, 'of Ro Hail.'

'I apologize, Stone Dog. But hate us or not, we don't want to fight any more.'

'So, it's time to talk,' said Bronwyn.

Fallon spoke quietly to the general, gesturing calmly and cooling the situation. His face was open and friendly. He wasn't flustered or even surprised at what was happening. She'd never seen a knight – or an ex-knight – behave like this. What had happened to him?

'Let's keep things diplomatic, shall we?' said the general, forcing a polite smile.

Bronwyn puffed out her cheeks, preparing to deliver Fynius's terms. The moment would never be right, so she chose just to blurt it out.

'The Free Companies and Moon clans of Ranen demand that you prepare to withdraw from the Freelands.' She paused. 'Fynius

Black Claw, captain of Twilight Company wishes to meet with you, once South Warden is liberated.'

'Liberated?' exclaimed Frith. 'I understand Scarlet Company are no more. Who's going to live there? We'll arrest the Purple clerics in due time and then we'll talk to this captain fellow. But withdrawal takes time . . . and no one makes demands of me and my men.'

Bronwyn exchanged a nervous look with Micah before she replied. 'You won't need to worry about arresting them?' she asked hesitantly. 'I am here primarily to keep things calm when . . . the clerics are dealt with.'

The Red general was a considered and intelligent man. He peered at her, leaning in and digesting the words. 'And how will they be dealt with?' he asked.

* * *

Fynius hadn't stopped smiling since the Red knights filed out of South Warden. It was a simple kind of glee. The happiness of being proven right. Things were moving forward nicely, at a pace confusing to normal people. He'd kept everyone going at breakneck speed, twisting them left and right, making strange demands and generally being a pain in the arse. It had worked brilliantly. They had all done exactly what he wanted.

Outside the gates of South Warden a massive army waited. They thought they were in control, picketing their men, digging ditches, building fences, settling in. They would deal with the Purple men eventually. Bunch of idiots.

The clerics themselves still lined the outer walls, with the boss clerics assembled in front of the mount, nicely clustered in a few big groups, like mould on cheese. They fawned over the chief idiot – Mobius, he was called – and pointedly thrust out their chins at the mere suggestion that they were fucked. They knew the Red men wouldn't kill them, so at worst they'd have a stern talking to about killing their king, before tea, cakes and a welcome return to Tor Funweir. None of the men of Ro gave a shit about the mess they had left behind or the people they had killed and displaced. They would march back to the lands of Ro and forget about the men of Ranen.

'Time to learn a lesson, you bastards,' he muttered.

Fynius was skulking in the cheese tunnels with a good view of the central square. The men of Twilight Company were spread out on either side of the Purple men, hiding in basements and forgotten tunnels. Mathias Flame Tooth and the survivors of Scarlet Company were under Rowanoco's Stone, poised to join the men of Old Gar when the time came. Two hundred Purple clerics were going to pay for the invasion of the Freelands. If Fynius had been a follower of Rowanoco, the price would have been much higher. They were lucky it was he and not his brother who was about to kill them.

He pulled himself up out of the tunnel and skulked down next to a building. Two dozen men in dark blue tabards followed him, silently moving into position. He signalled to Vincent Hundred Howl on the opposite side of the square, and the rest of Twilight Company ghosted their way through the streets of South Warden. Five hundred fully armoured men could move as quietly as mice when they wanted to.

He passed the word to Scarlet Company. The men and women of South Warden were not gifted with unnatural stealth and had been told to wait until the clerics started screaming. Fynius needed the element of surprise and didn't want sweaty, bearded, shouty men ruining it. They were tough, dangerous even, but not subtle. Not in the slightest. Luckily, they were doing what they were told.

He drew Leg Biter. The blade was heavy, wide and perfectly balanced. The men of Old Gar were unique among the Ranen. They used swords instead of axes, preferring precision to brutality. Twilight Company were all similarly armed and moved forward with their captain, gliding over grass, cobbles and dead ground.

The central square was lined with overgrown pathways, lancing out into the deserted city. The steep walkways leading to the mount and Rowanoco's Stone were doused with purple – banners, tabards, people – and the new colour scheme clashed badly with the scarlet of South Warden.

'Let's redecorate this place.'

At the corner of a building he stopped. His men encircled the square, tantalizingly close to the Purple clerics. They had guards, lesser clerics tasked with protecting their commanders, as small ice-spiders cluster round their Gorlan mothers. They were unaware that they were about to die.

'Now!' he whispered, letting the command be carried round the encircling men of Twilight Company.

They moved as one, breaking cover with a hundred sword thrusts all at once. The men of Ro grunted, wailed, opened their eyes as wide as they would go, and slumped down dead to the ground of Ranen.

Fynius withdrew Leg Biter and took a second to make eye contact with the dying man at his feet. 'This is your lesson, man of the One.'

He strode into the square, taking his place within the huge semicircle of Twilight Company, each blade dripping with blood.

'Men of Ro,' he growled. 'Men of fucking Ro.'

The boss clerics were almost bowled over with surprise. They fumbled at their scabbards, pointing at spreading pools of blood.

'Consider this a lesson,' he boomed. 'This lesson will result in your death. If you have words, say them now.'

Lord Mobius, the man most responsible for the troll shit they found themselves in, stood to the fore. He was flanked by dozens of his minions and dozens more were quickly assembling behind their glorious master. They emerged from buildings and ran down roads, swarming like maggots across a rotting corpse. None of them looked superior now. Their chins were not thrust out and their noble foreheads were creased with confusion.

'You have killed noblemen of the One,' replied Mobius. 'Who in the stone halls beyond do you think you are? We are men of Ro . . . of Tor Funweir. You are nothing . . . it is our right to rule you and your peasant nation . . . who are you?'

Fynius chuckled, splitting his face into a broad smile. The Purple fool still thought he had authority. He still thought he had power. 'Who do I think I am?' he replied. 'Well, we could speak about that for decades. Unfortunately, your lifespan is not measured in such huge quantities. And those are shit last words. Try again.'

'Kill them!' shrieked the Purple man.

He was a fool and he had ordered his men to attack before they were fully assembled. Most had not buckled on their sword belts and many had still to enter the square. The clerics who were ready ran at them in small pockets, with no organization or unity. So much for the fabled military craft of the Ro.

'Let me end Mobius,' he said with a smile as his men attacked.

The clerics were skilled. They wore strong armour and knew how to use their swords. Their weakness was that their foolish leader had ordered them to fight a superior force. Each cleric had at least two opponents and died in a futile attempt to cover his fellows. It was a shame. They were good fighters and deserved a better death. Fynius decided to take it out on Mobius.

He outflanked a cleric and drew Leg Biter across his neck. He thrust at the back of an exposed leg, driving another to his knees. There was no duelling or honourable one-on-one fighting, there was just an outnumbered force being cut down.

Then Scarlet Company arrived and things grew much worse for the men of Ro. The new combatants appeared from the mount, rushing down the hill with frenzy in their eyes. For the people of South Warden, this was more than a fight. They were killing the men who had conquered them, killed their families, their friends, and had tried to enslave them.

Fynius dodged a well-aimed thrust and saw the attacker decapitated by Vincent. Then he was face to face with Mobius. The chief Purple man was vibrating with anger. Veins pulsed on his face and his sword hand shook. Not with fear, but with readiness. He was about to explode.

The cleric appeared mad. He attacked with suicidal abandon, swinging his longsword in circles and forcing Fynius on the defensive. He knew how to fight. This would be difficult if they were fighting a duel. Luckily, Twilight Company didn't believe in fair fights and quickly had the cardinal surrounded.

'Is that foam in your mouth, Purple man?' he quipped. 'It's a shame when the mind goes before the body.'

He defended himself admirably, using his sword to keep the attackers at bay, but he couldn't fight all the men who wanted to kill him. He killed two, but his movements were wild and uncoordinated. An axe thrown from Scarlet Company hit his thigh, then a sword thrust caught his underarm. Fynius let them cut him, standing back until the Purple man was on his knees, bleeding from a dozen minor wounds.

'Leave him!' He waved the attackers back. They obeyed without question. A few men of Scarlet Company appeared to want to be the one to kill Mobius, but still they obeyed.

'Got any more words?' he asked, resting Leg Biter across his shoulders.

Mobius panted and his face screwed up. His mouth quivered and his eyes bulged. 'She loves me,' he gargled, blood and bile on his lips.

'She'll get over it,' he replied, swinging Leg Biter at the man's head.

Cardinal Mobius of Ro died suddenly, a Ranen broadsword embedded in his brain. Fynius tilted his head and followed the dying man's eyes. They pulsed and flickered, looking surprised or maybe indignant. A common barbarian of Ranen had killed a nobleman of the One God. The very idea!

Fuck him and fuck his God, thought Fynius.

* * *

'Well, they will be dealt with by those they have wronged,' replied Bronwyn, unsure whether she should speak the whole truth.

A Red knight rushed into the tent. He was fully armoured and flustered.

'My lord general, there is some commotion in the city.'

Malaki Frith turned slowly, keeping his narrow eyes on her face. 'Define commotion for me?' he asked.

'The clerics have abandoned the walls and we heard steel on steel.'

He reacted straightaway, rising from his chair and straightening his tabard. 'Dealt with, you say?' he addressed Bronwyn. 'Sinking feelings are a curiously common sensation here in the Freelands. I think the cold disagrees with me.'

'General?' queried the knight. 'Shall we enter the city?'

He paused, sharing a glance with Fallon and the other knights in the tent. He took a moment to breathe in deeply and close his eyes. Then he drew his sword and levelled the point at Bronwyn.

'What is going on in the city? Answer in simple words, and answer quickly.'

She was startled and raised her hands. Micah stood up and glanced around, looking for some way to defend himself and Bronwyn.

'Sit down, boy!' roared the general. 'Answer, my lady.'

The other men of the Red drew their weapons and stood stony-faced and solid as a brick wall.

'I thought you lot had honour,' barked Micah. 'What the fuck is this?'

'If something has happened to the clerics, the Ranen broke parlay first. What were you, my lady? A distraction? I suppose it's the only way you could defeat us . . . through trickery.'

He made it sound so much worse than Fynius. She thought of herself as a diplomat, even as the sword point hovered inches from her face.

'I have the men to annihilate your companies, however many you have left. You should appreciate your position,' said the general.

Fallon had not stood up or drawn his sword. His demeanour had not changed and he had simply leant back in his chair. If anything, he looked amused. 'You're not going to kill her, general,'

441

said the seated man. 'You and I agreed, enough have died. The One and Brytag agree on this.'

They all looked at him. For a moment he appeared taller and stronger. The words, simple but powerful, carried sufficient weight for Malaki Frith to withdraw his sword. They were more than words and more than a man spoke them.

'Agreed,' said the general quietly.

'What are you?' blurted out Stone Dog, squinting at Fallon.

The swordsman stood up. He smiled and the tent appeared to brighten. 'I'm an exemplar,' he replied. 'I speak for the One God.'

'And I'm a wheel of fucking cheese,' replied Micah.

Fallon didn't stop smiling. 'That explains the smell.'

The senior knights sheathed their swords. Whatever was going to happen in this tent, it would be at the behest of Sir Fallon of Leith, and he did not appear hostile. Something else was happening that she didn't understand. Though she felt it was a good thing. Whoever he was, Bronwyn was sure that he wasn't their enemy.

As Frith sat down, Warm Heart poked his head through the tent flap and growled, as if to ask if things were okay. She nodded at him and his huge bulk retreated back outside.

CHAPTER TEN

SAARA THE MISTRESS OF PAIN
IN THE CITY OF RO WEIR

T HE ABBEY OF Oron Kaa was imprinted upon her memory.
The smooth dome and the high minaret, the slave pens
and the jagged, rocky harbour. The sun-kissed fields
of blood and despair. The expressionless minions, responding
to the whim of their mistress. The buzzing insects, appearing
each sunset to maintain the structure. The visions were as real
as the bed she lay on, the flesh next to her, and the wind that
blew through the open window. She remembered the matron
mother. Her wrinkled face, full of hate, her craggy fingers, long
and thin, the whip-crack of her voice, denying rest and peace
to her acolytes.

An uncontrolled mind was dangerous. Saara was supremely
skilled at marshalling her thoughts and maintaining focus, but
pieces of her past were leaking into her present. A long life, spent
in beautiful pain and debauchery, was seeping from her broken
mind to pound at the back of her eyes.

She remembered men and women she had killed, their faces
screaming at her. She remembered the deepest deserts of Far
Karesia, the heat battering her face. She remembered days, years,
decades, centuries. Every moment.

Men spoke to her about the dark-blood. He was dead and
they wanted her to be happy, but she couldn't be. They said that
the Thief Taker was a broken wreck of a man. Her mind didn't
permit her to care. Keisha was gone, stolen by the one assassin

to escape her, and she was sliding further and further away from reality and couldn't concentrate.

She had lost many phantom thralls – King Sebastian, Archibald Tiris, cardinals Mobius and Severen, even the young squire, Randall – but the deaths of Shilpa and Sasha had almost destroyed her mind. She was still whole, but she had used up much of her power battling the Gorlan and now she was weak.

She didn't trust her eyes, her ears or her mind. They lied to her. She wanted to slip into a peaceful sleep, wrapped in a warm blanket of Shub-Nillurath's love, but her mind would not permit it. So much had happened. So much beyond her control. She bore the burdens of five dead sisters. Their thoughts, their memories, everything. Each dead enchantress was like a new section of her mind opening. An unwelcome intrusion into her already troubled thoughts. She had summoned Isabel the Seductress, her last remaining sister, and planned to use her mind to relieve some of the burden. It would probably send Isabel insane, but it would allow Saara some respite. She didn't care if the Seductress had to be chained in the catacombs, so long as it allowed the Mistress of Pain to think clearly.

Behind her eyes, vivid images chipped away at her reason. The Red Prince haunted her. He had been the last thing Cardinal Severen and Archibald Tiris had seen. They had both been afraid of him and both of them had died with his name in their minds. Saara was not afraid, but she knew now that conquest would not he as simple as she had expected. The foolish men of Ro and Ranen did not appreciate their own inferiority. They fought with tenacity, unaware of the serene path of compliance that was within their reach. If only they would give in, their pain would stop and they could live their lives in pleasure, forever lulled into beautiful servitude. But Alexander Tiris was attempting to rally these lesser men and he was not without power.

Her thoughts were unhelpful. To worry about a single man and his tiny army was a distraction. She had a hundred thousand Hounds mustered around Ro Weir, and more in the Fell. The

Red Prince could not reach her, let alone cause her harm. And the thousand Young were almost fully grown.

A knock on her bedchamber door.

'I am not yet ready to rise,' she snapped, reluctantly opening her eyes.

Next to her, blood seeped from the dead body of a handsome young wind claw. She had consumed his power before she slept and had been too weary to remove the corpse.

'My lady,' said Elihas of Du Ban through the door, 'your faithful are gathering.'

'They can wait,' she replied in a throaty growl.

'There are three hundred Ro and almost as many Karesians.'

She screamed. 'Then three hundred Ro and almost as many Karesians can wait!'

Elihas didn't respond and she heard his boots on the wooden floor as he strode from her door.

She flailed on her bedside table for her rainbow pipe and a candle. She sat up and rubbed sleep from her eyes and drool from her mouth. She lit the pipe and drew in a deep lungful of smoke. It took the edge off, but nothing more. She had servants searching the city looking for the strongest rainbow smoke available and she had been using it to calm her mind for months. The substance was called green in Kessia and was the most mellow of a rainbow merchant's wares. The black used by the Hounds was like a war-hammer to the head in comparison.

Saara had spent too much time asleep. Since her battle with the Gorlan, she'd woken for barely two hours a day. The rest of the time she had been at the mercy of vicious nightmares about Oron Kaa, the matron mother and the Red Prince.

She rose from her bed and washed herself in a free-standing basin of clean water. Dried blood and sweat coated her body and she wished for a trusted body-slave to scrub her back. The layer of grime came off reluctantly and she took an hour to make sure she was properly washed. Her large flock had been summoned to the lower courtyard and she must not appear slovenly.

The death of Dalian Thief Taker had been prearranged and the citizens of her new empire were looking forward to it. A huge party had been planned for the evening. As she looked out of her window into the dusk of Weir, Saara realized she had been asleep all day. The wine and food would already be assembled and the Thief Taker would have been taken from his hanging cell.

Footsteps in the hall and another knock at the door.

'My lady, are you ready to rise yet?' asked Elihas.

'Almost,' she replied, as she finished dressing. 'You may enter.'

Elihas of Du Ban, Black cleric of the One God, was never without his armour. She imagined his skin as toughened leather, calloused and hard from years of austere living. His face was no less harsh. He had sharply angled features and would have been handsome were his eyes not so dead.

'The lower courtyard is full, my lady.'

She looked at herself in the mirror and slowly brushed her hair. 'Have we heard from Cozz?'

'Not as yet. The last group of merchants to arrive said nothing of interest. Yacob is there with the cargo, I'm waiting to hear from him.'

'Inform me as soon as you do.'

She composed herself and took a long look in the mirror, assessing her appearance. She was not at her best, but she wouldn't be studied close-up and the festivities would allow her some anonymity, perhaps even a chance to slip away.

'Take me to the Thief Taker, I wish to see his face.'

'He has not woken,' replied Elihas.

'I will wake him.'

The Black cleric nodded and strode from the room. Saara followed and four wind claws joined them in close guard. The duke's residence was airy and many windows let grey light flood into the rich corridors. Duke Lyam had a fondness for classical paintings and the halls were lined with rich watercolours: noble knights battling barbarians and savage beasts, all rendered in vibrant colours.

Servants and guardsmen rushed to catch a glimpse of their mistress, but she ignored them, her escort keeping her isolated. Elihas led them past a balcony beyond which she could see a flood of people in the square below. They drank and shouted, chanting oaths to the Dead God and pledges of servitude to the Mistress of Pain.

Her flock was huge. Equal parts Ro and Karesian. Even a handful of Kirin rainbow merchants had joined the faithful. Powerful men and women were in love with her, they offered their fortunes and their influence to her new world. She received them gratefully but despised every one of them.

At the base of the residence, under the multi-levelled garden and above the catacombs, was the dungeon. Its only occupant was Dalian Thief Taker, greatest of the wind claws. Saara tuned out the braying cattle around her and followed Elihas to the bottom level. Somewhere in the middle of all this vileness, work still had to be done. Men needed to die, preparations needed to be made.

'The last cell, my lady. Shall I accompany you?' asked Elihas.

She paused, looking from the bottom of the steps along the cold stone corridor. There was no breeze and the air was fetid. Bodies had been left to fester, rats had been allowed to feed and those who cared for the place had been killed by Elihas for various minor indiscretions.

'I'll speak to him alone,' she replied. 'But stay close.'

She took the cell key and walked down the line of empty cells. The first was filled with torn sacking and straw, the second had rats feeding hungrily on splintered bones, the third and fourth were both bare with green streaks of mould for decoration. In the last cell was a dark heap, curled up in shadow and covered in a thick grey blanket. The shape was motionless. If she had been better rested, she would have laughed.

'Behold, the greatest of the wind claws. Humbled by his betters.'

A twitch of movement. A dirty hand appeared at the corner of the blanket, scratching at the stone floor. The forearm was bare, with blackened bloodstains and deep cuts.

Rust peeled from the hinges and the door opened with a high-pitched squeak.

Another twitch of movement. This time both arms were visible, but the face was still hidden. The only sound was a guttural mutter, almost a growl. As she glided into the filthy square room, the twitching stopped. His hands clenched against the floor, scratching into fists across the stone.

'Awake, Dalian Thief Taker. Awake and meet your death.'

The blanket was thrown off and he lunged at her. Blood seeped from the corners of his mouth on to his teeth. His eyes were wild and red as he was prevented from striking her, his fists frozen solid in the air inches from her face.

She laughed. 'You have always been powerless against me, you just needed reminding.'

An invisible barrier was between them. His veins strained against his bloodied skin. She could feel his anger, his frustration, his sadness. He had lost and it was destroying him. Defeat was worse than any torture she could conjure.

He slumped back to the floor, the last vestiges of his strength disappearing. His body had been partially repaired but he had not eaten or washed and many of his wounds had reopened. He bore cuts and lesions over his bare torso and his face was thin and stained red. He still had a taut muscularity, despite his age and wounds, but he had no fight left.

'Awake,' she repeated, permitting his mind to relax.

So much hatred. Touching his thoughts was difficult. His will was stronger than most men's, his faith in Jaa acted as a layer of protection, but he was vulnerable and his mind opened to her like a willing lover.

He sat against the far wall, looking at her, the blanket now around his shoulders. His body was still and his eyes focused, though the lids drooped and his fists were clenched.

'I . . . wish . . . you dead,' he murmured, the words dribbling out of his mouth.

'You have failed,' she replied, enjoying each word. 'Your assassin is gone, your allies scattered and broken.' A slow smile crept across her face. 'Your god . . . has fallen.'

'Then why do I live?' he roared, drool and blood spluttering from his lips. 'Just kill me!'

He lunged again, and was again stopped in mid-air.

'Just kill me! Kill me!'

She took a step, driving him back. His fingers flexed and reached for her, blood appearing around the nails. He was strong and his hatred of her was stronger still. Every inch of his flesh quivered against the invisible barrier, fighting against hope to deliver a final blow or to break the enchantment and strangle her.

'Do not spend your last moments in anguish,' she said. 'Calm yourself.'

He slumped again, scuttling back against the far wall.

His pain flowed over her like a cooling breeze. Waves of pulsating torment revitalizing her tired body and expelling the fog from her mind. The pain of the mighty was like the sweetest liquor.

Another moment and she called for Elihas. 'Bring chains and a hood. It is time.'

The Black cleric appeared with three wind claws. He took two strides into the cell and struck Dalian sharply across the face.

'Just to remind you of your place, Thief Taker,' he said, standing over the broken man.

'You're a filthy traitor,' he growled in response, spitting blood on Elihas's steel-shod boots. 'To your god and to the lands of men.'

'And yet I will not be executed today. Perhaps my god is more forgiving of my actions than you believe.'

Dalian tried to spit again, but Elihas kicked him in the stomach. The Thief Taker coughed, retched and curled up in a ball, sending more waves of pleasure through Saara.

The wind claws brought chains and shackled the prisoner at the wrists and ankles. They did not allow him to stand fully upright, causing him to hunch up as Elihas dragged him to his feet. The hood was placed over his bloody face and tied at the neck.

She looked at him – a bent and broken man, breathing heavily through the canvas sack and struggling against his restraints. He could have been her greatest ally. As it was, he would remain as no more than a footnote in the Lands of the Twisted Tree.

'Bring him,' she ordered.

Once out of the cell, Saara's headache slowly returned. By the time she had reached the stairs, she had to squint to alleviate the pain. Dalian's death would give her a few hours of respite before she would need to find another's life force to consume. Keeping her mind clear and her conviction strong was becoming a full-time duty, consuming her time and keeping her from her work.

She walked wordlessly past lines of armoured men standing at attention either side of the corridor. Karesian wind claws and Ro guardsmen, each wearing a black tabard displaying the Twisted Tree of Shub-Nillurath.

Distantly, she could still hear the clamouring of her flock, men and women squeezed into the lower courtyard awaiting their mistress and the evening's festivities. Many would already be drunk. More would be taking part in orgies and the ritual consumption of drugs. They revelled in the debauchery freely available in the new environment Saara had created.

Sycophants every one. Weak, but useful.

The curtains that led to the lower balcony were held aside and she glided into the evening air of Ro Weir. A few minutes of theatre and playing to the crowd and she could remove herself to her tormented solitude.

Her flock cheered her arrival. They raised their arms and reached for her. Every man and woman hungered for her. They believed her to be their purest love and the catalyst for their future prosperity.

Beyond her flock, soldiers encircled the courtyard. The gates were closed and only the elite were permitted to view Saara. Thousands more lined the streets outside, filling the old town. Any glimpse they could catch of the enchantress would be the highlight of their year, a story they could pass on to their loved ones.

She usually enjoyed the attention. But not this time. This time it tasted like bile in her throat. The noise was jagged to her ears, the sight of so many spewing idiots made her nauseous. Their longing for her was necessary but it felt like the love of infants, a petty end to a long game.

'Shh . . .' she said, holding out her hands to the adoring masses. 'We will adorn ourselves in flesh and become lost in sensation . . . all in due time.'

Men looked at women, women licked their lips, and every one of her flock imagined the sordid pleasures of the evening to come.

'But flesh feels better after a victory. A great victory. A victory for all who follow the Twisted Tree.'

More noise. They ranted oaths of compliance, their eyes bulged and they cavorted in a mad rapture. Flesh addicts threw off their robes and flaunted their bodies, daring men and women to touch them.

'Not yet,' she said. 'Soon.'

Elihas came forwards, flinging Dalian on to the balcony. The old Karesian appeared as a ragdoll, his limbs flailing limply within his steel restraints.

'A man who would see me dead will die this night.'

Discordant cheering from the crowd.

She nodded to Elihas. He held up the prisoner, grasping his neck and shoving his hooded face towards her flock.

'My beloved followers, my friends, I present to you, Dalian Thief Taker, greatest of the wind claws.'

Elihas removed the hood and pulled his head upright. The prisoner grunted and closed his eyes. Even the glow of twilight was too much for him.

His pain again soothed her mind and she allowed herself a moment of enjoyment at the spectacle of the enchanted people who adored her. They loved so freely, giving her their minds and their hearts in an instant.

However, the question of how to kill him still played on her mind. A swift decapitation? A slow draining of his blood? Elihas had questioned her decision not to enchant him, but Dalian was too strong for her to do that easily. Small commands were possible, but full enchantment could work only if he were unaware that it was happening. A mind of iron and fire would take time to break, and his death would be more useful to her than his compliance.

'In Kessia, you would be inched before this fine crowd,' she whispered. 'Thank your fire god that we are in a less civilized land.'

'I . . . will . . . fear . . . nothing . . . but . . . Jaa.'

'No, no, no,' she replied in a purr, 'you will fear me, and you will fear Shub-Nillurath.'

'Nothing but Jaa.' He began to laugh. His bloodied cheeks wrinkled up, his teeth were bared, his eyes, bloodshot and watering, stared off into the sky.

Why would he laugh? What did he know that she did not? It didn't matter. His laughter, like his life, would soon be snuffed out.

'Enough playing,' she whispered. 'These good and loyal people have come here to see a death, and a death they shall see.'

Her lip curled into a sly smile and her eyes became slits. 'Elihas, hand him a knife.'

The Black cleric hesitated. He glanced behind at the wind claws in close guard, then at Dalian's broken body.

'And unchain his arms.'

'Yes, my lady,' he replied, moving to do as she instructed.

Saara faced the prisoner, delving as deep as she dared into his mind. There was layer upon layer of righteous anger. He was protected by his unswerving conviction. No matter. She didn't need to enchant him, just to command his actions for a few moments.

'Take the blade, sweet Dalian,' she intoned, her words echoing in his weakened mind.

He resisted. Once his hands were free, he reached for her again. He could barely raise his arms and the strain caused his veins to bulge and his teeth to press tightly together. With tears of pain and regret, he took the offered knife.

'Good. Your pain is not my goal . . . your defeat is. Give yourself to me and it will be quick.'

He slowly turned the knife towards his chest. The crowd cheered and willed him to stab himself. They spat and waved their arms, chanting at Dalian.

Death! Death! Death!

His face changed. Anger gave way to despair, then resignation. But the hate never left his eyes. It just grew deeper as the blade touched his skin. A gap in the bloodied rags allowed the knife to draw blood.

'You know this is what you deserve. You chose the wrong master, Dalian Thief Taker, servant of Jaa.'

'He chose me,' he replied, plunging the knife into his heart.

She gasped. She had been slowly driving the blade towards his chest, intending to make his death slow. At the last, he'd taken matters into his own hands.

His eyes changed again. Now they were peaceful and defiant, staring at Saara as his limp body fell against her. An intense fire burned deep beyond the stare. A pinpoint of rage, barely held behind the eyes of a mortal man. She shoved him away in sudden alarm. The crowd cheered but a pounding in her head shut them out. Elihas grabbed Dalian's falling body but his blood still coated her dress.

She held her breath. He had killed himself. She hadn't expected it. Something defiant and beyond her control. The crowd didn't care, so long as the traitor was dead, but she cared. For an instant she saw true faith. When his dead eyes focused on her she was face to face with the enraged Fire Giant. He had further work for Dalian Thief Taker and she had gained little by killing him.

The cheering had become a dull squawk, as if her followers were a flock of geese pecking at their seed. It was too much. The roar of those below, the thick blood falling at her feet . . . and the surge of Jaa's eyes.

Dalian's corpse lolled to the side as Elihas dumped him to the ground. His head turned and the eyes again sought her out. She ran from the balcony, barely containing a scream behind the pounding in her head.

* * *

Saara's phantom thralls were like predatory animals, scratching at her mind when she was at her weakest. They pounced from corners and out of shadows as soon as she fell face-down on to her bed.

You cocky, Karesian bitch.

Didn't expect that, did you?

Ha ha, not so powerful now, sweetheart.

She couldn't shut them out. Some were dead, some still living. Their anger stabbed at her, unleashed as her control wavered.

'Leave me,' she wailed.

Make us!

You can't, can you? You're weak, aren't you?

She buried her face in the pillow and cried. She didn't want to know who spoke. The apparitions spoke with the voices of Sebastian Tiris, the squire Randall, Cardinal Mobius and others. They mocked her, viciously revelling in her failure. Had she failed? Had everything fallen apart? She had lost Ranen, for now at least, but Tor Funweir was in her grasp. Fjorlan was still in the balance as armies moved against her. Was this failure?

Of course it's fucking failure.

The speaker was Cardinal Mobius, an honourable man, living a life of servitude to his god. Then he met Katja in Ro Tiris and became a thrall. He had been the hardest to enchant. His will and faith were almost as strong as Dalian's. His weakness had been loyalty to his king, a man much more easily swayed.

We are free of you!

'You are lesser beings,' she whimpered, barely believing her words.

'No!' stated a new voice.

The chattering stopped. Saara panted heavily against her pillow, terrified of turning round. She knew who it was.

'Look at me,' said Dalian Thief Taker, his voice clear and sonorous.

She pushed herself away from her bed and slowly turned round. He was standing next to the window, wearing black armour and glowing with a hazy red aura. He wasn't real. At least, Dalian Thief Taker was dead and what was before her was more than a man.

'You remain just to torment me?' It was barely a whimper.

The apparition smiled. She could never remember Dalian smiling. 'I do not remain for you, but I choose to address you before I leave. You are a feeble creature, ignorant despite your centuries of life. You have not won, nor has your god the power you believe. All your endeavours, all your treachery, there is no great reward for you.'

Tears filled her eyes, flooding down her cheeks. They were salty on her lips and tasted like weakness. He was right. She couldn't summon the power to dismiss him, whether he were real or not.

'I am the shade of Dalian Thief Taker and I am beyond your control. You are a petty priestess of a dead god.'

'No!' she roared. 'I have power . . . I live while you die. Leave me!'

There was no reply. The shade just looked at her, slowly fading from view until it was no more than a wisp of red smoke. And then it was nothing, as if it had never been there.

* * *

Yacob Black Guard of Weir disliked Cozz. He'd been here before the Hound occupation and he hated the uppity merchants and their arrogant sneers. They'd got what they deserved when the Karesians swarmed over their tiny empire. Those that didn't learn their place had been burned alive. The Hounds called it 'immolation', as if that made it less violent. Yacob didn't care. He'd enjoyed seeing the smouldering pyres that lined the King's Highway. Their bodies were black and cracked, dropping flakes of burned flesh on to the 'hallowed ground' of Tor Funweir.

If you had to choose a side, you should always choose the winning side, and the Karesians were clearly going to win. Money was easy to come by when you could convince the powerful that you were useful.

Yacob was a killer and the new rulers of Tor Funweir needed killers. He'd already had much gold from the Karesian woman and he would receive more when the job was done. They had a lot of gold and he intended to see as much of it as possible. There were hundreds of people that needed killing. Clerics, knights, lords and merchants – anyone that didn't bend knee to the new rulers was a potential contract for Yacob. He hoped they wouldn't surrender too easily.

Izra Sabal was a strange woman. She had accepted Yacob and the Hounds with whom he'd arrived, but she hadn't conversed with him. She'd grunted out of her mangled jaw and returned to her duties, allowing him to wander freely around Cozz. He was one of few Ro who weren't in chains or locked up. Some merchants and nobles had surrendered to Izra, pleading their compliance and offering service. Like Yacob, they had realized when they couldn't win and had been sent with their fortunes to Ro Weir.

The majority of the enclave's citizens had not been so wise. Cattle pens had been set up at the four corners of Cozz, housing thousands of men and women. Rich merchants scratched in the earth next to the lowliest servants, trying to find food or clothing that wasn't soiled. The Hounds watched, playing sadistic games with the captives, revelling in their misery. Izra was reluctant to kill every citizen of Cozz and now she had prohibited her Hounds from random killing. However, that didn't stop them bullying, beating and degrading their playthings.

Yacob didn't like the Hounds. They wore identical armour and helmets, wielded identical swords, and appeared to have virtually no personality. Each day they stood in lines before huge covered wagons to receive their dose of drugs, and each day they twitched and laughed manically as their narcotic collars took effect. A steady stream of carts made the journey to and from Weir and the logistics involved in keeping the Hounds in pungent Karesian black was staggering. It was the one thing they were good at – keeping their faceless masses well stocked with drugs.

Izra and her captains didn't partake of the daily regimen. According to Pevain, they were kept in line by enchantment and by a deranged sense of pride in following their orders. They were only truly compliant when they were near an enchantress. Out here in Cozz, the Hounds would grow rebellious as well as cowardly if they were not tightly controlled by fear and drugs.

Kasimir Roux, a senior Hound with an ugly scar from his forehead to his chin, was on the wooden battlements watching the northern plains. He had some grievance with Izra and kept his distance from the whip-mistress. Yacob had been told to report to him.

'What's a Black Guard?' asked Roux.

'A member of a traitorous house,' replied Yacob, slouching against the wood and massaging his feet. 'My father . . . could be wicked.'

Kasimir sneered. The concept of wickedness was relative when speaking to a Hound.

'And you?' asked the Karesian. 'Are you wicked?'

'Not really, I'm just greedy.'

Kasimir nodded approvingly and turned back to the northern plains. The King's Highway was mostly empty. A few broken caravans and the constant stream of drug wagons lent texture to the otherwise barren horizon. Close to the northern gate was the stump of a darkwood tree, cut down by Marshal Wesson within the last year. The wooden mound was black and had started to rot within a few days. Yacob peered down at it. It didn't look anything special. To hear Pevain talk, the thing had some hidden power over the weak-willed. Clearly, that power had not been strong enough to prevent it being cut down. Swords and paid men to wield them would always trump sorcery.

'You clear on what you have to do?' asked Kasimir.

'I am. As long as the gold in my pack isn't counterfeit.'

'You have your coin. You'll have more when you get back to Weir.'

Yacob removed one of his boots and flexed his toes, relieving the soreness. His feet stank and his woollen socks needed repair. There was a time when he would have had servants to fix his clothing and massage his feet. And there was a time when he would have been able to rest indoors, out of the wind. The strong gusts that blew across Cozz did help soothe his aching limbs but they made him feel like a peasant. It was a miserable excuse for a town, built in a stupid place for stupid people.

'Do you know what you have to do?' he asked Kasimir.

'Don't worry about me and my men, Black Guard. When Izra falls we'll give them the surprise of their lives.'

'Your men are losing their edge, whip-master,' he replied with a sneer. 'Your Karesian black don't seem to be quelling their cowardice. Sure you're getting the purest stuff?'

'They're a long way from home. The drugs only do so much without regular enchantment.'

'If they run away, I won't get paid,' grunted Yacob.

'Think of them as cattle. They can be herded and used. In the end, their purpose is to die.'

From further along the battlements a woman called to Kasimir. 'Commander,' she said. 'Look two points off north.'

Kasimir followed the directions from the lesser Hound. It was early evening but not yet dark. The sun was low in the sky and a dusky glow covered everything.

'Two riders approaching,' said Kasimir.

'They're here,' replied Yacob.

CHAPTER ELEVEN

GWENDOLYN OF HUNTER'S CROSS IN THE MERCHANT ENCLAVE OF COZZ

THEY HAD RIDDEN for two days and two nights. On barely an hour's sleep, the small company was now approaching Cozz. The grassy fields and gravel roads melted into one as they covered the ground on tired horses. The sun was disappearing, casting a dull glow over the wooden stockade. Everything seemed unreal. The horses, the grass, the enclave, all were hazy and indistinct, as if she were still asleep and dreaming the moment.

Gwen rode with five hundred men and forty Dokkalfar. The largest company they could spare. The Hawks were stretched thin. They had sailed and fought, and had not rested. Despite that, every man was lean and hungry for combat. The majority of their force was still in Tiris, securing the city and calming a volatile population.

Cardinal Cerro and Captain Brennan were an odd combination, but they were now jointly in charge of the capital of Tor Funweir. A soldier and a cleric, perhaps that was the best leadership they could hope for. In time, a distant cousin of Xander might be found as a new duke. Perhaps a Tiris dwelling in Du Ban or the Falls of Arnon, but until then the reluctant duo would rule. Markos of Rayne, the White paladin, had left ahead of them, bound for Ro Arnon, intending to join them at Cozz with the White knights of the dawn.

She was riding behind Bromvy and Xander, allowing them to get a little way ahead of the column. The two lords of Ro looked to the front and had done so ever since they first mounted their horses. Their armour had been repaired, their swords sharpened and their minds were as focused as their tiredness would allow.

It was hard to read them. She made her judgement based on her own fatigue. Brom had sat in his hall for months and she hoped that he wasn't keeping up with Xander through stubbornness alone. He was hot-headed enough to get himself killed rather than admit he needed rest. Gwen would need to keep an eye on him during the coming combat. Or maybe Xander would be sufficiently intimidating to force a surrender. She hoped he would try.

Xander and Brom reached a rise within sight of Cozz. The glow of dusk spread over them, reflecting off their armour and making both men shine. They looked at one another and reined in their horses, trotting to a stop on the high ground. The general raised his arm and the column formed up in ranks behind them.

The merchant enclave of Cozz was smaller than she had expected. It was an irregular circle of wood, bisecting the King's Highway. There were trees and jagged rocks to the south, but otherwise the plains were featureless. The merchants who had established the enclave had insisted that the settlement be built in the centre of Tor Funweir, within easy travel of all the great cities of Ro. It was now the northern outpost of the invading Hounds.

Xander wheeled his horse in full view of the enclave. He shielded his eyes from the glare and studied the wooden structure. They had catapults, a large gateway and a perimeter wall of wooden poles driven deep into the earth. The walls were solid and perhaps twenty feet high.

Gwen smiled. The Hounds within Cozz had no organization. Their catapults were not loaded and they had no crews, the gate was not secured and the battlements were barely patrolled. They had two thousand warriors, but she did not consider them to be true fighting men.

'Brothers!' said Xander, his voice carrying across the plains. 'We are outnumbered . . . shall we surrender?'

A laugh rippled through the company.

'This is Tor Funweir and that is Cozz. It's not Kessia, Thrakka, or any city of Karesia. It's ours and we're taking it back.' He drew Peacekeeper. 'Who here remembers my old squire, Wesson?'

Men nodded. Gwen remembered the prickly man of Haran. He was a good squire and a good man.

'There is a Hound in Cozz who left him to bleed to death on the King's Highway.' He was shouting, his eyes bloodshot and emotional. 'That Hound does not get the chance to surrender. But the others may.' He turned back to the enclave.

He nodded to Brom, who ordered Sigurd and the Dokkalfar to dismount. They ran to the east, quickly disappearing into the glow of dusk. Their lord remained, mounted next to the general.

'With me,' Xander commanded, nudging his horse forward.

In a column, three ranks deep, they advanced. It was not a charge but a steady and considered approach, giving the Hounds a chance to see their numbers.

Gwen appreciated the benefit of making this kind of statement, but she also wished for some cover or a way to sneak up on the enclave. Luckily, the Karesians were not sufficiently organized to use the time they had been given to mount a proper defence. They didn't run to their catapults or position men on the northern battlements. Those that did appear, pointed and exclaimed, flapping their arms in the air like untrained peasants. One or two commanders ran along the walls trying to get their men to load the artillery, but their movements were sluggish and they caused further alarm by fumbling with boulders and breaking the controls of the winches. It was almost laughable how poorly coordinated they were.

'A mob, not an army,' she whispered, glaring through narrow eyes.

They rode to within a hundred paces of the enclave and stopped. Xander and Brom trotted ahead.

'Is there a man within who can treat with me?' roared the general, resting Peacekeeper across his shoulders. 'I speak for Tor Funweir.'

Faceless Hounds now rushed over the battlements, forming up into some kind of line. From the centre, above the gatehouse, three Hounds emerged without helmets. It was unusual to see them as people rather than as blank suits of armour.

Two men and a woman stood before them. All Karesian, one man wore a scar down his face, and the woman, standing in the centre, sneered above a mangled jaw. She looked barely sane, with drool falling from her mouth, and carried a two-handed scimitar across her back.

'Who the fuck are you?' asked the woman in broken language.

'The defender speaks first,' replied Xander. 'Tell me your name, Hound.'

She grunted and snarled. 'I am Izra Sabal, whip-mistress of Karesia. I command here.'

'Well met, Izra Sabal,' replied the general. 'I am Alexander Tiris, the Red Prince of Haran. I claim this land. You may withdraw.'

He maintained eye contact, glaring up at the Hound. He didn't waver or blink and the woman could barely contain her anger.

To the east, Gwen caught a glimpse of black shapes darting between shadows. The Dokkalfar were in position, flanking the enclave. They were inhumanly fast, covering the ground like a slick of darkness. The dusk light was now grey and shimmering, providing the forest-dwellers with additional cover.

Gwen nudged her horse forward.

'Sigurd lies in wait, my general,' she whispered to her husband.

He nodded, maintaining his glare.

'I say again, you may withdraw,' Xander shouted up at Izra Sabal. 'We are prepared to kill you, but we would rather not.'

'You are prepared to kill us?' exclaimed the woman. 'I will eat your heart and rape your corpse, man of Ro.'

Xander smiled. 'Are you the one?' he asked. 'Did you kill Marshal Wesson?'

Her face twisted into a frown, her cheekbones taut and her mouth asymmetrical. 'Easily,' she replied.

He nodded. 'Then you will remain . . . your men may withdraw south.'

Izra spluttered, drawing her huge scimitar. It was a cleaving weapon, with little elegance. She banged it against the wooden battlements and screamed in rage.

'I said . . .' roared Xander, 'you will remain. Your men may withdraw south.'

'Load catapults,' she ordered, sending men scurrying across the walls.

'Big mistake,' countered the general.

From out of nowhere, leaf-blades arced through the air, cutting down anyone near a catapult. Sigurd and his Dokkalfar appeared from the east, vaulting over wooden buildings and causing panic among the nearby Hounds. They had found a way into the enclave and were fanning out, clearing the gateway of soldiers.

'Sigurd, the gate,' shouted Brom, drawing his longsword.

The wooden frame began to creak and a sliver of light appeared in the middle. Grey, bloodied hands appeared in the gap and two Dokkalfar pushed the large gate outwards, opening the gateway into Cozz.

'Forward!' commanded Xander, leading the way.

They rode slowly, moving into a single column to pass through the gateway and keeping their formation tight. Gwen was near the front of the column, watching dead Hounds fall from above. Sigurd and his Dokkalfar were holding the gatehouse in a semicircle, cutting off any chance of the Hounds reaching their artillery.

The first dozen Hawks entered the enclave and met with no resistance. Within, she saw a town of broken wood turned into a military camp. Small black tents were squeezed between buildings and bedrolls lay around smouldering fires. Most of the buildings were intact, used as dosshouses by the Hounds. There were no men or women of Ro within view. Perhaps they were all dead, or corralled at the edges of the enclave.

The Hounds had pulled back from the gateway, following screamed orders to form up in the town square. Abandoning the wall was foolish. They had let the Hawks in, had not even tried to clog the gate or break the Hawks' formation. These Karesian idiots were not worthy to occupy a town of Ro.

'Easy, lads!' said Xander. 'Keep it tight.'

They fanned out within the enclave while the Dokkalfar finished clearing the battlements. So far, things had been easy. She wasn't optimistic enough to think that would continue.

The Hounds were in lines before them. They held black steel shields, but they were not formed up in a defensive position. They simply stood in a group, holding their swords and shields. Izra and her captains had not even put on their helmets. They stood behind the mass of Hounds, gesturing and shouting to their troops.

Xander and Brom formed the five hundred Hawks into a column and stopped. They had not been challenged and had taken their time, eyeing up their opposition.

'Things are never as simple as they appear,' she said to her husband.

'I'll take staying alive over simplicity,' he replied, reaching across and stroking her hand.

'When you're ready,' said Brom, pointing his longsword at the mass of Hounds. 'I could ask them to wait while you two fuck.'

Gwen smiled at him. 'We do that after battle, not before.'

The three of them laughed. Their laughter seemed more terrifying to the Hounds than any threat of violence. The Karesians had had everything their own way until just now, when a small company of Hawks had ridden into their world armed with swords, confidence and laughter.

'Right, I'm going to call her out,' said Xander. 'Kill their leader. Get the rest to surrender.'

He didn't wait for a response.

'Forward!' he shouted, riding away from the gatehouse.

The company moved as one behind their general. They rode past stables and densely packed wooden buildings. Sigurd and the Dokkalfar were ghosting them on either side, covering their advance and clearing the side streets of stray Hounds.

The advance halted at the edge of the square. Before them, the Karesians were a mass of shining black metal, covering half of the enclave and stretching back to the southern gatehouse. The sun was disappearing now and dotted campfires provided some light.

The Hawks dismounted and assembled behind their general. Their horses were led away and the two forces faced each other. This was not a battlefield or a large open space and the men on both sides stood amid broken buildings and detritus. Only the advance units were in the square, with the rest jammed into adjacent streets. Cozz was filled to the brim with armed warriors. Some stood in overgrown gardens, others had to perch on barrels or duck under planks.

'Can we now talk politely?' Xander asked of Izra, letting his voice rise.

'You may say your words before you die,' she replied, still hiding behind the ranks of her men.

'My words are simple – your army will withdraw, you will remain.'

'You're outnumbered, prince of Ro.' Her words were slurred and indistinct.

'And yet you haven't attacked or even defended your walls,' replied Xander, pointing Peacekeeper at the Hounds. 'I say you are a coward. It takes a brave warrior to kill merchants and common folk. Step forward and prove you're more than a butcher.'

Gwen found the faceless soldiers unnerving. Maybe they were scared and ready to run, or maybe they were fanatics, waiting for the opportunity to attack.

The senior Hounds were arguing now. They spoke softly and their words couldn't be heard, but she reckoned Izra's command was precarious. The man with the scar was pointing around him, to a nearby stable, a cracked well, a cluster of barrels. She didn't know what he was worried about, but Izra appeared not to care. She shoved her captains out of the way and pushed to the front of the mass of Hounds.

'I have killed hundreds of men,' she snarled, emerging into the square. 'I have severed arms, legs, heads and cocks. I will kill you slowly, man of Tiris. I will kill you slowly and your men will watch.'

Xander looked at his wife.

'Stay alive,' she whispered.

He signalled for the Hawks to stand at ease and took two long strides into the square. Izra followed his movements and the two warriors met between their soldiers.

The whip-mistress was tall and her bulky armour suggested a well-muscled physique. The black metal plates covered her from neck to thigh, ending in interlocked segments that gave her complete freedom of movement. She moved like a cat, keeping her steps light and her two-handed sword loose in her hands.

Xander was on guard, with Peacekeeper across his chest. His leather and steel armour was lighter than his opponent's, but his sword was smaller. He wasn't used to parrying such weapons, but Gwen could tell he was the better fighter.

Izra attacked, stepping forward and swinging her scimitar at Xander's head. It was a wide overhead swipe, using the heavy pommel to put maximum strength into the blow.

Xander didn't parry. He nimbly sidestepped and swung Peacekeeper at her arms, severing her left hand.

'His name was Wesson,' said the Red Prince.

Izra howled and dropped her scimitar. She grasped at the stump where her hand had been and dropped to her knees.

'My hand!' she wailed. 'My hand!'

The Hounds didn't react. They didn't move an inch as their mistress slumped in the main square of Cozz, spraying blood on to the cobbles.

'He was my squire,' growled Xander. 'And you cut off his fucking cock!'

Gwen could tell that he was fighting the urge to make the whip-mistress suffer. He should kill her cleanly, but his lips curled and his eyes betrayed his anger. He held Peacekeeper level, contemplating severing her other hand.

'My general,' Gwen shouted. 'The woman has admitted her crime. The punishment is death.'

'Aye,' agreed Brom. 'Let's get this over with. I need a rest.'

Xander nodded, pivoted on his right foot and decapitated the whip-mistress with a backhand strike.

In unison, the Hawks of Ro signalled their approval by striking their rectangular shields. Each man puffed out his chest and stood confidently. The Karesians had no faces to stare down, but the Ro glared nonetheless. It was a moment of victory.

'Scorch the earth!' roared the scarred man.

A series of bright flashes. A barrel exploded to her left, turning three Hawks into a bloody mist. Detonations rose all around them, tearing apart Karesian and Ro. Houses, stables, barrels and yards all filled with fire and dust in a dizzying instant. Gwen reached for Xander and began to speak, but a broken well next to her erupted in fire and her world turned to black.

* * *

Smoke, pain, burning lungs, hazy vision. She awoke, or at least she thought she did. Gasping for breath, she sat up and vomited. She could barely see her hands in front of her face. All she could hear was a high-pitched whine that cut into her brain and shut out all other sounds. She recognized the smell and the heavy fog. It was black wart.

She coughed, winced, spluttered and gritted her teeth. The fog was total, restricting her world to ten feet or less. Small fires smouldered in the distance, giving some light, but they were mere red spots and provided no orientation. Her ears were ringing. It was painful and repetitive, a whine that wouldn't abate.

A severed and bloodied arm lay next to her, a broken Hound hung from a wooden fence post. She had been blown backwards a great distance. Her back was dotted with points of sharp pain and her right leg was deeply cut.

'Think!' She couldn't hear her own voice.

Feverishly trying to clear her ears, Gwen crawled forward. She needed to know where she was. She needed to find Xander and Brom. She needed to stay alive. She felt as if she were under water, as if her ears were full and her limbs were being pulled down into a rough sea.

Black wart was a Dokkalfar explosive, and the Hounds had used a huge amount. The thick fog would remain for a time.

A figure appeared, a Hound with half his face burned away. He rushed at her, roaring soundlessly. His scimitar thrust down, but was poorly aimed. With a shriek of pain, Gwen tackled him, wrapping herself around his legs. The whine in her ears dulled everything, but she managed to crawl up his flailing body and ram her elbow into his throat. Four times she struck him, putting her body weight into each blow, until he was dead.

Who was still alive? How many Hawks, how many Hounds? They knew they couldn't win, so they had levelled the playing field. These Karesians were not true fighting men. They were barely men at all.

She took the dead man's scimitar and used it to help her stand. Her leg wouldn't bend at the knee and she tried not to look at the wound. It would take just enough weight to allow her to hobble forward into the dense smoke. She stumbled through small pockets of the dying until she reached the corner of a building. She couldn't see the roof or any adjacent structures.

'Help,' mumbled a young voice, which came to her as a vague grunt.

Gwen crouched as best she could and edged her back along the wooden building. A little way down the street was a young Hawk, trapped under heavy wooden logs. His head was wounded and blood stained his hair and face.

He mouthed some words, but she couldn't hear him.

'Speak louder!'

'My lady,' he said, the words echoing through a filter of dull sound. 'Please . . .'

'Easy, soldier,' she replied, gritting her teeth with the pain.

'Your back, my lady,' said the young man. She read his lips, rather than heard his words.

She reached behind and felt blood on her back. Small wooden splinters had stuck in her flesh and pinpricks of pain penetrated her.

'Let's get you out of there,' she grunted, unable to hear herself speak.

She used the scimitar to lever the wooden planks off the man's chest. He was strong, and between the two of them they freed him quickly.

'I can't hear,' he said, wiping blood from his eyes. 'And I lost my sword.'

Gwen leant against the wall and handed over the scimitar. The young man had a deep cut to the front of his head, but he was less badly wounded than she was. He could at least stand unaided.

'Watch my mouth,' she said, pronouncing each word slowly. 'Your hearing will get better . . . I'm sorry, I don't know your name, lad.'

He frowned, guessing at what she was saying. 'Sergeant Symon of Triste, my lady,' he replied. 'Third cohort.'

'Did you see the general or Lord Bromvy?'

He shook his head. 'I don't understand . . . the general? I didn't see him. I was standing near to Lord Bromvy. He flung himself at the general before the world went black.'

She leant in close to hear him over the whine in her ears, then nodded and tried to assess the situation as best she could. The Hounds had detonated the enclave, scorching the earth rather than surrendering it. The bastards had prepared their explosives well. They were poor soldiers, but they committed suicide with great skill.

'Come on, Symon, we need to move. There will be others still alive.' The young Hawk tore a strip of fabric from his tabard and she helped him wrap it around his head. The wound bled heavily but it was not bad. It would heal with an impressive scar.

He helped her stand and they moved along the wall towards a crater at the corner of the building. They were at the edge of the main square and the crater was filled with body parts. Unidentifiable chunks of dark and pale flesh among smouldering and broken armour. She was thankful that the darkness and smoke obscured much of the grisly scene.

Symon patted her shoulder so that she'd look at him. 'What happened, my lady?' he asked, mouthing the words deliberately. 'Was it Ranen pitch?'

'No. The Hounds have been killing Dokkalfar for a long time. It appears they've stockpiled a lot of black wart.'

She leant heavily against him. Stubbornness was keeping her upright, but her back would need attention soon.

'Identify yourself!' The voice was just loud enough to be heard over the ringing in her ears and came from a Karesian man.

Gwen and Symon looked at each other before he slowly lowered her into a seated position. Three Karesians appeared out of the mist and Symon raised the scimitar.

'We are Hawks of Ro, stand down or die,' he shouted.

The Hounds were not wounded and they rushed forward. Symon ducked a clumsy swipe and opened up the man's neck. The second man kicked the Hawk in the chest, pushing him to the ground. He rolled backwards into a crouch next to Gwen.

'Feint at his left and step right,' she mouthed, shoving him upright.

He nodded and faced off against the two remaining Hounds. He lunged at the first man's left-hand side, making him attempt a clumsy parry. Symon was skilled enough to pull back his blow and step to the right, striking the man in his exposed side. The last man tried to tackle him but received Symon's blade in his stomach. The young Hawk was a good swordsmen, in spite of his wound, and he made sure all three were dead before he returned to Gwen.

'You did well, sorry I couldn't assist,' she said, accepting his help to stand up.

'I still can't hear,' he mouthed. 'Just every other word . . . I don't like this scimitar, it's poorly forged.'

They stumbled away from the crater, further into the square. Points of firelight danced across her field of vision, but everything else was dark and misty. Symon found a longsword and discarded the inferior Karesian weapon. Gwen found her stride and the pain in her leg softened. She still needed his help, but her knee would now bend a little.

A Dokkalfar appeared, lying in a heap on the cobbles. He had lost an arm and was not moving. Another forest-dweller sat nearby, holding his head in his hands. Blood seeped out from between grey fingers and broken leaf-blades lay at his feet.

'Brother!' said Gwen. The Dokkalfar didn't hear her. 'Brother . . . how serious are your wounds?'

He removed his hands and revealed a scorched face and neck. His eyes were intact, but his smooth features were a mess of burns and deep cuts.

'I am in pain,' replied the Tyr. 'My skin burns, but I live.'

Gwen and Symon drew closer and faced him, pronouncing their words carefully in order to be understood. The ringing in her ears had faded into the background but she could still only hear loud noises.

'Your name, friend?' asked Symon, collecting two more discarded longswords.

'I am Tyr Kalan,' he replied. 'I can still fight, woman of Haran.'

Symon gave the Dokkalfar one sword and Gwen took the other.

'He will need to be burned,' mouthed Kalan, pointing to the dead forest-dweller. 'But we have time.'

'How much black wart did they use?' she asked.

They were clustered closely together to hear each other's words.

'They chained the explosions,' replied Kalan. 'Each detonation caused the next to be larger, more explosive. The fog will remain for hours.'

The three of them walked tentatively away, towards where Izra and Xander had fought. She could just hear Karesian voices, pained and urgent, coming from all around them. The fog hadn't lifted and it was now night-time.

'Many Hounds ahead,' said Kalan, facing Gwen so that he could whisper. 'I can see them, standing over their dead comrades.'

'Your eyes are sharp, friend,' said Symon.

471

'I see better with no light,' replied the Dokkalfar. He wore the pain from his burns wordlessly, with barely a twitch of anguish on his grey face.

'How many?' asked Gwen, flexing her leg.

'Ten or more, spread out. Some wounded, most not.'

She stopped and tried to focus through the mist. Kalan's eyes were much better than hers and she could detect no movement in front of them. The voices grew loud as the Karesians struggled to hear each other. They came to her as wisps of sound, as if travelling through heavy air.

'Keep quiet,' she said. 'Kalan, lead the way. We'll attack from cover.'

'Aye, my lady,' said Symon.

'Clear,' said Kalan.

She tested her leg, feeling a dull throb. It hurt, but light movements were possible. She could still fight. Her back was now more numb than painful, making it easier to ignore it.

They stalked forward, weapons held low, until Gwen saw opaque figures swirling in the mist before them. The Karesians had gathered into a broken squad of men, with a few of the wounded being tended to. They spoke of retreat and spat out words of hatred about Izra and their masters. These were undisciplined men who had survived by chance.

She waved Kalan and Symon to flanking positions and the three of them attacked as one. The first sound was a gasp of surprise, the second a gurgle of pain as Gwen severed a man's neck. Kalan floored two, kicking one in the groin and driving his sword through the other's chest. Symon killed a man with a powerful strike through the helmet, splitting his head.

All three of them were wounded, but their skill was far superior. The Hounds swung and shouted, using strength and brute force, but their training was limited. Their parries were weak and they were permanently off balance. Each time Gwen engaged one it was easy to make him fall forwards or topple over. She was quick, and her leg hurt less and less as she fought.

The Hounds died cleanly, cut down by the superior warriors, until they stood again in silence. They had barely heard the ring of steel on steel and the encounter seemed surreal and dream-like.

'We have won,' mouthed Kalan, finishing off a wounded Hound.

She nodded. 'So, three of us are worth ten of them. Worth remembering.'

'We could have taken more,' said Symon, cleaning his blade.

'Hawks!' announced a gruff voice.

From the mist, men appeared. The sounds of combat may have alerted them, and five more Hawks joined them. They had red, sticky fluid coming from their ears and appeared disoriented.

'My lady,' shouted Sergeant Ashwyn. 'Good to see you.'

'Ash,' she replied, moving close to the Hawk. 'Have you seen the general?'

'He was still standing when I flew backwards,' he replied, still shouting. 'Somewhere around here.' He swept his arm across the bloody cobbles. 'Near where the whip-mistress died.'

'And Lord Bromvy?'

He shook his head. 'I think he died just after you disappeared. Well, he threw himself across the general and bore the brunt of a big bang. He might have lived.'

She bowed her head. Hundreds of men had died, maybe thousands including the Hounds, but she hoped that the luck of Brytag would have followed the lord of Canarn. To hope that Brom was still alive was to hope that Xander was still alive, and she wouldn't allow herself to hope for anything less.

'We killed a dozen or so further east,' said Ash, rubbing his ears and wincing at the blood. 'Saw a load of Hounds running out the gate. Saw a man carrying his own leg too. They fucked us hard, my lady.'

Ashwyn's men had suffered cuts, burns and large splinters, but they were still in the fight.

'Sergeant, over here,' said a Hawk called Benjamin.

He was pointing at a severed arm lying across a pile of masonry and armour. On the hand was a ducal ring with a black raven. Brom had at least lost his arm. Gwen knelt down and removed the ring. Pain lanced through her leg and Symon had to help her stand up again.

'He may still be alive, my lady,' said the young Hawk.

'It's his left arm. Do you know which hand he fights with?' she asked.

'Sorry, no,' replied Symon, his words a little clearer now.

She flexed her leg again. The wound was swelling and would soon prevent her from standing entirely. For now, she had to tough it out.

'Tyr Sigurd has healing salves,' said Kalan. 'Your wounded leg is not severe. Your back needs more immediate attention.'

The Dokkalfar's voice was easier to hear, as if its pitch could cut through the ringing in her ears. 'I can't see it, so it's easier to ignore,' she replied, trying to smile. 'We need to keep moving. Towards the northern gate. We'll rally there.'

'Aye, my lady,' replied Symon and Ashwyn in unison.

There were now eight of them and they moved in loose formation across the cobbles. The discovery of Brom's arm had filled her mind with thoughts of Xander. She would lament the loss of Brom, but hope remained so long as the Red Prince lived. If he lived. The lord of Canarn had tried to shield him from the black wart, sacrificing himself in the process, but the general could still be dead.

Strangely, it was not his face or his voice that she brought to mind. It was the feel of his skin. It was the moment, late at night, when he turned in his sleep and their bodies met. When the world went away.

It was easy to daydream in the otherworldly mist. Easy to picture herself far away, safe and happy. Glimpses of dead men poking their heads, arms and legs through the opaque twilight lined their route north, but didn't touch her thoughts. They progressed from Xander's skin, to his touch, his smile, the feel of his lips, the sound of his voice, the snuffling sound he made when he was cold. These things meant more to her than a hundred victories and a thousand dead Hounds.

'Where are you, my love?'

It was easy to find the King's Highway from the square. Between the mist and the darkness, they had to use the buildings to orient themselves. Ashwyn's men had torches and they moved slowly northwards. Whenever they encountered Hounds, the Karesians ran from them, sensing that eight warriors would be too many to fight. Whatever loyalty they felt towards their commanders, it was fragile, and now they fled southwards.

'These men aren't soldiers, my lady,' said Symon, when their ears had cleared a little more. 'This isn't war, it's folly . . . sheer folly.'

'Fools can still invade,' she replied. 'And they die and kill the same.'

'What happens,' began the young sergeant, 'if he's dead, the general? What happens?'

She didn't want to answer that question. She didn't want to think about it – the question or the answer. But he deserved an answer. She was just Xander's wife. To the Hawks of Ro, he was much more.

'I don't know,' she replied. 'I really don't know.'

Sergeant Ashwyn, at the front of the group, slowed and fell in beside Gwen and Symon.

'Don't mean to eavesdrop, my lady, but I've got an answer,' he said. 'If the general's dead, if Lord Bromvy's dead . . . well, we won't miss a fucking step. We fight, we kill every Hound in Tor Funweir. We are the Hawks of Ro, soldier, we remain so . . . with or without a general.'

'Strong words, Ash,' she observed. 'And I thank you for them.'

'You won't go far betting against him, though. Your old man is a tough old man.'

No more words. Symon didn't ask again. He may have been satisfied by Ash's answer, or he may have sensed Gwen's anguish.

He was a soldier and he would remain loyal either way. He just nodded and kept his eyes to the front.

The northern gate was close now, just visible through the gloom. The gatehouse was gone and broken bodies hung from wooden splinters. Mostly Hawks, their chain mail torn and their faces burnt beyond recognition. A crater lay in their path and several others were nearby. The Karesians had made sure the gate had been detonated, killing off the back ranks of Xander's force. The dark grass beyond the gate was littered with bodies, the remnants of their rearguard.

'Find some cover,' she ordered. 'We hold here until the fog clears.'

'Aye, my lady,' answered Symon and Ash.

The eight of them fanned out and moved towards the ruined gate. The outer wall was still intact, with a few dented planks, but all the structures nearby were reduced to rubble.

Cozz was gone. There wasn't enough of it left to bother rebuilding it. The merchants who had fled south would have little to gain from returning, and so many men had died here. It was now a graveyard, a monument to the brutality of warfare. The forces of Karesia had killed thousands when they took the enclave. They had killed thousands more when they detonated what remained. They were bastards of the highest order. At least their masters were.

* * *

The night lasted forever. The fog stuck to the air like mould on stone, leaving them nothing to look at and nothing to do but wait. The eight of them had split in two groups, under partial roofs, either side of the gate.

Within a few hours they had picked up some more stragglers and seen some more fleeing Hounds. The Hawks were dazed and wounded, and the Karesians had no fight left in them. But Xander didn't appear. If the Red Prince was dead, they would need to sort through the grisly remnants of slaughter to identify his body. If anything was left to identify.

Tyr Kalan had disappeared into the enclave several times, fetching healing salves and finding his brethren. He moved better than the men, especially with the lack of visibility, and refused any suggestion that he should wait. He found two surviving forest-dwellers and sufficient healing supplies to help the wounded.

'I'm not a healer, Lady of Haran,' said the Dokkalfar as he tended to her back. 'You are strong, but these salves need skill to minister and I have not found Tyr Sigurd.'

'I'm alive, that's enough for now,' she replied, staring off into the darkness.

'It will be morning in a few hours,' he said. 'The fog should clear shortly after.'

'And then we'll search. We'll search for survivors and we'll send the dead on their way.'

CHAPTER TWELVE

UTHA THE GHOST IN
THE CITY OF THRAKKA

THE CITY FELT as if it had woken from a dormant state. Viziers, wind claws and templars emerged from slumber and brought life to the web of walkways and towers. A Gorlan mother had been seen, one of the Seven Sisters had been killed, and martial law had been enacted. Wealthy viziers and their paid guards patrolled the streets, hunting for the spider. Utha heard tales of a grand hunt, with every young warrior of Thrakka declaring his intention to slay the beast and avenge the enchantress.

He didn't care about any of it. He had lost his squire. Randall had become enchanted, a slave to the Seven Sisters, and Utha had not been able to help him. The one person who didn't deserve any of this had fallen. What was Utha's journey worth? Was it worth Randall's life? The staircase, the labyrinth, the guardian, did any of it matter now he'd lost the one person who cared for him, the one person who followed him out of loyalty?

'Pull yourself together,' said Voon from the window.

They were in Shadaran Bakara's tower, hidden far above the walkways. Voon had insisted they flee and hide there. Bakara himself was missing, presumed dead, but Voon thought the higher levels of the tower to be safe. Sasha had been there before them, probably torturing Bakara, and now it was the last place they would look for them.

Utha sat on a divan chair in an opulent, carpeted study. His head had been in his hands for over an hour and he had said nothing. The tower responded to Voon and allowed him to alter walls and remove staircases, ensuring them a degree of isolation. The magic was commonplace to Voon, though wondrous to Utha. The three levels beneath them had been divested of staircases and he had seen each one slowly disappear before his eyes until the two of them were well hidden up above.

The disagreeable Karesian had cut him off whenever he'd suggested they look for Randall or Ruth. He assured him that Randall was gone and Ruth was in danger. Not that they were particularly safe, but at least they weren't being hunted with nets and spears.

'Pull myself together? Is that the best you got,' he replied. 'How about patting me on the head and telling me it'll all be all right.'

'I'm not your friend or your mother, old-blood. We need each other.'

'Fuck off!' spat Utha. 'Where I'm from we don't leave friends behind.'

'Where I'm from we do, and I'm from Karesia.'

'So it's a country full of bastards. What the fuck am I doing here?'

'You are here because you must be here, because you are the last old-blood,' replied Voon. 'So pull yourself together, we have far to travel and I have much to teach you.'

'Teach me? What are you going to teach me? You've barely spoken since we left Kessia. Without Randall, I'd rather just fuck off back to Tor Funweir and watch it burn from a tavern window.'

The exemplar walked calmly across the red and black carpet. He went to a drinks cabinet and retrieved a crystal bottle of dark liquid.

'This is Kessian desert nectar,' he said, thrusting a glass towards Utha. 'Bakara loved the stuff.'

'So?'

'So, maybe a drink will help,' replied Voon.

'I don't want help, I just want Randall not to be enchanted.'

Utha ignored the glass and snatched the bottle. It was a sweet and sickly liquid which coated the tongue, but it was blessedly alcoholic and he gulped down a large measure.

'Ruth offered to guide me, you offer to teach me . . . the only thing Randall offered me was loyalty.'

'This is making me weary,' replied Voon. 'You are making me weary. We still have far to travel and this is a poor way to begin. I thought you a man, not a child.'

Utha stood. He faced the Karesian and smiled. Voon was a strapping man with solid limbs and a wide, muscular neck. His spear was resting against the far wall. Like Utha, he was currently unarmed. He was tall, taller than Utha, but the old-blood punched him in the face anyway.

'Don't call me names when I'm angry,' he said, as Voon held his wounded jaw.

The Karesian hadn't fallen and had responded with a powerful sideways kick at Utha's stomach, driving him against the wall and winding him.

'Don't make me hurt you,' growled the exemplar.

Utha snarled and ran at Voon, tackling him into a powerful grapple. He trusted his strength and lifted the taller man from the floor, dumping him in a heap. The Karesian tried to tie up Utha's arms and kick out, but he struggled to break the powerful bear hug.

Voon slammed his forehead into Utha's nose and shrugged him off. Pain flooded through the albino and tears rushed from his eyes. The Karesian followed up with two quick punches to the stomach. He fought strangely and Utha backed away, assessing the laconic exemplar. He was quick and well trained, using odd combinations to cause injury, but Utha stubbornly refused to yield.

He advanced again and threw powerful punches at Voon's face. None of them connected, but he drove his opponent back. He received a sharp kick to the shin, but the pain was minimal. The bastard wasn't fighting fair.

Utha charged again, using his strength to tie up the faster man. He was stronger and turned Voon round so he that couldn't headbutt him. He lifted him up and flexed his arms, driving the Karesian into the wall. His nose throbbed, but he kept smashing Voon's shoulder into stone.

'Enough!' wheezed the exemplar of Jaa.

Utha released him and deposited Voon on the floor, grabbing his shoulder and breathing heavily.

'Don't call me names when I'm angry,' he repeated. 'And that sneaky Karesian shit doesn't mean anything when you can't move.'

Voon sat up, flexing his arm. They were both bruised, but none of their injuries were serious.

'You fight like a wrestler,' said the Karesian. 'Difficult.'

'And you fight like a fucking girl,' he replied. 'Who uses a spear anyway?'

'It's called Zarzenfang, a gift from Jennek of the Mist, the last Fire Giant, old-blood.'

Utha was not impressed. The man was sincere and saturated with faith and conviction, but he was also a fucking contrary bastard. It felt good to have punched him in the face.

'Is your head clearer now?' asked Voon. 'Did that help?'

'Strangely, it did. Beating up an idiot is pretty cathartic.'

Voon chuckled, the most humour he'd expressed so far.

'I have been called many things, Utha the Ghost, but never an idiot. I will let it pass for the sake of our cooperation.'

He still managed to be intimidating despite the fact that he had been soundly beaten and was now lying on the floor. Utha was not easy to scare, but Voon would be terrifying to common folk.

'So, where next?' he asked, letting the Karesian stand up and retrieve his glass of desert nectar.

'The Jekkan causeway,' replied Voon. 'It's the only way of getting ahead of those that pursue us. There will be more now the enchantress is dead. My face is known and I was seen.'

'But you're the high vizier!'

'I am a follower of Jaa, a heresy in the new Karesia. The death of the enchantress has not helped us.'

He didn't say it, not wanting to make Voon weary again, but the death of the enchantress had not helped Randall or Ruth either.

'So, we're running away?' he asked.

'Yes, we are. Does that bother you? You were going south anyway, this is just a quicker way and now you are not burdened with useless hangers-on.'

Utha wanted to punch him again. To beat his face red until he never insulted Randall again. Useless hanger-on? He was an idiot and a bastard, but hurting him would not help. 'You're pushing it, Karesian.'

'If I appear harsh to you, I apologize, but I know this country and I am harsh in order to keep you alive. You don't need to like me, you just need to trust that I will protect you with my last breath.'

He still wasn't impressed. Voon was far more in tune with the gods than was Utha and his point of view appeared strange. Utha had always been a terrible cleric, even more so since he had turned his back on the One God. His journey south was a vague quest, an insistent pull, one from which he never intended to return, but the exemplar of Jaa was treating it as a pilgrimage, a spiritual journey to rouse the Giants.

'What is the Jekkan causeway?' he asked.

'A relic,' replied Voon, picking up his spear and gathering his pack. 'It runs from Thrakka to Oron Kaa. It was here before Jaa claimed these lands and old magic dwells there. The journey would take months overland . . . or over the sea, as Ruth wanted. The causeway will get us there in weeks.'

'Is it dangerous?'

'Extremely. Karesians do not travel the causeway for fear of the servitors. They remain, waiting for their masters to return.'

'I won't ask what a servitor is,' said Utha, sheathing his sword and strapping his mace to his side in prepation to leave.

'Hopefully, you won't need to find out,' replied Voon, motioning Utha to leave the room.

He strolled from the high tower and turned to where the staircase had been. Now, there was only bare stone, and he waited for Voon to access the strange Jekkan magic that would allow the towers to take a new shape.

'This weird craft of yours is unknown in Tor Funweir.'

The wall flowed downwards to reveal a new opening. The stone appeared to melt and form new lines and structures at Voon's touch.

'That is the reason I had us stop in Thrakka,' replied the Karesian. 'Bakara's tower sits atop an anchorhead that leads to the causeway.'

'An anchorhead?' queried Utha.

'An old Karesian term. They bridge the gap between the lands of men and the remnants of the Jekkan caliphate. There are few known.'

Utha didn't respond, unsure whether Voon was being deliberately obtuse. Lots of new words, concepts and ideas had been flooding into the old-blood's head of late. 'Caliphate', 'anchorhead', these were just new terms to bewilder him.

'Follow me,' said Voon.

The stairs formed as they descended, each new step answering to the Karesian's command and weaving round the inside of the tower. Utha hadn't realized how high up they had been, over a sheer drop, with no banisters. Voon had removed three or four levels of Bakara's tower and reconstituted the staircase, leaving no level ground.

'Randall would hate this,' he muttered to himself.

If Voon heard, he didn't respond. The monosyllabic Karesian just strode down the steps, not looking back as Utha tentatively followed him. Soon they were a good distance apart, maybe three rotations of the tower. He tried to catch up, but his progress was hindered as he desperately tried not to look down. At least it meant he didn't have to watch Voon contorting the bottom levels of the tower.

'Hurry up,' said the Karesian, disappearing into a newly created corridor.

'Fuck off!' he muttered in response. 'I'll follow in my own bloody time.'

He deliberately slowed down, lingering in the wide, dark stone cylinder. What a strange place. A strange country, full of strange people and stranger magic. They didn't even realize how strange they were, which made them stranger.

'Hurry,' repeated Voon from the darkness.

'Why?' he asked, loud enough to be heard. 'As I understand it, this tower only has doors when you ask it.'

He reached the bottom of the steps. The corridor Voon had created contained more steps, delving into the bare rock. It might have been a part of the tower, or they might be walking into the earth. Either way, Utha was glad he no longer had to look down.

'Where does this go?' he asked, unable to see Voon.

There was no reply.

With a sigh of annoyance, he followed, hurrying into the dark staircase. The steps were steep and he used the walls to steady himself. He walked downwards for ten minutes or more.

Now there was light coming from somewhere. No more than a blue glow, but enough to see by. Studying the construction of the stairway, he could see cracks in the cyclopean stone blocks and ribbons of blue light emanating from them. Wherever they were, this had not been newly created. Voon had led him somewhere. To this anchorhead maybe.

'Voon!' he shouted down the steps. 'Are you still there?'

No reply, but footsteps were gradually approaching. For a moment, Utha felt fear. He didn't know why. As Voon appeared, he breathed out deeply.

'Where the fuck are we?' he asked.

'We're under Thrakka. Do you need to know more?'

Utha stroked his hand along the stone wall. It was smooth and cold. There was something odd about the stairway. Some trick of the light making the angles appear irregular.

'I don't like this place . . . it's eerie.'

'It is. And much more,' replied Voon. 'Let us stay together. And perhaps advance more slowly.'

'Okay,' he said, welcoming the unexpected offer.

They walked slowly now, delving deeper into the ancient bedrock of Karesia. Hours came and went, and Utha had no idea of how deep they must be. The stairway didn't change. The slivers of blue light, the huge blocks of stone, the eldritch prickle at the back of his neck.

'We're almost at the anchorhead,' said Voon, breaking the silence. 'We will cross over soon.'

'Cross over into what?'

The exemplar of Jaa stopped walking and faced Utha, his eyes shadows in the blue glow.

'It is time to grow up, Utha of Arnon.'

'Do you want another punch in the face?'

'Now is not the time for your temper. I am being serious. Your upbringing has been sheltered, your world mundane. If you were astonished by the towers of Thrakka, your mind may not be prepared for a Jekkan ruin.'

'A ruin? Like an old building?'

'An old, old building,' replied Voon, his lip twitching. 'It was once part of a city called Oron Desh. The magic the viziers wield in Thrakka leaks from the ruins below. It twists up from ancient chaos and madness. Though the Jekkans have gone, their magic infests the brick and stone.'

'So, what? I might go mad?'

Voon bowed his head and frowned.

'I don't know. Jaa has gifted me with strength enough to withstand it. I don't know how an old-blood will react. You may be stronger than me, or you may die in tortured insanity.'

Utha felt like hitting him again. Not because he was feeling angry or violent, but because he was feeling naive and foolish. He had followed prophetic dreams and bizarre counsesl and they had led him to a world he didn't understand.

'Will I get any warning, or will I just start dribbling on the floor?'

'Your eyes may bleed first,' replied Voon.

'Nice. Let's go then, shall we?'

Voon led the way and the staircase stopped, blending into a large walkway. It was higher and wider than the passage down, but was made of the same smooth stone blocks and emitted the same blue glow.

'Where is that light coming from?' he asked, the web of blue stinging his eyes.

'Not known,' replied Voon. 'I imagine it was their way of doing without lanterns.'

Before them, the tunnel ended in a solid wall. The blue lines were duller and the stone appeared to crumble as they approached.

'We're crossing over into the Jekkan ruin. Prepare yourself.'

Utha was about to make a sarcastic comment when he felt his world assaulted. The grey stone fell away to reveal a sickly blue vista, dripping and coagulating into walls and ceiling. Every sense was heightened. The colour was too vibrant, the screaming in his ears too loud, the rank smell of death too strong. He could even taste the chaos. It left a metallic sheen on his tongue and tightened his throat. Time and space felt elastic. He imagined he fell to his knees, but he couldn't perceive the floor on to which he fell. He imagined he screamed, but the sound was drowned out by the roaring in his ears. He closed his eyes, but the blue shone through his eyelids.

Voon clapped his hands together in front of Utha's face. 'Wake up!'

The old-blood grabbed at the air, reaching for his companion. When his hands grasped the other man's shoulders, his head cleared. Panting, clenching his fists against Voon's robes, he regained his senses.

'You are strong. You weathered that far better than I did the first time.'

Utha coughed violently, his lungs burning. He looked around hesitantly. The cavern was vast, melting into far darkness beyond thousands of carved pillars. There was no ceiling, just more black, endless emptiness. The blue light remained, but it was now just a glow framing each flagstone of the smooth floor.

'That was an anchorhead? So we're beyond the world?' His voice was disjointed.

'No, we are still in the world, just not in the lands of men. The Jekkans could shift reality, hiding themselves from lesser species. They knew the power of their magic and they sought to protect it. What we just did would have killed any common man seeking entrance.'

Utha stood and rubbed his eyes. His legs were sore and struggled to carry his weight. There was fear nagging at the back of his mind, a fear that came from the very stone. Every inch of the Jekkan ruin emanated an aura beyond its simple architecture. Magic infused the place, as mortar infused a castle of Ro.

'How long do we have to spend here?' he asked, accepting Voon's help to stand up.

'Perhaps two weeks. The causeway will lead us to Oron Kaa, but the distance changes. We'll still be there well ahead of our pursuers.'

'Is it all like this?'

The endless, irregular forest of pillars was all he could see.

'Mostly, but it changes,' replied Voon, offering his spear as a crutch.

'Why can't I fucking stand? My legs are fine.'

'You'll get used to it. The rules aren't always the same. I think metal weighs more here.' He tapped the heavy steel mace at Utha's side. 'The Jekkans had no knowledge of metal, I understand.'

'There is metal in my boots, metal in my belt, metal in my pack. I'm not leaving everything behind.'

'Then grow stronger,' replied Voon, gesturing to his own fabric robes and wooden spear.

'Yes, very funny. What do we eat down here? I don't see any game.'

'We won't need to eat.'

'Do we still get hungry? Because being hungry without needing to eat sounds shit.'

Voon ignored the question and began to walk. He appeared to pick a direction at random. Utha hoped he knew where he was going.

Leaning on Zarzenfang, the old-blood limped after the exemplar.

* * *

Time had no meaning in the Jekkan causeway. Utha felt neither tired nor hungry and their progress was good, though the unchanging surroundings were disorienting and made it hard to assess how far they'd travelled. He grew used to the weight of metal and the stark vibrancy of his senses, but the fear at the back of his mind didn't abate.

Randall would doubtless have had something blunt and witty to say about the place. All Utha could think was how otherworldly everything was. Even simple things like stone and carved pillars had a strangeness not found in the lands of men.

Within hours he had begun to study the endless carvings. Each pillar, from floor to darkness, was covered in elaborate designs. He guessed that the cat-like figures, which dominated the carvings, were Jekkans. They were thin and sensual, with extravagantly long claws and luxuriant whiskers. Once his interest was peaked, Utha found it hard to turn away.

'They tell a story,' said Voon. 'It'll pull you in if you let it. Jekkan art is addictive for humans.'

Utha was looking at a grotesque scene of cavorting Jekkans. They danced round a central mass, beckoning tentacles and eyes to form on its surface. It was black and the carving appeared to ripple.

'That's a servitor,' offered Voon. 'Made from flesh and madness.'

'It's a blob,' he replied, the fear more acute now.

'It's a tool, a pet, a minion. They fought wars for their masters. They had other pawns called builders . . . strange insects.'

Utha nodded. 'A pillar back there seemed to show that the servitors rose up. Some kind of revolt.'

'You shouldn't look at the story. You can't have knowledge and safety.'

'Safety? Since when was that an option?'

He turned back to the carving. It seemed the Jekkans were proud of the beings they had created but feared them gaining their freedom and minds of their own. All their wars – and the carvings suggested there had been many – had been fought by the servitors and the ancient Jekkans had become reliant upon them.

'Utha, you need to trust me. This magic is insidious and seductive. It will crawl into your mind and make you its plaything. You won't even notice.'

'Okay, let's go. Do we need to rest down here?'

Voon shook his head and ushered Utha away from the carved pillar.

* * *

More hours of walking and he wished for conversation. Any kind of conversation. Left to his own thoughts, he was steadily worrying himself into knots. Perhaps Voon had interests or hobbies, things he could talk about. He was a miserable bastard, but maybe Utha just hadn't found the right topic of conversation. Everything was muddled and confusing, even his own thoughts.

'Why have you stopped walking?' asked Voon.

'What? Sorry, I didn't notice.'

He was motionless, staring at another carved pillar, his eyes drawn far into the design. The servitors bubbled and blasphemed from the stone, twisting the will of their masters into forms and functions. The art had layers of texture, eliciting meaning from bare stone. They were talking to him, addressing him directly.

'Stop looking at the carvings!' demanded Voon, turning Utha round.

They locked eyes. He felt drunk or drugged. 'I think I need to sleep. Or at least sit down.'

The Karesian studied his face. Utha smirked, feeling light-headed, but oddly in tune with the Jekkan causeway.

'I don't think this place likes old bloods,' said Voon.

Utha grinned like a drunken fool. 'It doesn't know what to make of me. It's scared.'

A sound echoed between the pillars. It came from far off but was deep and insistent. Voon's hand went to his spear and he looked terrified.

'Don't worry,' said Utha, slurring his words. 'It just wants to see me.'

'We need to leave!'

'It won't hurt us,' he replied, not knowing how he knew, or why he was no longer afraid.

Voon grabbed him by the shoulders and shook him. 'Your mind is being twisted, man,' he snapped, turning Zarzenfang towards the noise.

'But I want to see it.' He was so sure, so confident.

A repeating cry, the same few sounds over and over again, bouncing off the pillars and growing louder. It gurgled and coughed, each note echoing into the next. A shape appeared. Just a shadow, low to the ground, oozing into view from between the pillars.

'Run!' shouted Voon, grabbing Utha.

He let himself be led away, but he had to see it and stole a backwards glance.

Over the Karesian's shoulder was a pool of bubbling black. Its shape flowed across the stone, rolling and bubbling after them with surprising speed. For a moment, Utha thought it was a moving shadow, until it flickered into the blue light close to them.

'Fuck!' he bellowed, his mind recoiling from the abomination, and the fear returned like a war-hammer to the head.

It was huge. A shapeless, protoplasmic mass forming pustules that turned into eyes and disappeared. It conformed to no law of nature that Utha understood, and the repeating cry was now deafening.

'*Tekeli-li, tekeli-li, tekeli-li, tekeli-li.*'

Each sound was unnatural and coughed from the depths of the iridescent shape.

They ran. Utha no longer needed persuading. The servitor had shaken his mind to pieces. He pulled himself past pillars and sprinted after Voon. The sound followed, each syllable causing pain. He rubbed his face and felt blood, as if the servitor was cutting him with its mocking cry.

He screamed. No words or meaning, just a primal shout of despair. The thing, the servitor, the insane, black mass. He had no way of comprehending what he'd seen. He just ran and he just screamed.

'*Tekeli-li, tekeli-li, tekeli-li, tekeli-li.*'

It was still there. Could they outrun it? Voon was ahead, sprinting through blue-tinged stone. He hadn't looked back.

Tentacles appeared, reaching for him. Arms of rippling tar, snapping at the air as he ran. They caressed his face, leaving a sticky residue on his skin, but they didn't grab him.

Instinct took over and he narrowed his eyes. Utha the Ghost was not going to die in a cave under Karesia. He turned sharply, running in another direction. He threw himself past pillars, weaving in chaotic lines and pumping his knees as high as he could.

The sound died down, but he didn't stop running. His lungs burned and his legs ached, but still he ran. The Jekkan servitor was still there. He glanced back and the shapeless blob of black bubbles was stationary. It reached into the air after Utha and Voon but did not know which of them to follow.

He couldn't see the Karesian. The causeway looked all the same. Pillars, stone and the blue glow. Utha kept running, more concerned about ourunning the servitor than with finding Voon. After what seemed like an age, he could no longer hear the repeating cry of the Jekkan beast.

* * *

He could handle the monotonous hours of solitary walking. He could ignore the carvings. He didn't feel tired, metal was no longer heavy, and he was trudging on with stubborn determination, but the blue glow was driving him mad. Why blue? Did the Jekkans not know about other colours? Their servitors were black, their stone grey, but their lights were all blue.

He was unimpressed with their architecture as well. Pillars and huge, square flagstones. Not very imaginative. No rooms, no corridors or walls. Just the bloody pillars.

Why was he here? The staircase, the labyrinth and the guardian? The halls beyond the world? The exemplar of fucking Jaa? His dreams, so vivid for months, seemed far away now. The certainty that he had worn like armour was now a thin veneer of hope which offered him no protection. He just wanted to go home and forget he was an old-blood. Being an albino wasn't so bad. People were scared of him, but it didn't preclude a quiet life.

Quietness had a resonance. The Jekkan causeway had no ambient sound. No whistle of wind or background chatter of animals. He began to talk to himself just for company.

'Sorry you're not here to see this, Randall. I'd like to share my abject misery with an unsympathetic ear.' He smiled. 'And I could have thrown you to the servitor while I ran away.'

'How long have I been down here? Not tired, not hungry.'

He puffed out his cheeks and stopped walking.

'Voon!' he shouted, surprised when there was no echo. 'I don't suppose there's a tavern or a fuck-shop down here?'

No answer. Utha imagined he was lost, separated from Voon by the endless stone pillars. There was no point in stopping, but was there any point in continuing to walk? He had always been lucky, but finding Oron Kaa amid such monotony would be a tall order. In fact, it edged into the realm of the impossible.

'Voon! I'm getting fed up of this place.'

Still no answer.

'Does it change? Do the lights turn green at some point?'

His eyes were drawn back to the pillars. The carvings were just as vague and shadowy, but his mind felt stronger and he allowed himself a look. The stories were told in interwoven pictograms, with one pillar connecting to adjacent pillars. He found that the story dictated the direction he walked, each thread of story leading him in a different direction.

The Great Race of Jekka had held these lands for millennia. They had built an empire on chaos and sensuality. He wouldn't call them evil, just amoral. Or perhaps he just didn't understand their morality. They warred with ancient creatures, all of which were lost in the catacombs of deep time, forgotten by the Jekkan caliphate that had quashed them.

A symbol made him pause in his journey through the history of the Jekkans. It was a humanoid, superimposed behind a bright star, and he knew that it referred to the old bloods. In the Jekkan age the blood of Giants was still strong and the warlords of the time had wielded this power to build their own kingdoms. They had fought each other and they had fought the Jekkans until few remained. The old bloods fell from might and were hunted by the Great Race, who both feared and hated them. The fear was stronger. But why? The carvings were vague and he felt the very stone recoil, bringing him to a halt.

The Jekkan causeway was afraid of him. The servitor had not been trying to kill him, it had been trying to scare him off, to make him leave. But why? What power did he have?

He followed the story, lost in his journey between the pillars. The stone columns had appeared identical, but now each one was as different as steel and snow. Jekkan art was experienced in layers, depth chiselled out of stone by unknown craft. Or was it art? He was beginning to doubt. It felt as if he was reading a book or watching a performance. It was in his head, an experience both visual and sensory. Voon had said it was addictive, but he now drew his eyes away easily.

He looked around, taking in the still air. The metal was no longer heavy and his head was surprisingly clear. In fact, he felt good. Well, not exactly good, but certainly not as bad as his situation would dictate.

He kept following the Jekkan story, slowing to a stroll and concentrating on the images. Old bloods were forbidden in Jekkan lands. In ages past, the Great Race had been terrified of those with Giant's blood, believing their presence drained the Jekkan magic. The last symbol was harder to translate. Maybe *drained* wasn't the right word. *Leeched, consumed.* He wasn't certain.

He stopped again, rubbing his eyes and swearing in a low mutter.

'Fuck me, this is weird. I'm in a world of blue shit, lost, looking for a Karesian shit, while reading some carved shit . . . on stone shit.'

He turned away from the pillars and slumped to a seated position on the huge flagstones. He wasn't tired, but defiantly he plonked himself down anyway.

'Randall, what do I do? What's my move, how should I react? Come on, you're so good at moralizing . . . tell me what's right.'

The blue glow began to fade. Slowly at first, the criss-cross lines disappeared. Centred on Utha, the immediate area darkened. The pillars still had their eerie light, but the blue of the floor was repelled by him. He could feel its fear.

He stood. 'You are right to be afraid of me.'

The light held its position, pulled back in a circle, unable to encroach into his space. Every second he felt stronger, every second he leeched more power from the Jekkan causeway. Reading the story had unlocked something. The art was more than carved images, more than decoration. It had transferred knowledge to him. Knowledge that he struggled to put into words or any sort of usable form, but it was there, scratching at the corners of his mind.

Jekkan magic was bastardized from the divine spark of the gods. It was the remnants of the true magic of the Giants, mighty in the lands of men, but vulnerable to those who possessed a true hint of the divine.

With clarity, Utha the Shadow realized that he was more than he thought. The stories called him something else, something more than an old-blood. He was a demi-god. Millennia had wiped out his legacy, but the power remained, hidden in the depths of his blood. Somewhere, clinging to a vein or sitting in an artery was a drop of divine ichor, the blood of the Giants. It gave him power.

The Jekkans understood this and knew what the old bloods could do and what they represented. Though he was still vulnerable. He and his Shadow Giant ancestors had no power of belief . . . maybe a distant sliver from the remaining Dokkalfar, but nothing of true worth.

'Right, what else do you have to tell me?'

He returned to the pillars and located his place, letting the story take him where it wished. As he walked, the lights retreated from his step, illuminating nothing but the carved pillars. He felt stronger with each step. Larger, more upright. As more of the Jekkan power passed into him, Utha breathed in deeply.

'You'll show me what I want you to show me.'

He pushed his will at the Jekkan causeway, forcing it to answer to his command. His eyes took him back to the halls beyond the world. The pillars showed him the dreamscapes that had plagued his nights – or perhaps he was now reading his own story. Either way, he felt powerful and in control.

The shadow hall was still there, a broken wreck of black, twisting shapes, a graveyard for a long dead god. But there was more. The place called to him as if they were intertwined, as if his spark of the divine was all that was keeping the hall intact. There was no Shadow Giant, not any more, but Utha knew now what he had to do. Within him was the seed of a new god. In the lands of men, his destiny had been vague and unformed, but now that he was infused with Jekkan magic he was more confident than he had ever been. He was the distant descendant of a god, a creature of lands both terrestrial and beyond.

'I can rebuild the hall. I can revive the Shadow Giant.'

* * *

As the hours melted together and formed an endless journey, Utha learned more and more. He could shape his story with a thought, forcing the causeway to obey him. He had been a simple man with a simple view of the world, but that view had been challenged, eroded, cut away and finally splintered.

'You're not so scary really,' he said to the causeway. 'You're all big and tough with men, but you're fucked when someone stands up to you.'

He had followed the pillars in meandering lines and chaotic circles. The stories were also a map, a guide through which a knowledgeable traveller could find his way. Oron Kaa was just a chapter heading, a place to bookmark the journey if he so wished. He could halt his journey at any one of a hundred different locations, none of which he had heard of.

Imrya, the Nar Scopian Deeps, Mordja, the twin cities of Klarkash and Skavan. He hated feeling ignorant. The magic he leeched made him feel powerful, but did nothing to alleviate his ignorance. These lands, these kingdoms, these cities, they had existed in the distant past of the world. Perhaps they existed now, but Utha didn't want to visit them.

He located Oron Kaa and walked.

EPILOGUE

FYNIUS BLACK CLAW, captain of Twilight Company, was staggeringly bored. He sat at a table opposite a bunch of people, most of whose names he couldn't be bothered to recall. There was the tall one, the drunken one and the one with bizarre eyebrows.

On his side, Mathias Flame Tooth, Al-Hasim, Federick Two Hearts and Lady Bronwyn spoke for the Ranen. Even recalling their names was a struggle.

'The law is the law,' said the one with bizarre eyebrows.

'The law of Ro doesn't apply here,' replied the fat one, Mathias Flame Tooth to those who could give a shit.

'Two hundred Purple clerics are dead,' said eyebrow man. 'Someone must answer for that.'

'For fuck's sake,' muttered Fynius, not realizing that he'd spoken aloud.

Everyone looked at him.

'What? What did I do?'

'You killed two hundred Purple clerics, you obstinate bastard,' replied the eyebrows. 'And a cardinal.'

'I only killed five or so . . . but the cardinal, yeah, that was me.'

'Fynius, keep your mouth shut for a minute,' snapped Lady Bronwyn, the up-her-own-arse one. 'Diplomacy is not one of your gifts.'

He slumped back in his chair. 'Yeah, okay, just wake me up when the Ro bastards have fucked off.'

The tall one kept the peace as the eyebrows started swearing.

The drunken one just smirked, sipping from a brass goblet and nodding politely. They whinged and bickered, making stupid threats and feverishly masturbating over their Ro superiority.

'Please, gentlemen,' said Bronwyn, interrupting their words with raised arms. 'Fynius does not represent all of us. The Ranen of South Warden wish for a peaceful resolution.'

'As do we,' said the tall one, who appeared to be more reasonable than the eyebrows. Fynius thought he was Fallon of Leith but would continue to think of him as the tall one until he was sure.

'Where are you bound, my Lord Frith?' asked Bronwyn. 'Tor Funweir could use its Red general.'

Good girl, she was flattering him. Old men liked that.

'My destination is not pertinent to the current situation,' he replied. 'The murder of the clerics is.'

'Murder!' exclaimed Mathias. 'Just so we know, where does conquest end and murder begin?'

They carried on talking. Some of it may have been arguing. Most of it was dull babble, infused with a sense of entitlement. These men, this moment, all of it was a click of the fingers or a speck of dust in the ocean. They would never understand, so he let them argue. He let them argue and he gradually stopped listening.

Once eyebrows had stopped whingeing about the murder of the One God's noblemen – a ridiculous title, with many levels of misunderstanding – he moved on to the state of his country. Fynius began listening again.

'How fairs Tor Funweir?' asked Lady Bronwyn. 'We have had little news . . . little opportunity to ask questions. Since I left Canarn . . . seems like years ago . . . I really don't know what's been happening in the lands of Ro.'

Frith shrugged. 'We've been on the road for months. The last I heard, an enchantress had turned up in Ro Arnon. Something about Hounds around Ro Weir, but that wasn't our problem. The king commands and we obey.'

Another man of Ro appeared. An old man, robed in brown and with an open, friendly face.

'I may be able to offer some information,' said brown robes, standing over the tall one's right shoulder. 'I was in Canarn more recently than Lady Bronwyn.'

'And?' prompted eyebrows.

'Well, the reports were sketchy . . . and obviously my Lord Bromvy wasn't first in line to receive any juicy information.'

'Speak!' said Frith, his bizarre eyebrows dancing about on his forehead.

Brown robes flapped a little, uncomfortable at the Red man's tone.

'Lanry,' said the tall one, 'anything you can offer would be helpful.'

'Yes, I'm sure . . . just give me a moment, I am somewhat flustered by all this activity.'

He looked around the table for a spare seat. When he saw none, he looked imploringly at a nearby Red servant, lackey, bound man, Ro idiot – what was the correct term? wondered Fynius.

'If you wouldn't mind, dear chap,' said brown robes, 'the old legs let me down sometimes.'

A chair was placed next to the tall one and brown robes sat down with a weary grunt.

'Please, brother, if you would,' said eyebrows, rapidly losing patience.

'Well, it appears that the Seven Sisters of Karesia are steadily annexing Tor Funweir. Bromvy had a . . . friend, called Nanon. He had ways of getting information. I think Hounds already occupy Ro Weir. That was . . . maybe six months ago.'

Bad news. For Fynius it was bad news. For the tall one and the eyebrows, it was terrible news.

'Is Brom . . .' began Lady Bronwyn. 'Is he alive?'

Brown robes nodded. 'Alive and well, last I saw. Nanon said he was waiting for someone called the Red Prince.'

'That's Alexander Tiris,' offered the tall one. 'Maybe some good news.'

'Maybe,' replied Frith suspiciously.

His eyebrows rose and fell in tune with his inner monologue. He was a general, a cardinal, an important man it seemed, and his country was fucked. At least Ranen was free of Hound influence.

Fynius frowned. He didn't like feeling sympathy. Especially for a man, or cardinal, of Ro.

'Bastards!' spat eyebrows. 'We've been dragged to this hole in the One God's arse while they strut around Tor Funweir unopposed.'

He started muttering to himself. 'Ten thousand men here. Maybe five still in Arnon, another three or four spread around the north. Some knights in Du Ban and Voy. A few holds, some yeomanry.' He turned to the tall one. 'How many Hawks does Xander have at Ro Haran?'

'No idea. He hates the Red, remember,' replied Fallon. 'But if the Hounds have occupied Weir, there would have to be a lot of them . . . an awful lot of them.'

'As I said,' interjected Lady Bronwyn, 'Tor Funweir could really use its Red general.'

The eyebrows puffed out his cheeks. 'Months here, months back. We don't even know how many men they've got or how far they've marched. Weir is on the other side of the fucking world from South Warden.'

'You could go via Canarn,' said the drunken one, his eyes unfocused. 'There must be hundreds of ships along that coast.'

'Best get going then,' blurted out Fynius. 'No time to waste.'

* * *

Some time after midnight Fynius was slouched against a tree in Brytag's grove. He deserved a rest. Everyone was doing more or less what they were supposed to do. The tall one and the eyebrows were mustering the Red men, Lady Bronwyn and her Karesian pet were waiting impatiently to return to Canarn, and the Ranen had moved into the city. Rowanoco's Stone was in ruins, but the rest was intact. The men and women of Scarlet had lost thousands, but they were tough, tougher than Fynius had expected. They would survive. They might even get tougher.

As for the Red men, they'd be themselves. They'd be Ro, but at least they remembered their god and they were getting the fuck out of Ranen. Ro Canarn wasn't far, but it was far enough. If they reached Tor Funweir they might even make a difference. Probably not, though.

The World Raven hadn't told him what would become of the Ro, whether they'd triumph or be crushed under the weight of the Dead God's rising. He imagined that eyebrows and his men would put up a fair fight, given the chance. But those that think with their swords seldom prosper in the long run.

Fynius didn't think with his sword. He didn't really think with his head either. Things occurred to him and he acted on them. Others saw how often he was right and began to listen to him, to follow him, even to kill for him. Apparently, he was divinely inspired. In fact, he just listened to the voices rather than try to silence them. They spoke clearly if you gave them the chance.

Still, a shade would be useful. His thoughts were flighty and hard to marshal sometimes. With someone to converse with, his moves would be sharper and easier to explain to others.

As a biting breeze cut through the darkness, Fynius saw a figure emerge through the grove. He strode purposefully over the snow, though his feet left no prints. It was a young man with short, black, curly hair and a close-cut beard. He wore a longsword, topped with the well-made cast of a raven. His eyes were haunted and his clothing poor.

'I am the shade of Bromvy Black Guard and you are the exemplar of Brytag.'

'Finally,' replied Fynius. 'Though I suspect Lady Bronwyn will be a little upset.'

BESTIARY

COMPANION WRITINGS ON BEASTS
BOTH FABULOUS & FEARSOME

THE TROLLS OF FJORLAN,
THE ICE MEN OF ROWANOCO

*History does not record a time when
the Ice Men did not prowl the wastes
of Fjorlan. A constant hazard to
common folk and warrior alike, the
trolls are relentless eating machines;
never replete, they consume rocks, trees, flesh and bone. A saying
amongst the Order of the Hammer suggests that the only things
they don't eat are snow and ice, and that this is out of reverence
for their father, the Ice Giant himself.*

*Stories from my youth speak of great ballistae, mounted on
carts, used to fire thick wooden arrows in defence of settlements.
The trolls were confused by bells attached to the arrows and would
often wander off rather than attack. Worryingly, there are few
records of men killing the Ice Men, and those that do exist speak
of wily battle-brothers stampeding them off high cliffs.*

*In quiet moments, with only a man of the Hammer for company,
I wonder if the Ice Men have more of a claim on this land than us.*

FROM 'MEMORIES FROM A HALL' BY ALGUIN TEARDROP LARSSON,
FIRST THAIN OF FREDERICKSAND

THE GORLAN SPIDERS

Of the beasts that crawl, swim and fly, none are as varied and unpredictable as the great spiders of Nar Gorlan. The northern men of Tor Funweir speak of hunting spiders, the size of large dogs, which carry virulent poisons and view men as just another kind of prey. Even the icy wastes of Fjorlan have trapdoor Gorlan, called ice spiders, which assail travellers and drain the body fluids from them.

However, none of these northerners know of the true eight-legged terror that exists in the world. These are great spiders, known in Karesia as Gorlan Mothers, which can – and indeed do – speak. Not actually evil, they nonetheless possess a keen intelligence and a loathing for all things with two legs.

Beyond the Gloom Gates is a land of web and poison, a land of fang and silence and a land where man should not venture.

FROM 'FAR KARESIA: A LAND OF TERROR'
BY MARAZON VEKERIAN, LESSER VIZIER OF RIKARA

ITHQAS AND AQAS, THE BLIND AND MINDLESS KRAKENS OF THE FJORLAN SEA

It troubles me to write of the Kraken straits, for we have not had an attack for some years now and to do so would be like tempting fate. But I am the lore-master of Kalall's Deep and it must fall to me.

There are remnants of the Giant age abroad in our world and, to the eyes of this old man, they should be left alone. Not only for the sake of safety, but to remind us all that old stories are more terrifying when drawn into reality.

But I digress. The Giants of the ocean were formless, if legend is to be believed, and travelled with the endless and chaotic waters wherever tide and wind took them.

As a cough in Deep Time, they rose up against the Ice Giants and were vanquished. The greatest of the number – near-gods themselves – had the honour of being felled by the great ice hammer of the Earth Shaker and were sent down to gnaw on rocks and fish at the bottom of the endless seas. The Blind Idiot Gods they were called when men still thought to name such things. But as ages passed and men forgot, they simply became the Krakens, very real and more than enough when seen to drive the bravest man to his knees in terror.

FROM 'THE CHRONICLES OF THE SEAS', VOL. IV,
BY FATHER WESSEL ICE FANG, LORE-MASTER OF KALALL'S DEEP

THE DARK YOUNG

And it shall be as a priest when awake and it shall be as an altar when torpid, and it shall consume and terrify, and it shall follow none save its father, the Black God of the Forest with a Thousand Young. The priest and the altar. The priest and the altar.

FROM 'AR KRAL DESH JEK'
(AUTHOR UNKNOWN)

THE DOKKALFAR

The forest-dwellers of the lands of men are many things. To the Ro, arrogant in their superiority, they are risen men – painted as undead monsters and hunted by crusaders

*of the Black church. To the Ranen, fascinated by youthful tales
of monsters, they are otherworldly and terrifying, a remnant of
the Giant age. To the Karesians, proud and inflexible, they are
an enemy to be vanquished – warriors with stealth and blade.*

*But to the Kirin, to those of us who live alongside them, they
are beautiful and ancient, deserving of respect and loyalty.*

*The song of the Dokkalfar travels a great distance in the wild
forests of Oslan and more than one Kirin youth has spent hours
sitting against a tree merely listening to the mournful songs of their
neighbours.*

*They were here before us and will remain long after we have
destroyed ourselves.*

FROM 'SIGHTS AND SOUNDS OF OSLAN'
BY VHAM DUSANI, KIRIN SCHOLAR

THE GREAT RACE OF ANCIENT JEKKA

*To the east, beyond the plains of
Leith, is the ruined land. Men have
come to call it the Wastes of Jekka
or the Cannibal Lands, for those
tribes that dwell there are fond of
human flesh.*

*However, those of us who study such things have discovered
disturbing knowledge that paints these beings as more than
simple beasts.*

*In the chronicles of Deep Time – in whatever form they yet
exist – this cleric has discovered several references to the Great
Race, references that do not speak of cannibalism but of chaos and
empires to rival man, built on the bones of vanquished enemies
and maintained through sacrifice and bizarre sexual rituals. They
were proud, arrogant and utterly amoral, believing completely in*

their most immediate whims and nothing more.

Whatever the Great Race of Jekka might once have been, they are now a shadow and a myth, bearing no resemblance to the fanged hunters infrequently encountered by man.

FROM 'A TREATISE ON THE UNKNOWN', BY YACOB OF LEITH, BLUE CLERIC OF THE ONE GOD

THE JEKKAN SERVITORS

The war did not last long. The Great Race of Jekka had no desire for the forests. At length we fought them back to their mountains and threw down their altars.

But their pets had to be defeated. As the masters fled, their servitors covered their retreat. They were terrible, amorphous things of no fixed form, shaping their flesh as their masters ordered.

Fire did not burn them, arrows did not pierce them, blades did not cut them. Only the touch of cold caused them to flee. The mightiest Tyr wielded swords of deep ice and the wisest Vithar conjured snow and freezing winds.

The servitors were defeated, though it cost many lives. In the long ages that followed, whispers remained of the terrifying beasts, that they skulked in Jekkan ruins or guarded long-forgotten lore, but they were never again seen by Dokkalfar.

FROM 'THE EDDA', AUTHOR UNKNOWN BUT ATTRIBUTED TO THE SKY RIDERS OF THE DROW DEEPS

VOLK WAR HOUNDS

In ages past, the Volk of the northern ice were bound in an eternal war with their cousins, the Dvergar. The came from the dark lands, scratching like insects across the snow. Generations, beyond the understanding of men, were consumed with bitter conflict until the Dvergar gained the ascendancy.

In their darkest moment, the Volk priests screamed to the sky, asking Rowanoco for aid, and the ice giant sent the white pack.

Great hounds from Sovon-Kor gained intelligence and allowed the Volk to saddle them. They felt no fear and valued loyalty above all. They plunged into battle as a wave of death, annihilating any Dvergar that stood before them.

The white pack bred until there were thousands of war hounds, each one bound to a Volk master from birth to death. But as their masters died, the ageless hounds went forth into the world to do the work of Rowanoco.

FROM 'THE NINTH BOOK OF HIGHER XAR'
BY ORRIN SCARLET BEARD OF VAN CLOS

CHARACTER LISTING

The People of Ro

The house of Canarn – descended from Lord Bullvy of Canarn
   Hector of Canarn – duke of Ro Canarn – *deceased*
   Bromvy (Brom) Black Guard of Canarn – traitor lord of
      Canarn, soldier of the Long War, son of Duke Hector
   Bronwyn of Canarn – the Lady of Canarn, twin sister to
      Bromvy and daughter of Duke Hector
   Haake of Canarn – Duke Hector's household guard
   Auker of Canarn – city guardsman
   Hawkin of the Grass Sea – city guardsman

The house of Tiris – descended from High King Dashell Tiris
   Bartholomew Tiris – the king's father – *deceased*
   Sebastian Tiris – scion of the house of Tiris and king of Tor
      Funweir
   Lady Alexandra – wife of King Sebastian
   Christophe Tiris – son to King Sebastian, prince of Tor
      Funweir – *deceased*
   Archibald Tiris – regent of Ro Tiris, cousin to King
      Sebastian
   Clement of Chase – watch sergeant of Ro Tiris
   Lux – watch sergeant of Ro Tiris
   Elyot of the Tor – watchman of Ro Tiris
   Robin of Tiris – watchman of Ro Tiris

The house of Haran – descended from High King Dashell Tiris

Alexander Tiris, also known as the 'Red Prince' – disgraced
son of the house of Tiris, brother to the king, duke and
general of Haran

Gwendolyn of Hunter's Cross – the Lady of Haran, wife of
Alexander Tiris

Ashwyn of Haran – a sergeant of the ducal army, the Hawks

Symon of Triste – a sergeant of the Hawks

Brennan of the Walls – a captain of the Hawks

Lennifer of Triste – serving girl to Gwendolyn of Haran

Clerics of the One God

Mobius of the Falls of Arnon – cardinal of the Purple

Brother Rashbone of Chase – Purple cleric, adjutant to
Cardinal Mobius

Severen of Voy – cardinal of the Purple

Brother Jakan of Tiris – Purple cleric of the sword, protector
to King Sebastian Tiris

Brother Cleon Montague – Purple cleric, bodyguard to King
Sebastian Tiris

Brother Torian of Arnon – Purple cleric of the quest – *deceased*

Animustus of Voy – Gold cleric

Brother Cerro of Darkwald – cardinal of the Brown

Brother Lanry of Canarn – Brown cleric, former confessor to
Duke Hector

Brother Daganay of Haran – Blue cleric, priest to the Hawk
army

Artus of Triste – novice of the blue, pupil to Daganay of
Haran

Brother Elihas of Du Ban – Black cleric, working with the
Seven Sisters

Brother Utha the Ghost – former Black cleric and last
old-blood of the Shadow Giants

Brother Roderick of the Falls of Arnon – Black cleric

Brother Hobson of Voy – White cleric

Knights of the One God

Malaki Frith – knight general of the Red

Tristram of Hunter's Cross – knight commander of the Red

Markos of Rayne – commander of the White Knights of the
Dawn

Mortimer Rillion – knight commander of the Red –
deceased

Wesson of Haran – knight marshal of Cozz – *deceased*

Bracha – old knight sergeant of the Red

Callis – sergeant of the Red

Ohms of the Bridge – knight sergeant of the Red

Dolf Halan – knight captain of the Red, adjutant to Malaki
Frith

Taufel of Arnon – knight captain of the Red, adjutant to
Knight Commander Tristram

Nathan of Du Ban – knight captain of the Red, adjutant to
Knight Commander Rillion – *deceased*

Fallon of Leith, the 'Grey Knight' – former knight captain of
the Red, exemplar of the One God

William of Verellian – former knight captain of the Red

Theron of Haran – former knight lieutenant of the Red and
adjutant to Knight Captain Fallon

Rashabald of Haran – executioner and knight of the Red –
deceased

Nobles

Vladimir Corkoson, the 'Lord of Mud' – lord of the
Darkwald and commander of the Darkwald yeomanry

Dimitri Savostin – major of the Darkwald yeomanry

Hallam Pevain – mercenary knight in the employ of the Seven
Sisters

Kale Glenwood (formerly Glen Ward) – forger of minor
nobility, companion to Rham Jas Rami

Leon Great Claw – a knight, first master to Randall of
Darkwald – *deceased*

Lyam of Weir – duke of Ro Weir
Yacob Black Guard – disgraced lord of Ro Weir, an assassin

Common folk
　　Randall of Darkwald – squire to, in succession: Sir Leon
　　　　Great Claw: Brother Torian of Arnon: Brother Utha the
　　　　Ghost
　　Broot of Weir – a mercenary under Hallam Pevain
　　Castus of Weir – bound man and gaoler – *deceased*
　　Parag of Weir – a mercenary under Hallam Pevain
　　Lorkesh – guardsman
　　Lyssa – child in the Brown chapel
　　Rodgar – child in the Brown chapel
　　Fulton of Canarn – tavern keeper
　　Mirabel of Arnon – brothel owner in Ro Arnon
　　Mott – a bandit
　　Tobin of Cozz – blacksmith and fixer

The People of Rowanoco

The Ranen of Fjorlan

The high lords of Fjorlan have, since the first, sought to keep their names alive through their children. Those of minor houses are afforded no such honour and many deliberately strike their father's name due to dishonourable actions.

The house of Teardrop – named for Alguin Teardrop, the first high thain of Fjorlan.
　　Ragnar Teardrop Larsson – father to Magnus Forkbeard
　　　　Ragnarsson and Algenon Teardrop Ragnarsson –
　　　　deceased
　　Algenon Teardrop Ragnarsson – high thain of Ranen, elder
　　　　brother to Magnus Forkbeard Ragnarsson – *deceased*

Magnus Forkbeard Ragnarsson – younger brother to
  Algenon Teardrop Ragnarsson, priest of the Order of the
  Hammer, friend to Lord Bromvy – *deceased*
Alahan Teardrop Algesson –heir to the hall of Fredericksand
  and son to Algenon Teardrop Ragnarsson
Ingrid Teardrop Algedottir – daughter to Algenon Teardrop
  Ragnarsson
Oleff Hard Head – chain-master of Fredericksand, survivor
  of the Dragon Fleet
Wulfrick the Enraged – axe-master of Fredericksand,
  survivor of the Dragon Fleet
Thorfin Axe Hailer – lore-master of Fredericksand
Samson the Liar – old-blood of the Ice Giants

*The house of Summer Wolf – an ancient and respected house,
named for Kalall Summer Wolf*
Aleph Summer Wolf Kallsson – thain of Tiergarten –
  deceased
Halla Summer Wolf Alephsdottir –axe-maiden, survivor of
  the Dragon Fleet, daughter to Aleph Summer Wolf
Tricken Ice Fang – chain-master of Tiergarten
Earem Spider Killer – axe-master of Tiergarten
Borrin Iron Beard – axe-master of Tiergarten – *deceased*
Rhuna Grim – cloud-mistress of Tiergarten
Father Brindon Crowe – priest of the Order of the Hammer
Heinrich Blood – novice of the Order of the Hammer

*The house of Hammerfall – home of the cloud-men and the Wolf
Wood*
Grammah Black Eyes – new thain of Hammerfall
Rexel Falling Cloud – axe-master, survivor of the dragon
  fleet
Moniac Dawn Cloud – axe-master and cloud-man of the
  Wolf Wood
Anya Coldbane (Lullaby) – wise woman of Rowanocoa

The berserkers of Varorg
   Rorg the Defiler – berserker chieftain
   Timon the Butcher – berserker of Varorg
   Unrahgahr – a troll allied with the Varorg

The house of Ursa – a new house with no honourable lineage,
they name as they see fit
   Rulag Ursa Bear Tamer – the Betrayer, now sits in the high
      thain's hall. Previously thain of Jarvik, father to Kalag
      Ursa
   Thran Blood Fist – lord of Jarvik
   Kalag Ursa Rulagsson – lordling of Jarvik
   David Emerald Eyes – chain-master of Jarvik
   Jalek Blood – axe-master of Jarvik
   Father Oryk Grey Claw – priest of the Order of the Hammer

The Ranen of The South Lands

Those of the Freelands – formerly Tor Ranen – are known as the
Free Companies. They are commoners who earn their names with
deeds of honour. They have never sought nobility or family names.

The Moon Clans – unconquered tribes of the Moon Woods
   Federick Two Hearts – chieftain of the Crescent
   Aesyr Two Hearts – maiden of the rowan oak, daughter to
      Federick Two Hearts
   Ossa Two Hearts – maiden of the rowan oak, daughter to
      Federick Two Hearts
   Theen Burnt Face – chieftain of the Crescent
   Dawn Sun Runner – night-raider of the Crescent
   Barron Crow Friend – man of the Earth Shaker
   Warm Heart Moon Father – Volk war-hound of the White
      Pack

Wraith Company – protectors of the Grass Sea
  Horrock Green Blade – captain of Wraith Company,
    commander of the destroyed Ro Hail
  Haffen Red Face – former axe-master of Ro Hail – *deceased*
  Freya Cold Eyes –wise-woman of Rowanoco
  Micah Stone Dog – young axe-man of Ro Hail
  Darron Moon Eye – priest – *deceased*

Scarlet Company – protectors of South Warden
  Johan Long Shadow – captain of the Scarlet Company
  Mathias Flame Tooth – axe-master of South Warden
  Dragneel Dark Crest – priest of Brytag the World Raven

Twilight Company – protectors of Ranen Gar, the northernmost stronghold of Ranen
  Fynius Black Claw – captain of Twilight Company, exemplar
    of Brytag the World Raven
  Vincent Hundred Howl – warrior of Twilight Company

The People of Karesia

The Seven Sisters – enchantresses, formerly of Jaa, now of Shub-Nillurath
  Saara the Mistress of Pain – leader of the Seven Sisters, bears
    no mark
  Isabel the Seductress – marked with the sign of a coiled
    snake
  Sasha the Illusionist – marked with the sign of a flowering
    rose
  Shilpa the Shadow of Lies – marked with the sign of birds in
    flight
  Ameira the Lady of Spiders – marked with the sign of a
    spider's web – *deceased*

Katja the Hand of Despair – marked with the sign of a
howling wolf – *deceased*
Lillian the Lady of Death – marked with the sign of a hand
– *deceased*

The wind claws – warriors who give their life to Jaa
Dalian Thief Taker – greatest of the wind claws and father of
Al-Hasim
Kal Varaz – servant of the Seven Sisters
Kamran Kainen – servant of the Seven Sisters
Larix the Traveller – *deceased*

The Viziers of Jaa – his faithful
Voon of Rikara – high vizier of Karesia and exemplar of Jaa
Sanaa Law Keeper – vizier of Thrakka
Shadaran Bakara – vizier of Thrakka

The Hounds – criminals serving as the Karesian army
Izra Sabal – whip-mistress of the Hounds
Turve Ramhe – whip-master of the Hounds
Kasimir Roux – captain of the Hounds and adjutant to
whip-mistress Izra Sabal

Common folk
Al-Hasim, the 'prince of the wastes' – exile and thief, friend
to the house of Canarn, son of Dalian Thief Taker
Claryon Soong – Kessian mobster
Emaniz Kabrizzi – book-dealer of Ro Weir
Jenner of Rikara – Karesian smuggler, brother to Kohli
Kohli of Rikara – Karesian smuggler, brother to Jenner
Makad Rarzi – smuggler and ship's captain
Walan Zeen – Karesian warrior

The Godless

Kirin – a mongrel race, neither Ro nor Karesian
 Rham Jas Rami – assassin, dark-blood and friend to Bromvy
   Black Guard of Canarn
 Keisha of Oslan – body slave to Saara the Mistress of Pain,
   dark-blood and daughter of Rham Jas Rami
 Zeldantor –body slave to Saara the Mistress of Pain, dark
   blood and son of Rham Jas Rami – *deceased*

The Dokkalfar – an ancient race of non-human forest-dwellers
 Tyr Dyus the Daylight Sky – warrior and Fell Walker
 Tyr Hythel – warrior of the Fell
 Tyr Kalen – warrior of Canarn
 Tyr Nanon the Shape Taker – warrior of the Heart and
   soldier of the Long War
 Tyr Rafn – warrior of the Heart – *deceased*
 Tyr Sigurd – warrior of Canarn, previously of the Heart
 Tyr Vasir – warrior of the Drow Deeps
 Vithar Jofn – shaman of the Heart
 Vithar Joror the Heart's Hand – shaman of the Heart
 Vithar Loth the Tree Father – shaman and Fell Walker
 Vithar Xaris – shaman of Narland

Mysterious others
 Ryuthula – Gorlan mother
 Magnus's shade – apparition and servant of Rowanoco
 Torian's shade – apparition and servant of the One God

ACKNOWLEDGEMENTS

I think I'm getting better. I hope I am . . . and I really hope you all enjoy this. Thank you for so many things.

Simon Hall, Kathleen Kitsell, Marcus Holland, Benjamin Hesford, Scott Ilnicki, Carrie Hall, Martin Cubberley, Tony Carew, Karl Wustrau, Mark Allen, Paolo Trepiccione, Terry and Cathy Smith, Mathilda Imlah, Melmo the Sinister Apothecary.